The WATERS of AVALON

PART 1 OF 'THE CREEPING TIDE'

PETER ROSSER

UK Book Publishing.com

Photo © Zannah Nesbitt-Green

Editing, design, typesetting and publishing by UK Book Publishing
www.ukbookpublishing.com

ISBN: 978-1-918077-34-6

The WATERS of AVALON

PART 1 OF 'THE CREEPING TIDE'

CONTENTS

Part 2   **154**

PART 1

CHAPTER 1

MIRROR FIRST IMAGES

And I rose-
In rainy autumn,
And walked abroad in a shower of all my days.
(Dylan Thomas; 'Poem in October')

Dan squeezes past the dressing-table mirror to get to the window. Fleetingly, the mirror holds his image as he moves to peer through the window's grimy glass which then in turn holds a shadowy reflection of saturnine facial features, brown eyes and hair which in better light would be clearly perceived as grey. In former times, he had to stoop to see out of the window but now such a deliberate act is becoming superfluous.

Seeing the scene outside he quickly realises he cannot afford to waste time. A breeze is springing up and already he can see ripples forming on the lake below and small waves washing beneath the house.

He turns and pushes his way back past the mirror. His animation is in marked contrast to the silent and unmoving solidity of the mirror's presence. Inevitably, like Dan, it is ageing – but more slowly – and there is a possibility that it will outlast him. It has occupied the same position by the window for many years now, silently reflecting the restless, unending cycle of days and nights.

Dan, though, cannot stop, cannot take time to pause in vain reflection for, this morning, events are imposing on him a timetable of their own; he must hurry.

He scurries about the room, getting ready to leave the house, peripherally aware of the flickers of his own movement. And soon, whatever the mirror has witnessed of him, has vanished from its glass.

After all, it is not, to all appearances, one of those 'solid state' devices that could conceivably record all that passes before it – and, of course, being static, how could it possibly have recorded the events of Dan's lifetime for he is not a prisoner, and it is only in recent years that he has returned to sleeping in this room.

Despite his hurry that morning, when the weather's timetable is not nagging him, he prefers to sink into his armchair and reminisce, indulging himself, as Dylan Thomas has written, long before the events of this ominous morning, 'in a shower of all his days'. And had the armchair retained its hold on him long enough, he might even have mused on the unreliability of his memory and how often it has now begun to let him down; his partner, Karen, frequently reminds him that not everything is as he recalls it, and although her comments irritate him, he consoles himself with the thought that nobody possesses the one and only accurate version of the past.

The apparent limitations of the mirror, however, are illusory. Dan bought it in ignorance of where it had come from and bought it simply because he liked it and thought it would 'fit in' but its design is such that it can only be known for what it is, in very specific circumstances and it is not about to 'clear' and suddenly reveal itself as containing some all-seeing, all-knowing twenty-first century device. That, however, is exactly its secret and it has access to remote memories that contain the events of Dan's lifetime with a clarity and detail of which his own memory is no longer capable.

It also has access to a great deal more that does not relate solely to Dan or even to the confines of the physical location in which it exists, but rather to events that are changing the world and changing the entire nature of the 'reality' in that world. Somewhere, then, if not in Dan's mind or bedroom mirror but in the depths of a remote server, a different kind of 'mirror' clears, and a microcosmic portion of its vast memory is ready to receive the minutiae that will contribute to this day....

CHAPTER 2

SHARDS

She had been woken by a sudden noise – a loud banging, a hammering and she was still fighting to free herself from the fog of her dreams when the banging gave way briefly to raised voices. Now Amanda was fully awake and aware of what was happening.

Her father had finally found his key and had made his way through to the lounge. The light was on – she could see it shining through the gaps around the edge of her bedroom door. Quietly, she opened the door and crept out to peer between the rails of the banister at whatever was happening below.

"No, Frank, we don't want you here!" Her mother's voice rang out across the room, shrill in its desperation.

"It's my fucking home too, Sharon! You can't stop me being here! Get out of my bloody way!"

Her father lurched towards the staircase but her mother, gaunt, pale, her lank hair straggling over the shoulders of her dressing gown, blocked his path.

Amanda pressed her hands over her ears, trying not to hear her father's anger as he picked up a dining chair and repeatedly crashed it down on the living room floor until finally it was smashed into its component parts.

"Go to your brother's, Frank! Sleep it off at his place. You're not going anywhere near Mandy or Edie in that state!"

By now Amanda's younger sister Edith had also woken and had slid alongside her.

"Edie, what are you doing?" hissed Amanda. "You shouldn't be here!"

4

Her sister said nothing but clung tightly to her, shocked and frightened by what was happening. Seeing that she would not go back to bed, Amanda put her arm firmly around her, intuitively trying to provide a safety that did not exist.

As she hung on to Edie, she watched in horror as her father snatched up a chair leg and lurched towards her mother with it. Sharon was no stranger to beatings, though, and as he approached, she remained calm enough to push the seat of the shattered chair towards him with her foot. Unable to sidestep it in time, he suddenly found that it had somehow wedged itself between his ankles.

He managed to yell "You bitch!" at his wife before he came crashing down at the foot of the stairs where he lay inert in a widening pool of vomit, his head twisted at an awkward angle and his body spreadeagled on the lounge floor.

"Oh my God, my God! What have I done?" Despite her actions, Sharon was aghast.

The two girls, seeing their mother's distress and the terrible sight of their father at the foot of the stairs also began to wail loudly. As if becoming aware of them for the first time, Sharon glanced up at them briefly, and then pulled out her phone. The call was quickly answered. Amanda could hear a woman's voice talking, asking questions, in response to which her mother knelt next to her father's body, trying to check that he was still breathing and that he had a pulse.

In what seemed quite a short time to Amanda, there was another bang at the front door. Her mother hurried over to open it; two paramedics came in and after the briefest of questions began to work on her father.

The atmosphere in the room began to calm. Such was the competence of the paramedics, a man and a woman, that Sharon immediately began to take hold of her own emotions once more. She looked around, remembering that Amanda and Edie had been watching from the landing. She spoke quickly to the female paramedic who, by this point, was kneeling on the floor, carefully supporting her husband's head. The woman nodded and Sharon came up the stairs, where, kneeling, she drew her daughters to her.

Eventually, she said, "Your dad's had an accident. He's got to go to hospital."

Amanda looked up into her mother's troubled face and said, "We know, Mummy. We saw."

Her mother looked down at her. Of course, she had known as much. For tonight, she would comfort and reassure her daughters and, in the morning...in the morning, it would be another day.

Together, the three of them went down the stairs to where the paramedics were now ready to move the girls' father to the ambulance. The wind through the doorway was cold and they stood huddled together, conscious of the ambulance's blue light flickering across the fronts of their neighbours' houses.

Then, after another brief conversation with the paramedics, Sharon closed the door, turned off the lights and led Amanda and Edie up the stairs.

That night, the three of them slept together in Sharon's bed.

* * *

From the window of her room, Amanda could study the street below. She pulled her dressing gown around her. It was still winter and although the room was heated, it somehow helped to feel the warm material of the dressing gown on the skin of her neck.

Her Aunt Joyce was looking after them well. Life was much steadier now. Her Uncle George was friendly and sympathetic. He always seemed to have as much time for Amanda and Edie as he did for his own children – Amanda's cousins, Simon and Gemma.

Perhaps the best thing of all, thought Amanda, was that she now had time to read – because it was in the world of books that she found her greatest escape. She read from her tablet computer or from books when she had them. When she had the chance to handle a physical book it gave her a particular delight; she enjoyed the covers and their designs, the quality and colour of the pages, and the and the illustrations that adorned them.

Her teachers soon began to notice a difference in her. She had always been a conscientious girl although, compared with many of the other children, she had seemed dour and care laden. Now she began to enjoy her work and to form numerous friendships. Such was the change that she began to be perceived no longer as a child who was struggling but one, instead, who was thriving and who was capable of making rapid progress beyond that which was expected for children in her age group.

* * *

It had been with dismay that Amanda learned she was still obliged to see her father. On alternate Saturday mornings she and Edith were taken to his dingy little flat near the railway station. He tried hard to entertain them with computer games or by having a few toys for them to play with, but the times that she and Edie enjoyed most though were those when he took them to the cinema. The cinema ran a Saturday morning kids' club, and the two girls would sit in the darkness enthralled by the ever-changing images and the stories portrayed on the screen in front of them.

Of the two of them, it was Edith who missed her father the most. Amanda, since she was several years older, understood a little more about her father's problems with alcohol and the violence that it had led to before they had moved to stay with their aunt and uncle.

Amanda's feelings about her father were complicated. He had never hit either Edie or herself but there had been many times when she thought that he might, especially when he had come back from the pub in a drunken rage – which in the last weeks before they had moved, seemed to have been on more occasions than she really wanted to remember. She had also sometimes seen the treatment he meted out to her mother whom she loved and adored; it was that, beyond anything else, that had led to her mistrust and fear of him.

For a while, whenever they met their father now, he no longer smelt like the pub that he had so often frequented. He seemed kinder towards both her and Edie, and showed interest in how they were doing at school. Amanda almost began to look forward to their Saturday morning visits, especially those on which they made a visit to the cinema.

Then, for no reason that Amanda was ever able to discover, he began to smell again of alcohol. It was on his clothes and on his breath. His manner towards both girls changed and when Amanda tried to tell him about the praise her work had been given at school, he was dismissive and seemingly uninterested. Finally, there came a Saturday morning when he took them to the cinema but once he had bought their tickets, left them to find their own way through to the auditorium. Edie had fretted but Amanda felt sure that she could find the way directly back to her aunt's house, if that proved necessary. In the event, they had found their mother waiting for them in the foyer as they had made their own way out of the cinema.

That was the last time during their childhood, that they saw their father. They stayed for some time with their aunt and uncle until, eventually, her mother found her way into a job which enabled her to rent a pleasant flat in one of the better parts of the town. By that time, Amanda was in secondary school and not only thriving but beginning to excel. Edie, too, was doing well and their mother, after the years of turmoil seemed quite content that it was just the three of them – a situation that did not change until Amanda was on the brink of going to university.

Her mother's second partner, when he came into their lives, was altogether different from her biological father – something that, in her late teens, took more than a little readjustment but then also reassured Amanda that not all men were violent and that, in a loving relationship, her mother could also develop her life in ways that had been impossible before.

* * *

Dan had been asked to see the Head of the Geography Department. It was a very warm summer's afternoon, and he was waiting in the Head of Department's office, aware of the fan on the ceiling rotating ineffectually in the humid air and of the noises filtering up from the campus beyond the partially closed blinds.

The Head of Department's desk sat squarely in front of a door through to an adjacent office. Dan could hear the Head of Department talking in a hushed voice to his personal assistant. He twisted in his seat, perspiring slightly and wondering why on Earth he was there. Ever since he had been told that he had to present himself, he had wondered what possible reason there could be for him to be summoned forth by the Head of Department's PA.

His mind ran through the usual gamut of potential reasons. Perhaps his work was not up to scratch? Maybe his choice of research topic in his final year had been thought to be a poor one? Possibly the party he had attended with his friends the previous evening had been beyond the bounds of acceptability.

He paused. If it was any of those things surely, they were matters that would be handled by the Course Tutor? They hardly warranted the firepower of a Professor of Geography. The more he thought about it, the more he was puzzled.

His thoughts were disturbed by the Professor suddenly appearing in the PA's doorway and then moving not to his desk but coming across to where Dan was seated. There was a casual chair nearby. He moved it a little closer.

"Hello Dan," he said finally. "As usual, I find myself wishing that I was able to spend more time with students here. Unfortunately, it's only in certain circumstances that I get to do so…"

By now Dan was agog and wondering what exactly the circumstances could be.

The Professor seemed to hesitate for a moment. Then he said, "We tried to get hold of you by a whole variety of means but in the end, it was my PA who managed to track you down. "I'm sorry, Dan – but this is not good news."

Dan looked searchingly and with a troubled expression at the Professor, who by now was almost seated at his side.

"Your father has died – very suddenly, I understand. Your uncle phoned us a little earlier. He'd been trying to contact you."

It was some moments before the news penetrated Dan's consciousness. As it did, he found himself involuntarily and unashamedly weeping into his shirt sleeve. The Professor waited, not trying to say anything but recognising that Dan would need time to deal with the news he had just imparted to him.

The Professor was no stranger to bereavements and waited, giving Dan time to regain some semblance of his self-possession. Eventually, a temporary emotional numbness settled upon him and he sat waiting for anything further that the Professor might have to say.

"I'm very sorry to be the bearer of such news. Your uncle did try to contact you directly but, when that proved not to be possible, he phoned here. We agreed that I would tell you as soon as we had managed to find you. I think it best, though, that you phone him.

Dan patted his pockets in search of his smartphone but, to his consternation, it seemed to be missing.

"I think I must have left it in my room," he said.

He raised his head to wipe away a tear that, unbidden, was rolling down his left cheek.

The professor continued, "It's no problem, Dan. Alison, my PA, can place a call to your uncle for you – and we will then leave you to talk. We both have some work to do in here so please take the time that you need. Speaking to your uncle is the most important thing for the moment."

Appreciative of the help that he was being offered, Dan looked up and was briefly aware of the earnestness of the Professor's expression, emphasised as it was by his tanned skin, furrowed brow and white hair.

There was a pause in which Dan wondered what on earth he had done with his phone but then, focusing his thoughts again he said, "Thank you – my uncle will know much more about...about whatever has happened."

The Professor stood and said, "In that case, Dan, if you'd like to follow me, I'll show you through."

Alison waited as they entered the office and crossed to her desk. She dialled Dan's uncle and, as soon the phone at the other end was ringing, handed Dan the receiver.

* * *

Barely an hour later, Dan was on the train home. It would be a two-hour journey – time to do little more than try to assimilate the brief details that his uncle had told him over the phone. It seemed that a neighbour had not seen the usual signs of life at his father's house that morning and had gone to check. Receiving no answer at the front door she had peered through the front window of the lounge from where she could see Dan's father lying face downwards on the lounge floor.

Events had then taken their own course. It seemed that Dan's father had had a heart attack and, according to the doctor subsequently in attendance, had died almost immediately. Now Dan was on his way to meet his uncle at his father's house – which was, at that point, still the place that Dan called 'Home'.

He wondered, in deeply sombre mood, what came next. His uncle would know, he was sure…but then, would he stay in the house or go to his uncle's place? No doubt, it would not take long to sort out. Then there would be his father's funeral and will – both things to which Dan had given very little thought. There again, no-one seemed to have expected that he would have spent time familiarising himself with the events that would follow his father's death. He was, after all, a nineteen-year-old student, without brothers or sisters. The previous evening, he had been at a friend's birthday party which had been both a rowdy and drunken affair – which, he dimly remembered, was how he came to be caught up with another friend in a besotted bet to see which of them could throw his smartphone the furthest…What a terrible difference, he reflected, a day could make.

In the year that followed his father's death, Dan learned that there was more to being an adult than simply accommodating the biological changes of his teenage years. With the agreement of the University authorities, he took a year out, eventually returning a little poorer although with some memorable travellers' experiences behind him. It was to take him much longer, however, to recognise that his father's death – and that of his mother, some years previously – was simply part of a cycle through which, in one form or another, everyone, without exception, has to pass – and to learn that if he needed something in life, it would be earned by the dint of his own efforts. Even there, though, the money he inherited from his father left him with much more of a 'cushion' than many of his fellow students had when they graduated, most of whom began their working lives with substantial university debts.

* * *

CHAPTER 3

SETTING OUT

He did not have a clue who she was although he had seen her many times. But the bar was crowded and if he did not sit in the space next to her, he would have to take his chances with the crowd of younger students currently spilling beer over one another and jabbering away about topics that were incomprehensible to the small number of older postgraduates who sometimes sought refuge there.

Dan slid into the space, self-consciously glancing sideways at the woman next to him and hoping that she would not make a fuss about his sudden intrusion.

"I hope you don't mind," he said. "There's very little room in here."

The young woman glanced up from her phone.

"Don't worry about it," she said. "I'm waiting for friends but they're not going to make it, and I have a tutorial in ten minutes."

However, now that Dan had got so close to the 'mystery woman' he had seen so often, he wanted know more. "I've seen you around here many times, but I don't know your name…"

She smiled. "There's no particular reason why you should… but since you're asking, my name's Amanda."

Dan returned her smile. Despite the noise and the crowd of students all around them, she seemed very relaxed – which surprised him, considering that they were now very firmly rubbing shoulders. She was tall, he remembered – but then so was he. Crammed together as they were, they had stretched out their legs together before them. Awkwardly he tried to crank his head round so that he could see her.

Her hair was long and brown, shoulder length and, as far as he could tell from such an awkward angle, she had green eyes. He was intrigued. Green eyes were unusual....

"So?" she said. He looked mystified – and she had to prompt him again.

"So, what's your name?"

"Oh," he responded belatedly, "I'm Dan. I'm on the Primary PGCE course."

"That makes you a rare creature..."

"Really?" he said. "What makes you say that?"

"Because there are very few men wanting to work in Primary."

"And you know that because...?

"... I'm on the B. Ed (Hons) course – and we get to know such things."

Trying to look at him sideways was awkward but she made the effort – and took in his slightly tanned skin, his dark curly hair and his serious but by no means unpleasant face. Unusually for a student, he was also wearing a wrist watch. She could not help but be drawn in by it...but then – "Oh hell!" she exclaimed, seizing his wrist and peering more obviously at the watch's face. "Is that the right time? I'm going to be late! My tutor will kill me!"

Dan quickly moved to one side to let her out.

"Tomorrow?" she asked, sliding past him.

"Yes," he said. "Same time..."

She had to push her way through the group of students next to them but managed to call back, "See you then!"

Dan tried to follow her with his eyes, but she had already disappeared into the crowd.

* * *

They had met the next day, as planned, Amanda reflected. She turned to look across at Dan, making out the silhouette of his shoulder against the orange light that filtered into the bedroom of their flat from the streetlamp on the opposite side of the road.

Did she love him? She certainly did – but this love she thought they shared was causing her a certain amount of soul-searching and anxiety.

They had graduated at the same time from the University's School of Education and since, at that time, the nearby town of Sedgewater was expanding, there were teaching jobs to be found either in the town or the outlying area.

During the final stages of their time at the university they had first become good friends and then, in the slang of the time, they had moved on to become 'an item'. The flat they had agreed to share had two bedrooms so that, for the first few weeks there, they had slept apart but then almost inevitably, it had seemed to Amanda, they had begun to share a bed.

She moved closer to him and kissed his naked shoulder. He was sleeping soundly and did not stir. The problem was, she thought, the way in which they were living was no different from that of a married couple – and, since she was not yet twenty-five, she did not feel 'ready' to be in that kind of relationship. It was clear, though, that Dan felt quite settled and she was anticipating that it might not be very long before he asked her to marry him. And then what? It would be just a short time no doubt, before they had children – and again, she simply did not feel ready for such a step.

She gave a quiet sigh. They had drifted into their present relationship, and to her, it had all seemed as though it was a matter of convenience as much as any matter of their mutual feelings. So far their relationship had not been 'tested' in any way – and she remembered well enough what had happened when her parents had found themselves in adverse circumstances.

She remembered the drabness of the house in which she had lived as a young child and, even more strongly, the feeling of always being hungry – all of which resulted from her father's addiction to alcohol. Where he had found the money to fund his drinking habit had always been a source of family tension because her parents had constantly struggled to put food on the table. That was why he had repeatedly abused her mother – because she had refused the money he needed to fund his drinking. The destitution that his addiction had brought upon them still haunted her and she was determined that in her future, she would avoid any hint of such poverty – and, above all, the insecurity of always living on the brink.

Her mind turned, a little guiltily, to someone she had met one evening recently – someone with more than a hint of wealth and dependability about him; so how, she wondered, would a future with Dan compare with marriage to someone such as him.

* * *

It was early evening, and she was whiling away time before going home. She had come to the pub with some teaching friends following a school INSET day, but they had now deserted her, gradually moving on to whatever or whoever was next. The choice of pub had been her suggestion because it was here that she had briefly met the person she was hoping to see again.

As she sat at the bar nonchalantly sipping her drink, she noticed a business card, seemingly left there for some unknown reason by a previous customer. She extended a nail to turn it so that she could scan its contents. She got as far as 'James Ashworth, Residential and Commercial Developer' when a voice behind her said, "Ah, do you mind if I reclaim that? I don't particularly want it used as a coaster."

She turned quizzically towards the speaker, realising with a mild and pleasant shock that this was the person she had hoped to see.

"No of course," she had said, moving slightly aside so that he could reach it.

She looked at him as he came closer to her. He was just a little taller than her, well-built and casually dressed – handsome, she thought, in a rather rugged sort of way. His card told her that he was a developer although he seemed rather young to be claiming such a role.

Tucking the card in his pocket, he said, "I was here earlier – hoping to meet a potential client – although it looks as though he's a non-starter."

Amanda politely feigned a lack of interest. He was not to be put off, however and he ostentatiously looked at a large wristwatch. "Hmm, next one's not due for half an hour."

"I think you were here earlier, as well – with some friends?"

She nodded. Her attention must have been focused on her companions although she wondered how she could have failed to notice him.

He persisted. "Teachers, I'm guessing?"

"Yes," she said, a little bleakly. "Most people seem able to guess what we are. It must be printed on our foreheads."

He shrugged – and moved a little closer to her.

15

"Actually," he said, "I think we've met before?"

"I think we have…"

"Hmm, one of your friends introduced you to me, I recall. You're 'Amanda'?"

"I am indeed," she confirmed.

He smiled as if satisfied that he had just remembered her name – although he had known from the start. He turned and signalled to the barmaid, who made her way along the bar towards them.

"Can I get you something?"

She was about to say "No", but she was still a little tipsy from the earlier session with her friends and Dan had an evening meeting at school so, spending a little time in James' company was a choice she could easily make.

"That's kind. I have to leave soon – but I can keep you company whilst you wait…I'll have a small Pinot Grigio, please."

They chatted amicably until James' client, slightly to Amanda's surprise, duly arrived. Minutes later, she was making her way back to her flat, her work – a tedious pile of assessments – and the reheated remnants of a meal that she and Dan had cooked at the weekend.

* * *

It was a simple observation on Amanda's part that it was James' occasional practice to meet some of his potential clients in the same bar on an informal basis before deciding whether he might have interests that were worth pursuing with them. Consequently, it had not been difficult for Amanda to 'bump' into James again – and it was from there that they began to see each other on a regular basis. Sadly, there would come a point in the future at which Amanda would wonder if she had ever been much more than a 'client' or, at best, a business associate.

Inevitably, however, her life with Dan at the flat became difficult. She moved back into the second bedroom and although she tried to be fairly gentle about letting him know about 'James', it was still something of a blow for him to find that any assumptions he had entertained about the future of their relationship, had been wide of the mark.

Reluctantly and with a sense of loss akin to that of a bereavement, Dan realised that Amanda was keen to 'move on'. There was little point in making it difficult for both of them, so he generally avoided the company of their mutual friends and meanwhile, moved to a smaller flat. He was there for about six months before he decided to use the remainder of his capital to put down a deposit on a house.

From the first, however, his choice of house had come with warnings. "It was out on the Levels," he was reminded. "Was he aware of the problems in that area?" It was suggested to him that such a move was unwise, even perverse; at some time or other, it would almost certainly be flooded which, not unnaturally, would affect its value, should he decide to sell it in the future. And, of course, getting insurance would be so expensive as to be prohibitive.

He listened politely – but it was a spacious, modern house, of the kind that, in other locations, he would have struggled to afford. His travelling had also widened his horizons beyond those of many of the people offering him advice; he knew that he did not want to wake up every morning in suburbia and also that, if it became necessary, he would rather adapt the house of his choice than let himself be talked into following conventional wisdom. After several years on a university campus and then another year in a Sedgewater flat, he did not want to be constantly surrounded by buildings but instead, to live in a place that was more closely connected to the natural world around it.

He went to talk to a firm of solicitors. They handled a range of conveyancing, but the local office spent much of its time dealing with the domestic variety. There he found himself dealing with an experienced solicitor – who promptly asked him if he had any objection to the inclusion of his young assistant, Susan Meadows, in their dealings. The 'assistant' had smiled confidently at him – and Dan thought that he would have no objection at all.

Events were such that Susan and Dan found themselves discussing aspects of the house purchase together and eventually, after the house purchase had been completed, Dan decided to ask her out on a date. Unlike Amanda, she was not immediately striking to look at but she was pretty, not particularly tall, but attractive to him and, importantly, someone he had felt immediately at ease with. Accustomed to the normless cynicism of so many of his friends, she also seemed open, confident and possessed of a sense of where she was going. A further recommendation was that she was not a teacher;

Dan had already decided that in his domestic life, he would not want to find himself always gravitating towards the various aspects of his work.

* * *

Amanda, meanwhile, was continuing to move on. One Saturday morning, at James' suggestion, she took herself off to Sedgewater Guildhall and was browsing through an exhibition of plans for housing and a school that was to be built just to the east of the town, when James appeared at her elbow.

"So, what do you think of my latest project then?" he asked.

She laughed,

"Is it yours then?" she had asked, not knowing if he was joking with her.

"Every bit of it," he replied. "It's going to keep me in work for some while."

"I can imagine it would," she said. "It looks very ambitious."

"Of course," he said, adding with a laugh. "What else would you expect?"

She looked again at the plans. She was impressed – which was probably what he had intended. She too was ambitious – but she was also intelligent enough to see that beyond the project displayed before them was a level of ambition on a very different scale to her own. Was that something, she wondered, that she would be happy living with?

James, however, saw Amanda as someone with 'people skills', someone whose looks and general intelligence would make it easy for her to mix with the clientele he was steadily developing and to accommodate herself to a business in which the boundaries of work and leisure sometimes became rather blurred. Of course, there was no denying that he was attracted to her in the usual way but he could also see that she was someone with enough wits to be independent of him during the long hours of his absence, and who also aspired to something better than the 'average' that Sedgewater and district had to offer.

It was in the second of these thoughts that he came closest to supplying a solution to Amanda's initial disappointment with her chosen career. As she was slowly drawn, as if by social osmosis, into his lifestyle she began to realise that her hopes of moving beyond the constraints of her previous life might, after all, be realised and when, eventually, he asked her to marry him, she was sufficiently convinced to agree, with just the faintest shade of a suspicion that she had been swept along or that she might eventually miss the carefree times she had shared with Dan; if she paused at all to wonder what sort of life she might have had with him, she could not imagine that it was likely to be in any way as attractive as the prospect that lay before her with James. She was, she felt, on her way to changing her whole outlook on life.

* * *

Dan, having moved away from the circle of people he had, to quite a large extent, shared with Amanda no longer had many people who he thought of distinctly as friends and instead, had a fairly consistent group of acquaintances whom he thought of as being 'friendly' and whose experiences, to one degree or another overlapped with his. In general, people other than those with whom he worked barely noticed him in daily life but some of those who did, tended to pigeonhole him as 'a loner'.

He was, though, not lonely and he made sure that he never quite lost touch with Amanda – as did Amanda with Dan. They each invited the other to their respective weddings, believing that it would be churlish not to do so – and besides, they convinced themselves, whilst they were seemingly not destined to marry one another, they could at least continue to have an empathetic and mutual regard.

In quiet, solitary moments, Dan sometimes reflected on the amount of time that he spent thinking about his own situation. Perhaps that was why he was searching, as he had in his travelling days, for that vista beyond the window and something that lay outside of himself? Was there, indeed, any such thing as objective reality? But whatever was going on in the natural world, whatever he was seeing, hearing, reading about out there was becoming ever more energised – and that would have consequences, he thought, for all living things on the Planet.

* * *

CHAPTER 4

A WATERY DARKNESS

It was a different day, another morning. Dan paused to remember how long he and Sue had been married – although, of course, he knew how long it was anyway. It was seventeen years. And the house in which they usually lived with their two children was in a sorry state. He crossed the damp and chilly room to peer out of the window.

After the incessant winter storms, the glass was grimy but as he stared miserably out, he could see the wind-driven water rippling across what was, in drier times, his lawn. He swept his fingers through his dark but slightly greying hair and momentarily caught a glimpse of himself in the mirror of his wife's dressing table. Then, he straightened up, having stooped to look out of the window; being tall sometimes made him feel a little clumsy and awkward, even when he was only keeping his own company.

The call handler at the Fire and Rescue Service had said that it could be some time before the rescue boat got to him. He looked down again at the depth of the water and thought that getting into a boat from his back step would not be the easiest thing he had ever done.

The battered old backpack into which he had stuffed a few clothes, his razor and tooth brush, sat on the bed, waiting for him to pick it up. The upper storey of the house had remained dry but he knew that if he opened the bedroom door and peered down into the lounge area, it would be awash with filthy grey water in which various household objects they had not had time to move – such as the logs, wood basket and small wooden stool – were now drifting about in the gloomy darkness below. When the storms were at their peak, they had been in such a rush...

* * *

He perched on the battered old sofa he had hauled into a space between the piles of personal and household belongings.

He was in a difficult situation, that could not be denied – but waiting for the boat was also going to be tedious. He took out his phone. He couldn't be bothered about texts, e-mails or social media not least because, for a number of days up until that morning, none of it had been working. He twiddled with the 'phone for a moment or two longer, listlessness guiding his fingers; the messages and news would all date from the time that the whole system had begun to totter – and then fall over.

Today, though, there was at last a signal. That was how he had been able to contact the Fire and Rescue Service – so that was something, at least, about which he could be positive.

His thoughts turned to his children. That morning, they were sitting in another house, not too dissimilar to the one in which they usually lived, about three miles away. Like him, Sue was probably feeling marooned – and irritable as well – and, if that was how she was feeling, Josh and Emily would be feeling the weight of her annoyance. Gwen, meanwhile, would be trying to hold the ring – the very small 'ring' in which they were all penned together.

He decided to look at his messages after all. He had not heard from Amanda in days. That, of course, was easy to explain. In their present situation, they always felt bound to keep their communications strictly to school matters but, even as he strayed into thoughts about her, Dan could not help but be aware that where she dwelt in his thoughts was a place to which he liked going.

He sighed – and he sighed because in that previous time, he had failed to see how quickly Amanda would become dissatisfied with the limitations of her lot as a young teacher – and, apparently, with him. It must have been easy, he thought, for James to come along and charm her down from her tree – James the property developer with the expensive cars and the big ideas and his friends at the Golf Club.

Such feelings were not helpful, but she had been a loss. When she had first moved out and then had gradually stopped seeing him to any significant extent, it had been a difficult time. He wondered if he would ever be able to forget about it completely. Eventually, he had decided that he needed to be his own person and to live his life in his own way. That was why he had decided to buy the house in which he was now sitting.

The deposit had not been a problem. The probate on his parents' estate had been a simple matter; he was their only child. To a large extent, the money that came to him following his father's death had financed much of his travelling and the deposit that gave him the keys to 'Moorside'.

He rehearsed the sequence of events in his memory. Out here on 'The Levels', he recalled, getting a mortgage, had been less of a problem than getting house insurance – which had proved difficult and expensive. Along with the conveyancing of the house, though, had come Sue, the senior solicitor's keen young assistant – pretty, easy to talk to, mercifully free of the cynicism he had encountered so often on his journey through Academia. In the early days, at least, she had seemed to understand his yearning for 'wide horizons' and a desire to live in a place that still had some semblance of connection to the natural world.

Dan looked at his watch. The Rescue people had not been joking. The boat was certainly taking its time getting through. He glanced across again to the window with its vista of grey skies and grey, watery expanse reaching almost to the thinly defined horizon.

The word 'marooned' came into his head again and not just in relation to Sue or the house in which he was stranded.

The instance that came most immediately to mind was his job – which he loved – but about which he often had cause to wonder where it was taking him. Just as almost everyone had advised him against his choice of house, his choice of career as a Primary teacher had also met with surprise – and a certain amount of disapproval. Few could see, as he did in his youthful idealism, that it was in those early years that the foundations of children's lives were laid. No doubt that was why he had stuck with what was sometimes called 'the classroom job', when others had gone after promotion and moved on.

Now, on this morning, where was he? He was washed up on this battered old leather sofa, a middle-aged man with the familiar problems of middle-aged men. At that point, Dan paused in his thoughts – which, he recognised, had fallen into an all-too frequent groove – and one that was now far short of the truth. Surely, if the flood outside did little else, it would wake him from the dream through which he and all the other people of his world seemed to be drifting. Just like the waters beyond his windows, his troubles, and those of everyone else were no longer trivial. They stretched to the horizon – and beyond. He felt himself wanting to shout –.at himself and the world in general, "Wake Up!".

His phone rang. It was the Rescue people. The boat was just a short distance away. He decided that he would make a last check round. He left 'the bedroom' but made a point of not looking down the stairs to the lapping chaos below. Instead, he crossed the landing to the second bedroom, wove a path through the muddle of small table, chairs and bed he had been using in what had become his living space and stared in the opposite direction from the house, out of the back window.

Short though it was, his tour encompassed the tiny living space in which he had spent the last few days. His attention like the flood waters below drifted. Then, suddenly, his ears picked up the sound of the rescue boat's outboard motor. He looked around for his waterproof jacket which he had left on a chair nearby – and his boots, which he had salvaged at an early stage when water had first begun seep into the house.

Hauling on his jacket and boots, he thought about the depth of the water in the hallway; it would probably be close to the top of his boots. He was putting on his backpack when he heard a shout from outside the front of the house. "Anyone at home?"

He worked his way quickly back to the nearest front window, and shouted down to the two yellow jacketed men in the inflatable boat that was now just outside his front door.

"Am I glad to see you!"

"No problem!" shouted one of the boatmen, his face turned upward in order to peer at Dan in the window above him. "If you can come down to the front door, we'll take you off the step here."

"Right!" responded Dan. "See you in a minute!"

He lurched, in ungainly fashion, out onto the landing and down the stairs until, in the darkness, he could barely see where he was going, and water was lapping round his boots on the bottom step. Cautiously, and still hanging onto the stair rail, he lowered first his right foot and then his left, onto the submerged floor of the hallway.

Feeling the water sloshing round near the top of his boots, he edged slowly forward towards the door. He had heard rumours that thieves had targeted the deserted houses nearby. He fumbled in his pocket for the door key. Then, once he had checked it was there, he began to turn the door handle; fortunately, the mechanism had not been affected by the water washing around the door's lower half. Regrettably, though, the same could not be said of the door itself. He gave it an initial pull but to little effect. He tried again, giving it a much more determined tug. This time, the door came flying open, sending a wave of water past him and towards the stairs and kitchen, and causing him to lose balance so that he nearly fell backwards into the hallway.

"Whoa there!" shouted the waiting boatman, as Dan grabbed the door to steady himself; he waited momentarily and then said, "If you can make your way forward onto the step, I can get you into the boat!"

Dan managed to do as he was told. Then, balancing precariously on the submerged front edge of the step, he turned and, with difficulty, shut and locked the door before finally reaching out a hand to the waiting boatman. Seconds later, he was in the boat, having been given a firm pull just when his height might have caused him to dither. Momentarily, he stood awkwardly, until motioned to sit down in the mid-section of the boat.

He sat, musing on the novelty of his situation before nodding briefly to the two other passengers, distributed fore and aft, so as to maintain the stability of the boat. The boatman who had helped Dan aboard, picked up an oar and used it to shove the boat away from the house and then, recognising that the water was deep enough to use the outboard motor again, eased the boat out over the submerged road that now lay beneath them.

Somehow, the experience did not seem that peculiar – even, at first, a little exciting. The hedgerows slid by on either side of them as if they were travelling along a canal, albeit a rather narrow one. The wake of the boat slid out behind them and disappeared amongst the trees and bushes. Then, for a moment or two, the steersman eased back on the throttle in order to negotiate a way past an obstacle to the right (or was that 'starboard'?) side of the boat. As they drew level, there were small gasps of surprise from the passengers as they caught a glimpse of a car, submerged to its roof, the aerial projecting just a short way above the water.

Emerging from the narrowness of the gap between hedgerow and car, the steersman opened up the throttle again and the boat began to skim rapidly along the waters of the submerged lane once more. With the noise of the outboard motor, there was little point in trying to talk, so instead, Dan peered about him, taking advantage of the boat's height above the road and the gaps in the hedgerow to get a glimpse of the countryside on either side.

His house had been surrounded by water for three days, so the view across the landscape should not have been a surprise. All the same, the fleeting views of the watery world through which the boat was now passing, caused him to draw breath. Ordinarily, he would have expected to see a mosaic of fields, hedgerows, patches of woodland, an isolated farmhouse or two and the occasional row of cottages. The houses were still visible although they were flooded up to the window ledges of the ground floor in most cases. Where the level of the land fell away towards the river, hedgerows had in many instances disappeared or were represented only by their vestigial upper tips; the tops of taller trees stood out above the water although many smaller trees were almost submerged, so that only the topmost parts of their crowns appeared above the huge lake that now stretched away in every direction, rimmed only by the gradual rise of the hills in the distance. In all, they were travelling through a watery and largely featureless expanse punctuated solely by occasional hints of the drowned landscape around them and the haunting, wilderness cries of water birds.

They travelled on in this way for some twenty minutes, the fresh breeze of the boat's forward motion streaming past them, until the still visible lines of the hedgerows between which they were travelling began to curve steadily around to the right, or starboard side. Then the passengers saw coming into view the small settlement of Monk's Hill, sitting atop what had now become an island.

The people of the village had used scaffolding poles and planks to build a small, temporary pier or quay, but the steersman ignored it and began gradually to throttle back the outboard motor, relying on the boat's momentum to take them in to a point where the passengers would be able to slip out of the boat and paddle to the water's edge. Slowly he turned the boat so that the bow was presented to the road's surface. He had already raised the propeller out of the water and now, with a small amount of crunching and scraping, the boat came to rest.

The still anonymous boatmen had risen from their places in order to help their three passengers ashore. Dan thanked them and slid from the rubber side of the boat until his boots entered the shallow water. Then he waded his way up the surface of the submerged road and walked until at last he stood once more in surroundings where water was not immediately visible and from where he could find his way to the house in which the rest of his family was staying.

* * *

CHAPTER 5

TIGHT LITTLE ISLAND

Dan made his way from the main road through connecting alleys to the small street on which his mother-in-law's house stood. It was familiar territory since he had first become a regular visitor when he and Sue were still getting to know each other. As he drew nearer to the house, he reminisced about the early days of his relationship with Sue.

They had been out on several dates by the time that she had first tried to inveigle him into the 'Sedgewater Singers' – a local choir of which she was a member. Dan made no great claim to be a singer, but he had been a member of his school's choir and, having unwisely let this information slip out, he was lured into going along to a practice session.

It was soon discovered that he had 'a fine tenor voice' – which in the light of the choir's shortage of tenors was none too surprising. Sue had lured him into joining but it meant that he got to spend a little more time with her, and the singing made a welcome break from the daily round of book marking and lesson preparation. It also helped that some members of the choir usually adjourned to the pub – the 'Lamb and Flag', just around the corner from the rehearsal rooms – and it was there that he was able to socialise with a group of people he might otherwise not have met.

Now, several years later, Sue was still an active member although Dan had long since fallen by the wayside. The choir itself was much as it had been before, consisting, as it did, of local people who liked singing as a way to unwind and providing for some of its older members with a source of social contact.

Dan's mind returned briefly to the time when, to her mother's consternation, Sue had gone with Dan to have a look at 'Moorside', the house her legal work had helped him to buy and was soon spending a good deal of her leisure time there. Her mother, Gwen, sensing the direction of travel in her daughter's relationship, had insisted that, by way of compensation, they spent some evenings with her.

Despite some initial formality in their relationship, Dan and Gwen had gradually come to like each other. It was a distinct advantage too, from Dan's viewpoint, that Gwen's gregarious nature often manifested itself in her willingness to feed others.

Sue's father, on the other hand, had died some years previously and, although Gwen had greatly mourned his loss, she was pleased to have a man's presence in the house again.

So it was that when Dan and Sue had decided to get married, she had found it difficult to adjust to their decision to live at Moorside and she became a frequent visitor. The visits had increased when the children, Josh and Emily, had been born – and Dan and Sue had often been grateful for Gwen's support.

Dan paused in his reflections as he arrived at his mother-in-law's front gate. The incessant rain of recent times had encouraged the briars in the front garden to grow vigorously so that they trailed along the front wall of the house and thence to hang down over the door. Carefully, he tucked the latest offender behind the edge of the trellis to one side of the door, and went in.

The front room of the cottage at this time of the day was generally gloomy so resident and visitors alike were probably occupying themselves at the back of the house. Dan wove his way through the open doors to the kitchen. Gwen had heard his arrival at the front door and as he entered the kitchen, she looked up from the lump of dough that she was kneading.

"Hello Dan!" she called across to him. "We were all wondering when you'd arrive."

"Sorry about that," replied Dan. "I tried my mobile but the service at the house has always been poor. Then, in the boat, I forgot all about it. I was too busy hanging on – and gazing at all the water."

Gwen gave a smile of understanding. "A bit of a shock, I should think," she said. "It's the worst I've ever seen it."

Dan paused for a moment, still feeling disconcerted by his watery start to the day.

"I can well believe what you say – it's a changed world out there. I found it difficult to know where I was. It felt more like the Lake District than Somerset."

Gwen returned to kneading the dough that she was working on but shook her head.

"Flooding to the west of the village is somethin' we're used to, but we've never been completely surrounded by water before," she said.

"I agree", said Dan. "It's quite something to see, although for the farmers around here, it's a disaster."

"Well, the farmer at the lane here, Ted Gilmore, is in no doubt about it," continued Gwen. "I met him the other day. I wouldn't like to repeat what he said about the Environment Agency. He's moved all his cows inside now – but not before he lost two of his herd."

"How did that happen?" asked Dan, sorry, though not surprised, to hear of the farmer's misfortune.

"Well," said Gwen, "Ted told me that he found most of his herd on a small patch of higher ground over towards the Knoll but when he checked on them, he found that two were missing. He thinks that they were simply swept straight down the river."

She paused for moment and turned aside from working on the dough.

"It's no good, Dan…I shall have to sit down. I find it hard these days to stand for long spells at this worktop." She dusted off her forearms and then washed them under the cold tap by the sink.

"Would you like me to make a cup of tea?" asked Dan.

She gave a chuckle. "I certainly would. A cuppa would be very welcome just now."

Dan busied himself with the kettle and tea cups but then, as if suddenly remembering his wife, he said, "Where's Sue?"

"She's working upstairs. She's a bit happier this morning. Broadband seems to be working again, and her bosses have sent her something she can get her teeth into."

"Oh, that's good," said Dan. "She'll be pleased – although I probably should go up and see her…"

"I'd give it a few more minutes if I were you, Dan. Josh and Emily have been a bit of a handful this morning and I think she'd appreciate a bit of uninterrupted time on her work."

"Ok," agreed Dan, a little reluctantly. He had not seen Sue for the three days in which their house had been completely cut off by the flood waters. "I guess it was fortunate that she was already here with the kids when Friday night's deluge came down."

There was no doubt plenty of catching up that she needed to do on her work, but Dan found it difficult not to feel peeved.

The switch on the kettle gave a pronounced click as the water boiled and Dan turned aside to make the tea. A few minutes later, Gwen, contented for the moment, was sitting with her drink and gazing out of the window at the wet and gloomy tangle of plants in her front garden. Dan, meanwhile, had gone in search of Josh and Emily.

He found them in the dining room. They had clearly been told by Sue that they had to spend some time on their school work. They seemed to be unaware that he had been in the house for some minutes, because when Emily saw him, she immediately looked up from her books and then came and threw her arms around him.

"Oh, Dad, what kept you?" she asked. "We've been waiting and waiting for you."

"I'm sorry, Em – but just thank your lucky stars that you were here on Friday night. Otherwise, like me, you'd have had to wait for the rescue boat."

"Em thinks you should have swum." After three days on his own in a flooded house, hearing the gruffness of Josh's voice had a welcome familiarity to it.

"No I don't!" Emily responded to her brother's taunt, forgetting that it was never a good idea.

"Ok you two." Dan wanted to stop them before they got into an argument. "I didn't come in here to cause a fight. Let's have a look at what you're doing."

Both of Dan's children were becoming tall and the casual clothes they wore when not at school, made them seem more adult and less like children – which, it seemed to him, was probably why they were usually keen to get out of their school uniforms the moment they got home.

Josh's frame was much too big for Gwen's furniture, and he seemed to spill out beyond his chair and all over the work on the table before him. Dan started to look through the page of Maths homework that he had been working on. Josh, however, pushed back a slick of dark hair and stood up, his complexion seeming a little sallow as it caught the weak light from the window.

"I just want to take a break for a few minutes," Josh explained. "Working on Gran's table is killing my back."

Dan gave a wry smile. "I'm not surprised," he said. "Why don't you take a walk down the garden?"

"Yeah, good idea, Dad – I could do with a few minutes to myself." He glanced at Emily. Then, turning away, he picked up his mobile phone, and headed for the back door. Dan suspected that Josh was dating one of the girls at school and probably welcomed the chance to get away from Emily's scrutinising glances.

"So, what are you doing?" asked Dan, settling himself on the chair next to Emily.

"Oh, nothing much," she responded.

Her father looked sideways at her. Even though it was only a few days since he had last seen her, the brief separation made him aware again of the recent changes in her.

She was in the early stages of transition from slender teenager to young woman. Her blonde hair was shoulder length and that morning, she had painted her fingernails a pastel green.

She saw her father's glance and said, a little defensively, "Mum and Gran don't mind. They said it's alright while I'm not at school."

Dan smiled. "I didn't say a word. If it's alright by them, it's alright by me. Besides, your nails look very nice."

"Thank you, Dad." She spread her fingers as if to scrutinise them further and then looked away, towards the back window.

For a moment she seemed to drift away from the conversation but then returned to it, her tone changing as she did so.

"How much longer do you think we'll be here?" she asked. Dan noted the boredom, perhaps even frustration, in her voice. "I love Gran's house but there's nothing to do. And all our friends are miles away."

He was readily sympathetic. Compared with their usual existence, both his children must have felt as though they were in a prison – a prison surrounded by flood waters and with no return to normality in sight.

"I think we'll be here for some days yet," replied Dan. "At the moment, the water can't be pumped away fast enough."

He looked at his daughter and could see clearly now that she was finding their enforced stay in their grandmother's house very trying.

"Why can't they do something, Dad?"

Unthinkingly, Dan slipped momentarily into teacher mode. "It depends on who you mean by 'they'."

It was not the response that Emily was looking for, and she snapped back at him. "Oh, Dad – you know who I mean – the 'Powers that be' as Gran calls them!"

I'm sorry." Dan raised his hands, belatedly understanding his daughter's viewpoint but also a little surprised by her sensitivity. He paused momentarily before saying, "The Environment Agency have brought in some bigger pumps. They've had to get them from Holland so I guess it will take two or three more days before they begin to have an impact."

"Well, I just hope I can stay sane that long. You have no idea what it's been like here whilst you were stuck at home. Gran's done nothing but moan – and Mum's been on my case the whole time!"

Dan was not surprised. They had all been under each other's feet for much too long. He paused to think of ways in which he could help to ease the situation.

Finally, he said, "I may be going back to the house tomorrow. You and Josh could come with me if you like – just to get a break from here."

Emily brightened visibly at the thought. "Oh, could we, Dad? That would be great! I could phone Phoebe and perhaps I could go over to her house?"

Dan looked doubtful for a moment. "Just remember that everywhere around the house is flooded."

Emily briefly slumped in her chair but then suddenly sat up again. "Don't forget our boat! Don't forget 'The Happy Prawn'!" She gave him a meaningful look. Dan though tried to look unimpressed having wondered how long it would be before they got around to the subject of the dinghy.

He gave a small sigh. Everything had taken a beating on Friday night and he had not had a chance to check on the state of the boat. Despite its cover, it might well be full of water. He had certainly not wanted to try his luck with it when travelling the watery miles between the house and Monk's Hill.

"Well, we'll see," he said cautiously, "but, if nothing else, a chance to get outside these walls would do you and Josh some good."

"Thanks, Dad, you're a star! I'm going upstairs to see if I can get through to Phoebe."

Dan let her go, knowing that it was often easier to send a text from the upper part of the house although, as far as he could see, Josh was still managing very well from the bottom of the garden. He watched his son for a moment, taking in his apparent readiness to use up the credit on his phone. Turning away from the window, he reflected that he did not particularly envy him – going through teenage anxieties, and with the constant pressure of exams always in the background.

There was also another small matter which had only just occurred to him; he had yet to ask Sue what she thought about Josh and Emily returning with him to the house. He was guessing that she would be pleased. They would be out of her way and would also be his responsibility for a few hours.

He walked back from the dining room towards the kitchen and found it empty. Gwen's coat was gone from the hook on the back of the kitchen door. Footsteps on the landing and stairs announced that either Sue or Emily was on the way down to the hall. A moment or two later, Sue appeared.

"Oh, hello," she said, as if slightly taken aback by her husband's presence. "I didn't realise you were here. Why didn't you come up?"

"Your mum thought you could do with some peace and quiet." Dan tried not to sound too defensive.

"She had a point. I haven't been able to get through to the office for the last three days, and Josh and Emily have been an absolute pain."

Dan looked at his wife for a moment. Apart from the incongruity of her red slippers, she had dressed much as she would for the office. Her black skirt ended around mid-knee and the creamy blouse, which was probably not warm enough for Gwen's house, was partly covered by a stylish grey cardigan.

He moved to put his arms around her. She accepted his hug and briefly returned his kiss but then let her embrace slip away. Distractedly, she wandered off into details of her e-mails and phone calls.

"On the positive side, I did manage to get through to James this morning. We seem likely to get some more work on a new development in Bristol – so, for once, he was in a fairly good mood. Apparently though, Eric is still pushing hard for completion of the work on the Wellington site. Silly man doesn't seem to realise that I'm still in the middle of the Great Flood with next to no means of communication." She looked exasperatedly at Dan, and he felt for a moment that, perhaps, in some way, he had been the source of this conjunction of circumstances. Then, unusually, she remembered for a brief moment that he had been occupied with something other than her work.

"Sorry... I imagine you've had enough to think about at home. It's just that no-one else here seems to understand how difficult it can be."

Dan nodded whilst also thinking to himself that everyone else in the house probably felt that they knew a great deal more about the problems of Sue's office than they really wanted to. Then he acknowledged to himself that she had not been able to talk to the people at work in the last few days.

Remembering that he was supposed to say something, he tried to describe the situation at the house.

"It's quite a lot worse than when you came over here with the children. The whole of the valley is like one enormous lake – except that the water is flowing, of course."

"That's what we've been hearing," she affirmed. "But what's the situation at the house?" She sounded slightly impatient; there had been endless news reports about the general situation, but it was the state of her house that she particularly wanted to know about.

"Not good, I'm afraid. When the three of you came over here just the garden had flooded. Now the whole of the ground floor is full of water. When I left this morning, it was nearly up to my knees. Dan glanced at his wife, realising that, despite her apparent preoccupation with work, she was both frustrated and angry about the damage to their house.

"Damn the Environment Agency!" she suddenly exclaimed. "Damn them to hell! They're supposed to protect us! What on earth have they been buggering about at all these years?" Her shoulders sagged. If she had cared to admit it, she had no idea why the valley had flooded.

His wife's question hung in the space between them. Dan realised that she was lashing out at an easy target, but it was not the time to fill the air with words. He moved closer to put an arm around her, only to think that she might push him off. For a moment it seemed as though she would, but then her shoulders began to shake with the release of pent-up emotions, and she sank her face into his chest.

The moments passed slowly. Dan was aware of Gwen's kitchen clock ticking as Sue continued to sob into his pullover. He held her firmly but sympathetically. Despite the awful situation at the house, it was good to know that she still came to him for comfort when there was trouble. Slowly, her sobbing subsided.

Eventually, she lifted her tear-stained face towards him. "I'm sorry, love," she said, "I've been bottling it up for days. You must think I'm an awful wimp."

Dan had thought no such thing and shook his head. "No," he said, "I feel the same way myself."

They stayed with their arms around each other a little longer, and then gradually disengaged.

Although neither of them had directly said so, having a house that was full of filthy flood water was an experience that was beyond awful, and Dan felt sure that Sue was feeling it just as much as he was – perhaps more.

Aware of the fading light, she went to the window and peered out.

"Not much of today left," she commented. "No-one from your school has phoned so what have you got planned for tomorrow?" Sue's question brought him back into focus.

"Well, I thought I might take Emily and Josh over to the house. Josh could help me and Emily is hoping to meet up with Phoebe."

"Mm sounds like a good idea. They need to get out of here for a while. I could do with a break too, but I need to get some more work done."

Dan nodded, wishing that, if only for an hour or two, she might forget about work for once.

"You could come with us." He had said it before thinking.

She hesitated, as if momentarily tempted by the idea, but then said, "No Dan, you take the kids. They'll be out from under my feet – and I've got more than enough to do."

"OK," Dan acknowledged, "I'm sure you have. Come to think of it, I haven't been able to contact anyone from school since last week and from what you've said, no-one has rung here. I'm certainly surprised not to have heard from Amanda."

He stopped himself. Sue and Amanda knew each other quite well but Dan had been trying not to discuss the fact that he was now working with his former partner.

Turned momentarily away from his wife, he tried to think about what he should do, but when he turned back again in expectation of her response, she was already at the top of the stairs.

* * *

CHAPTER 6

BRIEF ESCAPE

Later, in the evening of that day and after they had all eaten, they chatted together for a while but then, one by one, decided that sleep was the preferred option and went off to their rooms. Dan, though, waited for a little while, taking advantage of the quiet to continue thinking about what, if anything, he could do to get back in touch with his colleagues at school. There was, after all, a signal on his phone but despite now having made various attempts to contact his colleagues, their numbers were still unobtainable.

His thoughts did not detain him for long; he had had enough for that day and there was some evidence from Gwen's phone that the landline network was recovering, although it seemed clear to him that it would be some days before travel, other than by boat, was going to be possible.

He made his way up the stairs and along the landing to the bedroom that he and Sue were sharing whilst they were staying with Gwen. He pushed open the door. The bedroom was lit with a soft yellow glow from the bedside lamp on Sue's side of the bed. She was lying propped up by pillows, sipping a cup of coffee and pulling a wry face at its taste.

Dan glanced across at her, as he began to undress.

"Why are you drinking that stuff if you don't like it?" he asked, surprised that she was drinking coffee at that time of night and faintly amused by the expression on her face.

"An old habit from my teens and twenties," she replied. "Mum always bought instant coffee. She and Dad always thought that cafetieres were too posh."

She continued sipping at her cup as Dan pulled on his pyjamas. He sensed, however, that it was not coffee that she wanted to talk about and as he was hanging up his clothes, she returned to the theme that she had taken up with him, earlier in the evening.

"I really hope we can soon get back to normal, Dan. I know we've only been here three days, but we can't go out anywhere – and before the flooding, there was all the other bad weather we had in the run up to Christmas. Sometimes in this country, I wonder if the rain will ever stop."

"It's not as bad as the Pandemic some years ago – and both of us got through that…"

"I know…I know…We won't have to wait around for a year or two while it goes away, but at least at that time, we didn't have a house full of water and except during 'lockdowns', we could still usually travel around."

Dan searched for a reply. He remembered the Pandemic as a particularly bad time for everyone, and he had no intention in talking about it or trying to minimise the harm that it did – but at worst, pandemics were periodic whereas, the Climate Crisis…

He left the thought unfinished. Now was not the time to say any such thing to Sue.

He slid into bed beside her. At home, they sometimes enjoyed a brief spell of 'pillow talk' before settling down for the night but this evening, having suffered enough frustration for one day, she decided to slip down under the duvet. If she was going to say anything further, he would struggle to hear it. He snuggled in closer but, perhaps because she was already feeling irritated, she mistook his intentions.

"Don't go getting ideas," she said, her voice muffled but full of emphasis. "I'm not in the mood – and anyway, Mum will hear us."

It was not the response that Dan had hoped to hear. "That's not what you said to me when you used to smuggle me in here years ago," he retorted.

"Well, things were different then. We were both a lot younger. We didn't have kids and we didn't have a house flooded with filthy water."

With a sigh of resignation, Dan withdrew into his own space; clearly, this was not a night for 'pillow talk' – and still less for anything else. He noticed too that, despite her annoyance, Sue's voice was beginning to tail away. Although she usually only took sleeping tablets when the pressures of work were getting to her, the situation they were in had pressures of its own. He glanced across to the bedside table. The packet of tablets lay open.

He rolled gently away from her, though not too far; the bed was narrower than the double bed at home and he did not want to find himself sliding onto the floor.

She was probably right. Perhaps he had harboured the thought that they might comfort each other for a while but the walls in the cottage were thin and sounds easily passed through them; they might reach not only Sue's mum in the bedroom next door but also the two children, sleeping in the bedrooms beyond that. Emily would be sure to hear, even if Josh did not; she was alert, to the point of jumpiness. And the disruption of their 'normal' lives had also clearly unsettled her. Dan was concerned about the effects of the situation on all of them, but he was always aware that, from the earliest times, Emily had been a sensitive child.

He made a conscious effort to change the direction of his thoughts, although as always, he was only partly successful. He began mulling over the topic that was surely close to everyone's thoughts but which no-one ever seemed to discuss. In fact, the more pressing the general situation became, the more unwilling people were to talk about it.

The flooding, though, was only the latest local manifestation of what was happening globally. It was natural for everyone to wonder how long it would be before the floods receded and they could all begin to get back to 'normal', but then, it was almost impossible to know any longer what 'normal' was supposed to be.

For the moment, they felt shut in, confined by the floods to the small world of the house and the village, with no immediate end to the confinement in sight, whilst in the world beyond, everybody else had problems of their own. Beginning at last to feel drowsy, Dan resolved that in the morning he would at least make good on his offer to Josh and Emily – and make sure that they got away from the house for a while.

* * *

When he woke, a grey light was already filtering between the curtains. He could not remember falling asleep. He turned away from his position facing the window and tried to make out Sue's shape amongst the bed clothes – but further searching revealed that she was already elsewhere.

He climbed out of bed, hoping that he would not be in competition for the shower, and slowly made a start. The cottage at least still had hot water and the shower helped to raise his mood. Fortunately, he also had some fresh clothes, so that by the time he went in search of breakfast, he had begun to feel more positive about the day ahead.

He was mildly relieved to find that, as with the shower, he was not in competition for a seat at the kitchen table. He set about finding cereal, milk, a bowl, and a spoon, and then placed himself so that he could see through the open door to the dining room and the front window. He glanced at his watch. It was 7.30. Emily and Josh would probably be in bed for some time yet unless Sue had plans to rouse them. He decided to make the most of his few minutes' peace whilst he had them.

From his seat, he could see that there were few people about in the street outside. Gwen's house was not on one of the village's 'beaten tracks' so he was not surprised. His quiet viewing of the scene outside, however, was interrupted by Sue's voice. She was still upstairs.

"You need to be up and dressed. There's plenty to do so you're not spending half the day in bed!" Dan was not sure if it was Josh or Emily who was the subject of Sue's ire but when a bleary-eyed Josh shambled down the stairs, Dan had his answer.

"What's the matter with Mum these days?" he complained as he fumbled about with the cereal and milk. "She's always in a bad mood."

Whilst silently agreeing with him, Dan felt that he should at least try to show some loyalty. "I think the floods are getting to everyone. Besides, you know what your mum's like. She loves her work and when she can't get there, it makes her fed up."

"Huh – 'fed up'? Is that how you describe it? She's on everybody's case, Dad – and, anyway, since when has work been so all-important?"

Josh began to pour himself a bowl of cereal but as he did so, they were aware again of Sue's voice.

"Come on, Emily. It's time you were out of there! You should have been up long ago!"

Emily emerged a few moments later, pulling on an all-too short dressing gown and shuffling her feet into a large pair of fluffy slippers. The door to Sue's adopted 'office' slammed as Sue, having achieved her purpose, went back to whatever she was doing.

Emily picked her way down the stairs and came through to sit at the kitchen table with her head in her hands.

"Ooh," she moaned. "What on earth is the matter with Mum?"

"I think we'd all like the answer to that one," muttered Josh.

Dan gave him a slightly impatient stare and then, thinking to change the subject, said, "Well, since you are both out of bed now, why don't we think about our plans for the day."

Emily's rude awakening from sleep had caused her to forget her conversation with her father the previous evening, but now she remembered it and her face visibly brightened.

Realising that Josh so far knew nothing about his conversation with Emily, Dan said, "I was wondering if you and Emily would like to get out of the house for a few hours today."

"Out, Dad? Did you say 'out'?" Josh could hardly believe his ears. "Sounds fine to me – but 'out' where exactly?"

"Well, despite being 'rescued' there's more I can do – more I must do – at the house – so you could both come with me and either help me or take the chance, perhaps, to visit your friends. If you are going to visit friends though, I suggest you phone them first and make sure that they haven't had to evacuate – and, of course, that it's ok with their parents for you to visit. If it is, then hopefully, I can get you over to them in 'The Prawn'.

Inwardly, Dan still had his doubts about the dinghy and wondered if he was being rash in even mentioning it, but Josh and Emily had no such qualms.

"The Prawn! The Prawn! The Happy Prawn!" they chanted as they began a mad impromptu caper around the kitchen.

"Look at the pair of you," commented Dan, seemingly bemused. "How old are you?" He paused before reminding them, "Make sure you check with your friends – and their parents."

He found that he was apparently talking to himself since both of them were already on the way to get their phones – which Dan and Sue had always banned at mealtimes – but Emily turned back briefly to say, "As if, Dad…Anyway, I checked yesterday. Remember?"

Dan winced at the noise level as they arrived together on the landing. Sue would be out of her room to shout at them all if it continued. He also wondered where Gwen was, before remembering that on a Tuesday

41

morning, she usually went to help an elderly neighbour, Mrs Down, to get up, dress and eat some breakfast; it gave Mrs Down's daughter, Kate, a chance to 'escape' for a few hours.

Dan ardently hoped that 'The Happy Prawn' was in a fit condition to use. He had last checked it a few days ago but, at the onset of the previous week's storms, had left it tethered in the flooded expanse of the back garden and during the cataclysmic storm of Friday night, all his concerns had been for the house itself. It was fortunate that he and Sue had made an early decision to get Josh and Emily to Gwen's house – and, with the exception of himself, they had all been marooned there.

Involuntarily, Dan smiled as he remembered happier times and Emily's naming of the inflatable dinghy which they had bought with their trips to the coast in mind. He smiled, again, as he also remembered Josh's comment that the name sounded more like that of a Chinese restaurant than of a boat, but the three of them had laughed about it and somehow the name had stuck.

His memory paused for a moment; in his mental picture of the event, there were just the three of them. He remembered now. It had been a Saturday afternoon. He had taken Emily and Josh to collect the dinghy from a friend some miles away. 'Where had Sue been?' he wondered. Ah yes, she had been tidying up the legal details on the sale of an office block. Home life had to come second. It had been like that for several years now.

This morning, however, Dan also needed to do one or two things before they left. First, he would phone his nearest neighbour, Jack Briscoe, and ask him if he would mind doing a visual check on the dinghy, if only to see that it was still in place and in one piece. He knew from past experience that Jack was able to see the dinghy at its mooring point, near the back door of the house.

It was at that point that he realised to his horror that he had not checked that the temporary boat service to Sedgewater would be running that day. He quickly decided that, phone services permitting, he would get through to the operators of the service; having raised Josh and Emily's hopes, his name would be mud if it turned out that they were marooned in Monk's Hill. Fortunately, though, when he made his call he was in luck – and he breathed a small sigh of relief.

Next, he wrote a note to Sue and Gwen, just to let them know that, as he had planned, he was taking Josh and Emily over to 'Moorside' and that they would be back before dark, at about 4.30.

Sue, of course, was still in the house but it seemed best not to disturb her. Then again, he wondered, was that the 'best' option – or was it simply the easiest?

* * *

Josh and Emily duly presented themselves in the kitchen a suitable time before the boat to Sedgewater was scheduled to arrive at the improvised jetty down at the other end of the village; the service, which had been operated in the past during spells of flooding, had been quickly resurrected to meets the needs of the villagers.

Together, they walked through the winding streets of stone and thatched cottages, past the long green shed that served as the village hall and past the village's few shops to where the muddy brown flood water lapped at the improvised 'quay' and the road surface.

Dan had thought that Josh and Emily's temporary incarceration at their gran's house had caused them both to look rather pale but the walk down through the village quickly put a glow into their cheeks and already, they seemed livelier. Dan envied them their youth.

"So, you both managed to contact your friends then? And it's alright for you to visit them?"

Emily nodded vigorously. "You bet, Dad. Phoebe was really excited! It seems like weeks since we last saw each other."

"That's because it is weeks, Dumbo," commented Josh. "There was flooding over there long before we had it here."

"Ok, Mr Clever, so who have you got lined up today? None of your football mates, I bet! I know – it'll be Jayne, won't it? Jayne with a 'y'!"

She smirked at her guess, feeling sure that she was right.

Josh gave Dan his 'girls can be so annoying' look of resignation and decided that he could not escape his sister's abilities to guess what he was up to.

"As a matter of fact, yes, I will be seeing Jayne!" he confirmed, feigning indignation. "She wants me to help her with her homework."

Dan was never sure whether Josh was naïve in his responses to Emily or whether he simply took a perverse delight in presenting her with an 'open goal'.

Emily gave a small whoop of delight. "That'll be the best offer you've had all winter, Josh my boy! And tell us now, will Jayne's mum be there as well?"

"Of course, she will! She's stuck at home like the rest of us."

Ignoring his last comment, Emily said, "I thought you were sick of homework. At least, that's what you said at Gran's." She was rarely ready to give up.

"You're right, I am sick of it – but anything to help a 'damsel in distress'. Anyway, Jayne always has trouble getting down to it."

"That's not what I've heard..." Emily briefly glimpsed the ghost of a smile on Josh's lips and went off into peals of laughter.

Amused though he was, Dan commented, "Come on, you two. The boat should be here in a minute. Why don't you listen out for it?"

His appeal to them, based as it was on the techniques he used as a Primary school teacher, was barely successful and Emily continued to snort helplessly with laughter into the sleeve of her coat whilst trying to look away, across the flooded road and fields. Josh, meanwhile, shuffled his feet and readied himself to step onto the jetty; he had already heard the boat approaching, and shortly it rounded the long, hedge-lined bend in the road, coming in to manoeuvre alongside the temporary and slippery structure. Dan and Emily followed, as did three other passengers, also seeking to get away from the village for a few hours.

* * *

The pilot of the 'water taxi' (as Emily had decided to call it) gave each of the passengers a hand down into the boat, although Josh and Emily needed minimal assistance. As soon as everyone was seated, the steersman opened the throttle and swung out into the middle of the flooded lane. In moments, they were watching the widening lines of the boat's wake rippling out to the hedgerows, and then beyond, into the flooded fields.

At first, Josh and Emily were clearly excited by the novelty of the ride. They tried to call out comments to their father, but the noise of the engine and the movements of air and water made it difficult to hear them; after a few moments, they gave up and instead devoted their attention to the ride.

Although Dan had made the journey in the opposite direction the day before, he thought that it would take him a while to become accustomed to it – and it was more than likely that the floods would have receded before that happened. He sat watching the water slide past, staring out beyond the lane where he could, looking for signs that the water level was falling but, finally concluding that, if there were any such signs, they were imperceptible. The water's expanse stretched across the fields on both sides, as far as the eye could see, further isolating solitary farmsteads, outbuildings, trees, pylons and poles carrying power cables or phone lines. They were crossing the floodplain of the River Sedge and, therefore, the entire landscape was vulnerable to periods of inundation; the question that was exercising local inhabitants, however, was whether or not the Climate Crisis was making the situation worse.

Dan became aware that Josh and Emily were showing renewed interest in the journey; familiar road signs and a tall willow tree on one side of their route told them that they were about to arrive. The steersman throttled back the engine and took the boat, at a gentle speed, through the almost invisible gateway and up to the front steps with barely a moment's hesitation. Moments later, with assistance from the other passengers, all three of them were scrambling out of the boat and onto the upper steps by the front entrance. Then, with a cursory wave from the steersman, the boat reversed away until he could turn it round into the lane again and continue the journey.

When Sue had evacuated Josh and Emily to Monk's Hill, the flooding had been less than it was now and seeing their home again was something of a shock to them.

"Ooh dear!" said Emily as she used her father's key to unlock the front door.

"What the...?" Josh's comment was no more articulate than his sister's.

It took a hefty shove from Dan to open the door, swollen as it was by the water, but as they slowly pushed it further ajar, they could see that the flooding extended right along the hallway and, indeed, all through the ground floor of the house. Although they had taken the precaution of wearing boots, they had to move carefully to avoid water spilling over the tops of them and soaking their feet.

* * *

Emily and Josh went to explore the flooded house and also to let their friends know that they were in the vicinity, while Dan waded round the outside of the house until he came to the dinghy. It was still where he had moored it – tied to a post he had adopted for the purpose. The trailer, semi-submerged, was a yard away. Water sloshed about in the cover that sagged into the centre of the dinghy but he managed to release it without decanting its contents into the boat's interior. There was still fuel in the tank and despite it being 'old fuel', the dinghy's engine was a reliable starter; he thought there was a good chance that he would be able to get it going – and then to take Josh and Emily to see their friends. He folded away the dinghy's cover and looked up as the sound of splashing announced their arrival. Josh was frowning.

"Are you alright?" asked Dan.

"It's a mess in there, Dad – and Mum's right. With every day that goes by, it will be getting worse."

"I know," agreed Dan. "But that's exactly why I've decided to come over here today – to do what I can. Other than that," he said with a sigh, "we have no choice but to wait it out."

Emily was also subdued. "Will Phoebe's house be in the same state?" she asked.

"It might be," replied Dan. "But she wouldn't have agreed to your visit if she thought it would be a problem. I'm sure that you and Phoebe will be absolutely fine."

Josh grinned. "Well, I'll be alright!" he announced. "Jayne's house is on stilts. The workshop and garage are on the ground floor, but the rest of the house is well above water level."

"It's good to know you'll both be warm and cosy," Emily chipped in sarcastically.

Josh opened his mouth to reply, but Dan got in first.

"Ok – let's get you two into the boat." He held on to the dinghy so that Emily could scramble in and then between the two of them they prevented the boat from rocking whilst Josh clambered aboard. Finally,

Dan used the 'mooring post' to steady himself as he too climbed into the boat. Moments later, he felt a small wave of relief as the motor started first time. There was an oar in the boat, and they were not going far, but it would still have been a slow and laborious process without the dinghy's engine.

Dan slipped the mooring line and began carefully manoeuvring the boat out of the garden. The water's depth was just sufficient, and he had an anxious moment, skirting the rock garden. Then, he steered them round to the front of the house and began tentatively finding his way into the lane.

From the gateway, it was just a short distance to the first turning that they needed to take. With the 'Water Taxi' in operation, the flooded road over which they were travelling had probably been checked for debris, but the side lanes were another matter. The flood water had carried along with it tree branches and a collection of farm and household refuse that could damage the boat before they were even aware of its presence.

Dan took the anticipated turn and had gone only a short distance before their route was obstructed by a very large tree branch, grounded at the end from which it had fallen but floating at its furthest tip. Dan took it very slowly, the engine chugging as he did so. Emily and Josh helped to fend off the branch as they edged past. Then, with sighs of relief, they floated into deeper, unobstructed water.

Emily's friend Phoebe lived in a small close, just to the left of the lane along which they were travelling. Dan swung the dinghy into a circular area, bounded by four white cottages, the second of which was Phoebe's house.

He attempted to get as close as he could by turning off the motor and raising it out of the water. He then used the oar to push them closer to the submerged steps by the front door. Phoebe's mum, Sarah, opened the door and Phoebe appeared at her mother's side. Both of them were wearing wellington boots. Phoebe, thin and as tall as her mother, blinked as if emerging for the first time from a burrow. Sarah, middle-aged and comfortably rounded in figure, pushed a lock of brown hair out of her eyes and gave a wan smile.

"How are you doing?" Dan hailed them from the dinghy, whilst he and Josh steadied it so that Emily could climb out.

"Oh, alright I guess," replied Sarah. "Phil's had a rough time at the farm but we're surviving here. How about you?"

"Moorside's flooded – so we're staying with Sue's mother. It's comfortable there – but we can't wait to get back home."

By this point, Phoebe was ushering Emily into the house. Sarah made way for them and called down to Dan, "Don't worry about Emily. We've been cut off for weeks, but we'll be staying upstairs. It'll be good for Phoebe to have Emily's company."

"Likewise for Emily," replied Dan. "She desperately wanted to meet up with Phoebe – so thanks for having her. We 'll need to catch the water taxi back at 3.30. Shall I give you a call at about 2.45?"

"That's fine," replied Sarah. "It's good to see you – and to know you're all OK."

Dan gave her a final smile and began using the oar to push the dinghy away from the steps.

Sarah waved, and closed the door, disappearing back into the house and away from the flooding.

Back again in deeper water, Dan re-started the engine, turned the dinghy around and steered back out to the lane. It was just a short distance to the submerged entrance to Jayne's house. A tarmac drive was murkily visible beneath the muddy brown flood waters and Dan used it to guide him towards the concrete steps that ran up the side of the house to a balcony area on the first floor.

Josh scrambled onto the bottom step and then made his way up to the balcony where he rounded a corner onto the balcony's front section. Dan caught a glimpse of a slim white hand waving to him as Josh disappeared through an open glass door.

Jayne's father, Jeff Myers, was a local contractor to the farming community and was known for his shrewdness and occasional ruthlessness. Dan knew that he had prospered but briefly wondered how anyone could have enough money to build a house such as the one before him. Such a project, he thought, was a long way beyond his present means.

He gave a sigh and then steered the dinghy around so that it was once more facing in the direction from which he had come. Moments later, he was once more feeling his way past the fallen tree branch and out into the wider expanse of water covering the main road.

* * *

Unlike Jeff Myers' place, it was all too evident that the ground floor of Dan's house was not built to withstand the ravages of flooding; of that, he was savagely reminded as he gloomily tethered the dinghy by the back door so that he could step out of the boat into shallow water. Once on the back step, he opened the door and paddled his way across to the foot of the stairs.

Unsurprisingly, the atmosphere in the house was cold and dank and he was aware again of a foul and pervasive smell, the source of which, he had little doubt, was the detritus in the floodwater.

He gazed around him in the half-light, reflecting that there was so much to do and wondering when he and Sue would ever be able to get the house back to what it had been. He hated to think about what the water and its contents were doing to the floors, skirting boards, and ground floor structure generally. He paused at the foot of the stairs, thinking about whether he needed to take his boots off before stepping onto the stair carpet. Then he decided that there was little point.

Once at the top of the stairs, he made his way through to the bedroom, where he found his slippers. Taking off his boots at last, he stood them on the remnants of an old newspaper, put on the slippers and made his way through to the larger room at the front of the house.

It was all as he had left it, except that in coming back to it, the damp atmosphere, the smell, and the sounds of lapping water that echoed through the otherwise lifeless silent gloom below, seemed doubly depressing.

He searched around for a small saucepan. There was no water available from the taps, but he had left a large bottle of water on a nearby table, and he poured enough into the saucepan to make a cup of tea.

Back in the room that he had previously used as his living quarters, he found the tin tray on which was standing his primus stove and a box of matches; like everything else in the room the box felt damp, but he managed to get a match to light and then, in turn, lit the primus stove. Whilst he waited for the water to boil, he busied himself with tidying the room and finding the filing box that held the house insurance documents. Having found them, he put them in his backpack to ensure that he took them with him.

Finally, the water in the saucepan began to boil. He looked around for a cup but the only one that he could find was an old one he had adopted as a pencil pot; he emptied it, wiped it round with a tissue and, exhuming the teabags from beneath a mound of papers on his desk, finally made himself a cup of tea. The fridge was not working and there was no milk, so he took his cup of black tea and retreated to the battered old settee that he had previously retrieved from his study and there, sat sipping away at it, drawing some comfort from the familiar things around him.

Then, sadly, he found himself reflecting again that it might be weeks, perhaps months, before the family would be able to move back into the house, always assuming that the flood would subside sometime soon – and, as he had already seen, there was no immediate sign of that happening.

He enjoyed the tea, despite the lack of milk, and its warmth briefly helped to alleviate his gloom, but it was incapable of dispelling his problems with Sue and the unrelenting dreariness and depression that had accompanied his return to the house. There had been times recently when, waking in the hours of early morning, his situation had seemed to him like an endless black wall around which, or over which, he was unable to see.

It was his plan that day to photograph the damage done to the house by the flooding but now he wondered if such an activity would only add to the depths of his mood...

He took a few more sips of tea then looked around for a space to put down his cup; to his surprise, his mobile phone began buzzing.

He picked it up and answered. At first, he could barely hear the caller at the other end but then he attuned to it and he recognised the voice of Anne Moresby, a peripatetic teacher with whom in normal times, he sometimes worked.

The call ended and he put the phone back down. The gist of it had been that her husband was on a business trip to the States and was not due back for another two weeks. Meanwhile, although her house had not been flooded, she had been marooned by the inundation of the surrounding landscape and now she was badly in need of help. Dan recalled that before the flood, she had been struggling to cope with her job.

Anne had explained that prior to the arrival of the floods, she had been taking medication for anxiety, and now she was getting towards the end of her stock of tablets. She could arrange an on-line prescription from her GP but, because there was no help forthcoming any time soon from the prescription delivery service, she was in need of someone able to collect the medication and get it to her.

Dan realised that, under the circumstances, she was asking quite a favour of him, but he had already planned to go into Sedgewater, the nearest town of any size, and he could easily add her tablets to his list. Delivering them to her would be quite a problem but now that he knew the dinghy was usable, he agreed to help her. He explained where he was but said that he would contact her later to make firm arrangements.

He busied himself with the reason for his return to the house, began to forget about the phone call and started to focus instead on his intended inventory of the flood damage to the house. With a sense of resignation, he pulled on his boots and tramped down the stairs to make a start on the dreary task before him.

He worked for as long as he could, photographing the obvious signs of damage, recording his comments, and taking a careful look at the more insidious examples of deterioration, such as the gradual ingress of water into the fabric of the walls and into furniture that, for whatever reason, they had been unable to move to the upper floor of the house; this included fitted bookshelves in the lounge and all the recently installed units in the kitchen.

As he worked, the dampness seemed to seep into his clothing and his hair, and when he later remembered that he needed to contact Josh and Emily he was grateful for a reason to stop. He clambered to the fourth step on the stairs, where he was sufficiently above the level of the water, sat down, tugged, and swore at his boots as he took them off and then, in stockinged feet padded back up to the landing.

Neither Josh nor Emily were particularly eager to hear from their father, but they both knew that, bearing in mind they needed to meet up with the water taxi scheduled to be passing the house at about 3.30 pm, he would have to collect them some time in the next forty-five minutes.

Having made his calls, Dan went again through the laborious procedure of hauling on his boots, wading through the kitchen, locking the outer door and picking his way through the water to where he had tied the dinghy. Once more, he slid into the boat, and carefully set off past the rockery, the dinghy putt-putting its way out onto the road, now doubling as a canal. After a short distance, he repeated his earlier turn into the side lane, planning to collect first Emily and then Josh. By now, he was getting used to navigating the dinghy through narrow spaces; 'The Happy Prawn', he reflected, was proving to be a useful asset.

Later, in contrast to the exuberance they had shown on the outward journey, Josh and Emily sat sullenly in the water taxi, as it fled through the gathering dusk of the winter's afternoon towards the village. Emily sat near the stern, mesmerised by the boat's creaming wake. Where he could, Josh gazed over the hedgerows, at the expanse of water all around them, gliding steadily and inexorably towards the sea. When they arrived at the temporary quay, the two teenagers scrambled out and set off at a brisk pace along the route that led to their grandmother's house. Dan trailed along behind them, hoping that their 'day away' would not simply serve to heighten their sense of frustration with the restrictions imposed by the flooding.

Meanwhile, he tried to remind himself of the temporary nature of the flooding. Despite his earlier despair, it would surely not be long before he, Sue and the children, were once again in their own house, dank and damaged though it might be, and looking forward to the gradual amelioration of their plight.

That evening, as Josh and Emily chattered away through dinner, Gwen showed interest in what they were saying; she knew many of the families in the area and always wanted to stay abreast of any 'gossip'. Dan also listened but was wanting to catch the latest weather forecast and news, if only to remind himself that, beyond the claustrophobic captivity imposed by the flood waters, there was a much greater world in which, for the most part, people were able to get on with their lives. Sue looked a little happier so he guessed that something in her work must have gone well that day.

After dinner, Josh and Emily went through to the lounge. Between them, the three adults cleared away the remnants of the meal and shared in the business of washing, drying, and putting away Gwen's cups, plates, and cutlery.

Eventually, and contrary to standard form, Sue retreated to the settee with a book of Sudoku puzzles for company. Dan fished the home insurance details from his backpack and sat in an armchair poring over them, trying to make sense of the 'Claims Procedure' and wishing that he had employed more patience in reading the 'small print', when he had signed the forms.

Gwen had taken a little longer over tidying the kitchen but came through to join them.

"So how did you get on today?" she asked Dan. "Is the house surviving?" She gave a wan, empathetic smile.

"Oh yes, it's surviving – just. The water level has steadied but it's still lapping around the bottom of the stairs. For the moment, there's little we can do although I did rescue a few bits and pieces that, in our hurry, we'd previously managed to miss – things like the fruit bowl and one of the breakfast stools."

"I've hardly dared to ask you about it," commented Gwen. "Moving the furniture upstairs must have been very hard work."

"It's amazing what you can do when you have to," replied Dan, "and fortunately we'd already moved a good deal of it while there were still four of us in the house. It was only after Sue, Josh and Emily had left that the water rose some more and started to enter the house. Then, of course, I realised, that there were smaller items that we'd missed but the problem for me was that the water was rising so quickly – and I had no idea when it would stop."

He shook his head as he remembered the chaos. "Unfortunately, during Friday night's storm, I found myself scrabbling simply to do what needed to be done. There was no electricity of course and I was trying to save the power in my phone battery in case of dire emergency – and then, the network went down anyway. It felt very unsafe to be there."

Sue looked up from her Sudoku puzzle. "You certainly had me guessing, Dan. Until you phoned yesterday I was feeling incredibly anxious."

Dan stared guiltily at the papers in front of him. They had already had this conversation, but he said, "I'm sorry, Sue. I wish I'd been able to let you know what was happening, but the storm was so intense, that I was simply trying to keep myself safe."

"The storm was terrible," said Gwen, tactfully agreeing and playing her familiar role of peacemaker. "I thought we'd had our dose of storms and could all get on with clearing up. How wrong I was..."

Sue, though, was not ready to give up. "It was a long, stressful weekend not knowing what was happening to you and the house. I breathed a very big sigh of relief when you got back in touch."

Dan could think of no reply to Sue's comment. He had had to fight a sense of panic that had risen steadily with the flood waters. He had done it by busying himself with securing the dinghy and moving what items he could still reach on the ground floor up the stairs and into the jumbled assortment of household goods that had been hastily assembled in the spare bedroom. He had found himself with little choice but to pile them up whilst hoping that such hasty and random storage would not simply add to the damage caused by the water.

Seeing Dan's distraction, Gwen asked, "Anyone fancy a drink?"

Dan nodded. He needed something to dull the memory of his recent ordeal.

Sue smiled, the first smile from her that Dan could remember, since he had arrived the previous day.

"Ooh what a good idea, Mum. Anyway, I was just waiting for the right moment to announce that I have a little bit of something to celebrate."

Their eyes swung towards her, as they realised that whatever it was, it must be something impressive given that it had clearly lifted the dark clouds that, in recent times, had been permanently parked over her head. They waited.

"Today," she announced, "I finished all my legal work on the Bristol project."

Dan immediately beamed his broadest smile at her but then turned his facial expression towards Josh and Emily, hoping that they would quickly follow his lead. Alarmingly, they continued to look non-plussed.

"It's taken a huge effort," continued Sue as if talking to her work colleagues, "and there's still a lot to be done before 'Opening Day'."

She looked around the now attentive faces turned towards her. "But, overall," she went on, "it looks as though it will be a complete success."

Taking her cue, Gwen quickly set out the glasses on the dining table and poured the adults in the room a good measure of Prosecco. Then, looking to Sue for agreement, she motioned that she was about to pour similar measures for Josh and Emily. Sue beamed and nodded her agreement. Gone instantly was the teenage nonchalance of moments before.

"Cheers everybody!" said Sue, tipping the glass to her parted lips.

"Bottoms up!" exclaimed Dan.

Gwen followed suit but smirked, "I remember that you always used to say that when you and Sue were courting."

Josh and Emily swigged their Prosecco, trying not to look at each other.

Dan glanced at Sue, their eyes meeting over the rims of their wine glasses. He reflected that Gwen was the only person he knew who still used words like 'courting'. To everyone else he knew, words like 'courting' were echoes of a past that had all but disappeared into recent history.

The wine glasses were filled twice more and then Sue said, "Dan, I'll fill in those insurance forms if you like." She glanced across at Gwen. "I know he hates filling in forms. It'll be worth it, to avoid all the huffing and puffing." She briefly imitated Dan huffing and puffing.

Gwen smiled and drained her glass. "Well, I'm really pleased about your excellent news, Sue, and it's good to see you both smiling again – but, if you don't mind, I'm off up the 'wooden hill'. I was up very early this morning, and that wine always goes straight to my head." She giggled, causing Emily to splutter into her sleeve just as she had earlier that day. Then, she lurched a little unsteadily to her feet and began to make her way up to bed. Dan smiled. 'Wooden hill' was yet another of Gwen's phrases, another echo of the past.

Sue was not long in following her mother up the stairs and Dan followed soon after that, having substituted for Gwen in checking that the outer doors were locked. Josh and Emily also went to their rooms although Dan thought that they would spend time on their phones or computers before settling down to sleep.

He climbed the stairs and made his way along the landing. In the bedroom, Sue's lamp once more lit the room with a soft yellow glow. Sue, meanwhile, had huddled down under the duvet and Dan thought that he caught a glimpse of naked shoulder. He began to undress but glanced across at her, wondering how much of a difference her good news and the glasses of wine had really made. Deciding to forget the caution that had grown up around their bedtime routine, he asked, "Are you wearing pyjamas?"

There was no response other than the sound of gentle snoring. He reached out a hand towards Sue's shoulder and his fingertips quickly told him that his glimpse of 'naked shoulder' had been no more than wishful thinking.

He knew the routine and decided that rather than brood on his frustration he would simply get a good night's sleep.

* * *

CHAPTER 7

FATEFUL ENCOUNTER

It was about 8.40 the next morning when Dan slipped away from the house. Josh and Emily were still sleeping. Gwen had already gone out on a local errand whilst Sue had left earlier on the first water taxi of the day to Sedgewater. From there, a car sent out by her solicitor employers, would collect her. She would be gone until early evening.

There had been no time to fall into a routine with the 'pop up' water taxi service, but Emily had found a timetable on the internet, had printed off a copy and pinned it to the kitchen notice board. Dan had consulted it and found that the next boat would be along at 9.00. It would take him about ten minutes to walk through the village to the temporary quayside. He would have time to buy a cup of coffee at 'Mo's Snack Pod', which the enterprising Mo had set up near the quayside at some distance from her coffee shop, in order to draw on any trade that there might be from travellers.

Soon, he was sitting on a small stack of pallets by the quayside, gingerly sipping a very hot cup of coffee. There would just be time to finish it, he thought, before the boat, a larger version of his own, would be manoeuvring its way in to where five local people were patiently waiting.

He had barely disposed of his still warm cup when the water taxi arrived, its wash sending large ripples over the otherwise dry section of the road. Dan, together with the other travellers, was helped aboard by the two orange-suited crewmen, and then off they went again, the boat's wake churning behind them, along the 'canals' formed by the flooded roads.

He was not intending to visit his flooded house until later that day. Instead, there were jobs to be done in Sedgewater. The journey took some time but now that he was getting used to travelling in such a way, he had begun to use various features along the route as distance markers. The throb of the engine receded into the background of his thoughts as he watched the outer reaches of the town drifting past and into the background.

The first part of the journey lay along the flooded road that passed Dan's house. For the time being, no-one had been able to recover the car that was still submerged at the point where its owner had abandoned it; the water taxi slowed to squeeze past it but then sped on between the hedgerows demarcating that part of its route. Dan's attention lapsed for a while and, at some point imperceptible to Dan, the boat left the flooded lanes and joined the swollen River Sedge gliding sullenly on its way into Sedgewater. Borne along by the current, it slipped past dilapidated wharves and warehouses which, prior to the flood, had become inaccessible to craft coming up the river; now, for the time being at least, there was no such problem.

Eventually, the crewman piloting the boat began to throttle back the engine and took them in to a short flight of stone steps leading up onto a quayside. The other crewman threw a rope from near the prow to a waiting worker, who fastened it round a bollard; the process was repeated with a rope from the stern of the boat. Helped by the crewman, the passengers then slowly disembarked onto the steps and climbed the short distance on to the wet stones of the quay.

Dan stood for a moment or two at the end of the quay, watching the other passengers disperse into the town. He had made a mental list of the jobs to be done but with the morning stretching before him, there seemed to be no immediate rush. He decided that it was time for yet another cup of coffee and he remembered that there was a coffee shop at the end of the street. He decided to take a few minutes to gather his thoughts.

Soon, he was seated at a table near the window, watching the passers-by in the shopping precinct outside; their constant movement caused a flickering of light and shade across the table as the pleasure of the hot coffee vied with a feeling of aimlessness and drift akin to that he had felt at some points during his waterborne journey.

He wondered how Sue's day was going. She would be happier now that she had been able to get into work. Briefly, he pondered his growing anxiety about their future as a couple. Did she have similar worries?

The missed opportunity for shared intimacy the previous evening had been disappointing, but he found himself, as Sue sometimes suggested, trying to be grateful for those occasional moments that still came their way. The situation with the house was also a nagging worry, despite the fact that they could do little until the flood waters receded. He felt a sense of relief that Sue had taken on the task of dealing with the insurance company.

With leisure to think, he had to admit to himself that it was rather hypocritical of him to feel a sense of grievance about Sue's obsession with her job. In 'normal' times, as a school deputy head, he also lived and breathed his work and for every work-related thought buzzing around in Sue's head at the end of the day, he always had his own share of thoughts spilling over from the hours he spent preparing, teaching, marking, assessing, meeting with colleagues and all the other activities that made up so much of his daily life.

Thoughts about school prompted thoughts about Amanda. He had not heard from her since the week before the last major storm. That, however, was not entirely surprising. Local communications had proved all too susceptible to lightning strikes and to the enormous volumes of water that fell right across the region. Like Dan, Amanda and James had also chosen to live in a small hamlet which was several miles out from Sedgewater.

Despite warnings at the time about the effects of the growing climate crisis, the school where Dan worked served an estate that had been built on the floodplain of the River Withy; both houses and school had been flooded. Pupils and their parents were either stranded or had been evacuated. The school's staff were in similar situations; so, for the time being, everyone was held in water-bound limbo.

He remembered, though, that the local phone networks were gradually becoming operational again and told himself that he needed to phone Amanda as soon as he could. He also felt frustrated with himself that, as the Deputy Head of Wellsprings School, he had not made a more concerted effort to contact other members of the school's staff. Whatever the problems presented by current conditions, it was surely something that he should be doing – or should already have done? Did he really need Amanda to take the lead, especially in a situation where the communications in her village were probably even worse than those at Monk's Hill? He had an uncomfortable feeling that the flooding was exposing him – and perhaps others – to a desire to see the return to 'routine' delayed for as long as possible – and prior to the flooding, that was not a feeling that he would have anticipated.

His thoughts moved on to his plans for that day. He guessed that his mission on behalf of Anne Moresby would take up the next few hours. Getting over to Anne's house and back again would be anything but routine. He felt a small sense of trepidation as he thought about it.

His mind wandered back again to his work. Despite the closure of the school, there would be plenty that needed doing – and he was also curious to know how Amanda had coped with the isolation of the hamlet in the aftermath of the storm. Of course, he mused, now that the phone networks were recovering, there was no reason why Amanda could not phone him.

He finished his coffee and headed for the street. He would be finished here in less than two hours and at least the bustle of the town might help to renew his own sense of purpose. He needed one or two things from the hardware shop and then he would collect Anne's prescription from the pharmacy. He made his way amongst the shops and small businesses that had survived the ravages of the 'online revolution'. Their brick and rendered facades had changed little when Sedgewater had entered the new millennium but now there was a succession of 'To Let' and 'For Sale' notices; the High Street had struggled to survive in anything like its old form and was now having to reinvent itself. Fortunately, thought Dan, that did not seem to include 'Lawton's Hardware', the shop that he was now about to enter; he ducked into the old fashioned and labyrinthine interior. There were too many things in the store that simply had to be handled before deciding that they would 'do the job'. Besides, he thought, if there was anywhere that would help him to forget about the flooding at the town's threshold, this was it.

* * *

Sometime later, he was back on the quayside waiting again for the water taxi. This time, at least, he had been able to use his phone to book and pre-pay for his seat; the use of cash was now almost extinct even for the most mundane of daily transactions.

He was travelling back earlier than most of the passengers he had seen on the outward journey and there were no familiar faces. As soon as they were all safely seated, the steersman throttled up the boat's engine, reversed away from the quay and swung out into the wide expanse of the flooded river, where the air streaming past them pushed back their hair and made their eyes water in the breeze created by the boat's forward motion. For a few minutes, Dan almost forgot that this watery landscape that he was travelling through was the source of a great deal of misery for local residents, businesses and farmers.

Eventually, the steersman began to slow the boat down so that he could steer it once more into the lanes leading back to the village. Now, after plenty of coffee and fresh air, Dan was sufficiently awake to be aware of the transition. He would soon be back at the house and organising himself to deliver Anne's prescription.

The steersman took the boat as close as he could to Dan's front steps so that he was able to scramble out; in a moment or two, he found himself standing once more in front of the house and unlocking the door to peer into the watery gloom. Because the phone network had been unreliable, he had left a map that he would need in one of the improvised spaces he had made for himself upstairs. He already had a vague idea of how to find Anne's house, but the map would be essential if he was not to waste a lot of time looking for it in what might be difficult conditions.

The map was amongst a pile of papers he had sorted through the previous day. After a few moments, he located it and opening it out, he soon found the hamlet in which Anne's house was situated. Looking at the journey, he realised that he had given an undertaking to get to her without really appreciating the problems that it might entail. He looked again at the map. He would need to travel north-east through the lanes towards Harrowbridge, then on towards Eastmoor Green and finally to Blunden's Knoll. Like so many others in the area, her house on the 'knoll' had not been flooded but, with boats and the rescue services overstretched in the last few days, her situation had not been considered 'urgent' although she was well and truly stranded.

It was time he sent her a text. He quickly found her in his 'contacts' but felt a little awkward. The context in which they always met was that of work; they met quite often – but as colleagues. However, he had offered to help, and he had now collected the prescription, a rather bulky package that took up most of his backpack and which was now waiting for him to get it to someone who would shortly be running out of much needed medication. With a small sigh, he quickly typed into his phone.

"Have your prescription. Can reach you in about 30 mins."

There seemed to be barely a pause before Anne's reply came back to him.

"Thank you so much. Let me know when close. Will put kettle on."

To confirm that he was setting out, he sent back, "See you soon."

That was it. He had better make a start.

* * *

He checked the fuel supply in the dinghy's tank; it looked more than sufficient for his intended journey – although he noted that he would soon have to concern himself with the quantity of fuel left in the storage tank. Next, he looked at his watch. Despite his journey into Sedgewater, it was still just a little after midday. The journey to Anne's house was only a few miles, perhaps two or three – no distance at all under normal circumstances. These, though, were not normal times and it was not hard to see that, as time passed, what was considered to be 'normality' would be almost meaningless.

Dan paused to think for a moment. It might take him as much as three quarters of an hour to get there. He had already studied the OS map in some detail but he folded it carefully and put it into a transparent, waterproof bag so that he could confirm the details of his route as he travelled. He thought it unlikely that he would get lost or unduly delayed but, as a precaution, he put a compass and torch into the pocket of his anorak.

As on previous occasions, the dinghy's engine sprang quickly to life, and he was soon easing his way past the now familiar obstacle of the submerged rockery and towards the gateway. There, he turned and continued for some distance along the route he had come in the water taxi until, after about a quarter of mile, he slowed the dinghy's speed so that he could look for the signpost to Harrowbridge.

Despite the gloominess of the day, he eventually spotted it sticking up from beneath the muddy waters. He looked for the lines of the hedgerows that would show him the route of the submerged road and guide him in the right direction. Sure enough, he could see the twin lines he sought running away from him into the middle distance, where they seemed to disappear beneath a group of trees.

Feeling apprehensive, he set off between the parallel lines of the adjacent hedgerows. The wake of the boat churned away behind him and he steered an unimpeded course along the centre of his route. His sense of uneasiness, however, was beginning to deepen.

As he approached the trees, the tops of the hedgerows disappeared beneath the water, presenting him with a featureless stretch of water but then to his relief they re-emerged, and he was able to follow them into the partial darkness beneath the trees.

His relief did not last long. A jarring thump against the side of the boat made him aware that, as he had found in other places, the storms had brought down a great many branches. He quickly throttled back and began to pick his way between the fallen boughs, straining to see them in the gloom. Several times, he found himself letting out a long sigh, having unwittingly held his breath as he carefully steered the boat between one hazard and the next. Finally, as he was about to let out another such sigh of relief, he found himself confronted by a huge branch, lurking like a shadowy predator and which, despite being partly submerged, seemed to span the entire width of his route. Squinting into the darkness, he could see that there was a short section where the depth of water covering the bough was probably just sufficient to allow him to pass above it. He cut the throttle so that the propeller was turning at very low speed and passed gingerly through the narrow space and into the unimpeded water beyond. There, at last, he emerged from beneath the trees and into the light once more.

For a while, the hedgerows continued to provide him with a clear channel to follow. Soon he was approaching Harrowbridge. Looking at his map he saw that the road was shown as making a detour around the village and then on the lower lying area that led to Eastmoor Green and from there to his destination, Blunden's Knoll. It looked simple enough.

Soon, however, he began to find that his reliance on the hedgerows could not be sustained. As he navigated his way past Harrowbridge, he could no longer see a clear channel ahead of him. He travelled slowly on for a short distance with the hedgerow providing him with little more than hints as to where he was going. Then, as he had feared, their guidance disappeared beneath the water so that he now found himself floating on a huge and featureless lake.

He set the engine to idle and then began quickly to check his course with the map and compass. Having just left Harrowbridge, the map showed that, allowing for a wood projecting into his line of travel from the east, Eastmoor Green lay north of his position. If he skirted around a line of trees that marched down into the water on his starboard side, he should see Eastmoor Green.

Once more, Dan's heart was in his mouth as he skirted the outer trees of the wood. The water on which he was travelling now seemed deeper than any that he had crossed so far but then rounding the point at which the spur of woodland projected into the water, he was relieved to see Eastmoor Green come into view just ahead of him. It was far from being a warm day, but Dan had suddenly begun to feel hot. He unzipped his coat and then set himself to finding the last point on his journey – Blunden's Knoll.

The route to the Knoll lay roughly northeast from his position. By this time, Dan had also taken to looking carefully at the map in order to be aware of the underlying contours. He had not, for one moment, supposed that the flooding would be as extensive, or as deep, as it was. Despite having had plenty of time to get used to the situation in the areas adjacent to Sedgewater, the reality here seemed much worse.

The tips of tree branches projecting from the water just ahead of him caused him to go forward slowly for a minute or two. As he did so, he glanced down into the water on the boat's port side. It was indeed much deeper there. He watched, certain that despite the murkiness of the water, he could see the shapes of fish moving in the water. Seemingly, the inundated terrain had quickly become a hugely expanded domain for the aquatic creatures of the area.

Dan drew his attention back into the boat. After all his earlier trepidation, he could now look towards Blunden's Knoll. Continuing on his northeasterly route, he could see it rising from the flooded expanse ahead of him, perhaps a little over a quarter of a mile away. He turned the dinghy a little further to starboard so that it was now heading directly towards the island that Blunden's Knoll had become. Remembering the steep gradient leading up to Anne's house, he speculated that the water beneath him must be as deep as any in the area he had just crossed. Disconcertingly, he began to feel the dinghy being carried to port, away from the road surface sloping up towards Anne's house. He looked quickly at the map. Immediately, he could see that the course of a small river crossed the area beneath him, and the current created by its flow was pushing the dinghy along with it. He opened the throttle. For a few moments, the engine had to work a little harder but then he was into calmer water again. He paused to send Anne a quick text message after which he searched for a shallow place in which he could safely land.

Manoeuvring the last few feet without damaging the dinghy was tricky, but he managed it. The boat was now in just a few inches of water, and he jumped out with his pack on his back and the mooring rope in his hand. Finally, he was able to tether the boat safely to a road sign on the nearside of the road that led past Anne's house and trudged a squelchy path towards her driveway. He looked at his phone just before he rang the doorbell and decided to turn it off. For reasons he did not pause to think about, he did not want to be bothered with texts or calls whilst he was talking to Anne.

* * *

He rang the doorbell. It had been a while since they had last met – and that had been at a teachers' meeting. As he waited, he was aware that his heart was beating a little faster than usual; he supposed it was the result of the journey he had just undertaken.

She seemed to take a long time answering the door and he was just beginning to wonder if, despite his text and the efforts demanded by the journey, he would be left standing on the doorstep, but then he heard the unmistakeable sounds of a security chain being slid back and a key being turned in the lock. The door opened.

"Hello Dan," she said and smiled, kissing him lightly on the cheek and leading him into the house. Tugging off his boots, he left them by the door.

"Sorry if I was a bit slow answering the door. I was at the back of the house, and I only just managed to hear the doorbell."

As she talked, she was walking along the hallway slightly ahead of him. At the end of the hallway, they emerged through a doorway on the right into a very spacious room with a high ceiling and lit by large windows facing onto the garden.

She seated herself on a two-seater red settee and gestured to Dan to have a seat in a red armchair, of similar style, next to the settee. Between them was a small coffee table, elegantly carved in a dark wood. The surroundings of the room made Dan awkwardly aware that he was still carrying his backpack; he slid it from his shoulders, put it down next to him and then settled himself into the chair's comfort.

"This makes a welcome change from the seat in the dinghy," he commented.

"Oh yes – I can imagine. I feel rather guilty getting you to come all the way over here – especially in the present conditions. What a journey you must have had…!"

He was momentarily tempted to describe 'the conditions' to her but instead, he simply replied, "It had its moments – but I'm pleased that I can help. I bought the dinghy for use on family trips to the coast, but with the flooding, it's proved to be invaluable."

"It certainly is," she replied. "I would have been in something of a fix if you hadn't been able to help. I'm very grateful to you."

Dan heard the sound of a kettle coming to the boil and an audible click as it switched itself off.

"Ah, at last," she said with a smile and went off to the kitchen to make the tea. She returned several minutes later, bearing a tray with cups, teaspoons, steaming teapot, milk and sugar. To Dan, it all seemed suitably calming after the hazards of his journey.

Whilst the tea was brewing, he plied Anne with questions. He was impressed by the size of the house and of the rooms, although he was largely guessing that they were of a similar size to the one in which they were sitting.

"I'm assuming your husband is not in teaching?" he said.

Anne gave a wry smile. "No – he isn't," she confirmed. "George has his own business, making machine parts. He's developed it from a small, two-man operation to one that employs about a hundred people. You're right though – if we had to depend on my salary, we'd never be able to afford a place like this." She poured them both cups of tea and handed one to him.

Dan cradled the hot cup in his hands. "He sounds like a busy man."

Anne nodded. "He is. We used to be able to spend late evenings and weekends together but since the business has developed, George has had to travel much more. At the moment, he's in California."

The conversation briefly lapsed as Dan gazed about him, wondering what it was like for her spending days on her own in such a place, especially now, in flood enforced isolation.

"You must find it rather lonely here – in a house this size, on your own...?"

His question sounded absent minded, almost abstract. He faltered, realising that it could also be seen as presumptuous.

She noticed his hesitation but replied, "I suppose you're right – although I try not to spend time dwelling on it."

"Do you have any friends or relatives nearby?"

"Oh yes – both. And I also visit family members in London. Much of the time, of course, I'm busy teaching, especially since I often teach outside of school hours."

Dan nodded, remembering that a small number of Anne's pupils were talented pianists and needed more of her time than was available during school hours.

In the soft afternoon light of the room, they sipped at their tea in companionable silence. Dan's eyes strayed across to her and she returned his look with a smile. As he watched her, a lock of hair fell across her face, and she paused to push it back into place.

He drew back his gaze but found himself reflecting that meeting Anne at home was quite different from meeting her at work. To say that he was 'seeing her in a different light' was no more than a statement of fact but although he had recognised that he liked being in her company, he saw now that his had been a strangely grudging recognition; whilst he tried not to prolong his gaze and thereby cause her embarrassment, his eyes were drawn again to both her grace – and now that he had time to contemplate it, her beauty.

The echoes of his professional ethic prompted him that although he had always viewed Anne as a friendly, thoughtful colleague, albeit an unusually talented one, he could never think of her as more than that. But then, here, in the unhurried space of her home, chatting as friends and particularly after his journey to reach her, he found himself briefly forgetting their professional relationship.

He reined in his thoughts and glanced at his watch. Reminding himself of the purpose of his mission, he realised with a small shock that he had not yet handed over the prescription that had had brought him there in the first place.

"Oh!" he exclaimed. "If I'm not careful, I shall be forgetting the purpose of my visit."

He reached out to his backpack, opening it wide to retrieve the large bag of medication that had been the cause of Anne's anxious request for help. He placed the bag on the table, taking care not to knock over the now empty teacups.

She laughed. "I'm afraid I'm as bad if not worse – I'd almost forgotten it too. Thank you so much for getting it for me."

"My pleasure," he said but aware that the light in the room was beginning to fade, he did not want to be making the homeward journey in the dark. It was a pity; after the trouble he had had getting to her, they had only been able to spend a very short time together.

Anne rose, reloaded the tea tray and took it through to the kitchen.

Whilst she was out of the room Dan went to the window and gazed out at the flooded landscape.

As she returned, he said, "I'm sorry, Anne, I'd love to share your company for longer, but I was late arriving, and I think I need to make a start on the return journey."

"Of course," she replied. "I was about to prompt you anyway. It's already beginning to get dark out there."

She walked him to the front door, where he put on his backpack, pulled on his boots and began to make his exit. He bent to give her a customary farewell kiss on the cheek but then, as they parted, he hesitated, smiling for a moment and causing her to remind him, "You need to go, Dan. Have a safe journey – and text me when you get home. Perhaps we could meet up for a chat again – perhaps when the floods have gone?"

"Yes, of course, I'd love to," he replied.

Anne watched him with a degree of concern as he made his way across to the dinghy where it was gently rising and falling in the chill ripples at the water's edge. It would be nightfall by the time he got back to Monk's Hill.

* * *

CHAPTER 8

LATE

Despite the gathering twilight, the first section across the lake by the knoll was simpler than it had been on the outward run. At least this time, he was heading back towards the lanes and not out across a largely featureless expanse of water.

The problems began once more, though, when he struggled to find the entrance to the lanes. Although he judged himself to be in the right position, he remembered that just before the stretch across open water, the hedgerows were submerged and that, only by using his compass and one or two features, such as the church tower in Eastmoor Green would he be able to relocate the route he needed.

It took him several anxious minutes but, finally, he found his way back into the channels along the lanes and soon he was once more under the trees and picking his way, in almost complete darkness, amongst the half-submerged branches. His torch proved to be invaluable, enabling him to avoid the larger boughs, but occasionally, he would come almost to rest with a jarring shudder as the dinghy came into contact with an immoveable object. There were several times when, just as on the outward journey, his heart was in his mouth as he wondered what damage he had done to his boat. By this time, a sliver of new moon had risen to illuminate the sky sufficiently for Dan to see that it was a largely clear and starlit night but, despite the cold, he felt himself perspiring again, if not with effort then with the intense concentration needed to avoid sinking or overturning.

At last, he emerged into the flooded lane that ran all the way past his house to Monk's Hill. There would be no water taxi now that darkness had fallen. He would have to navigate his own way back to the village and moor the dinghy at the makeshift quay for the night. The moonlight shone on the ever-widening ripples of his wake as he eased into the final stretches of the journey. At least here, other than the submerged car, the route had been cleared of obstructions, and he relaxed sufficiently to begin feeling the evening's chill.

The lights of Monk's Hill had a welcome warmth to them as the dinghy puttered its way to the water's edge. Cutting the engine, Dan beached the boat where the road ran up into the village and then slid over the side, into the shallow water. It was largely with a sense of relief that he felt for the rope in the dinghy's prow and used it to tow the boat along to the quay. There, he found a length of scaffolding pole projecting above the quay and tied the dinghy to it. He could hardly pretend that it was safe from thieves but, for this one night, he thought that it was a reasonable risk to take.

* * *

He began to walk up through the village. The streets were lit once more but only here and there and sometimes he found himself walking in darkness. As he walked, he began to think about what he would say to Sue, having left the house without telling anyone about his plans – and then leaving Gwen to keep an eye on Josh and Emily. For some reason that was not quite clear to himself, he felt reluctant to mention that he had spent a good part of the day helping a friend – perhaps because the friend was female and, although Sue often spent long hours away from home, she would be quick to become jealous if she knew that Dan had spent time in another woman's company, outside of the work context. Then he remembered that, having switched off his phone whilst at Anne's house, he had not yet switched it on again; he took it from his pocket, restarted it and paused in the street as he waited for it to display the familiar 'Home' screen. He had no sooner put it back in his pocket than a succession of 'pings' told him that a number of messages were waiting for him.

Moments later, he arrived at Gwen's front gate, steeling himself as he did so to relate the full story, even if it met with disapproval, and not to resort to so-called 'white lies', especially over something that he regarded as not very important. The lights were on in Gwen's front room, illuminating the small garden at the front of the house and providing sufficient light for him to find his key. He slid the key into the lock and had begun to turn it when the door was pulled sharply open. Dan blinked a little in the sudden brightness of the light.

"Dad, thank goodness! We were worried sick about you! Where have you been?"

Emily, managing to sound concerned whilst also conveying her relief, stood to one side as Dan, smiling at her, shuffled around the door and into the house.

"It's a long story," was his uninformative reply. "Where's your gran – or your mum?"

"Hummph," snorted Emily. "Everywhere is flooded, you go missing all day – and you expect us not to ask where you've been?"

"No, I'm not at all surprised Em' – but I do need to let your gran and your mum know that I'm here."

At that moment, Gwen came into the room. "Ah Dan, at last. We'd really begun to wonder where you were." Her tone was slightly accusatory, but she was prepared to let it go until Emily had returned to the computer game that she had temporarily abandoned.

"I hope you're hungry. I've kept you some dinner."

"Great, I've almost forgotten about food today."

"Now that takes some believing, Dan. Sometimes, I get the impression it's all you think about."

He grinned. "And sometimes, you'd be right…"

Taking the hint, Gwen went off to the kitchen and returned with a steaming plate of potatoes, chicken and vegetables. She placed it on the dining table and waited whilst Dan returned from washing his hands. As he seated himself, she said, "It's been keeping warm in the oven for a while, I'm afraid, but I thought you'd prefer something hot on an evening like this."

"Thanks, Gwen!" he said, immediately beginning to tuck into the food. "This is just what I need."

She nodded, then returned to the kitchen, made herself a cup of tea and came back to seat herself at the table, opposite him. "So, what happened to you today?" she asked.

"I'm sorry I didn't contact you or Josh and Emily. I thought you'd be busy anyway. I caught the water taxi into Sedgewater and then went back to the house. Then, unfortunately, I managed to miss the last water taxi for the day and had to use the dinghy. By then, of course, it was dark, and the journey back here was a bit of a nightmare."

Gwen sensed that he was being economic with the truth, but Dan was not the only source of irritation at that moment so, for the time being, she let the matter rest. There was an awkward silence which, after a moment or two, Dan sought to break.

"Is Sue back yet?" he asked.

"No, she's had to work late so she's stopping over for the night," Gwen replied with more than a hint of resignation. "She's trying to ensure that the initial work for the Bristol project is completed on time. I think the deadline is Friday."

Despite having a mouthful of food, Dan pulled a wry face.

"That's a pain," he said. "I'd hoped we could all do some catching up."

"That would have been a nice idea," agreed Gwen. Although Josh and Emily are teenagers now, they still need you to spend time with them. If it comes to that, you and Susan hardly ever spend time with each other these days."

Dan noticed Gwen's use of 'Susan' rather than 'Sue'. Perhaps the conversation was a little more serious than he thought.

Dan agreed. "I know. You're right, although in fairness, I did take Josh and Emily to see their friends the other day."

"You did," affirmed Gwen. "On the other hand, that isn't the same as spending the day with them yourself."

Dan was sceptical. "How many teenagers do you know who want to spend a full day in their parents' company?"

"With some families that might be true but when they were younger, you were always telling me that it was important for parents to spend time with their children. Besides, as a teacher, I would have thought that you above all people would have appreciated how important it is."

Dan struggled to find a suitable reply. "Normally, I'd agree with you. But the last few weeks, particularly with all the recent flooding, have hardly been what you'd call 'normal'.

"I'd agree with you there. But you've hardly heard from your school – and Susan is dealing with the insurance company so I can't imagine what you found to do all day."

He felt stung by Gwen's comment – and, though he tried to resist it – a certain amount of indignation that he was getting what sounded like 'a telling off' from his mother-in-law. He decided that it was time to tell Gwen about his expedition; it had, after all, simply been an attempt to help a friend and colleague and was nothing to feel guilty about.

"Ok, Gwen – you asked me before. I'm sorry that I didn't tell you the full story. The truth is that I went to visit a colleague. Her house is surrounded by the floods. She'd run out of some important medication and had no means of getting to the pharmacy, so I went for her. Then, of course, I had to get it to her. It all took much longer than I thought. The journey in the dinghy was quite difficult and unfortunately, by the time I left her house, it was already beginning to get dark. That's the main reason that I was late – and also why I didn't contact you or the children."

…Even in his own ears, the story sounded less than convincing…

Gwen was not inclined to be empathetic. "So, this colleague of yours, does she have a husband or a partner? Why didn't she have anyone else who could go to the pharmacy for her?"

Inwardly Dan was becoming even more indignant but for the moment he decided to go with the run of the questions. "She does have a husband. He's a businessman. The problem is that at present he's in California. I only volunteered to help because there seemed to be no-one else."

He paused but then added with a certain asperity– "And, anyway, why should I not help? She's a colleague and a friend. I don't know her all that well, but we have both worked in this area for a long time."

Resentful though he was that her questions had begun to seem like an interrogation, he stopped short of telling her to mind her own business.

Gwen pursed her lips and looked sceptical but then decided that, for the time being, discretion was the better part of valour. It was, after all, Dan's failure to let them know that he was safe that had caused them unnecessary concern so, as a parting shot she said, "I still don't see though why you couldn't have phoned one of us here? It would only have taken moments to do it."

Dan had to admit that, on that score, he had been unduly dilatory. "I'm sorry," he repeated. "I'll try to get it right in future, and to spend some more time with Josh and Emily tomorrow. Besides, I can't imagine that this situation will continue much longer. The weather's more settled now and the Environment Agency will probably have a chance to get to grips with the flooding. Then, all being well, we can get back to something like our normal lives."

"I'm sure we would all welcome that," said Gwen, in what appeared to be sincere agreement.

She turned in her seat, preparing to leave the conversation, but then remembered that there was something else she had to say.

"Oh, Emily took a message for you earlier on. I think she wrote it on the pad by the hallway phone."

"Right, thanks," said Dan, slightly puzzled. "I thought the landlines weren't working?"

"No – they're back in use. I don't know when they were restored but they have been."

Gwen left the room, and Dan went in search of the message. It took him only moments to find it.

It was from Amanda. He had been wondering why she had not contacted him...but there again, he asked himself, why he had not taken the obvious step and made more effort to contact her?

He paused, wondering why he was giving himself a difficult time over something that was so inconsequential. He had, of course, he explained to himself, been pre-occupied first with the flooding and then with the need to get Anne's medication to her.

The truth was though, he reflected, that neither of these considerations excused him from not having made more conscientious efforts to contact other school staff, especially Amanda.

He looked at Emily's note.

"Hi Dad, Mrs Ashworth called at 15.03. She wants to speak to you about the re-opening of the school. Please could you call her to discuss? Emily."

"Hmm, very efficient," reflected Dan. She must get it from her mother rather than him. He looked again at the message. Despite the huge problems caused by the flooding, the message that Amanda had left with Emily had an optimistic tone to it; surely, he should welcome any sign, however remote, that everything was on the brink of returning to normal? Of that, for reasons he had not stopped to think about, he was by no means sure.

He briefly continued trying to make sense of this seemingly strange thought – but then recognised that although, for the present, he did not know the answer, there would come a time when it would be clear to him.

It was late but he decided, nonetheless, to phone Amanda from his smartphone, discovering in the process that she had left him a string of messages that day. He could hear her phone ringing but eventually his call went to the messaging service. He left a brief message whilst deciding that he would make another attempt to phone Amanda in the morning.

After that, he went to put his head round Emily's door so that, if she wasn't asleep, he could thank her for the note. Then he thought he'd talk to Josh for a minute or two as well.

* * *

Dan cautiously pushed open the door of Emily's room. She was in bed but still awake – though only just.

"Hello, Dad." Her voice was suitably sleepy. "Did you find your message? I forgot to mention it before."

"Don't worry. Your gran remembered – and thanks for taking it. I'm sorry I haven't spent any time with you today. Perhaps we could all do something tomorrow?"

"Sounds good to me. Would you believe school have actually sent out loads more work for us to do? I've started it, but a break tomorrow would be welcome." Her voice began to trail away.

"Alright then, love. It also sounds like you need to get your head down. I'll see you in the morning." He walked across to his daughter, her fair hair spread across the pillow and her skin pale through lack of sunlight and fresh air. He looked at her for a moment before stooping to kiss her on the forehead. She was already asleep. He turned and quietly went out of the room, closing the door behind him.

Josh was still awake and was lying on his bed, listening to music; as Dan appeared in the doorway, he slid his headphones onto the bedside table. "Hi Dad. Glad to see you're back. We missed you."

"Yes, so I've been told. I'm sorry, Josh. I suggested to Emily that tomorrow we might all spend some time together."

Dan was by no means sure that he would get the same response from Josh as he had from Emily, but he need not have worried.

"Oh, yes! I've had enough revision to last me a lifetime. That would be great!"

"Ok then. I have to deal with some work-related issues first thing, but the rest of the day should be ours. Don't let it get too late before you get some sleep."

"No problem. It seems to have been a long day!"

Dan gave him a thumbs-up sign and turned to go but Josh had another question.

"Dad, where's Mum tonight?"

It seemed that Gwen had forgotten to tell Josh that his mother's work precluded her from coming home.

"She's working on a big project at the moment, so she decided to stay overnight in Bristol. What she's doing has to be completed by Friday."

"Oh, really? She always seems to be at work these days."

"It might seem that way," said Dan, "but she's had to spend several days here without being able to do any of her regular work. I expect she has a lot of catching up to do." He inwardly agreed with Josh but still felt he should support Sue in her career. No doubt when life was back to 'normal', they would all be busy and her absence from home would be less noticeable.

Josh thought otherwise. "I suppose I also meant before the floods arrived. She was always at work then."

"That's how it is sometimes in the adult world – as you'll gradually find out."

"I hope not. It can't be much of a life if all you ever do is work."

"Someone has to earn the money – lots of lovely money so that we can all continue living our luxury lifestyle."

Josh caught the tone in his father's voice and grinned.

"I wish…." he said, not finishing the sentence.

"We can talk about it again tomorrow. Now, I need to get some sleep – and so do you."

He went back on to the landing and headed for the bathroom. He was physically weary and quite dirty from the day's efforts in the dinghy. A shower might help him to feel better. Minutes later, the hot water was having its usual therapeutic effect but, afterwards, as he climbed into his pyjamas and then into a bed that, unlike his usual feelings about it, felt both cold and too big, he was irritated again that whilst Gwen had taken him to task for his day's absence and lack of contact, she never seemed to take the same approach to Sue. He reflected that Gwen and Sue's mother-daughter relationship was an interesting one – and also one that he would probably never fathom. He lay for a while turning over the day's events in his head before finally lapsing into sleep.

* * *

CHAPTER 9

IN DENIAL

Dan woke quite early the next morning. The curtains were slightly parted from the previous night, and he lay gazing out at a dreary prospect of grey skies. He had not studied Macbeth since his school days but the oft-quoted line, "Tomorrow, and tomorrow, and tomorrow, Creeps in this petty pace from day to day…" ticker taped through his memory; he had seemingly forgotten for the moment his escapades of the previous day and, besides, it was too early to be positive.

He slowly clambered out of bed, hauled on his dressing gown, pulled on his slippers and went down the stairs in search of breakfast. A bowl of cereal was the simplest thing to put together so, a minute or two later, he sat munching away at cornflakes, looking through the open door of the lounge to the front window and into the street outside. Then, shortly, when he had finished his cereal, he progressed to toast.

Sounds of activity came from elsewhere in the house. Josh and Emily were still asleep, so it was Gwen he could hear bustling about. She came into the dining room with a bowl of cereal and, as on the previous evening, sat opposite him.

Dan was already on his second piece of toast but went to make tea for them both. He returned with a pot of tea, cups, milk and sugar.

"I'm phoning Amanda shortly," Dan announced after a rather awkward silence. "She wants to talk to me about re-opening the school."

"Sounds rather optimistic," Gwen commented. "Last I heard, it was knee deep in water."

"You know that – I know that – but the Academy is probably being leaned on by the Local Authority, the regional Commissioner etc. And, no doubt, the Government is leaning on everyone."

Gwen shrugged. "I suppose you can understand. The children have already missed a huge amount of schooling."

"Of course, but the whole area is suffering. The farmers are probably having the hardest time. Goodness knows what the flooding has done to them."

"Yes, you're right, I'm sure – but you were talking about Amanda and the school – and I assumed it would be them that you were most concerned about."

"Well – yes – I am," Dan reassured her. "But during the last few weeks, the School has been the last thing on my mind. Now, suddenly, here we go again – and everything is expected to be back to 'normal' as fast as possible…"

For once Gwen was inclined to be sympathetic. "I guess if you don't live in this area, you probably have no idea about how bad the flooding is. But I agree with you – it will take a lot to sort out the mess and, of course, everybody expects it to be done yesterday. I don't envy you."

She began clearing the remnants of their breakfast in anticipation of Josh and Emily's presence at the table. Then, turning to Dan, she asked, "Why don't you make your phone call to Amanda? It's probably better to do it now than wait until Josh and Emily are down here."

Dan nodded. That would make sense – although, after glancing at his watch, he decided that it was still a little early and that he would leave it for just a few minutes longer; he also knew that, in Sue's absence, Josh and Emily would sleep until he went to wake them.

He went quietly up the stairs to get dressed.

* * *

Later, back in the kitchen once more, he skimmed through the notes he had made on his laptop. He had a fairly long list of questions – and ideas – but, with time on his hands, he had already reviewed them a number of times. In the first instance, what he most needed to know was how Amanda intended to move the situation forward.

He mused for a moment or two on the train of events whereby, this morning, his job required him to phone her. Had the flooding occurred in the previous winter, he would have been phoning Georgina – or Gina – Bootle, the previous Head of Wellsprings Primary. It was all rather ironic, in view of his previous history with Amanda – something that both of them had so far been careful not to air in public; and it had, after all, been Gina and the interview panel at Wellsprings that had appointed him.

When Dan first knew Gina, she had been Gina Williams but in the course of events, she married and became Gina Bootle. Subsequently, she also became Head of Wellsprings Primary School where her talents as a teacher and Deputy never fully translated into an appetite for the job she was then expected to do – an integral part of which was dealing with OFSTED inspections.

Gina's first OFSTED at Wellsprings did not go well. Shortly after the Inspectors' report, she had begun to 'self-medicate'; Dan had found her one afternoon when they were due to meet, head down on her desk, her office reeking of alcohol. From there, it was but a short time before she was 'fast tracked' into early retirement.

Amanda, meanwhile, as the former, very reputable Head of Wellsprings had found herself having to return there and to combine what was, in itself, a demanding task with the role that she now also occupied – that of Academy Deputy CEO. Much as Dan admired Amanda, he wondered how long she would last.

He glanced at his watch; even given that he had eaten an early breakfast, she would probably be up and fully functioning by now. He went straight to her number in his contacts list. The signal for mobile phones was poor in Monk's Hill but eventually he could hear her phone ringing.

"Hello?"

"Hello Amanda, it's Dan, returning your call from yesterday."

"Ah, Dan – after all this time, we're back in contact. How are things at Monk's Hill?"

"Not so good I'm afraid. The whole area is flooded. The only way we can get around at present is by boat. How are things there?"

"Much the same. James and I have been unable to contact anyone. After the last big storm our mobiles were useless and, as you probably discovered, the landlines were already out of action."

"Yes, I tried to get in touch – but all the phone networks were down."

"Well, as you will have gathered, it was only yesterday that we were able to get back in contact with the outside world."

"I think it's been much the same everywhere," replied Dan. "Emily gave me your message. I'm sorry that you had trouble getting hold of me but, flooding or not, I guess everybody now wants to get back to some sort of normality."

"Exactly – and, of course, there's immediate pressure to re-open the schools."

"Yes, I'd heard. But we can't complain. We must have had the longest Christmas break ever."

Dan was attempting to be light-hearted but belatedly realised that his comment must have seemed rather flippant.

Amanda was not amused. "Yes, we have – but, not surprisingly, it's causing a lot of irritation – with parents, councillors, and, of course, our very vociferous MP. We have to get started on re-opening and, in order to do that, we need to meet."

"I'd assumed that we would need to hold a staff meeting but how do we get around the fact that many of the staff will find it very difficult to get to a meeting – wherever it's held? I assume we could hold a 'virtual meeting' – just as we've done before."

"Of course, I'd thought about that, Dan, but I've been told that the recent storms have made conferencing unreliable. I also think that our sense of being a 'team' will be very much reinforced if we can all meet in one room. Hopefully, though, the networks will be fully up and running again soon though – because we're going to need them."

"You mean we'll have to resort to 'virtual teaching'?"

"Yes – I'm sure we will – for reasons that I'd rather explain at the meeting."

"I'm sure I can guess…"

She did not reply to his comment but said, "Unless, you feel otherwise, Dan, I want our first meeting to be SLT only."

Dan did not disagree. Getting all the staff together for a full meeting would be almost impossible whilst much of the surrounding area was still under water – but it seemed much more likely to be feasible if just the members of the Senior Leadership Team were involved.

"Do you have a time and place in mind?"

"I do – we've been offered the use of The Winstanley Room in Sedgewater Guildhall next Thursday at 10 am but I'd hope that we can be finished by midday. I'll put an agenda together – and keep the

Governors and Academy up to date on progress. Meanwhile, I'd like you to contact the other SLT members – firstly, to make sure that we can actually contact them, and secondly, to confirm that they can get to the Guildhall."

"I'll get on with it as soon as we finish our call. I don't think it will be a problem for the others to attend. They all live in Sedgewater – and I'll be able to use the shuttle service – or as Emily calls it – 'The Water Taxi'. How about you, though, Amanda? It could be difficult for you to get there."

"No, on this occasion I don't think so. I'll check with the Council, but my information is that they intend to re-open the Sedgewater road later today – so it shouldn't be a problem."

"Uhh, I almost hate to ask, but what's the timescale for the re-opening of the school?"

"Unfortunately, I simply can't tell you that." She gave a sigh that was audible over the phone. "As you may be aware, the school site is under water, and it will almost certainly be a number of weeks before the buildings are in any fit state to be used again."

"Yes, I'd heard that the school was flooded...So presumably, we'll all be in some sort of temporary accommodation for a while?"

"I'm afraid so – but that's one of the things that we need to discuss. All in all, it looks as though we're both going to be very busy for the rest of term, not to mention the rest of the school year."

"Nothing new there," laughed Dan, "and some of the decisions we'll have to make will not go down well with everyone."

Amanda silently agreed with him; having to accommodate children and staff in temporary buildings would not be popular.

"I'm sure you're right," she said. She paused. A moment she had anticipated, had now arrived.

"You realise of course that in the situation we have to deal with we will have to work closely together. And I'm sure it will come as no surprise that I'm wondering if you will find that difficult..."

Dan had already given it plenty of thought. "No," he said, "I won't find that at all difficult."

"Well, I hope not, Dan." She hesitated for a moment. "I think you should know that it was the CEO's decision for me to return to Wellsprings. And she was, after all, faced with having to make a rather unexpected decision." She paused again before adding, "I didn't feel able to tell you that last term, but I think it's important for you to know that I did not immediately offer to step into the situation left by Gina. But the Academy had very limited choices…"

"Does the CEO know about our past relationship?"

"No, she doesn't – and it would be best if we keep it that way."

"I can't see how it would come up," replied Dan. "We'll have more than enough to keep us busy."

"We certainly will. Anyway, our past private lives are very much our own business, and we need to focus more than anything else on getting Wellspring's children back to school even if that isn't on the Wellsprings site. They have already lost a good deal of time this year – and that's something that we have to make every effort to address."

"Absolutely!" agreed Dan, although he privately thought that making good on all the lost time would be an uphill struggle.

"Meanwhile, there is an urgent need to get back to normality and with that in mind, I'll be putting together the agenda for the SLT meeting today. I'll forward it to you for your comments but then it needs to be sent on to the other SLT members as quickly as possible."

"Fine – I'll deal with it the moment it arrives."

Amanda's sense of urgency made him feel uncomfortable about the relaxed approach he had inwardly taken during the storms and flooding about the resumption of the school's work. He should not have so readily accepted the situation forced on them all by the weather… and he should not have used the difficulties as cover for his lack of motivation or his guilty feelings about his intended visit to Anne.

He became conscious that Amanda was still talking.

"Excellent! Best wishes to everyone else there, Dan – and thanks to Emily for delivering my message to you. Hopefully, now that communications are up and running again, it won't be so hard to contact you next time…"

Her comment was a very minor sting in the tail. For a moment or two, he stared blankly at his phone but then brought his thoughts back to his plans for that morning. He would use his phone to pick up the expected e-mail from Amanda – so he could still spend part of the day with Josh and Emily – but then he would have to begin giving much more attention to his work which had now so suddenly reappeared, seemingly from the abyss.

After the enforced break caused by the conjunction of the storms, the Christmas holiday and the severity of the post-Christmas flooding, the sudden outbreak of activity necessitated by his work seemed like an imposition. More than that, after the events of recent years, including the massive disruption that had been caused by the global pandemic, talk about 'getting back to normal' had come to seem rather meaningless to Dan. For decades now, news from across the world had contained a constant procession of environmental disasters. He thought back to the previous summer when large parts of Texas – many times the area of Somerset – had been devastated by a Category 5 hurricane. No doubt he could comb through previous statistics and find similar events in the past for both places – but it was their accelerating frequency and intensity which had steadily increased global anxiety about what could be done. In the face of the way the world was changing, what was 'normal' supposed to mean now? And yet...?

And yet, he needed to wake Josh and Emily. True to form, there were no sounds of activity from upstairs, so he had better get on with it. He decided that he would not now have time to take them into Sedgewater. Instead, they could go to the coffee shop in the village which had the advantage that it also provided light meals. If Josh and Emily agreed, they could go there and spend some time together before he tried to engage once more with the demands of 'normality'.

* * *

Half an hour later, the three of them were heading up the steeply sloping road that would take them into the centre of the village. Generally, it was a busy road, but this morning, most people were on foot, welcoming the freedom of being outdoors. The air also seemed fresher – possibly because there was a breeze blowing from the east but also because, for the time being, there was little traffic.

They arrived outside the coffee shop, their pulses a little faster after the walk up the hill and their cheeks glowing. For Josh and Emily in particular, it further helped to dispel the feelings of staleness that had overtaken them whilst confined in their grandmother's house.

"Hey, look at that!" Josh had turned to look across the largely empty car park at the view spread around the hill. Dan and Emily also turned to follow his gaze.

Their view to the north and east was partly obscured by the village centre buildings but to the south and west they could see a watery vista of marooned hamlets, drowned hedgerows and trees. The colour of the inundated expanse was somewhere between grey and brown but overhead, the breeze had begun to break up the cloud and here and there, the sun was managing to penetrate, lighting wind-driven ripples that sparkled in the sunlight.

Dan looked reflectively at his children. "It's an impressive view," he said, "although, sadly, the floods have caused a lot of damage and misery. It will be a long time before we're all back to normal."

"I'm sure you're right, Dad. Only you have to admit that in its own way, it does look rather beautiful."

Emily did not usually disagree with her father, but she was still young enough not to dwell on the disruption caused to the lives of people in the watery landscape below. Josh, a little older, thought that the problems could be solved without too much difficulty.

"My friends at school just think that they need to dredge the rivers properly."

"And who might 'they' be?" asked Dan although he had already been thinking about exactly who would be deemed to be responsible for the colossal task of draining the water from 'The Levels'.

"Well, the authorities of course. Whoever it is, 'they' have to do something. We can't go on living in our present state."

Dan could hardly disagree with that, particularly since he and his family were numbered amongst those who had been displaced and whose lives had been disrupted.

"Let's go inside," he said. "It's warmer there – and it'll be easier to talk without the wind in our faces."

They trooped inside. The café exuded quaintness and rural charm, which seemed to go down well with the summer tourist trade but at that moment, it was busy with local customers. Despite the number of people, Emily managed to find them a table in a softly lit corner. Dan went to the counter to order drinks and snacks.

A few minutes later, he returned with the drinks and whilst waiting for their food to arrive, they picked up the conversation again.

Now, with his drink in front of him, Dan tried to get Josh and Emily to give some more thought to the comments they had made outside the café.

"I'm still puzzling about who's supposed to be responsible for draining away the flood water."

Dan realised that involuntarily they were dropping into the roles of teacher and pupil. It was not what he wanted to happen, but it often did; he smiled at his daughter.

Emily said brightly, "It'll be the Environment Agency."

"Yes, you may be right – but what an almighty task they'll have."

Josh though had no time for any doubts. "I've heard that some new pumps are arriving from Holland. Once they're set up and working, it'll be just a few days before we're back to normal," he said.

"How Amanda would love your optimism!" Dan thought to himself but rather than try to puncture Josh's buoyancy, he asked blandly, "How many days do you think it will take then, Josh?"

"About a week to ten days, I would say." He managed to sound very authoritative, but Dan guessed that both Josh and Amanda had been drawing on the same news source – probably the BBC.

Emily's absorption with the smoothie she was drinking lapsed momentarily into frustration.

"What I'd like to know is why we get all this flooding in the first place. Don't we just need to dredge the rivers more, as Josh says?"

"I wish it was that simple – but no doubt that will be seen as the so-called 'solution'."

It was Josh's turn to feel frustrated. "Oh, come on, Dad, surely it would help – for a while at least?"

"You could be right. And at the moment everybody, including me, wants a 'solution' but decisions need to be made not just for the short term but for the medium and long term as well."

Josh was not to be persuaded. "The problem with The Levels is that the rivers don't carry the water away fast enough. They're all blocked up, so we end up with a massive flood. If the water could flow away more quickly, there wouldn't be time for it to build up. Dredging must be the answer."

"It might be the answer for us out here – but people in Sedgewater wouldn't be very happy. All that water cascading down the River Sedge would probably inundate the town centre."

"So…? They could build bigger flood defences in the town." The answer seemed obvious to Emily and, for once, she was inclined to side with her brother.

"Exactly," agreed Josh. "If flooding in Sedgewater was the problem, then the Environment Agency could put their efforts into improving the flood defences there."

Dan was beginning to feel that he was under siege. He went back to his daughter's earlier question. "You were asking, Emily, why we're getting all this flooding. I don't think it is as simple as needing to dredge the rivers more. I think the problems are much bigger than that."

Josh resisted the temptation to roll his eyes. "So, what are the problems, Dad?"

"Well, firstly, I don't think that all the engineering we're talking about can be kept up for the indefinite future. It's hugely expensive. And, secondly, it seems certain that our rainfall is going to intensify and that the total amounts of rain we get every year will increase."

Having been glued to her computer for a number of days, Emily knew about the many views that had appeared in social media and the more traditional news outlets.

"There are lots of experts around here who don't think the rainfall is increasing. They say we've had much worse rain in the past and the rivers have coped with it. They say it's the lack of dredging that's the problem."

"Well first of all," Dan advised her, "some parts of the media are happy to refer to people as 'experts' when they're no such thing – and also, I think you'll find that many of those 'experts' are self-appointed. I'm decidedly not an expert but the information I'm relying on comes from The Met Office and they say that the oceans and atmosphere are warming. That means more evaporation and, in everyday terms, 'What goes up must come down' so we get more rain and, sometimes, perhaps, more snow – anyway, more precipitation in general."

Emily pulled a face and pouted as she said, "We haven't had snow for years. I wish we could have snow."

Josh, however, was looking thoughtful. "You might be right about that, Dad. In Physics at school we had to experiment with evaporation rates and temperature," adding, "Mr Bryant has a thing about climate change as well…"

"I'm pleased to hear it." Dan smiled, ignoring the taunt contained in Josh's remark but also hoping that all the earnest discussion had not adversely coloured that morning's opportunity to spend some more time together.

He glanced at his watch. "We don't have to go back just yet. Do either of you want another drink?"

"Ooh yes! Another smoothie would be great. But what's happened to the snacks? We've been waiting ages."

"Yeah, Dad, tell 'em to shift their arses. I'll have another diet coke – please."

Dan grimaced. "I will tell them, Josh – though perhaps not in those terms." He set off towards the counter.

As he went, Josh and Emily were laughing.

"Dad can be so prim sometimes. I guess it comes from being a teacher." Josh silently prayed that no such fate would befall him.

Emily smirked, "I don't think it's because he's a teacher. It's just Dad. I can't imagine him ever knowingly doing or saying anything that he thought was wrong."

"Really? That's a lot to put on him. We're all human…"

"You don't say," retorted Emily sarcastically. She paused. "I wish Mum was around a bit more. I really miss our 'M and D' time."

"Yeah," agreed Josh, I could with some 'M and S' time – I need some new T-shirts."

Emily sniggered. "No, come on, I mean it. Maybe she'll be back at the weekend."

At that moment, a red-faced and dumpy waitress in black dress and white pinafore arrived at the table bearing a tray with their food on it. She was clearly feeling harassed.

"I'm sorry," she apologised. Then, as if taking them into her confidence, "We're short in the kitchen today. 'Tis only those of us from the village as can get to work."

Josh, however, was not feeling co-operative.

"Another unforeseen consequence of climate change," he intoned, imitating his father's voice.

"I beg yer pardin, sir?" replied the waitress.

Josh relented and did his best to present her with a solemn facial expression.

"Oh, excuse me," he said. "Just something we were talking about…"

"Well then, I'll leave you to enjoy yer food," replied the bemused waitress and scurried away.

Dan, returning from the counter with the drinks, noticed Emily's almost puce expression and Josh's studied engagement with the Cornish pasty that had arrived in front of him.

"What have you two been up to?" he asked.

"You don't want to know," squeaked Emily, trying to suppress her laughter.

* * *

CHAPTER 10

REFLECTIONS

Prompted by nagging from the volunteer who kept an eye on the temporary 'quay', Dan had decided to take the dinghy back to Moorside. Early that morning, he had started the motor and set off along the flooded road that led directly back to the hamlet in which he lived.

Returning to the house, he felt as though at that point in time there was nowhere that he really thought of as 'home'. Living in his mother-in-law's house was a temporary and occasionally awkward arrangement, but here in his own house the general picture was one of flooding and decay.

He also wondered for how long now he would be able to use the dinghy as a means of transport; the formerly mythological pumps had arrived from Holland, had been installed and were now operating on a continuous basis, pumping water into channels that were thought capable of carrying it away downstream and ultimately, to the sea.

The pumps had been working for five days now and had begun to make an appreciable difference. As he moored the dinghy at the back of the house, he could see that the water was already much shallower and that it would not be long before the dinghy was grounded. He splashed his way back to the front door, unlocked it and went through the by now familiar routine of climbing to the third step and then removing his boots – except that, this morning, had it had time to dry, he could have seated himself on the second step.

Clambering up the stairs, he tried not to look at the places in the hall and kitchen where plaster had come away from the walls and tumbled into the squalid stew of materials that was swilling about in the lower part of the house. He found his slippers, which mercifully seemed not to have absorbed the general dampness of the air and pressed the ignition button on the Calor gas heater.

The throw on the settee had also stayed relatively dry and he used it as a barrier between himself and the clammy leather surface on which he seated himself. He did not have long. His excuse for escaping that morning had been the need to return the dinghy to its usual mooring place. His reason for returning to the house was that he wanted yet more space to think. The pervading dampness of the house was a source of serious concern but its brooding, watery isolation suited his mood – and there was plenty to think about.

It was now five days since the school leadership meeting at the Guild Hall in Sedgewater had taken place. Dan's quiet suspicion, that it would not be a harmonious affair, had proven correct. The various SLT members had retained their professional ethos but each one of them was distracted, to a greater or lesser degree, by the situations they had left at home. Dan, however, was still struggling to re-establish his former level of motivation. Nagging at him constantly was the sense that whilst they could all pretend that there was a 'normality' to which they could return, their situation was merely a temporary one and that it would not be long before it began to deteriorate around them.

* * *

He had spent a number of hours in Gwen's living room working on his computer thinking about the location and logistics of ensuring that they had the resources needed, sharing in the plans to provide safe access to the temporary school site and communicating with parents,

At the meeting, Amanda had opened the discussion, outlining the general situation, whilst Sue Nicholls, representing the Regional Commissioner via video link, had provided news about help that was being channelled through the Local Authority and professional associations – and the need, belatedly expressed, for MATs and schools to demonstrate improved flood 'resilience' and to have in place strategies that would enable them to minimise the loss of time at school, despite the increasing incidence and severity of flooding.

Because she was speaking to them by way of video link, Dan had wondered if Sue had realised how much the teachers in the meeting had bristled at her apparent failure to understand the severity of the flooding and a perceived implication that school staff were in some way reluctant to engage with the unfolding realities of the climate crisis. What, he briefly wondered, had both central and local government been doing during the preceding decades?

He, in his turn, had presented the various plans for practical aspects of the re-opening – most of which had been uncontentious – and the Special Educational Needs Co-ordinator had also had an opportunity to make an effective contribution.

At the end of the meeting and as expected of her, Amanda had enthused about their abilities to work as a team and to motivate the other members of staff. She had "every confidence", it appeared, that they were more than equal to the challenges.

No-one had lingered after the meeting. Dan was aware of Amanda's eyes upon him as he made his way out of the room. They needed to share thoughts and feelings with each other but in that time and place it would have seemed 'unprofessional' to both of them – so they had gone their separate ways, laying open the possibility that in the time ahead, they would continue to privately fret about their relationship, working or otherwise, and increase the likelihood that they would regularly misunderstand each other.

* * *

Dan's thoughts returned to his café conversation with Josh and Emily. It was probably to be expected that they had seen the flooding simply as a temporary problem and one that could be dealt with through simple solutions which would then allow their lives to go ahead in the anticipated fashion – good exam grades, university degrees, professional careers and comfortable, if not wealthy lifestyles.

He had a dilemma. As their father, he loved them – and it was his role to provide them with a sense of security, to ensure that they would be able to make their own way, and to take part in the general effort to provide an environment in which they, and any family they might have in the future, could flourish and prosper. But, day-by-day, the news media were telling him, and millions like him, about heatwaves, wildfires, hurricanes and colossal floods, not to mention the evolving failure of antibiotics, the threat of pandemics and the ever-present threat from nuclear weapons. Seen in that way, the world was a nightmare.

If, today, Josh and Emily preferred the imaginary worlds of their computer games or chatting with friends through social media, despite the problems that these obsessions brought with them, was it his duty to get them to look over the digital wall at the way in which what was represented as the 'real' world was developing?

Was he disappointed in their responses when he had tried to get them to talk about the flooding? There was, he thought, an element of such a feeling – although, given their age group, he thought they had done well to discuss it at all and, even though he did not agree with the simplistic ideas gleaned from friends and a multitude of local 'experts', they had, at least, not come out with the usual teenage epithet of 'boring'.

In any event, if Josh and Emily did not want to engage with the ways in which the climate crisis was going to fundamentally affect their lives, it was a characteristic that they shared with a large percentage of the adult population. Sue, meanwhile, was probably more typical than Dan in her daily concerns. She had returned to her mother's house tired after her long hours of work but still enthusiastic about the project with which she had now been engaged for weeks.

Dan and Gwen had listened, for what seemed like most of an evening, to the details of what she had been doing, how the project was all but complete, the apparently vast sums of money involved, the wealthy 'tenants' who would soon be moving in and the not-too-distant opening of the new office block. They had dutifully tried to follow half-understood details, to make seemingly intelligent comments at appropriate intervals and to sustain a level of interest beyond that justified by the length and content of Sue's monologue.

Eventually, Gwen had produced bottles of wine and poured them all a glass each, in the hope that Sue would gradually relax and start to talk to them about events at home. Unfortunately, it was not to be. Instead, she had quickly drunk several large glasses of wine, becoming ever louder and more detailed in her outpourings until at last, she slumped back on the settee and announced that she was 'shattered' and wanted only to go to bed.

Dan had moved forward to help her get to her feet and with some effort, had made sure that she climbed the stairs safely. Gwen, meanwhile, scooted round ensuring that lights were off, and locks were locked. Upstairs, Sue found just enough energy to get into her pyjamas, into bed and into a sleep from which it would have been difficult to rouse her.

Using the torch on his smartphone to check on her, Dan was not surprised. He had decided to return to the lounge, which Gwen had recently left in darkness. He had switched on a table lamp then gone to the drinks cupboard to find a bottle of whisky that he had tucked at the back, during the Christmas holiday. Resisting the temptation to pour himself a full glass, he had settled nevertheless for what would, in the village pub, have been a large measure.

The house itself had seemed to be sleeping along with all its residents other than him; he, by contrast, had felt himself to be wide awake and his mind sufficiently attentive to do the kind of calm thinking that he had wanted to do all day. For a while, it had worked but then the next thing he had remembered was waking at 2am and, realising that it would not be a good idea to be found next morning, asleep in the lounge with an empty whisky glass in his hand, he had crept off to bed, making sure that the evidence of his late night drinking had been hidden away.

* * *

So here he was, the next day, back out at the house, still seeking space in which to think, still trying to confront the aspects of his life that were troubling him. Restlessly, he got up from the sofa and went to stare bleakly out at the flood waters surrounding the house. The glass was not too thick to prevent him from hearing the cry of a wild bird – a curlew, he thought. His head throbbed from the previous night's bout of drinking but the wildness outside his window, the lack of visible landmarks, the winter cold and the cloud of dark troubles hovering around him pushed him, for a moment into an otherworldly detachment and he remembered a line from a T.S. Eliot poem, 'The Dry Salvages' – "Not fare well, But fare forward, voyagers". The question, however, that he next muttered to himself as he gazed into the wind rippled greyness of the flood waters was, "So, which way is 'forward'?"

He returned to the damp settee. For a while, the room developed a rather steamy, fuggy warmth as the gas heater did its job. He found himself dozing as the throbbing headache began gradually to ease. For a while he dreamt, and, in his dream, he was a teenager again, delivering newspapers. The problem was, however, that the newspapers would not go through the letterboxes – and nobody seemed to want them, despite his attempts to put them into their hands. It was a dream, he realised, that went around and around; he was no further forward at the end of it than he had been at the beginning. Eventually, he woke with a start.

Despite his dream, he felt better, rested – although he had not been sleeping for long. It was just as well. His reasons for making the journey that morning had been to return the dinghy to its usual place and also to make yet another check on the state of the house. He had better make his inspection, he thought. Sue would need the details for the insurance claim. He would also check the garage where he and a friend had previously managed to get his car up on a ramp so that it was above the level of the water.

He made his way back downstairs. Pulling on his boots and paddling once more around to the back of the house, he noticed that the water level had fallen a little more since he had first arrived. In a short while, the water taxi would be unable to get along the lanes. He checked for messages on the water taxi website and, sure enough, the service had been suspended for the time being. He returned to the front of the house, having carried out all the checks that he had needed to do and made sure that the front door was locked. Now that the water level was receding, looters would probably become even more of a problem than they had been at the peak of the flood.

With the water taxi out of action, he would have no choice but to walk through the shallow water back to Monk's Hill. It was a distance of about two miles, but he welcomed the chance to have some more time to himself. Ironically, he had splashed about twenty yards along the now shallow waters of the lane when his mobile phone began to ring. Seeing the name on the phone's display, Dan smiled to himself. It would be good to hear a friendly, uncritical voice. He quickly responded. "Good morning, Anne. How are you today?"

CHAPTER 11

DRYING OUT

Emily scrambled down from the school bus, shouldered the backpack she used to carry her schoolbooks and notebook computer and set off along the dusty lane. She would be the first home, although Josh would be along in about an hour. The bus ground on its way and Emily watched as it disappeared around the bend in the road, sending fresh clouds of clay dust into the air.

She came to the wrought iron gates that her father had put back in place now that the winter flooding had largely disappeared from the landscape. Pushing one of the gates open, she made her way up the short tarmac drive to the front door. She was not in any hurry, so she paused to look for a moment or two at the rock garden and the borders that her parents had worked to re-establish after the flood waters had receded. Daffodils, tulips and primroses nodded together in the breeze and the warm sun of the spring afternoon. One or two of the low-lying areas of the garden were still a little boggy but Emily thought that it was remarkable how well the garden had survived its winter inundation.

She slid off her backpack and fished in the front pocket for her house key, musing that it was a pity that the house had not recovered in the same way as the garden. A sudden gust of wind brought with it an eye-watering cloud of dust, causing her to open the door quickly and to scramble inside. Immediately, she was aware of the contrast. Outside a recovery was taking place; in here, everything was going at a much slower pace.

The first things that always caught her eye as she entered the house were the areas in the hallway where plaster had come away from the walls. Her dad had remarked that he was thinking about giving up teaching and going into plastering, such was the demand for plasterers throughout the district. Her second impression was subtler but more insidious. The whole house was pervaded by a dank mustiness that persisted despite sustained efforts to ensure that it was dry enough not to cause them all health problems.

Despite her youth, Emily was capable of sustained and thoughtful reflection and in the present situation, she could empathise with her parents' underlying distress. All four of them loved the house and had lived there long enough for every room and corner of it to have been fashioned to suit their needs and tastes – but now? Now there was a mountain of work to be done simply to restore it to a state in which it could survive into the future – intact, weatherproof as far as possible and their shelter from the restless world.

She paused to reflect on the meaning of her thought – 'weatherproof as far as possible'. Indeed, what did that mean now? The weather had shown that it was far mightier than any human ability to manage the countryside in which the house had been built. She could not see a time when human beings would be able to control the environment in such a way as to effectively contain the worst that the changing climate could throw at them. Once, perhaps, decades ago, people knew with a fair degree of certainty what it was they were contending with. That, however, was history. It was the period of 'Now' that worried her and, beyond that, caused her to wonder what sort of future lay in store for her, her family and friends.

For she could see for herself that something had unleashed the forces of the weather. And now, nobody knew any more the topmost limits to which the weather could go. Even this familiar place in which she lived would become a place of terror.

Was any of it, though, worth thinking about, she asked herself, because such thoughts made her depressed – and she was already being reproached at times for being 'too serious' or, less perceptively, 'grumpy'? Perhaps none of the terrible things that some of her friends talked about would come to pass? Besides, her friends were far from united about what would happen in the future. Whilst a few talked about such things as catastrophic storms, prolonged flooding, intense summer heat and sea level rise, others seemed to spend their time thinking about little other than music, clothing trends or the ephemeral 'lives' of celebrities. She imagined they reflected their parents' thoughts and views in which the future was seen as an indefinite extension of today's 'business as usual', only with today's wealth, today's devices and gadgets, today's towns and cities becoming only bigger and better. It was a totally different vision of the future than the one that was in her head – but, perversely, like the forces underlying the climate and weather, had to it no upper limit.

Emily sighed. She wanted to think about something else. It was no good mooning about in the largely unusable lower part of the house. She would go upstairs to her bedroom and watch television for a few minutes. Then she had to get on with her homework. Tonight, it was English Lit, and Maths. Before that, however, she would distract herself with a few minutes of entertainment.

She flopped onto her bed and used voice commands to 'wake up' the set. The wide screen of her TV sprang into life with a rapid sequence of images and colours, only not the usual variety but instead, a charity appeal on behalf of children in a war-torn African country, a country where mining and destitution determined that there was no clean water to drink. The narrator's voice told her to text the word 'water' to the charity if she wanted to make a donation. Emily wondered vaguely about how she could do that – but she had no credit left on her phone and, although she had some savings, access to them was controlled by her parents. The idea seemed to be a non-starter.

She was about to turn off the TV when she heard the front door open, and bang shut again. "Josh?" she called out. It should be him at this time.

Reassuringly, Josh answered, "Hello Em. I'll be up in a minute."

There was a thud as Josh dropped his sports kit on the floor, took off his shoes and padded up the stairs. The door of Emily's bedroom swung open and Josh's dark, tousled hair followed by his beaming, slightly red-faced features appeared.

"Hi Josh!" Emily called to him from where she was lounging on the bed. Then, looking at his red complexion, she commented, "You look hot. What have you been up to?"

"It's Thursday, Em!"

"So?"

"Thursday is football practice."

"Oh yes, of course. You decided to go then?"

"Well of course I went!"

Emily suspected otherwise, having heard that Josh's attendance at football practices had recently been poor, but she decided not to pry into Josh's affairs. She also thought she knew where he had been. There was just one attraction strong enough to prise Josh away from football.

"Anyway, what are you doing now? It'll be ages before dinner." Josh always seemed to be hungry.

"There are some of those little pork pies in the fridge if you want one." Emily had already looked and decided that she would wait until dinner.

"Do I want one? You should know the answer to that, 'little sis'!" Josh knew she hated being called 'little sis' but, as a teenage boy, annoying others came naturally to him.

"Any chance you could help me with my maths?" Emily asked. In fact, she was perfectly able to do that night's maths homework but thought it might be a chance to quiz him about Jayne, his girlfriend now for several months.

"Okay, no problem. But I want to chill out for a while. Ask me later."

Emily nodded her agreement.

Josh sauntered off, leaving the door open. Emily knew that he would head straight for the fridge and then go to his room. And if Jayne had not been very co-operative that afternoon, he would not feel like talking anyway.

Her thoughts ran on. There seemed to be a number of things – important things as it seemed to her – at home and at school, that no-one wanted to talk about.

Perhaps, instead of feeling frustrated, she should just get on with her homework? Gloomily she reflected that it was all her home life seemed to consist of these days. Reluctantly, she closed her bedroom door, unzipped her backpack and pulled out the poetry anthology that her class had been studying that afternoon. She preferred to start with the poetry. It suited her mood at that moment.

She enjoyed learning but the thought that she would have to spend four more years in formal education was daunting. And, beyond the compulsory subjects, what would she choose to do? She was 'good' at most subjects, without being particularly talented in any of them. What on earth was she going to choose as her future career? What could she see herself doing for all those years stretching into the future – always supposing, of course, that the human race had not starved, cooked, drowned or blown itself up by then?

Emily opened the poetry book and skimmed down through the headings. She enjoyed the poems – and would soon be able to write a 'good exam answer' about many of them, but what experience could she bring to them? She was still an observer, a bystander. In that sense, her life had yet to begin.

She remembered that Kevin Lang had been her discussion partner that afternoon; after they had read one or two, he seemed even more reluctant to discuss them than she was. Even so, she had enjoyed working with him. They had been in the same English group now for some time, but she still did not know him that well. Perhaps she could get to know him better?

She began to feel more cheerful. Her dad would be home in about half an hour and would cook dinner for them all. His pile of books to mark would be on one end of the kitchen table and the dinner ingredients on the other. It was fortunate that he enjoyed cooking – that, and the usual glass of wine that he drank as he worked. Her mum should be home in about two hours. Hopefully, she would have some time to spend with her that evening. Even though her mother worked long hours, there was still a special bond between them – one that was somehow different from the way she related to her father.

* * *

The house was surprisingly quiet when Dan opened the front door. In a way, he was grateful for that; he was feeling far from sociable and wanted some peace and a little time to himself. It had not been a good day at school. He had been drawn away from his class to take phone calls, the children had become progressively rowdier and finally, Amanda had called into question his judgement in dealing with an angry parent.

He dropped his briefcase on the kitchen floor, poured himself a glass of red wine and slumped onto a chair at one end of the kitchen table. Relationships in the school could be brittle at the best of times, but the floods had made them much, much worse. He needed just a few minutes to let the knots inside him untie themselves.

In what seemed moments later, he stared at his wine glass. It was empty. He could not remember drinking the wine although, as he ran his tongue round his mouth, his taste buds reassured him that he had. He poured himself another glass. As hoped, the knots in his stomach were beginning to disappear. In a moment, he would get the ingredients of dinner up together and start cooking. He should also go and say 'Hello' to Josh and Emily – but he still wanted just a few more minutes… just a few.

He felt his phone buzz in his pocket. He pulled it out and studied it for a moment; the Curriculum Group meeting planned for the late afternoon of the following day had been postponed. For a moment, he felt a sense of relief – life was quite full enough – and the meeting would have been just another thing to engage with, but then, he reproached himself, the Group's work needed to be done, and it simply meant that he would have to spend a different late afternoon slot at school rather than the one that was in his diary.

He found himself downing his drink and then refilling his glass once more. He supposed he had better get on with cooking the dinner or the day would end on the same note of discontent that had characterised the rest of it.

He stood up to gather the necessary ingredients but then lurched into the table. It was not a good start. He busied himself and began to feel a little more in control again. At least after a drink or two, he had the energy to get on with what he needed to do. And he was pleased that, of the rooms on the ground floor, they had decided to prioritise the kitchen, drying it out, repairing it, redecorating and finally, restocking it with food, appliances and kitchen utensils. It was the one downstairs room that they could really use at that point in time. He tugged open drawers and drew out herbs and spices. He opened the fridge, took out some chicken pieces and slammed it shut. He went to the utensils drawer and picked out sharp knives and wooden spoons, clattering them down on the worktop.

Suddenly, an upstairs door opened, and a halo of light appeared on the landing. Emily emerged from Josh's room where, the poetry homework completed, she had gone, ostensibly, to seek help with her maths. She called down the stairs.

"Dad, is that you?"

"Yes, Emily – of course, it's me. Who else d' you think it would be?" He noted that he was rhyming with himself and felt faintly amused.

"Oh, ok, Dad, it's just that I could hear all this slamming and banging and wondered what was going on."

"I'm trying to get started on the dinner. Otherwise, we'll have nothing to eat this evening."

"Do you need any help?"

"No, it's alright. It'll be something straightforward tonight. I can manage – but thanks for asking."

Emily closed Josh's door and, returning to her own room, closed her door behind her, so that the light from the landing was extinguished. Dan felt chastened – and sobered a little by Emily's concern about the noise. If this was what he was like when feeling sorry for himself, he had better try to come home in a better frame of mind. There was, however, an uneasiness inside him which said that he was not being realistic with himself.

He busied himself with the preparation and the cooking. This was, at least, something he did most days of each week. Dinner would be ready in time – but only just.

* * *

Sue parked the BMW on the drive, switched off the engine, grabbed her briefcase and, opening the door, swung her feet down onto the tarmac. She was feeling tired but satisfied. The Bristol project had gone well. The city centre complex had opened on time and on budget, and the efficiency of her legal work had been a vital link in the chain. Now, there was just the usual, residual tidying up to do – and then, it would be on to the next 'project'. Steve Paton, director of the company of solicitors for which she worked, had been very complimentary and she was due a handsome bonus for ensuring that all the conveyancing deadlines had been met. If she could only continue in this way, the family could begin to aspire to a better house, Josh and Emily's student debts, when incurred, could be paid, and meanwhile, she and Dan could think about taking some well-earned holidays.

The porch light was on. It was so good to be back in their own home, even if it meant that they were largely restricted, for the time being, to the upper floor. Living at her mother's house had been a trial and with

Dan, Josh and Emily all swanning around whilst the schools were closed, it had been difficult to stay on top of her work. The severe damage to local communication networks had also delayed the final stages of the Bristol project by several days; had it not been for that, the work would have been completed ahead of time. She had needed to strive might and main to keep her work 'on track' and had been able to give very little time to Dan and the family. Perhaps now, she would be able to give them some more of her attention – for a few days, at least.

As soon as Sue opened the front door, she could smell the food cooking. Maybe that evening, for want of any other celebration, she would drink a few glasses of white wine. She called out from the hallway.

"Hi Dan, that smells good. Do you need a hand?"

"No, love, it's all just about ready. You could give Josh and Emily a shout."

Sue went to the foot of the stairs. "Josh! Emily! Dinner!"

Dan bustled around the table, setting out dishes of chicken and vegetables so that they could help themselves but then he was able to sit and wait for the others. It was mildly frustrating that, after his labours in the kitchen, nobody seemed to be in much of a hurry...

The food, however, was still hot when they arrived in their seats and began ladling food onto their plates. Dan still felt moved, however, to say rather testily, "Come on, let's eat this food before it gets cold." He did not want his efforts wasted, having battled through the self-imposed haze of several glasses of red wine.

For a while, Josh and Emily concentrated on eating, pausing only briefly between mouthfuls to talk about their day at school. Dan was judiciously circumspect about his day. Eventually, however, Sue decided that she had an announcement to make.

"Since none of you asked," she said, "I had a very good day because today, the big project in Bristol has finally come to a successful conclusion. A date for the opening ceremony has been announced."

Josh and Emily gave a brief cheer.

"Does that mean we can spend a bit more time together?" Emily's innocent question could have been construed as having a hint of sarcasm in it.

Sue laughed. "I thought you might show a little bit more curiosity about it all?"

"We haven't seen you that much, Mum, but I think you've managed to keep us up to date." Josh did not want to hear any more about his mother's work. They had, after all, he thought, had a very similar announcement whilst they were still at his Gran's house.

Seeing Josh's reluctance, Dan realised that he had better intervene so, glancing at Josh and Emily, he said, "It looks as though the new Complex is set to be a big success. All the messages I've seen on social media look very positive. I think we should congratulate your mum on a job well done."

Sue beamed whilst Dan raised his glass of red wine. She raised her own glass of wine and chinked it against his, with Emily and Josh joining in.

"Congratulations, Mum – Sue – here's to present – and future – success!"

"Thank you," responded Sue. "It's good to have an evening when I don't have to think about work – and we can all have some time together."

Dan began to clear away used plates and dishes and then said, apologetically, "There's not much for dessert, I'm afraid. It's yoghurt or what's left of the apple pie from Sunday."

They made their choices and stayed at the table a while longer until it seemed as though everyone had eaten their fill.

In the lull that followed the meal, they began to drift off to their evening activities. As they did so, Sue said in a low voice to Dan, "Do you mind if we sort out the kitchen a bit later? I could do with having a chat to Emily. It seems like a long time since we had one of our mother-daughter sessions."

Dan could hardly disagree and smiled at her. It also reminded him of something that he needed to do. "No, go ahead. I need some time with Josh – and then perhaps the two of us could do a bit of catching up after that?"

Sue nodded in agreement and disappeared off to Emily's room whilst Dan moved plates, bowls and cutlery from the table to the dishwasher. Josh's voice carried down the stairs to the kitchen and Dan supposed that he was talking to someone on his mobile phone. He decided that he would wait a little while, knowing that Josh's conversation was unlikely to finish in that time.

* * *

Sue seated herself in an old leather armchair that had been 'donated' to Emily because there was no room for it elsewhere. Emily sat cross-legged on her bed, seemingly comfortable in a position that Sue would have found impossible to sustain.

Emily was pleased to have her mother's attention, even if it was not likely to be for long.

"It's so good to be able to talk to you, Mum. I've really missed our mum and daughter chats."

"I know, Emily. I'm sorry. It's just that the flooding coincided with the busiest time on the project, so it took everything I had to stay 'on track'. But we'll have some time now – and probably for the next few days as well."

Despite Josh's remarks at the table, Emily was interested in her mother's work. "I really admire what you've been doing, Mum. I think I want to do something like that when I leave school."

Appreciative as she was of her daughter's comment, Sue thought for a moment and then said, "In a way that's very flattering, Emily. But are you sure that it would be the right direction for you? The last time we talked about it, you said you had no idea what you wanted to do in the future."

"I know – but it's not that long before I have to decide on my exam options, and I don't want to leave it until the last minute."

Sue sympathised. "I know it probably won't be easy for you to decide but you still have quite a while to think about the subjects you want to do. I also think you need more information. Your dad and I could help you with that."

Sue remembered that there had already been a letter and e-mails from Emily's school about pupils choosing their options, and she felt guilty she had given only passing thought to the information that they contained. She said, "Have you talked to your dad about this? He is a teacher, after all. He probably understands the system better than I do."

"No, we haven't talked about it, not yet anyway. I'm not sure that he does really understand. He is a teacher of course – but he's a Primary teacher – and I don't think he knows about the details that I need."

"You may be right, but in fairness to your dad, I think he would be very willing to help you find out what you need to know – so I still think you should talk to him about it. However, I think you need to keep your options open for a while and I also remember that when I was at school, I was told that I needed a 'good spread' of subjects in my GCSEs."

"I think I will have quite a 'good spread'," replied Emily. "I'll be doing English, Maths, Geography, History..."

Sue had, at least, heard the list several times before.

"Doesn't sound any different from the last time we talked about it, Em."

"You're right, it is exactly the same, Mum – but the point is that I think I will have to drop some subjects."

"So which subjects do you think you will have to drop?" Sue asked, not wanting the conversation to become a guessing game.

"Basically, French and Music."

Sue pondered her daughter's use of the word 'basically' for a moment but then thought that she could see another reason for Emily's apparent reluctance to talk to her father about her options. Dan had decided views about the importance of 'Music' and 'Modern Foreign Languages'.

Sue thought she had better ask Emily the obvious question. "Why are you thinking about dropping those subjects?"

"I'm never going to make a career in Music. And since 'Brexit', I'm never likely to work in Europe."

"Hmm, I can understand your point about Music. I'm not sure about your other comment. I think you might still be able to work in Europe if that's what you eventually want to do. Anyway, I thought you were rather good at French – at least, according to your reports. Of course, you don't have to study a European language. Your school does offer other choices..."

At that moment, Emily's phone pinged, as a message arrived, and she stopped to read it. Sue waited with unaccustomed patience, dully aware of Dan and Josh's voices from a little further along the landing. She was more tired than she had thought and the topic of conversation, despite its relevance, was not what she had anticipated when she had sought out her daughter for some 'M and D' time. Naively, as it appeared, she had thought they would probably talk about friends, TV programmes – the sorts of topics that Emily had always wanted to talk about before. Even the subject of boyfriends might have been preferable.

* * *

Dan, meanwhile, was hardly faring any better. Like Emily, earlier that evening, he had a shrewd idea as to why Josh had been missing football practice. The question was one of how to approach the subject.

He slid into Josh's room which was lit only by a desk lamp and the light from the display on his laptop. Josh, used to his father's way of entering the room, turned away from his computer screen and said, "Hi Dad! What can I do for you?"

Dan, by then, was perched on a rather rickety folding chair, one of a pair, the other serving as Josh's desk chair. They sat facing each other in the dim light of the room.

It was, felt Dan, a difficult topic. He hardly knew how to start.

"I had a call from your Games teacher, this afternoon."

Josh feigned surprise. "Oh? What about?"

"The fact that you've now missed three football practices in a row." Dan paused. "So why is that?"

Josh tried to deflect his father's sudden directness. "You're kidding me, Dad. It's nearly the end of the season. We don't have any important fixtures left – and, besides all of that, have you seen the state of the school's football pitches? Every time we play, it's like a mud bath. How can we play half decent football in those conditions?"

Dan looked sceptical. "I've never known you worry about mud before," he commented. Josh's last remark was the flimsiest in a line of feeble excuses. "I can understand that with your GCSEs coming up, a few end-of-season fixtures might not bother you too much, but I think that you should, at least, have talked to Mr Bridges about it."

"I know, I'm sorry. I keep meaning to do it, but every day is full on at the moment. I will speak to him, I promise you."

Dan tried to look mollified. "I'd be pleased if you would. Mr Bridges has always taken an interest in you, and he's spent a lot of time with you over the years. However, my other concern has to be about where you've been, when supposedly you were at football?"

Although he had anticipated the question, Josh still felt defensive and more than irritated by it.

"I don't really see why you are concerned, Dad. I'm sixteen, as I'm sure you remember, and in a few months' time, I hope to be in the Sixth Form – where, hopefully, I'll have a bit more freedom."

"I understand that, Josh – but I'm bound to be concerned about you."

There was an awkward, rather angry silence, eventually broken not by Josh but by Dan.

"Alright, if you're not going to tell me where you've been, I think I already know. My guess is that you've been round at Jayne's house. Am I right?"

"What if you are right? We're friends, Dad, and Jayne's sixteen – the same as me. Surely at sixteen, we can choose who we're friends with…"

"Yes, Josh – but at your age, I think that from time to time you still might need some advice."

Josh paused. He knew that neither he nor his father would want the conversation to become a shouting match, and he did not want to say anything impulsive.

"I don't see why you think I'm in need of advice when all we're doing is our homework," he said as calmy as he could.

"Maybe, Josh – but then perhaps it's your definition of 'homework' that I'm concerned about."

"Dad, if you've got something to say…"

"Alright, Josh, I'll spell it out. I think that you and Jayne are doing your homework – there's every sign of that but…"

"But what…"

Dan had hoped to avoid this moment, but it had to come. "…The 'but' is, Josh, that I think you and Jayne have started having sex." It was Dan's turn to pause. He looked at Josh before continuing.

"Tell me I'm wrong and I'll drop the conversation – although, if I do drop it and then I find out later that you've been telling me – uh – 'less than the truth', I shall be very disappointed in you."

Josh, red with embarrassment, looked away, seeming to think before muttering angrily "…Really, Dad, just to remind you – we are sixteen so…"

"So…what?"

"So, we're not legally 'children' anymore."

Dan sighed inwardly but felt that at least they were probably moving towards the truth.

"Legally, Josh, you're right, but I have several things I want to say to you about what you're doing."

"So, what's that?" asked Josh, with more than a hint of annoyance.

Dan understood his son's impatience, but he continued, "Well, firstly, Josh, I want to know that the two of you are taking precautions."

"Of course we are, Dad – and, before you say anything else about it, we have had lessons about it…"

"I know all about the lessons but there are some things that can't really be taught at school."

"And what's that…?"

"Well, for a start, to be plain with you, Josh, once sex comes into the equation, both people usually begin to become much more serious about the whole thing. It all starts to move well beyond the hugs and kisses stage…"

Again, Josh paused before reacting and Dan inwardly gave him credit for that.

"All right, I can see that, Dad but I'm not sure why you're concerned. What's so bad about me and Jayne having feelings for each other?"

Dan drew a breath. "I don't want to say that there's anything wrong with the pair of you having feelings for each other," he said, "but it does concern me that you're getting into what I would think of as 'deep water' whilst you're both still very young – and in a month's time, you and Jayne have important exams. It seems to me you're expecting a lot of yourselves if you think you can handle exams and deal with…well, deal with what used to be called 'getting serious'."

To Dan's surprise, Josh began to grin. For a moment he felt annoyed.

"Look, Josh, this is nothing to grin about."

"I know, Dad…I know… it's just that you were having a go at me about my idea of 'homework' but now you're telling me that 'getting serious' is what older people say went they want to talk about having sex."

Josh's apparent flippancy was beginning to annoy Dan, so he decided that he needed to change tack.

"Do Jayne's parents know what you and Jayne are doing?" he asked.

Josh gave an audible sigh. "If they do, they've never said anything. They're hardly ever at home anyway. Besides, would you rather we met up in some farmer's cow shed?"

Dan let Josh's question pass and said, "Regardless of that, Josh, I think that Jayne's parents have the right to know what is happening in their own house. If you and Jayne are not going to talk to them about what you're doing, perhaps I should pay them a visit?"

Josh's face reddened immediately, and Dan knew that his remark had hit home.

"Ok, Dad," he replied quickly, "if it helps...Jayne and I have talked about the exam situation already."

"And what, if anything, did you decide?" asked Dan.

"...That we're not going to see each other – outside of school, that is – until we've both finished all our exams."

"Well, that, at least, sounds like a sensible idea..."

He got no further because, at that moment, there was a loud knock at Josh's door.

The door opened, and Sue's head appeared. "Hello both of you. Emily and I have finished our little chat so I'm going to the lounge."

"Okay," said Dan. He turned to look at Josh. "I think we're just about finished here anyway."

His son nodded, a sense of relief flooding over him. He hoped that their conversation was not only over for that evening but that it was one to which they would not return.

Dan turned to say 'Goodnight', but Josh had his back towards him and was busily packing his bag for the morning. It seemed better to leave him to his thoughts. Dan slid out of the room and went to check that all the lights had been turned off. The wine he had drunk earlier in the evening – and also possibly his talk with Josh – had given him a headache.

* * *

A few minutes later, under his bed covers, Josh found himself mulling over the conversation again and then, after a little while longer, about a different conversation that had taken place at school. One of Jayne's friends, he recalled, had told her that because the world was such a dangerous place, the last thing she wanted to do was to have children. Jayne had agreed with her. It was one very good reason that he and Jayne had been taking precautions from the beginning although, of course, at that point in their lives neither of them had the least ambition to become parents anyway – intentionally or otherwise.

It also seemed to Josh that the long running demonstrations by pupils and students had caused many of their friends to think much more seriously about the Climate Crisis and about whether or not the kind of future that most parents seemed to want for their children would even be possible. And Josh asked himself, what was the point of slogging away at GCSEs, A-levels and perhaps even university, if the sort of world they were all being prepared for was simply going to collapse in anarchy and violence...? It was strange, he thought, that given the views his father held about the Climate Crisis, he should still be concerned about such things as GCSEs. In the kind of world that Josh and his friends were talking about, GCSEs would be meaningless. Sometimes the adults around him simply did not join the dots...

* * *

Sue was already in the room that had been adapted, for the time being, as the family's 'lounge'. She was watching television as Dan padded across to the settee but switched it off as he settled beside her.

"Drink?" Sue held up her glass of white wine to show him that she had already started.

"Uhh – no – thanks," he muttered.

"Are you alright to talk?"

Dan thought he could manage that, despite wanting to go in search of the paracetamol bottle.

"How was Josh?"

"Oh – he's ok. Working hard – I think."

"Is he still seeing Jayne?"

"Yes, but he's doing a bit more than 'seeing' her – if you see what I mean."

"Really? Do you mean they're having sex?" She sounded rather shocked.

Dan nodded. "Yes, that's just what I mean."

"So how did you get to find out?"

"I had a note from Jeff Bridges, Josh's football coach, asking if I could shed any light on why he's been missing football practices – apparently he's missed three in a row...and of course I knew that he's been seeing Jayne."

"I imagine you talked to him about it..."

"I certainly did."

Sue took a sip of her drink. "They're a bit young to be getting into that, aren't they? Do they know what they're doing?"

"Well, Josh assures me that they do – and, of course, in doing that, he also gave the game away."

"But they've both got exams in a month's time..."

"Yes, I did remind him about that."

"And what did he have to say?"

"That he and Jayne have agreed not to see each other out of school hours until they've both finished all their exams."

"Well, that's something to keep him to...Perhaps we should speak to Jayne's parents?"

"Yes, I've thought about that. But as Josh reminded me, in legal terms, they're no longer 'children' – and it's consensual."

"I suppose we only have Josh's word for that..."

It was Dan's turn to be shocked. "Do you really think that Josh would...?" His sentence tailed away.

"Not for one moment but you must admit, it's a difficult situation to deal with." She took another sip of her drink.

"I certainly agree with you about that," replied Dan. "Fortunately, providing they keep to their plan not to see each other during their exams, we have a chance to think about what we're going to do."

"Good thought." She turned aside to fish in her bag.

"Here, Dan, I can't stand that pained expression on your face any longer. Why don't you take these?"

She held out two paracetamols which Dan gratefully took from her before heading down the stairs to get a glass of water. When he returned, he felt in need of a change of subject and asked, "How did you get on with Emily. Is she alright – or is anything bothering her?"

"Probably lots of things," said Sue with a faint smile, "but the one she decided to ask me about was the question of her exam options at school."

"Were you able to help her?"

"A little – I mean I understand that she needs to choose them carefully or she could be handicapped later in her A-level choices – always assuming of course that she wants to go on to the sixth form, but, other than that, I don't really understand why choices made at fourteen or fifteen should have such a big effect on their opportunities. I'm sure she doesn't have a clue about what she wants to do in the future." Sue paused. "Perhaps you could talk to her?"

Dan sighed. His colleagues – friends – in the local secondary schools had often talked to him about pupils' problems in choosing their 'options' – and the difficulties pupils could cause themselves by making careless choices.

"Yes, of course I will."

He paused. "So, what about us? What about the 'grown ups'? How are we coping – post-flood, I mean?"

Sue had wondered how long it would be before they got round again to the subject of the flooding, but progress was slow. For the time being there was little that she could report.

She said, "I've spoken to the insurers. I've also completed all their forms. Unfortunately, they're coping with a huge backlog of claims and are refusing to commit themselves as to when they will be dealing with ours. I can keep phoning and e-mailing them – although, other than that, I don't know what more I can do."

After the frustrating day he had experienced at work, Dan could manage little more than resignation. "Ah well, it will take as long as it takes, I guess – although it does make you wonder why we pay for insurance when it takes so much time to settle claims."

"We have submitted a very detailed list of the damage done by the flood water…"

"Yes, it's quite a collection. All the same, I'm wondering how much we should do, for the time being – in the way of repairs, I mean? Perhaps you could go through the policy again?"

"Mm, I will." Sue sipped at her wine. "I think though, that we should just carry on doing what we can to get life back to 'normal'."

Dan agreed. "At least the kitchen is usable."

"Yes, that's something we have been able to sort out. And thanks for tonight's meal, Dan. It's so helpful that we don't have to wait for me to cook the food."

"That's alright." The paracetamols he had taken had now taken effect and his headache was beginning to ease. The pile of children's books was still waiting to be marked, and the dishwasher had to be loaded, but he would have to get up early in the morning and deal with them.

Sue's glasses of wine had made her feel sleepy. "I don't know about you but I'm ready for bed."

Dan nodded and they headed for the bedroom. Although it was April, it was not particularly warm so as soon as they were in bed, they huddled together.

Dan said, "I can tell you've had a really successful day. Do you think we could…?"

Sue, since she was in a mellow mood and appreciating the warmth of Dan's body, said, "Why not…so long as…well, you know…although I suppose Josh and Emily are further away from our room here than they were at Mum's…"

After more than a month's abstinence, Dan thought that she might have managed a little more enthusiasm but then, he did not suppose for one minute that he was 'God's gift' to Sue – or indeed to any woman. He moved to hold her in his arms but found that she had already passed into a softly sonorous sleep.

* * *

Next morning, grateful for the early morning light to aid the rather feeble glow of the kitchen light bulb, having loaded the dishwasher, Dan sipped at a cup of black coffee and set to work marking his pile of pupils' books. He felt fairly certain that he had 'dried out' enough to be under the legal alcohol limit when he drove to school, although it was largely a question of safety; police cars were rarely seen in the lanes that led to Wellsprings Primary School.

Sue had left about half an hour before. Josh or Emily would lock up as they left the house. Finally, the last book marked, Dan put the pile into his school bag and picked it up. He headed for his briefcase and then the door. Just then his phone buzzed; it was awkward timing for a message but, deciding that he had better read it before getting into the car, he fished it from his coat pocket. It was Anne. Could they meet up at her house so that she could thank him properly for his help during the floods? It sounded like a good idea – but then was it? Perhaps Anne was telepathic. It was as though she had known that Dan's Curriculum Group meeting had been postponed. He would have an hour, perhaps a little more, to drive over to her house and then back home.

He wondered for a moment about the guilty feeling that came to him as he made his time calculations, whilst also remembering the frustration of Sue's involuntary response the previous night. Then he dismissed his thoughts as silly; Anne was a colleague and friend. Why should he not visit her in time that was now his own? Making love with Sue would have been wonderful – or so he told himself – and, for the time being at least, would have helped to rekindle their mutual affection. The trouble was that, from Dan's point of view, any such rekindling had become a rare occurrence. He found another brief moment to confirm that he would see Anne after school that afternoon and then made his way out to the car from whence it would be the beginning of another 'enjoyable' day.

* * *

CHAPTER 12

ONCE THERE WAS A WAY...

As usual, the level of the day's activity and the focus needed had been such that Dan had not been conscious of the time passing. Now that he was alone, he was quickly tidying his desk, trying to ensure that the resources that he needed for the following day were where he would be able to find them in the morning and that the classroom looked as though someone cared about it.

The day had, at least, been better than the previous one. He reflected that for much of the time, he had been able to focus on teaching his class which, he felt, often suffered as a result of his role in the school; consequently, pupils' behaviour that day had been much better.

With the postponement of the Curriculum Group meeting, he was now free to get away earlier than usual. He gathered up his laptop, briefcase and work for marking and headed down the steps of the temporary classroom in which he now taught. To one side of the cluster of temporary classrooms which, following the flood, currently housed Wellsprings Primary School, there was an area that had been hastily covered with concrete and tarmac to provide a parking area for teachers and parents.

Dan made his way there, laden with his bags and opened the boot of his small Toyota hybrid; he tried to look unhurried but as he put the bags into the boot of the car, he noticed that his hands were trembling slightly. Perhaps it was not a good idea to be meeting Anne? He reminded and reassured himself that she had been a colleague for a number of years but, because only a small part of her work took her into schools, he met her just occasionally. Her invitation would, at least, allow them to get to know each other better. He could also consider it relevant to his work because she sometimes taught music at Wellsprings Primary or helped to organise music events there. He had about an hour or an hour and a half. Then he would have to repeat his usual evening performance at home.

He swung his car out of the car park in a cloud of dust. After the winter's inundation, it seemed strange that the weather had now been very dry for about three weeks. For the time being, the lack of rainfall was a blessing and enabled everyone in the area to get on with the business of recovering from the flood.

Compared to the previous saga with the dinghy, when the landscape had more closely resembled an enormous lake, the journey to Anne's house would be a very simple one; it was about three miles from school – roughly the same distance as that from Dan's house, only today, getting there would take him minutes where, during the flood, it had taken more than an hour.

The very straight route ahead of him ran across a flat landscape, cut into variations on rectangles and squares by tall hedgerows along the perimeters of the fields and roads. Willow trees, alders and poplars helped to punctuate the monotony of the flatness. The straightness of the road along which he was travelling was unusual since in general the area was criss-crossed by lanes of the usual winding English variety but, in this section, it followed the course of an old Roman 'Way'.

It led across the countryside for what seemed some distance but was probably no more than a mile. The sky was a dull, uniform grey, compounding the monotony of the scenery but then, to his right, Blunden's Knoll had come clearly into view. An outlier of the hills to the north, it rose steeply above the fields, roads and ubiquitous drainage ditches that formed the grid-like area through which Dan was driving. Eventually, he came to a crossroads at which a 'finger' signpost indicated that Blunden's Knoll was a further distance of one and a half miles to the right. He made the turn, and the road wound its way in the more usual fashion amongst the hedgerows, many of which still contained such flood debris as rags, shredded pieces of black plastic and a great deal of flotsam from trees and bushes that had probably come from the annual hedge cutting, in the autumn.

After a while, the road began to climb steadily and, in places, quite steeply until it met with a wide lane which ran in a large circle around the Knoll. The hamlet of the same name as the hill was on the western slope, so that Dan found himself making another right turn and driving about half a mile with the hill sloping upwards on his right and sharply downwards to his left, so that he had an excellent view of the flat and geometrically divided landscape below him and across which he had come. As he approached his destination, the grey uniformity of the clouds parted momentarily, so that a single wide shaft of sunlight illuminated the many streams, ditches, ponds and puddles spread across the fields below. The greenness of spring was, at last, bringing touches of life to the weariness left behind by the flooding.

He drew his attention back to the last section of his short journey. The loneliness of the road enabled him to focus on finding the entrance to Anne's drive. Glimpsing the road sign to which he had tethered the dinghy a number of weeks before, he was amazed and slightly shocked by the depth to which the flood must have covered the area below. Then, before he could think any more about it, he was at the entrance to the drive. The tyres of the Toyota ran smoothly over the tarmac, bringing him to the front door of the house.

Unlike the occasion of his previous visit, when he rang the doorbell it was quickly apparent that someone was at home. A light appeared at the end of the hallway and in a moment, the door was opening, and Anne stood there before smiling. He dipped his head to kiss her on the cheek.

"Come in, Dan, come through to the lounge."

The hallway was quite wide. Dan padded along the carpet, following a little behind her. He thought she had probably spent a good part of the day at home because she was casually dressed in blue jeans, white shirt and a stylish v-neck cardigan. There again, she was the sort of woman capable of flattering whatever clothes she wore…

She took him into the lounge that he remembered from his first visit, ushering him towards the armchair. The daylight outside was steadily fading so she switched on the wall lights, bathing the room in a soft, yellow warmth.

"So how was your day?"

"Good – thank you."

"I've driven past Wellsprings' site a few times. What's it like to work in those temporary classrooms?"

She was not a devotee of small talk but could see that he was feeling a little tense and wanted him to relax.

"It's fine. I like the one I'm working in. It reminds me of the old classroom I had in my first teaching job – although this one is new – and we can still smell the paint."

She had another reason for asking. "As you know, I'll be coming over to Wellsprings next week. Do you have any idea what sort of space I'll be working in, bearing in mind that Amanda wants us to be working towards an end of term performance for the parents?"

"Hmm, good question." Dan smiled. "Each classroom is basically just a box and none of them is large, but I've found a room in which I think you'll be able to work with your protégés."

She laughed. "Protégés? Is that what they are? Actually, to be fair, Wellsprings does have some very promising pupils, musically speaking – so perhaps I should feel complimented..."

Dan smiled and mused for a moment. "Space in which to practise is one thing – but finding a space big enough for the performance, that's another matter altogether."

"I'm sure you, or Amanda, will come up with somewhere suitable."

She was, he thought, being very optimistic. At that moment, he had no idea where he would find space for some five hundred parents and their children.

Anne wanted the conversation to change direction, so she said, "Do you have time for a glass of wine?"

He thought about it for a moment; he would have to drive back through country lanes which might well be in darkness by the time he left but for some reason, he was still feeling slightly tense, and a glass of wine might help him to relax.

"Oh – I shouldn't really. But if you're having one..."

She had anticipated his answer, so she asked, "White – or red?"

"White, please." He guessed her preference and thought that he would share it – on this occasion, at least.

She left him for a few moments, returning with two glasses and a bottle of Pinot Grigio. She uncorked the chilled bottle and poured him a small amount of wine, handing him the glass.

Dan, co-operating in the usual ritual, tasted the wine. She looked quizzically at him, and asked, as if mimicking a previously encountered wine waiter, "Is the wine to your taste, sir?"

He nodded. "Mm, it's very good."

Anne duly filled his glass, poured one for herself and returned to the settee. Then, she raised her glass. "Here's to you, Dan – with a big 'thank you' from me for your act of kindness."

Dan raised his own glass. "It was no problem, Anne – something that you might expect one friend to do for another."

She thought that, in the circumstances of the flood, it was rather more than many friends would have done but said, "Then here's to friendship!" and tipped her glass to her lips.

Dan mirrored her movement. A short silence ensued, whilst they both sipped their wine and then she asked, "How's everyone at home?"

"Oh – they're all well. Josh and Emily are back at school, of course. Josh is already revising for his GCSEs and Emily is fretting about her 'options'. Sue is on one project after another– so we see her sometimes." Remembering that Josh and Emily would soon be at home, he realised that his time with Anne would be short. "How are things here?"

"Much as usual."

"So, you should be seeing George later then?"

Anne gave him a slightly bitter smile. "I did say that life here is 'much as usual'..."

"You mean he's on another business trip?"

"Yes, in Germany this time." She glanced at him. "I don't mind though. He's after an important contract – important to him and to his company, of course."

Dan said nothing but thought, as he had previously, that she must lead a rather lonely existence.

Aware of the irony, he glanced at his wristwatch. "Unfortunately, I don't have long this afternoon, Anne. I'll have to be going again quite soon."

"I know." She looked at him, seemingly to appeal to his realisation that she would be spending a solitary evening. Pausing, she wondered how much to say. "I think that on the day you came over I was grateful for your company every bit as I was grateful for the prescription."

"It was no problem," replied Dan. "It was an effort to get here but I enjoyed every moment of my time with you."

"It's curious," said Anne. "We've worked together for several years now but until that afternoon – well, it's almost as though I didn't really know you before. Now I feel that I do – or at least, that I'm beginning to..."

Dan nodded, aware of the warmth of feeling between them. He had felt it on his previous visit…but where could any such feeling go? He glanced around him. It was such a grand house, such a symbol of worldly success…He could never aspire to anything like it. He could never aspire to Anne.

He decided to change the subject. "It must be lonely for you here – especially with George having to be away on business so much."

She smiled. He had broached the subject before – but whilst she needed company there were also times when she enjoyed the time on her own. "Yes, it can be difficult sometimes, but I also need the solitude."

"What do you do here – all on your own?"

The question was intrusive, but he seemed concerned, so she said, "I spend most of my time playing the piano – that and listening to other people's music whenever I can."

"Hmm," said Dan. "Music seems to be your life. But is there anything else that drives you…that you feel passionate about?"

Her smile broadened. A conversation that had begun with small talk was becoming a little intense. "Well, since you've asked," she said, "yes – I am driven by other concerns."

Her words hung in the air for a moment as Dan waited for her to speak again.

"On the day of your previous visit, I had spent hours gazing out over the water that surrounded this place – and wondering what on Earth is happening to this world."

Dan shifted in his seat. Music was not his province, but this at least was familiar territory. "My trip in the dinghy helped me to understand that, even for the Somerset Levels, what's happening is not 'normal'."

She nodded. "It isn't," she agreed. "We've all known that now for a long time, but we've ignored it. That afternoon, though, I couldn't concentrate on my music and as I gazed out over the floods, I had plenty of time to wonder about the future of this place. I love this house – and it would have to be a mighty flood indeed to destroy this place but that isn't what really concerns me."

"So what is it then, Anne? If you don't mind me saying so, you seem to have everything here that you need – but I get the sense that there's something weighing you down."

She gazed at him for a long moment. "So is this what I'm here for, Dan?" she finally asked. "I'm a privileged woman, a musician with time to explore her music – and yet, what should I be doing in a world such as this? What can I really contribute?"

Dan shook his head. "I wish I knew the answer to that – on behalf of us both," he said. He looked up at her and gazed into her eyes. "That's probably not the reply you might have hoped for, but I've asked myself the same question many times – and I simply don't have the answer."

He looked down again. There were problems here that he wished he could solve – but there would always be a price to pay. He was not sure that he wanted to pay that price. He was generally content living the quiet life that he had. Unthinkingly, out of habit, he glanced at his watch.

Anne noticed and said, "I can see you need to go, and I expect Josh and Emily are already at home. It does me so much good just to talk to you – but we can do this another time."

They got up together and Anne led the way to the door. Dan paused just as she was about to open it. Absentmindedness had bred certain habits in him. "I'm feeling that I've left something behind."

"No," she said, "this time you brought only yourself – but I was very grateful for that –and for your company."

He placed his hands gently on her hips and softly kissed her on the mouth. She did not resist but after a moment, she carefully drew back from the kiss and placed a finger on his lips.

"I don't want us to do anything that would annoy Sue – or George for that matter. And we have so much more to talk about the next time that we meet."

Dan smiled, bleakly aware that he had been on the brink of complicating a friendship that he was hoping would continue into the future.

He kissed her again but this time briefly and lightly on the cheek and then he walked across to his car and, with just a momentary backward glance, climbed into it. Anne drew her thin cardigan around herself as he pulled away, his headlights probing the slowly fading light.

Somewhere in the growing space between them there was the realisation that this was a different flood, a different darkness and, despite the time shown on Dan's watch, it was already too late.

* * *

He mooned around the kitchen where his laptop stood open, the next week's lesson plans on the screen, as he used the quiet of Saturday afternoon to prepare for the week ahead. It was difficult, however, to know how to prepare. Amanda had emphasised the need for everyone to support one of the PTA's main fundraisers, the Summer Fayre and the concert, which was scheduled for the Wednesday evening. Meanwhile, he was aware of the lack of curriculum time before the National Tests in Maths and English, which were due to take place shortly – even though all the children for many miles around had lost a huge amount of school time because of the flooding.

The sunshine of the late spring afternoon fell through the kitchen window, illuminating the far end of the kitchen table, and Dan watched for a moment the innumerable motes of dust drifting in its beams. The warmth of the weather was helpful; it would continue the long drying out process that was needed after the flood. Outside, at the back of the house, was a pile of wreckage from the previous kitchen units, waiting to be taken to the recycling centre. It would be a long time before the house could be restored to anything like the 'normality' they had formerly taken for granted.

Before they had moved back to the house, Dan was aware that not all the damage to its structure would be immediately apparent, but they had inspected it all as thoroughly as they could and once the gas, electricity and water supplies had been checked, he and Sue felt satisfied that it was safe to return. In preparation, they had shared in clearing out the filth and the debris left behind by the flood water, although everywhere on the ground floor, walls were stained, plaster ruined and wooden flooring badly damaged.

Somehow, they had managed to carry out basic repairs and then buy some usable kitchen cupboards and drawer units from second hand shops and stores in Sedgewater. Of the food they had stocked in the kitchen, only the contents of tins had survived the flood. For safety reasons, the electricity supply had been cut at an early stage and so, when they returned, nothing else was fit for consumption.

Taken together with the effort needed to relocate and reopen the school in temporary premises, it had been a time of incessant activity. For Dan, the Easter break had hardly come quickly enough.

All too soon, though, the holiday had flown by and now ahead of him were all the usual events of the Summer Term. Thinking about the week ahead, he persuaded himself that detailed planning for the following week would largely be a wasted exercise. Instead, he outlined the items that he thought would be essential, saved his work and closed the laptop. Sue and Emily would be in Sedgewater for some time yet, whilst Josh would not be back from Bristol for several hours. He would have the rest of the afternoon to himself.

His phone buzzed in his pocket. He fished it out and retrieved a text from Anne.

"I'm at a loose end here. Do you fancy coming over?"

He placed the phone thoughtfully on the table. He certainly did 'fancy' going to see Anne – but was it a wise thing to do?

There again, there seemed little harm in going to visit her – so long as they continued their relationship as friends; this was probably a useful opportunity to do exactly that. Anne was a beautiful and gifted woman. He wondered briefly how many such people he had met in his life – so why now should he pass up the opportunity to know her better? He quickly sent a brief reply to Anne, reached down his jacket from the hook on the back of the kitchen door and checked his pockets for his keys to house and car.

His car was standing on the drive. He climbed in, switched on the engine and pulled away. Already, he felt guilty that he was going to visit Anne without first having told Sue. When he thought about, it seemed bizarre although he had to admit that having received Anne's message he wanted more than anything to be with her.

The roads ahead of him had remained dry and were still covered with fine layers of silt left by the flooding and, as he drove away, the now familiar clouds of dust rose behind him.

* * *

Anne greeted him at the door and took him through to the lounge. The room was warm, though whether it was warmed by anything more than the sun that streamed into it, Dan did not know. She had taken account of the spring day by wearing a light, elegant floral print dress, drawn in at the waist and revealing a little of her arms and neck whilst subtly bearing witness to her figure.

There was no sign of the seemingly mythological George, and Dan assumed that Anne was not expecting him to return that afternoon. She poured them both glasses of white wine which they sat quietly sipping.

Eventually Anne said, "Thank you for coming over, Dan. It's good that you live just a short distance away."

He smiled in acknowledgement. "Well," he said, "it seems unnecessary for you to sit alone here and for me to do the same at Moorside simply because others have gone off on missions of their own, and although we've worked together for quite a long time, I feel that we don't actually know each other all that well."

"I agree," she said. "Why don't you start by telling me about how you came to be living at Moorside."

Dan related the details of his decision to live in a place that others generally regarded as highly vulnerable – and the part that Sue had played in helping him to buy the house. He kept any mention of Amanda out of the narrative since he had agreed with her that their former relationship was a matter for them – and no-one else.

Anne listened intently but as he drew towards the end of his account, there was still more that she wanted to know. At last, she said, "I still don't understand, Dan, why you're choosing to live in a place that, as this last winter has shown, is so vulnerable to flooding. I don't mean this in an unpleasant way – but it seems almost perverse."

Dan was not surprised by her reaction; it was one that he often met when talking about his reasons for living at Moorside. "I think it's simply that I wanted to live in a place that still has some connection to its environment. When I lived in Sedgewater, the flat I had there was like any other flat of its kind and could have been in almost any town in England. Sedgewater's also an ugly place. It has little to recommend it."

Anne laughed. "You should be careful who you say that to. I know a number of people who love living there. It's also reasonably safe. Where you're living now, though, is far from safe. Any time we have a wet winter – or summer – large areas of the Levels disappear under water. Even the sceptics are having to admit these days that the climate is making our lives increasingly difficult. Surely, you and Sue must be worried – even very worried – about the storms that we get now and the way that the water out on the Levels can rise so quickly…"

"Yes, of course we're concerned, Anne. But I have absolutely no intention of living in a town or a city. Too many people, cars, buildings – I grew up in such a place but these days it would drive me mad."

"So what are you going to do – because the situation is only going to get worse?"

"We'll just have to adapt the house…"

She nodded. She had seen such adaptations in other parts of the world.

"Yes, I think I know what you're talking about, but it will probably cost you a great deal to do it."

"Yes, it will – but if I want to stay where I am, I have to find a way." He smiled. "So far we've talked about me, Anne. But you haven't told me anything about yourself."

"Well, you know some of it already."

"Hmm," he said, "I know that you're an amazing musician and that you own this beautiful house on top of a hill in the middle of nowhere. Other than that, despite the fact that we've worked together for about six years, I know very little."

She laughed. "Well, the first thing I have to admit then, is that I don't own this house."

Dan raised an eyebrow but was not surprised. He had not supposed for one moment that Anne would be able to afford such a house on the basis of a teacher's salary.

"So, the house belongs to George…"

"Yes – and as I think I've mentioned before, he has his own business. It started as a very small enterprise but over the years, he's built it into a much larger one."

Dan nodded. "You have told me that. I also know that he's a benefactor of local schools including Wellsprings. I don't think, though, that anyone has ever told me about the nature of his company."

For the first time that he could remember, a frown crossed her face. "Hmm, that does seem rather strange – especially since he's well known to the Governors at Wellsprings."

"I'm sure he is, Anne, but although I know his company makes pumping equipment that's all I know."

"Well," she said warily, "the pumps that George's company make are all destined for the gas and oil industry."

Dan sat silently watching her and slowly taking in what she had said. So that was it – the reason for Anne's wariness was that she already knew from somewhere that Dan would be strongly opposed to the nature of George's business.

It took some moments for Dan to absorb what Anne had just told him. So far, he had looked forward to visiting Anne, to enjoying the spaciousness and comfort of her beautiful house, but now it seemed it was all founded on the wealth that George had earned from his dealings with oil and gas companies.

They talked for a while longer. Anne began to hint at the details of how she had first met George, and Dan talked a little more about why he had chosen to live at Moorside, but both were aware that a shadow had fallen between them. Their conversation ended well short of the mutual understanding that Dan had hoped it would achieve.

* * *

Later, as he drove away, his feelings about Anne were heavily conflicted. She was a beautiful, intelligent and talented woman. He had felt already that he was falling for her and that being with her lit up his drab and mundane existence.

Then, however, he thought about the flipside of his feelings. He was married and had two children. He was expected to be a stable and reliable component of the little world of which he was part. And Anne, for all her talent and apparent virtue, relied for the essentials of her daily life on someone who had become wealthy on the back of the fossil fuel industry – an industry that had been for many years, a byword for greed, selfishness and environmental destruction.

It was late afternoon when he drew up once more on the drive of his own house. Despite having sought only a platonic friendship with Anne, he still felt a deep sense of guilt about his motivation for wanting to be with her.

He checked the garage, thinking that Sue might already have put her car away but there was no sign of it. He was not surprised. She had said before leaving that she hoped to enjoy her shopping trip with Emily and that the pair of them would not be in a hurry to get back. Josh too, Dan recalled, had said that he would be catching an early evening train back from Bristol.

The spring sunshine now came from a point further west, as late afternoon wore on into early evening. Dan seated himself at the kitchen table and eventually managed to think again about his plans for the following week. He had been working just a short time when, through the kitchen window, he saw Sue's car drawing up on the drive.

"Once there was a way to get back homeward" – although the song had been written before he was born, Dan had heard its words many times. It would seem, as Sue and Emily came into the house, that he had spent the whole afternoon working in solitude, but he knew that his willingness to let appearances deceive them was also a sign of his own self-deception.

He had to get Anne out of his thoughts. She was a distraction. He had his wife, his children, his work and a life that, in his own belief, was already meaningful. What he most needed to do, after the disruption caused by the flooding, was to refocus.

* * *

CHAPTER 13

BIRD OF PASSAGE

A little over two weeks after Dan's Saturday afternoon visit to Anne, Amanda asked him to meet her in her office after school. The purpose of the meeting, she said, was to look at some new data about the return to Wellspring's former site. She wanted his thoughts about it before it was discussed with the Governors.

Dan closed the windows of his classroom, thinking that in the afternoon's heat, it would have been better if he could have left them open but with laptops and notebook computers distributed across the room, it was too much of a risk.

Amanda's office was a short walk from Dan's classroom. The school administrator had gone home by that time of day, so he had to use the security device at the door to the building. He pressed the button of the buzzer that would tell Amanda that someone was waiting at the door. A small speaker on the device came briefly to life.

"Hello …?"

"It's Dan, Amanda…"

It seemed a little bizarre because the security camera above the door would already have told her as much, but he heard a click from the door as she released the lock.

He entered, closed the door behind him and made his way along the narrow corridor to Amanda's office. The door was open, so he knocked on it lightly and then made his way to the seat she had placed for him at the work table they generally used when they were jointly discussing school documents and plans.

Settling into his seat, he waited for her, but she remained for a short time at the large window that formed a large part of the office's end wall, and which looked out over the Somerset countryside. She seemed lost in thought.

Dan was content to wait and unobtrusively studied her as she stood silhouetted against the light from the window. He knew her figure well. There had been a point earlier in their lives when he had thought they would marry but... Unwittingly, he gave a small sigh and that was sufficient to rouse Amanda from her reverie.

"Ah, I'm sorry Dan," she said, smiling as she came to join him at the table, "I didn't hear you come in. I'm afraid I was far away, lost in thought. However, we have one or two difficult things to talk about, so we had better make a start."

She paused firstly to put on her glasses and then to retrieve a rather substantial looking document from her desk.

"This," she said, "is a report from the hydrologist contracted by the Foundation to look in detail at the school's permanent site."

"Oh?" said Dan in surprise. "I had no idea that any such work was being done."

"Hm, well, keeping it from you was not my idea, Dan, but I think when we start to look at it in a moment or two, you'll probably understand why I haven't been able to say anything…"

She flicked rapidly through the document until she came to the "Summary of Findings".

"There's a great deal of data in the report," she said turning to look at him, "too much to study at the moment – but if you have a look at the Hydrologist's findings, I'm sure you'll get the picture very quickly."

Dan drew the document across the desk so that it sat squarely in front of him. The 'findings' were bullet pointed so it took him just a minute or two to read through them. As soon as he had read the last of them, he turned towards Amanda, a frown on his face. She waited.

"I see what you mean," he said. "He doesn't spell it out to the last detail but there seems to be only one conclusion to draw from this."

"Yes," agreed Amanda. "But I still need to hear you say it…" She looked again at him, arching her eyebrows.

"It says, unless I'm much mistaken, that the school's permanent site is no longer viable and that, in less than five years, flooding there will be such a regular occurrence that urgent consideration needs to be given either to a complete overhaul of the buildings or…" – he hesitated – "or a permanent move to a new site on higher ground. How long have you known about this report?" Dan was eager to know.

"Oh," she said, "about a week – although I've known about the commissioning of the study – and that was three months ago."

Dan nodded thoughtfully. "I can see why the Foundation wants to limit its circulation – at least in the short term. It amazes me that none of the media has got hold of it."

"That's because the Regional Commissioner – and, of course, the Principal – have both insisted that we could only share a printed version of it. The report does exist in digital form, as you'd expect, but for now access to it is being very carefully controlled. As soon as we've finished here this afternoon, it will be going into the shredder."

"I can understand why it would be highly contentious – whenever the Commissioner and the Principal decide to release it." He did not envy them the task – which, despite being difficult, would also be inevitable.

"It will indeed," agreed Amanda. "The whole thing would be serious enough if it was just the school that was affected but, of course, it isn't..."

"No," said Dan, "the rise in the water table will affect the whole of that area, including the housing developments that the school serves. I hate to imagine what the repercussions will be when the residents get to hear about it."

There was a brief silence as they both contemplated the situation. It was Dan who spoke first.

"How on earth was planning permission ever given in the first place?"

Amanda looked thoughtful. "That would have been over ten years ago," she said. "As you might remember, the thinking then was completely different. For a start, many people, councillors included, still thought the 'Climate Crisis' was fictitious. There was data available indicating what would happen, but it was either ignored or treated as a 'worst case scenario'.

Dan shook his head. "The problem now, though, is that we're having to deal with the consequences of their lack of foresight."

"Yes," sighed Amanda. "Neither housing nor school should have been built in that location – and my great concern is that rectifying the problems will be financially impossible. It would cost enormous sums of money."

"What a mess!" said Dan, seeing no immediate solution to the problems. "Where do we go from here?"

"The short answer is nowhere," replied Amanda. "It looks as though we could be in the present so-called 'temporary accommodation' for some time to come."

"The Foundation will be very unhappy about that..."

"Of course – but for the time being, there's little choice. It also means that the planning we'd begun for the move back to the School's site will have to go on 'hold' – with the distinct possibility that it may be cancelled altogether. I'll have to tell the Chair of Governors about the problems with the return to the school's permanent site – even if I can't tell her about the Hydrologist's report."

She paused. "I'm going to need your help with some of this, Dan."

Expecting a sharp reaction to her comment, she looked at him, but he seemed unmoved.

"You don't seem very surprised, Dan, if I may say so."

"I'm not," he replied. "Any teacher who's used the playing field at Wellsprings knows how often it's too wet."

Amanda smiled – rather bleakly, Dan thought. "So now we know why..." She closed her copy of the Hydrologist's report and transferred it to her desk.

"When will the news be broken to residents and parents at Wellsprings?"

"That's a very good question – but I'm afraid I can't answer it. So far, no decision about going public has been made – which is why the information you've seen this afternoon has to remain secret – at least, for now."

Dan nodded in agreement. He had no wish to be identified as a whistleblower.

He could not resist one further comment, however. "I suppose that if you think about the name, the clue is there..."

"I'm not sure I understand what you mean?"

"'Wellsprings' wasn't a recently invented name for that area... It's been known as 'Wellsprings' for a very long time." He gave a wry, sarcastic smile.

Amanda looked at him over her glasses and said, "Hmm – amusing, Dan – but I'm not sure that anyone else will find it funny."

She looked rather cross – and Dan, realising that the colour in her cheeks was a warning sign said, "Is that it, Amanda? If so, I need to get away…"

"Not quite," she replied. "I did say I had one or two difficult things to talk to you about – and I haven't yet mentioned the second one." She indicated that they should move away from the table and pointed him towards one of two armchairs near the window.

When they were both comfortably seated, she said, "I won't keep you unnecessarily, Dan, but I just wanted to say how much I enjoyed the concert the other week."

Dan smiled. "Thank you, Amanda – it was Anne who did most of the work with the children."

"I'm sure you're being modest – but saying 'thank you' is not the difficult bit…"

He waited, wondering what was coming next. "Oh?"

"Yes, Dan. There's no easy way to say this – but I'm afraid that the two of you were far more 'obvious', shall we say – than was really wise."

For several long seconds, Dan did not reply. Finally, he said, "I don't really know what you mean, Amanda."

"I had hoped I wouldn't have to spell it out but whilst I think that you were fairly restrained, I can't say the same for Anne. And there are times when a woman's body language can speak louder than words – especially to other women."

Dan gave an audible sigh. It was pointless to deny what Amanda was saying. Why, he wondered, had Anne thought that there was such a thing as a private corner anywhere in Fairfields Secondary School…and why had Amanda had to come around the corner just at that very moment…?

She saw that Dan knew all too well what she was talking about, and she waited for him to speak.

"I'm sorry, Amanda – I have to admit it was a foolish thing. I think we both got carried away by the success of the concert."

Amanda held up her hands. "Please, Dan, don't feel you have to explain anything to me. I'm only raising it because I don't want to see either you or Anne getting hurt – and you know how easy it is for rumours to begin…"

Dan nodded; a single hug and a kiss – there had been nothing more to it than that. It was also unlikely, provided Amanda had been the only one to see them, that anything more would come of it.

"I don't know what to say, Amanda. I'm embarrassed. It was just a 'spur of the moment' thing. There's absolutely nothing going on between me and Anne."

She pondered what he had said for a moment but decided that it was best not to say any more.

Dan gave her a wan smile… "I thought we'd decided to leave the past in the past…" he said.

"And so far, we've succeeded."

There was another pause – this time, a longer one. "It's strange, though, isn't it, Amanda. It was all such a long time ago, but we've never quite forgotten."

She felt a flush of embarrassment. Dan was summoning feelings that she thought she had dealt with many years before. "There's nothing to admit, Dan. We both know that."

She drew closer to him. "All the same, I can't pretend that I felt only indifference when I saw you with Anne…"

She stopped herself, feeling that she was saying too much.

She turned away, shuffled together a few papers that still remained on the work table and then turned back towards him. "We both need to get home but there is just one more thing I want to add. I've known Anne a long time, much longer than you've known her – so I feel I can say this. Be careful. She's a lovely person, but she's someone who moves on. And I can already see what you feel for her…"

A space that Dan hoped Amanda would fill, hung in the air between them. If she truly knew what he felt about Anne, he wished she'd tell him – because it might be the only way he would ever get to find out. Amanda, though, simply busied herself again with the shredder so he picked up his briefcase, walked to the door and let himself into the corridor. There was, after all, nothing between him and Anne.

Amanda remained for a few minutes longer, dealing with the remnants of the Hydrologist's report whilst also wondering if, as she had tried to deal with Dan, she had discovered more than she really wanted about her own feelings. She had chosen the right time – of that at least she was sure. There was still a chance that he could step back from his rapidly developing obsession with Anne.

She thought again about the possibility that if Dan was seen too often in the company of Anne Moresby, it would be all too easy for rumours to begin – and neither Dan's wife, Sue, nor George Moresby were known for their patience. There was still a risk that the situation would not end well.

She sighed to herself as she finished her task – to what extent should she think of herself as having a role in Dan's private life? As he had said, their previous relationship was now long gone, and he was an adult capable of making his own decisions… The report about the situation at the Wellsprings site also clearly showed they both had much bigger things to worry about. Somerset's changing climate manifested new problems with every year that passed.

It was only a little later, as she sat in her car for a few moments before leaving for home that she paused to think more critically about how she had felt when she had seen Anne in Dan's arms. Seemingly, none of the three of them had made good decisions in their choice of marriage partner.

* * *

CHAPTER 14

DEGREES OF FRUSTRATION

Dan's daily life had begun to settle back into the familiar patterns that had been part of both his need for routine and, paradoxically, the sense of boredom that was the flipside of a life lived by daily routines and timetables.

On Thursday evenings in the past, however, he had generally tried to break away from school and home and go in search of male company for an hour or two, at one of his local pubs – the Fox and Hounds. It was one habit that, after the disruption of earlier months, he now wanted to revive.

A friend, Jethro, was already there. Dan had got to know him when he had taught first Josh and then Emily at Fairfields Academy School.

"So how are you doing, Dan? I haven't seen you in a while." Jethro didn't so much speak as rumble.

"Oh, I've just been busy. The house was a mess after the floods and school's been a bit of a nightmare."

Jethro glanced across towards the bar. "It sounds like you're in need of a pint – and I think I owe you one from last time."

Dan decided not to disagree and watched as his companion made his way across to the bar and its line of pumps. There was plenty of time to observe his companion as he bent his head to avoid the low beams of the ceiling; Jethro's very large frame was such that he always found it difficult to navigate the intervening space. His thick head of black hair and broad shoulders barely seemed to fit into the space above the bar.

Returning in like manner, he carefully set down on the table two brimming glasses of beer.

"They have a good head on them!" commented Dan.

"Hmm," grunted Jethro. "It's decent stuff. Cornish beer – 'Wreckers' I think it's called. Sounds appropriate."

"Well, I don't intend to get wrecked tonight!" Dan grinned, sipping at his beer and sporting a white moustache from the froth. "It might be Friday tomorrow, but I still have to survive the day!"

"Survival, Dan? I don't believe it. Rumour has it you and Amanda have the place running like clockwork."

"Rumours – didn't your mum ever tell you that you shouldn't listen to them."

"She did, I'm sure," replied Jethro, "but I still do it all the same." He laughed – a deep, rich laugh that drew the momentary attention of a couple seated near the bar.

"Listen," he said, bending closer to Dan, "any chance you could escape from Sue and the kids on Saturday?"

Dan shrugged. "Probably – Sue has one of her friends coming round. I'm not sure what Josh and Emily are doing."

"Well, the last time you were here, you were talking to some of my 'Green' friends about your frustration with the Fossil Fuel Industry."

Dan recalled the vehement conversation that had taken place. "I was," said Dan. "After all this time, CO_2 emissions are greater than ever. And we were worried about them ten years ago!"

"Sadly, you're right," agreed Jethro. "It's caused deep frustration and anger. The Oil and Gas industries are meeting concerted opposition right across the world."

"Huh! They're still making enormous profits though. How's that possible?"

"Because some people would deny the data even if the entire planet was going up in flames! But you know as well as I do, there's bitter opposition to fossil fuels everywhere."

"Yes – I do know that Jethro. It's just that I don't see much of it around here." Dan had long wearied of the stubborn refusal to move away entirely away from fossil fuels.

"Well, if you've been watching the news, worldwide protests are planned – big ones – this weekend!"

"Worldwide, eh? Is that likely to include Sedgewater?"

Jethro sensed the sarcasm in Dan's question but tried not to be side-tracked.

"You're too pessimistic by half," he said with a sad smile. "Sedgewater is very much included. In fact, one of the local companies 'Moresby International' is one of the worst offenders in this part of the country — which means it's a clear target for Westcountry Greens."

Dan grimaced. He could make excuses and try to wriggle out of any involvement, but Jethro seemed to be implying that local action might be focused on Moresby's plant – and, if so, he would have a decision to make.

"So, what's planned?" he asked.

Privately surprised that Dan was not part of the local 'loop', Jethro nevertheless went through the details of Sedgewater Green Alliance's intended protest. They were simple enough. Local Greens had been working the South West's social media networks trying to put together the numbers needed for a huge demonstration and march through Sedgewater. The march would end at Moresby International's factory on the edge of the town where, Jethro made clear, the protesters would be intent on putting an end to George Moresby's production of pumps for the fossil fuel industry.

"Hmm, a Climate Protest march is something Josh and Emily should be involved in – but it sounds as though what's planned at Moresby's is a whole lot more than just a demonstration."

"You're right, Dan." Jethro's reply was quiet but emphatic. "It'll be no place for Josh and Emily – at least, not this time."

By way of response, Dan cocked an eyebrow. "Oh?" he said. "Are you going to tell me more?"

Jethro frowned and briefly avoided Dan's gaze. "I can't – because I don't know much – and even peaceful protest is risky these days. So the police are sure to be out in force – and there are rumours of a counter demonstration."

"That could spell trouble. Do the police know about that?"

"I have no idea," said Jethro solemnly. "You're right about trouble, though – there could be plenty."

Dan nodded. Whilst clearly wanting him to take part in the demonstration, Jethro was being open with him. His thoughts momentarily raced across his unwillingness to do anything that might cause serious problems with Anne. But then he could not have a foot in both camps – and what exactly was the nature of his relationship with her? That was something he was still trying to work out.

"Okay, Jethro, I'll be there," he said. "But Josh and Emily will have to find something else to do." He could not back out of something that was of such basic importance to him – even at the risk of potential conflict with Anne.

"Good man!" said Jethro, placing a very large hand gently but firmly on his shoulder.

* * *

The protesters had arranged to assemble on a section of road that had now been replaced by the Sedgewater bypass. The wide strip of tarmac was about a quarter of a mile long, but it was soon filled almost to capacity by a huge gathering of buses, vans and cars – nearly all electric, although a smell of cooking oil also hung in the air.

Dan stood at the fringe of the proceedings feeling conspicuously unattached to any of the groups that were beginning to form; eventually, however, these began to coalesce, and activists busied themselves handing out placards to those who had not brought their own.

A large flatbed truck had been drawn up near the point at which the gathering crowd would make its exit. The protest organisers were planning to use it as a platform for the invited speakers after the march through the town had taken place. Dan, meanwhile, was keen to take part in the protest but, looking around, Jethro was nowhere to be seen, and he realised that there was no-one he recognised in the crowd.

Placards were still being handed out amongst the protesters. Dan meanwhile had brought his own. It read, "Save the Earth – End Fossil Fuels". There was no direct reference to Moresby's factory, but he hoped that the march would be more than enough to draw attention to its connections with the oil and gas industries.

Slowly, the march began to get underway. Their route would take them from the edge of the town and down into the town centre. From there it had been agreed that they would pass close to Moresby International's factory but, at the insistence of the police, would not directly approach it. Smaller protests were also planned at several garages along the route where petrol and diesel continued to be sold to those who refused to 'go electric'.

Negotiations with the police about the protests planned to take place at service stations had been the most protracted and controversial. The local news media had also chosen to make them the centre of attention – unaware that their choice of focus was secretly welcomed by a small group of activists who, meanwhile, were planning to be elsewhere.

Dan, now chatting with protesters from such places as Exeter and Bristol, was gratified to see that the march was attracting the attention of Saturday shoppers. Reluctantly, the police had agreed to divert traffic from 'The Parade' that led into the centre of Sedgewater for a period of 30 minutes and that the town's central square could be briefly used by local Green councillors to address the crowd.

The protesters listened, reacting with claps and cheers where they agreed with the speakers. All seemed civilized and peaceful. The speeches were along well recognised lines and passers-by were sometimes stopping to listen, although the younger ones amongst them had heard much the same slogans about 'Fossil Fuels' since they had first begun to learn the meaning of the words.

Dan's enthusiasm, however, was waning. The proceedings had a ritualistic feel about them, and the police officers stationed around the square were making it clear it was time for the marchers to move on. Cynically Dan reflected that police willingness to allow the protest was based on their belief that it would have minimal effect on the town's Saturday routine. Their task, they believed, was to control and contain the marchers and to see that they returned to their starting point, from where they could then be dispersed.

Slowly, the protesters began to move out of the square along a route marked out by police officers lining both sides of the road. Anger flared amongst marchers as a long bend in the road opened up spaces between them which were then used by people in civilian clothing to dart in and out of the procession, taking photographs of small groups and individuals. A few protesters in twos and threes attempted to chase off the unwanted photographers, but on each occasion the police were quick to intervene, prompting the belief that the predatory 'snappers' were police spies.

It was shortly after this that the first breakdown in police intelligence became apparent. At a junction with a side road on the right, there was suddenly a flood of demonstrators straight into the centre of the protesting marchers. It was clear immediately that the intention of the insurgent group was anything but peaceful.

Hit from behind by the violent crowd surging forward, three of the officers policing the junction were knocked to the ground and immediately targeted by people hacking and flailing at them with bike chains and batons. Individual protesters, seeing the police officers being beaten and kicked, tried to go to their aid but quickly found themselves to be under attack and embroiled in the widening melee. Dan yelled in pain as he felt a heavy punch to the right side of his head. He staggered into a space just to one side of him, lurched into a shop doorway and collapsed with his senses swimming and a nauseating taste of blood in his mouth.

Somewhere through the throbbing pain of the blow, he could hear the tinny blare of warnings now being crackled out towards the crowd of flailing combatants. He cranked his head painfully round to his left and towards the far end of the street, he could see police officers on horseback being assembled to break up the violence that had spread wherever opposing demonstrators were clashing.

Mounted police emerged from a reserved area and began to advance inexorably along the street, using their batons and the physical threat of being trampled to clear the route. As the front of the line drew level with Dan's position in the shop doorway, he was appalled to see four of the insurgent demonstrators heaving heavy containers onto the street, from which they began releasing large quantities of ball bearings straight into the path of the oncoming horses.

Dan pulled himself to his feet and began waving his arms and trying to warn the police riders only to find himself caught in the incriminating shot of a police photographer, snapping up images in the proximity, of those presumed to be perpetrators.

The leading horse and rider went down with a heavy crash onto the surface of the road. The rider lay prone in the road, whilst his horse then tried to raise itself again but, Dan guessed, was prevented from doing so by a broken foreleg; its piteous cries of distress began to panic the other horses and the line of riders came abruptly to a halt and then went into a forced retreat, since that was the only way in which they could avoid the ball bearings which now lay right across their path.

Seeing the fate of the horse and rider, police officers on foot and under the command of a nearby officer quickly formed into a counter attacking wedge and began to fight their way forward into a phalanx of demonstrators surging down the street to meet them. Dan watched in horror and despair, as the fighting took on a new vehemence and ferocity; anger had fully taken hold. He looked for an escape. In his present state, it was the only way that he was going to survive.

A small gap had begun to open up between the shop fronts and the roiling mob of combatants. Dan slid himself into the gap, keeping a low profile and sticking very close to the windows and doorways ahead of him. There were police, both mounted and on foot, just ahead of him, but who, seeing that he was clearly injured and making his way into the space behind their lines, left him to stagger out of harm's way.

The next occurrence, though, shook them all. Dan, by now dripping blood onto the pavement, belatedly covered his ears with his hands as the blast of a very loud explosion shook the town centre, cracking glass, stopping the police and demonstrators alike in their tracks and taking down every electrical appliance on the local grid.

* * *

Concerned faces swam into his vision and out again before returning once more to study him. Thirst and acute discomfort disturbed him. Then, for a time, there was nothing.

Eventually, another face swam into view and this time, it was one he thought he recognised.

"Welcome back, Dan!"

He managed a smile – a painful one. "Hello Sue," he said, finally recalling the owner of the voice. "It's good to see a familiar face."

"I'm glad you can recognise me," Sue replied. "You'll be in here a for a while though."

Dan looked at her quizzically. "I must admit I don't feel too good."

"That's hardly a surprise. Someone's tried to use you as a punch bag!"

She continued watching him as memories briefly clouded his eyes.

"Yeah," he said. "It's coming back to me. Someone hit me and I found it hard to stay on my feet."

"According to the account I heard, a policeman found you unconscious in a shop doorway."

"Sounds about right," replied Dan. "I was lucky. At the time, all hell was breaking loose."

Sue sometimes treated Dan's comments with a pinch of salt, but she had heard from elsewhere about the violence of the demonstration and knew that he was not exaggerating.

"You could say that!" she commented with a sigh. "This side of town has been without electricity for about four hours now. Someone's blown up a substation – and, according to social media, Moresby's factory is a wreck."

Dan was puzzled. "The last thing I remember is hearing an almighty explosion. A substation? And Moresby's factory wrecked?" He tried to whistle but the pain from his facial muscles was too great. "We seem to have electricity in here though."

"The hospital has its own generators," Sue reminded him. "It's fortunate that they have because it will be some while before the local grid is back to normal."

Dan grimaced. At that moment, he simply wanted to sleep, and Sue could see that he was finding it hard to stay awake. He needed more help. She looked around for a nurse. Conversation about what had happened that morning would have to wait.

* * *

CHAPTER 15

FEELING THE HEAT

D an took a while to fully recover from the injuries he had suffered during the protest, but eventually, he was deemed fit enough to work. The hot weather persisted to the point where he had become heartily fed up with it. Meanwhile, heat of another kind had radiated from a local scandal following the appearance on social media of numerous photographs taken during the anti-fossil fuel protest in Sedgewater; Dan had been horrified that a shot he had assumed to have been taken by a police photographer had now been seen by thousands of people. It distinctly gave the impression that he was trying to thwart the attempt by police on horseback to push back the protesters when in fact, he had been trying to warn them, following severe injuries to a horse and rider caused by the presence of ball bearings scattered across the road. The photo had been taken from such an angle that it was impossible to see any sign of the ball bearings.

The scandal had enhanced his reputation amongst many of Jethro's friends but with his friends and colleagues, he found himself having to explain the context of the photograph. For the most part, his explanation had been accepted but his wisdom in having taken part in a protest that had led to significant violence was questioned. It was through some of this that, Dan secretly admitted to himself, he began to understand the frustration that had led to the blowing up of Moresby's factory.

The anger about the disruption to the local electricity supply was to be expected although, as always, Dan thought that it showed a general failure to appreciate that a much greater disruption was now almost certain through the stubborn adherence to the use of fossil fuels. Initially, he tried to argue the point with those who saw him as a target for their anger, but obsession with the short-term seemed to be so widespread that he soon gave up.

As he returned to work at school, he was relieved to find that, in general, the attitudes of the children towards him continued to be as they had been before the Protest. He felt grateful that, if he had been the subject of parents' discussions, it had not been in front of the pupils he worked with. Amanda, too, completely accepted his explanation that he had been part of the peaceful demonstration and had known nothing of the violence that overtook it.

By this point, the Summer Term was approaching its end. Eleanor, the Chair of Governors, had by now been informed of the content of the Hydrologist's report – and was on the warpath. Ultimately, she had the Academy in her sights but for the time being, Dan and Amanda were the chosen targets of her wrath.

Consequently, Dan was yet again a reluctant participant in an afternoon meeting whilst his class were corralled in another practice for the end of term concert. Pauline Ewing smiled sympathetically as she warned him that, having been into Amanda's office with a sheaf of photocopies, the signs of battle were already apparent.

Dan knocked at the door and then scooted in as tactfully as he could. Eleanor did not raise her eyes from the copy of the Hydrologist's report that lay open on her lap. Amanda had already told her that she had given Dan a chance to read it beforehand and that they would not need to go over it again in what remained of the meeting.

Amanda pointed Dan to a vacant chair to Eleanor's left. He had barely settled in it before she said, "Eleanor and I have covered much of the territory already, Dan, but there are some points she wants to cover with you, so I thought it was best for you to be here."

Eleanor took Amanda's words as her cue.

"For the moment, Dan, I'm not going to ask you how long you've known about the existence of this report. I'm also not going to ask you about the destruction of Moresby's factory, in connection with which your photo seems to be everywhere. Those are separate issues, and I'll discuss them with you and Amanda outside of this present conversation.

"However, what I do want to discuss with you are your thoughts about holding a meeting between the Governors and all of the staff before the end of the term. I don't accept for one minute that the

Wellsprings school site and the housing estate are beyond saving – or, for that matter, that the area cannot be protected from future flooding. I want the Governors to hear, in the most direct way possible, the teachers' views about the effect of the delayed return on the children's learning."

Dan had already thought about the prospect of a rapid return to the Wellsprings site and was not in favour of such a move.

"All the staff have been concerned about the after effects of the flooding and the lack of access to the resources at Wellsprings. I think every one of them has worked even harder than usual to compensate for the loss of learning time during the flood and none of them has complained.

"I think we have to remember that during my absence, other staff have had to spend time on Sports Day, School visits, the End of Term Concert and the Pupils' Dance. Some have also had to work on Secondary School liaison, Parents' Evenings and the provision of purposeful learning between SATs and the end of term. They need the Summer break.

"I don't think that any of them would see a return to the Wellsprings site in the autumn as a realistic prospect. It would be helpful for their views to be heard by the Governors and the Trust, but a meeting for that purpose would be best held at the start of next term."

Eleanor looked up, annoyed by the tone of protest running through Dan's comments.

"I'm sorry, Dan, but, as we both know, it all goes with the territory. You know my views about such events as the Pupils' 'Dance' or whatever it is, particularly for Primary School pupils and I recall you once used the word 'circus' to describe the succession of events to the governors. However, whatever your views – or mine, the Governors' view is that the school needs to focus on more than just its academic role – particularly in the Summer Term."

Amanda, aware that Eleanor was straying well and truly into her domain, moved quickly to stop Dan from digging further holes for himself.

"I can empathise, Dan. We've all heard the notion that teachers' work ends at 3.30 each day and that school holidays are far too long. But we also have to remember that many parents have very long working days and constant pressures regarding childcare. None of us asked for the present situation but we also need to play our part in dealing with the problems it's created."

Dan felt the urge to snort in derision but instead, he restrained himself and looked back at Amanda as if appealing to her for a stronger response.

"Perhaps, Dan, you and I could meet during the Summer Break and think again about the way forward. Eleanor, as usual, it will be no problem for you and me to stay in touch. That would at least help us to keep things moving."

Eleanor nodded. It was not what she had wanted but she was also determined to speak to Dan on his own and she knew that, meanwhile, Amanda needed to be elsewhere. She looked at her watch.

"Amanda, am I right in thinking that you have to be at a meeting with the other heads?"

"Yes, that's right, I should have been on my way by now."

"Well, with your agreement, Dan and I can probably finish up here?"

Amanda smiled, knowing that Eleanor was manipulating the situation, but her meeting was decidedly a priority. Despite suspecting mischief, she stood and plucked her lightweight jacket from the back of the chair.

"I'll see you in the morning, Dan," she said reluctantly and with that, she headed for the door.

Dan sat bemused. He could remember meeting the Chair of Governors on his own before and his earlier unease returned.

She did not keep him waiting.

"There is something I must speak to you about. Normally, Amanda would have spoken to you first but it's a matter that directly relates to the Governors so it's more appropriate for you to hear it from me first."

Dan had a rather familiar sinking feeling in his stomach.

Eleanor, however, ploughed on.

"One of the governors was recently at a social function with one of the school's biggest benefactors. The person in question − you will know who I mean − said to the member of governors that you've been seeing a lot of his wife. In fact, he alleged that you've been having an affair with her."

During the sinking feeling, there had been just sufficient time for Dan to have recalled the only significant thing at that moment about which he had a guilty conscience.

He mused for a moment on Eleanor's turn of phrase – "seeing a lot of his wife". The comment could only be in relation to Anne and for a moment, the accusation that he had been having an affair with her, took his breath away.

Eventually, however, he found his voice. "I can only assume that you're talking about Anne Moresby?"

Eleanor nodded.

"I've been doing no such thing!" he exclaimed angrily.

"It's curious, though, isn't it, Dan. You immediately know who I'm talking about."

That at least was true. Her question had been a trap.

"Really?" replied Dan. "I got the impression earlier that it was the hydrologist's report and the explosion at Moresby International that you most wanted to talk about."

"Those are important matters," commented Eleanor. "But let's deal with one thing at a time. I've heard directly from George Moresby that you're having an affair with his wife. He says you've been visiting her at home when he's away on business and he also tells me that you and Anne were seen kissing after a recent concert at Fairfields!"

"Oh that again!" groaned Dan. "It was nothing – absolutely nothing! We were both carried away by the success of the concert. That's all there was to it!"

"You expect me to believe that?"

"Yes, I do, Eleanor. It's true that I've seen Anne much more recently but that's because we've been planning school events – and, yes on occasion, we have talked about personal matters. But that doesn't amount to an affair – and it's no more than men and women not married to each other often do these days – so I don't see that I need to explain myself. Anyway, if George Moresby has a problem about it, I'm more than willing to talk to him…"

"I can tell you now, Dan, that won't be happening any time soon. I'm amazed you can be so crass. George Moresby has been a major benefactor of the Wellsprings Primary over the years and what is his reward? I'll tell you. The school's deputy head decides that he's going to have an affair with his wife and, unbelievably, all too obviously connect himself with people who are known to be involved in the destruction of his factory! Just how stupid can you be?"

She paused, visibly angry and for the moment, out of breath.

Dan looked at her with a deep sense of frustration. "The police are investigating the explosion at the factory, so I'm not prepared to comment on it – or anything related to it. They have an entirely different account of events that day – for reasons that I'm sure will eventually come to light. The photo – well, the use of it on social media has been a complete and utter distortion!"

Eleanor returned to her previous line of attack. "Whatever the truth about the factory, Dan, your image is everywhere in connection with it. And anytime now, it'll be national news. As for your affair with Anne, I simply don't believe you! You're a liar – and I'm going to see that you pay for your lies! Women everywhere are sick of men like you!"

Dan slumped into the nearest chair, wondering what he could say that would stand any chance of changing the course of events he saw unfolding before him.

Eleanor, meanwhile, had almost finished. "Now, I've had more than enough of your presence for one day...I have other things to do – but I'm sure this is far from the last you'll be hearing about George Moresby's factory – or about his wife."

With that, she picked up the attaché case that went with her to every meeting and marched out of the room, leaving the door open behind her. Dan remained where he was, his head in his hands. Somehow he had to move on from this moment. Eventually he stood. Cleaners were still working in the classrooms so the caretaker would check on that area, but he needed to check the security of the administrative buildings.

He resolved to do it. After the anger of the last twenty minutes, the routine of checking security would be therapeutic. Then he would drive himself slowly home and pour himself a very large drink.

He checked the windows and doors, wondering if Pauline in the outer office had heard any of the angry conversation that had occurred. He listened but there were no sounds of activity further along the corridor. Pauline had her own children to collect and had left the office shortly after Amanda had gone to her meeting.

After the relative coolness of Amanda's office he had forgotten the strength of the sun that had beaten down on the landscape for so many days now. As he unlocked his car, everything he touched was almost unbearably hot. He had been in the driver's seat only moments when he was aware that he had already begun to sweat. He switched on the engine and immediately turned up the car's air conditioning as far as it would go. Pulling away, he wondered if the heat of the day had made the conversation any angrier than it might otherwise have been. It was possible. Not many people in stressful situations would remain calm and collected on a day as hot as this one.

* * *

He forced himself to concentrate and after about thirty minutes found himself in the final section of the journey. Normally, he enjoyed the drive through the lanes but, on this occasion, he felt oppressed by a sense that events were getting beyond his control. He had not betrayed his wife and children, but they would probably believe that he had.

Early evening sun fell across the hedgerows as he pulled into the entrance to his house. Almost immediately, he was aware that Sue's BMW was parked on the drive. That, of course, was very unusual. She never usually put in an appearance before about 7.30.

He parked his Toyota alongside her car, collected his briefcase from the front passenger seat and made his way through the open front door into the relative coolness of the kitchen. Sue was already there, seated at the table with half a glass of Chardonnay in front of her.

She looked flushed and angry, but Dan decided to assume that if that was the case, it must be about some situation that had occurred at work. It was also, he noticed, very quiet. There was no music playing from upstairs, no sign of teenagers trying to offset the tedium of homework.

"Hello Sue, this is a welcome surprise!" he said, thinking that it was not often that they got to spend time together at that hour of the day. He moved towards her, intending to give her a kiss on the cheek but she turned away, rather dramatically, with the simplest of prohibitions.

"Don't," she hissed. "Don't you dare!"

Her anger took him completely by surprise. "For goodness' sake, Sue, what on earth is the matter!"

For a moment, she looked as if she would explode. She stood up from her chair and came around the table towards him.

Then she said, in a studiedly icy voice, "You know exactly what's wrong."

"Do I?" After such an unexpected beginning, he had no idea what was coming next.

"Yes, you bloody well do, you stupid bastard!"

He was shocked – and alarmed. In the whole of their married life, he had never known her use that kind of vocabulary.

"I don't, Sue. I haven't a clue what you're talking about."

"You've been shagging that slut, Anne Moresby! That's what I'm talking about!"

"What? What!? Where on earth did you get such a crazy idea?"

"Well, let me tell you...! From more than one place for a start! I think I was the only one in the whole of my office not to have heard about it!"

"That's not possible! How can it be? Anne and I have done absolutely nothing. Wherever you've got this rubbish from, it's a complete and absolute lie!"

Dan had remained relatively calm up to this point, but the absurdity of the situation now began to get to him. First, he had heard these accusations at work – and now his own wife was coming out with them at home.

"Whatever you've been told, it just isn't true. It can't be true because absolutely nothing of the kind that you're talking about has happened between me and Anne. Someone has cooked up a pack of lies to suit their own purposes! And if you think about it, why would I do such a thing? It's simply not rational!"

"Rational? Rational! I can't believe you're using the word. Well let me ask you, is it 'rational' to wreck our marriage by bonking some stupid woman half off her head with pill-taking – because that's how she's been described to me. And, do you know, Dan, I actually thought – yeah, she sounds like the sort who would appeal to you these days – some poor simpering female who spins you a tale about needing your help. Appeal to your sense of 'chivalry', did she?"

"I did try to help her."

"Oh, don't tell me! I've heard all about it. And, of course, whilst you were so-called helping her, she was busily helping herself to my husband. How do you think I feel about that?"

"I can completely understand why you're feeling that way... But there is absolutely no reason, because absolutely none-of-it-happened!" He laid as much emphasis as he could on these words, adding angrily but unwisely, "Of course, if you're determined to believe such a pile of crap, then it's no surprise that you're upset!"

"Upset!? That doesn't even begin to describe it! How can you come out with such a pathetic word for how you've made me feel? In fact, let me tell you about just one of the things I'm feeling, Dan – I am feeling utterly, utterly humiliated – humiliated by your treatment of me, by your utter contempt for me after all these years – and, by the way, the utter contempt you've shown for Josh and Emily as well!"

"I can imagine that…"

"You don't seem to have been able to imagine anything, except what it would be like to get into that woman's knickers! I bet that's been giving you a steady little thrill, hasn't it? Oh, and whilst I'm talking humiliation, do you know how I had to find out?" Sue's voice had risen to yet another crescendo.

"I have no idea…"

"Yes, well, that would just about sum you up, wouldn't it? I found out because Edgar Prothero, one of the partners, came to see me at work. In case you're wondering, he belongs to the same golf club as your girlfriend's husband, George Moresby. By the time he'd finished telling me about your antics with Moresby's wife, I felt as though I was the stupidest, blindest, most self-deluded woman ever to be married to a lying, cheating scumbag like you!"

For the moment, she had exhausted herself. She hung her head and wept with sobs coming from deep down in her body. Dan, genuinely distraught by the grief caused by the fictitious accounts of his adultery, moved to put his arms around her but she pushed him away. Instead, she drew on the reserves of her strength and shouted at him.

"I don't want you touching me! I don't want you anywhere near me!"

"But this whole situation is a complete and utter farce!" Dan, too, had begun to shout. "And because it's all such a pack of complete and utter lies, I have no idea what it is that you think I should do about it!"

"Do? I'll tell you what I want you to do! I want you to get out of here and never come back! "

Dan was shaken. "Sue, you can't do that! I've every right to be here! I've done nothing wrong – and the house is as much mine as it is yours!"

"We'll see about that, shall we? By the time I've finished not one stick of this place will belong to you!"

Although Sue was the one with the legal qualifications, Dan knew that she would find that a difficult threat to carry out – but just at that moment there seemed little point in reminding her.

He turned away. Perhaps if he stayed in the guest room tonight, he might be able to talk to her again in the morning?

She had seen the direction of his gaze, however, and had other ideas. "Don't even think about staying here, Dan! You are not spending another night under this roof!"

His first response was to think that the last thing he should do was leave the house, but then, after the fractious meeting at school and Sue's devastating anger and humiliation of him at home, getting into a further struggle about staying there that night was going to be one conflict too many.

"Okay! Okay! Have it your way!" His shoulders slumped in despair and resignation. He would go and pack a bag. Sue, despite her humiliation that day, was a complete work addict and bound to go into the office sometime in the next day or two, even if they offered her time off. He would come back – but this time armed with whatever legal advice he could get.

Her voice interrupted his thoughts. "If you're thinking about a bag, I've already packed it for you. It was waiting in the entrance for you as you came in. But, of course, you didn't notice. You're still 'away with the fairies', because 'having it away' with Anne Moresby has completely addled that tiny little brain of yours!"

She almost spat the last of her bitter sarcasm into his face.

Without further comment, Dan retrieved his briefcase once more, found the bag waiting for him as described, and headed for the car.

From inside the house, she heard him open and then slam the boot of the Toyota. Sitting once more with her glass of wine in her hand, she took a long draught of the Chardonnay and then listened as the noise of the car's engine receded down the lane. Silence then descended on the house except that with Dan now gone, to her mind, forever from her life, she threw her arms down on the table, her face down on her arms, and wept until she could weep no more.

* * *

PART 2

CHAPTER 16

PIE NIGHT

Dan was filled with anxiety as he drove to a layby in the countryside where he might be able to pull off the road and begin sorting out his next step – finding somewhere to sleep for the night. The sick feeling in his stomach was in dramatic contrast to the beautiful summer's evening around him and the relatively gentle warmth that was beginning to replace the heat of the day.

The layby was near the top of one of the few hills in the area and Dan pulled into it to make a phone call. On occasions in the past, if he had drunk too much to drive home, a friend from his days as a probationary teacher had sometimes provided him with a bed. He scanned through the 'contacts' list on his phone. Greg Nolan was not amongst those he most frequently contacted but had generally proved to be a reliable backstop. Dan found his number and pressed the phone symbol to make the call.

At first, he was unable to get through and he spent a number of anxious minutes trying to think of alternatives to the course of action he had just begun to piece together. Eventually, however, he was able to breathe a sigh of relief as Greg finally responded.

"Hi there, Dan. Sorry I didn't get back to you immediately. I had some company here and…well, I'll tell you about it sometime. Now, what can I do for you?"

Dan hesitated for a moment but decided to plunge straight in. "I'm sorry to bother you with this, Greg, but the truth is, I'm in a bit of a fix and I was wondering if you could put me up for the night." His words came out in a rush, but Greg's reply was the first step towards easing his anxiety.

"Of course, mate. No problem. Why don't you come over right away – if you're free, that is?"

Dan gave an audible sigh of relief. "Oh yes, I'm free alright. In fact, if you don't mind, I could do with having a bit of a chat."

"You and me both!" agreed Greg. "Look, I haven't eaten yet this evening and it's 'Pie Night' at the 'Leg O' Mutton'. We could go there. Have you eaten yet?"

"No, I haven't. I'm not sure I feel much like eating but a visit to the pub is probably what I need just now."

"Right!" agreed Greg. "So it sounds like we have a plan then. Why don't you park your car here and we can walk? That would save any problems later – and the pub is only five minutes away."

"Good idea. I'll see you shortly then?"

"Sure thing. See you soon."

Greg went off the line and Dan closed his phone.

* * *

The drive across to Sedgewater took about twenty minutes. The final section of his short journey took him along a faded, tree-lined street incongruously named 'Imperial Avenue' which, nevertheless, on a warm, sunlit summer's evening, still managed to retain some hints of its original pretentions. Greg's flat was part of a large Victorian house in what had once been one of the more salubrious suburbs of the town. Like the street and house, Greg was also something of an anachronism because the area was mainly populated by college students and young people in the early stages of their careers.

The house stood on a plot of land that had formerly been part of a municipal garden, but which was now largely given over to parking spaces. Dan found a space intended for visitors and made his way over to the front door of the house. A grimy array of buttons with faded name tags next to them was located to the left of the door but Dan, having visited Greg a number of times before, unhesitatingly pressed the button without a tag. The distant sound of a buzzer could be heard and was followed by a rapid succession of steps down the staircase beyond the door.

"Ah, Dan, good to see you!" Dan caught a glimpse of the grand but well-worn reception area leading to the wide staircase behind Greg's head and shoulders as he emerged, hauling a corded jacket round his shoulders.

"It seems like some time since I was last here," commented Dan, gazing at his friend as he pulled the door shut. Greg was a little shorter than Dan, rather stocky in build, had a round face with a slightly reddened complexion and wore glasses with wire frames and round lenses. His work, teaching art at a local comprehensive school, had led him to squint habitually, as though perpetually examining a pupil's work. Dan always thought that, for someone with artistic sensibilities, he generally dressed in an unimaginative way; that evening, in addition to the corded jacket, he sported a grey sweatshirt, battered blue jeans and a well-worn pair of brown shoes.

Greg brushed a length of dark hair out of his eyes and said, "Look, I thought we might as well go straight round to the 'Leg 'O Mutton'. I'm starving and I could really do with a pint."

They set off together along the street, here and there stepping over the ridges in the pavement created by the roots of the trees. Dan, who was still in his shirt sleeves, wondered why Greg needed a jacket on such a warm evening but said nothing, knowing that his friend was a creature of habit and apt to wear much the same kind of clothing in all seasons of the year.

The 'Leg 'O Mutton' was of the same character as the area in which it stood and retained at least some of the tiles and the stained-glass windows that had been part of its decoration when it was built. Dan followed Greg up a short set of stone steps to an entrance area surrounded by dark woodwork and stained glass. Greg pushed open the door on his left marked 'Lounge', explaining, "I usually prefer the 'Public Bar' but if we want to talk, this is probably a better choice."

They found a table towards the back of the lounge area where there was just a small number of other drinkers. Greg bought them both a pint of beer and seating himself opposite Dan, they drank in silence for a short time until Greg said, "So, Dan, you wanted a chat..."

"I do," agreed Dan, "although it's hard to know where to start. Perhaps what I need to say is that it looks as though Sue and I may be splitting up..."

Greg looked at him slowly, curiously for a moment. "Really?" He appeared quite taken aback. "I always thought you and Sue had a 'rock-solid' relationship." He paused for a moment. "What's brought that about?"

"I…it was…absolutely nothing, Greg. But she thinks I've been having an affair." Dan put his hands over his eyes, not knowing if he could continue.

Greg waited. "Okay. She's thrown you out on …what? A rumour?"

Dan tried to keep a grip of his emotions. "That's about the strength of it. For reasons I can only guess, someone has invented a pack of lies about me – and Sue has completely believed them."

Greg waited. It was a situation he had not come across before. "So have you been seeing the woman you're supposed to have been having an affair with?"

"Yes…I have. But, Greg, that's really all we've been doing – meeting up, talking to one another, enjoying each other's company."

"Is this woman you've been meeting married or single?"

"Married."

Greg paused before saying sardonically, "Not really my territory, but if I had to guess, I would say that someone, somewhere is extremely jealous – almost certainly the husband. Do you want to tell me who we're talking about?"

Dan was unsure. It seemed too soon to be naming names.

"Not really, if you don't mind, Greg."

"So, who knows about these … allegations?"

"At the moment, Sue of course, the current Head at School – Amanda – and the Chair of Governors."

Greg put his lips together in a silent whistle. "That's quite a collection. How did they find out?"

"Amanda found out when she saw me and – well, when she saw us together after a school concert. The Chair of Governors supposedly 'found out' because she knows my friend's husband and Sue was told the same pack of lies by someone at work – someone who belongs to the same golf club as the husband of…"

He stopped again. He felt there was a good chance that Greg would know Anne since she taught pupils at the school where he worked.

Tactfully, Greg did not pursue it. He did not feel a pressing need to be part of the small but probably growing circle of people who knew the name of the person Dan was alleged to have been having an affair with.

"I think I get the picture, Dan," he said. "My guess is that – if you haven't already ended it with this...this mystery woman, that you still want to continue your friendship with her?"

Dan nodded.

"And my further guess is," continued Greg, "that nobody else, apart from the pair of you, thinks that you should?"

"I haven't directly asked them but I'm sure that's about the size of it."

For a short while, they sat in silence. Dan sat gazing disconsolately at an empty beer glass. Finally, he said, "Look at that! I've managed to talk and drink beer at the same time. Would you believe it?"

Greg downed his last mouthful of beer. "It's good to see you haven't lost your customary skills. Strangely enough," he commented, "I've managed to perform the same trick. Would you like another?"

Dan started to protest but Greg ignored him. "No, it's alright," he said, "I can tell that your need is greater than mine."

Whilst Greg was away at the bar, Dan reflected that the beer was beginning to serve its purpose. The pain of Sue's angry comments and the awkwardness of the situation at school, was beginning to fade – if only a little.

Greg returned with two more pints of beer. "I know you didn't specifically ask for a pie, but I have ordered you one. They should be out in a minute."

Dan tried to look grateful as Greg continued. "I know you said you didn't feel much like eating but I usually find it helps – and the pies here are very good."

"Thanks," muttered Dan. "I did leave the house in a hurry – and I probably should try to eat something."

When they arrived, the pies did indeed look unlike the anaemic offerings than he had previously encountered and, after a few mouthfuls, he was grateful that Greg had ordered them; also, as his friend had suggested, eating helped to lift his mood out of the depths into which it had sunk. He digested the last morsel of pie and remembered that Greg had said that he, too, was in need of having a chat.

"Well, that was much better than I thought it might be. Even so, we didn't come here just to eat pies and talk about me. I think there were some things that you wanted to talk about?"

Greg, now also arriving at his last morsel, put down his knife and fork and removed the napkin that he had tucked into the neck of his sweatshirt.

"Yes, that's right, I did… I do, I mean."

"Come on then, spill the beans."

"It's not as complicated as your situation – but it has its own little problems. As you might know, I've been seeing a girl called Julia for some time now."

Dan shook his head. "I'm sorry, Greg, I didn't know. Remember, we haven't seen each other for a number of months."

"Ok, so Julia, is a… well, I could draw her more easily than I can describe her. She's not quite as tall as me, has long brown hair, a really nice face – oh and she's a bit younger than me."

That was no surprise, thought Dan. Greg usually preferred women younger than himself.

"Well, the thing is, I'm a bit more serious about this one…"

"Tell me more."

"Ok, as you probably know, most of them have been good for a laugh – and usually not slow about jumping into bed. But, well, Julia's different. I mean, she's still good for a laugh – and we've been sleeping together for a while – but she has a serious side to her as well – which is unusual."

"It probably isn't," said Dan with a smile. "Only perhaps you haven't really been looking…?"

Greg nodded ruminatively. "You could be right. And perhaps it's simply that I'm getting older."

"It could be that too," Dan sagely agreed. "Is she an artist?"

"Of course. If she wasn't, we probably wouldn't have lasted as long as we have."

Dan silently reflected that Greg's reference to 'lasting' probably encompassed all of about three to four months.

"It all sounds good to me, Greg. But you say there are some problems in your relationship with Julia?"

"Well, not 'problems' exactly…" He paused. "She wants me to meet her parents."

Dan could not help grinning. For a sworn bohemian such as Greg, meeting Julia's parents would be anathema.

"I could imagine, on past form, that you would find that difficult," he said.

"Well, that's just it, you see. I don't think I'd find it difficult at all. In fact, I think I'd like to meet them. If Julia really resembles them, which I'm sure she must, I'd be fascinated to meet them."

Dan was at something of a loss. "Then I don't understand – what is it that's bothering you…?"

Greg paused, shuffling his feet a little. "Oh, I guess it's just me. It's responsibility, Dan. She wants us to get married, and I've never wanted that sort of responsibility. I said as much to Julia, earlier this evening."

"So is that why you were on your own when I arrived?"

"Yes – she went off in a huff."

"Probably because she doesn't feel it's true – about your problems with 'responsibility', that is. The Art Department came out really well in the school's last inspection – largely on the back of your work."

"It's kind of you to say so. I happen to know, as well, that Freddie Saunders is getting ready to retire and when the Head of Department has 'lost the urge' as it were, someone has to step up. The Principal's even suggested that when Freddie does decide to call it a day, I should put in an application."

"Huh," laughed Dan, "There you go! You'll be a member of 'The Establishment' before you know it."

"Now that would be something! Mercifully, there's a long way to go – a very long way – before I get to that!"

"Not least of which is that you need Julia to come back to you."

"True."

"And, assuming that she does come back, neither of you will be wanting a guest in your spare room."

"Also true – but look, Dan, that situation hasn't arisen yet. Even if it does, I think there may still be a way to help you."

By now, Dan was feeling impressively mellow. He did not want to return to thinking about his problems. He lifted his second empty glass of the evening and said, "One for the road, Greg?"

Greg thrust his empty glass into Dan's hand. "That's the spirit – one for the road!"

Dan made his way to the bar.

* * *

Dan's mellow state of mind persisted, and they took some time over the third pint of beer. The lingering light of a summer's evening gently illuminated the bar, its furniture and customers, with the colours of the stained glass in the pub windows.

"Have you recovered from the floods out there in the wilds?"

Dan came back from the reverie into which he had drifted and realised that Greg was speaking to him.

"What? Oh, yes – well sort of…I mean, the house is habitable again, but it could be a year or two before we manage to repair all the damage."

He paused, noticing how easily he had slipped back into using the pronoun 'we'. Was he still part of the family that he thought of as 'we' – or was that family which had for so long been the centre of his daily life now moving into personal history?

"We weren't much affected here in Sedgewater." Greg had continued rattling on with the conversation he had started. "The Sedge nearly overtopped its banks and for a while, it looked as though there would be a serious problem – but the flood defences did their job."

"So, nothing to worry about then?" Dan had managed to refocus.

"I wouldn't exactly say that. A few side streets down near the river were flooded and had to be evacuated. For people in those streets, it was a problem. Of course, we had all the wind and rain that everyone else experienced. Otherwise, I wouldn't have said it was that bad. It was winter after all."

"It was completely different out on the Levels. For a while it was like an inland sea. Farmers who've lived out there all their lives said they had never seen it as bad as it was this last winter."

Greg took a sip of his beer. "Hmm, the sort of thing people always say… and what's a human lifetime in the scale of things? If you go back through the records, it has been worse – much worse."

Dan remembered the instances that Greg was referring to, including one in which historians thought that a tsunami in the Bristol Channel might have been the culprit. He did not want to contradict his friend, but it had been a hard experience for people who lived and worked on the Levels.

"You may well be right, Greg," he said, "but I know of several farmers who say that if there's another winter like the last, particularly in the near future, they won't be able to continue farming on the

Levels. If they did move out, it would completely change the nature of the area."

Once again, Greg was sceptical. "I heard that – and saw them too – on television. They were trying to push the Government into action, or compensation – or something like that. I didn't take that much notice. I've lived down here most of my life. They make 'em tough out there... and they won't give up."

Dan thought the conversation was drifting into clichés – and into a dead end. Perhaps it was safer to stick to the personal topics, the ones about which they actually knew something. He stared into his pint of beer.

Greg noticed that his friend had drifted away again, and they both had about a mouthful of beer left in their glasses. Perhaps it was time that they went back to the flat.

"Come on," he said, draining his glass. "We both have work tomorrow."

Dan wondered briefly if there was a problem again with his hearing. Was this really the same Greg he had known for so many years, Greg the bachelor bohemian? He was right though. There were still two weeks to the end of the Summer Term and in a few hours' time, they would both be back in the midst of daily life at the schools where they worked. He, too, drained the last of his beer.

A few long, thin rags of cloud, washed with red and grey, drifted high above in an otherwise flawless sky, sinking away from the light and heat of day into a humid night. Dan paused to look up as they wandered along the street, once again negotiating the broken pavement and the tree roots.

Back at the house, it seemed a long way up the stairs to Greg's flat and Dan was relieved when, finally, they arrived at the door. Greg fished for his key and then let them in. A short hallway led into a lounge largely devoid of furniture and creature comforts other than a well-worn settee and a single armchair. Dan lowered himself onto a part of the settee that was not decorated with used sketchpads and items of female clothing.

"Ooops! I'll just get rid of those." Greg scooped up the 'evidence' of his home life, such as it was, and hid them under a newspaper on an adjacent coffee table.

"Julia will be back for those, if nothing else," commented Dan.

"Who says they're Julia's?" Greg gave him an arch look but on this occasion Dan was not in a mood to find it funny. "Can I get you anything else to drink?"

In Dan's previous experience, this would lead to an obligatory sampling of Greg's homemade wine – and he decided that the offer was best declined.

"Thanks, Greg. Some water would be fine. As you said, we're both working tomorrow."

"I did say that didn't I? Ah well, if you're sure? And anyway, you're right... I've got a big day tomorrow."

Generally, Dan would have asked about Greg's 'big day' but the beer had made him sleepy, and he knew that, if he did not get to bed shortly, he would find that he had spent the night on the settee.

"Right then, if I don't see you in the morning, the door will lock behind you as you leave – you just need to pull it to."

Dan nodded. He knew the routine – although it had been some while since he had used it.

Greg went off to his bedroom and with a sigh, Dan remembered he had left the suitcase in the car. He trudged down the stairs to retrieve it, returned and putting it on the bed in Greg's 'visitor's room', looked through the clothes that Sue, despite her anger, had still managed to pack in a neat and orderly pile. Fortunately, the pile included two pairs of pyjamas. He hardly felt like going to the trouble of putting on pyjamas but out of deference to Greg's bed clothes and any other visitors that Greg might have, he chose the topmost pair and put them on.

There was no table next to the bed, so he placed his glass of water on the floor. Sliding in beneath the duvet, the relaxation was immediately welcome, but he was aware, as always, that the mattress of Greg's 'guest bed' was quite lumpy. He wormed his way around until at last, he found a position in which he thought he could sleep and then, without consciousness of the process, sank into a fitful sleep.

* * *

He woke with a strong thirst, and an unpleasant, acidic taste in his mouth. He wondered if the pie was taking its revenge and reached down to the glass of water, becoming aware as he did so that his head was throbbing. He took a large mouthful of water, hoping that the headache was simply a result of dehydration. The dark curtains which hung limply at the window were largely effective in excluding the lights from the street, but an ambient orange glow still penetrated the room, feeding the sadness that was returning to his thoughts now that effects of the beer were wearing off. He had forgotten to take off his watch and he peered at it until he managed to make out that it was 12.30. He was surprised. His sleep, thus far, had been filled with eventful dreaming, so that in waking, he believed that many hours must have passed. Waking also brought with it returning memories of what had taken place in his conscious world during the preceding day. Sadness, anger and self-pity weighed down upon him, as he thought of the family life that he seemed to be about to lose. The room began to feel ever more humid as his thoughts led him to toss from this side to that in the uncomfortable bed, trying to find a position in which he might once again sink into the solace of sleep.

Sleep, however, eluded him. He tried to avoid thinking about Anne but found that he was unable to do so and fell into the depressing thought that she too was about to disappear from his life. Then he reproached himself, wondering how he could be so self-centred when it was his own lack of judgement that had lent credibility to the lies being told about him.

He did not notice the disappearance of the streetlights' orange glow as they gave way to early dawn. A sleep of exhaustion finally fell upon him, insufficient in itself to help him in the day that would follow, but enough, at least, for him to begin treading the self-inflicted road back from the foolishness of his own mistakes.

* * *

CHAPTER 17

SLOW ROAD BACK

Throughout the next day, Dan tried to lay low. His difficulty was, though, that in a school consisting of temporary classrooms, other than the toilets and the main stock cupboard, there was no such thing as a private place.

His class, anticipating the end of term, seemed noisier and less intent on work than usual, every staff member had a problem of some kind, and the continuing hot weather led to an ill-tempered staffroom discussion about the need for electric fans.

By the end of the day, Dan could claim that he had managed, despite the heat and the variety of perceived irritants, to keep his temper, but both children and adults were left with an awareness that he was not in his usual calm, organised and generally positive frame of mind.

His work, much of it done after school or in the evenings, was also beginning to pile up. He needed to leave the school not long after the end of the school day, but he knew that it would only lead to a further accumulation of teachers waiting to speak to him, of more texts and e-mails left without a response, and parents who, being unable to get to parents' evening, wanted individual appointments after school.

The need that nagged at him more than anything at school, however, was that of returning to his house, in the hope that Sue had calmed down sufficiently to tolerate his presence, if only for a short time – and then, perhaps, to talk about any chinks of light, of hope, that might still be left to them, for their marriage. He also needed to see Emily and Josh; although he had, so far, spent just one night away from home, he was already missing them and he wanted to reassure them that, although they were probably very angry with him, he did not want to make an exit from their lives.

Opting for speed rather than pleasant scenery, he used the main roads to drive back to what was still partly his house. The last two miles or so through the lanes seemed tediously slow and when at last he arrived, the gate to the drive had been closed. He jumped out of his car and, with relief, found that it had not been locked. He swung it open, secured it on its metal retaining hook, and then drove his car onto the tarmac parking area.

He sat for a moment in the cool of the car's air conditioning, before climbing out again into the hot afternoon and making his way across to the front door. He felt strangely furtive, as he did so, as though someone must be watching him. Then he tried to shrug off the feeling. Although Sue did not want him there, it was still his home. He took out his door key and attempted to push it into the lock.

Confusingly, the key slid part way into the lock and then became stuck; with some difficulty, he extracted the key and tried again – with the same result. When a third attempt also failed, he gave way to the realisation that this was not the lock for which his key had been cut.

He hurried round to the back of the house where he tried his backdoor key. To his relief, the key turned. Expectantly, he turned the door handle – but the door did not open. Rather desperately, he put his shoulder to the door and shoved. Then he shoved again. There was not the slightest movement. The bolts on the inside must have been drawn across. Sue had clearly anticipated that he might try to enter the house and had taken steps to keep him out.

Feelings of anger and futility jostled with each other, as he tried to bring calmer thoughts to bear on the predicament. Slowly, he wandered back to the front of the house. What could, or should, he do next?

As he pondered his next move, he became aware that something had lodged itself in the sole of his shoe; he stood on one leg and examined what had happened. Without too much difficulty, he extracted a masonry screw from the indentation it had made. Looking around, he found two more screws of the same kind.

He was not aware of having had any work done recently on the front of the house; and, he had certainly not done any himself. He looked up at the house façade – and found himself staring into a CCTV lens. The workmen must have been told to work quickly and, in doing so, had not been particularly scrupulous about clearing up.

The heat of the late afternoon was only slowly abating so he decided to return to the car, switch on the air conditioning and the radio, and wait for Josh and Emily to arrive. From behind the steering wheel, the car clock told him that it was 4.30 pm. There might still be a little while to wait. Josh and Emily were amongst the last to be dropped off and the progress of the school bus through the country lanes was inevitably slow. There had also been a recent occasion when it had broken down.

Together, the air conditioning and music from the radio helped to calm him. The sleeplessness of the previous night began to overwhelm him so that, despite the ongoing 'white noise' of his anxiety, his head began to loll and slowly sink onto his chest. For a while he resisted. He had fought with tiredness all through the day. Then deciding that, after all, there was nothing to be lost, he finally gave in to the drowsiness.

The mingled sounds of the music and the air conditioning seemed to recede to a far place. He drifted blissfully, his mind and body offloading for a while the worries of home and work. He could still see the interior of the car, the dashboard with its various instruments and through the windscreen, the deeply pleasant green of the summer countryside. Then, to his joy and relief, Josh and Emily appeared at the window on his side, laughing and pulling faces and gently rocking the car to wake him up.

He woke with a start. Strangely, Josh and Emily had disappeared – but then he noticed that his phone was buzzing. Retrieving it from his pocket, he saw rather blearily that there was a text from Sue. For a text, it was rather long – but to the point.

"By now, you've probably been trying to get into the house. Don't bother. If you do any damage, I will come after you. Don't waste your time waiting for Josh and Emily. They're staying with me at Mum's house – and will be until I decide we can return. Now just go away. My solicitor will tell you what happens next."

Despite the animosity that Sue had expressed the day before, Dan was surprised by the level of aggression in the text. Was it really all down to the humiliation and anger brought about by his supposed betrayal of her? He had behaved foolishly – but apart from that, he was innocent of any wrongdoing. For the time being, however, it looked as though there was going to be no 'second chance' with Sue.

She had always seemed 'driven', but Dan had assumed that it was largely an outcome of her work and the constant deadlines that she was forever expected to meet. Now he began to wonder. Perhaps she had been unhappy with him for some time? Generally, in recent times, they had rarely made time to talk to each other – at least, not without the presence of Emily or Josh – or Gwen. The only times they had been alone together were when they were in bed – and in those times, as Sue had frequently reminded him, she needed her sleep; she was there to sleep and do nothing else. Neither conversation nor, still less intimacy, was on the agenda.

He would not, could not, exonerate himself. He had been at least half the cause of this mutual disengagement. He thought about it for a moment but knew it would take longer to disentangle than he had available that evening. Now that he had been locked out of the house, he would once more need to find somewhere to sleep. He hesitated to ask Greg if he could sleep at the flat again because it was almost certain that he would be wanting Julia, not Dan, to spend the night there. He decided to drive over to 'The Withy Cutters Arms'. It was a beautiful summer's evening. He needed something to eat and drink, and he could give some thought as to where to stay overnight. It was possible that he could stay at the pub. In any event, there were plenty of 'B and B' places in that area. He could check first on his smartphone but decided that his need for food and something to drink came first. He would solve his accommodation problem afterwards. After such a dismal winter, why should he not try to enjoy the hot weather?

He started the car's engine, no longer in a mood to dwell anymore, that evening, on the problems that had arisen between him and Sue. An hour or two of respite was what he needed most. But as he drove on through the summer lanes, he thought, more than once, that he caught a glimpse of Josh and Emily's faces in his side window.

* * *

The 'Withy Cutters Arms' was on the banks of the River Bree. Built a little way back from the river on ground that rose towards the small town of Drainton (pronounced 'Drenton', Dan still bothered to recall), it had nevertheless been inundated by the floods, during the winter.

Having lost many of his picnic tables to the river, the landlord had installed wooden bollards to which the tables were now moored with stout chains. Fortunately, the bollards did not detract from the pleasure of eating at the tables, so Dan ordered himself a salad and a pint of beer, paid, and went to sit where he could watch the river and briefly forget about his troubles.

He had eaten most of his food and the beer had helped to soften his mood when he became aware that his phone was buzzing. At first, he ignored it, but then curiosity won, and he fished it out of his pocket. He missed the call but peered closely at the number; it had been from Anne's phone. Since their alleged affair had already caused so much heartache, he hesitated to call her back but then the phone pinged as a text arrived. It was from Anne. Despite his troubles, his heart was already beating a little faster. He opened the message, squinting at it in the strong light of the summer's evening.

"Deeply sorry I've caused you so much grief but am desperate to see you. Can you come?"

He agonised briefly but then replied, confirming that he would be with her in about twenty minutes. Then he finished his last mouthful of beer and left the remnants of his salad.

En route, he forced himself to drive at a steady pace. He wanted to arrive in one piece and the lanes were so narrow that if he met anything at speed, there would be no escape.

Despite his inner conflict, Anne's message had been a ray of light in two days of misery. His visit to Greg had briefly punctuated his depression but in the early hours of the morning, he had returned again to his previous anxiety and regret. Now he was on his way to the woman with whom his supposed relationship had caused both anger and sorrow.

Other than in the world of his obsession, it made little sense. This 'Love', that he had always thought of so positively as a source of joy, was also a great disrupter that brought in equal measure, moments of both great happiness and profoundly wrenching anxiety.

Despite having to watch his speed as he drove through the lanes, he arrived at Anne's house in just fifteen minutes.

* * *

Despite having claimed to be 'desperate' to see him, Anne looked palely attractive when she answered the door. Her hair, he saw, had been brushed, carefully arranged and worn 'up', perhaps because it was more comfortable to wear it that way in the hot weather. She was wearing a light summer blouse, open at the neck, and a slim waisted skirt. She looked the picture of coolness.

Looking over Dan's shoulder at his car parked on the drive, she said, "I think it might be best if you park at the back again. The outbuilding there is mostly empty except for a few bits of old furniture. If you drive round there, I'll show you."

Dan followed her out onto the drive and followed her in his car round to the back of the house. There, the drive divided into two with one branch going to the house and the other, to a huge shed largely concealed amongst a clump of trees. Unlatching the doors of the shed, she heaved them open and waved him forward to the coolness of the interior. He edged his way in, his sight only slowly adjusting to the darkness.

Climbing out of the car, he was aware of a curious mixture of smells – of wood, of oil and, despite the heat, of a musty, woodland dampness. She came forward to him and, before he had time to think about it, they kissed. For one sensuous moment, he was aware of the taste of her lipstick and the perfume that she was wearing, They moved apart a little, giving him an opportunity to look at her once more.

Usually subtle in her use of make-up, it seemed to Dan that she had used rather more than usual. In particular, it seemed to be thicker below her left eye, where there was an almost imperceptible shadow. Not having noticed it at first, he now felt concerned. Had her husband's anger been expressed in more than words? He decided to delay asking her about it until he had been with her a little longer.

Together, they shut the heavy wooden doors of the shed.

"Come on," she said. "We can go in through the back of the house."

She led him to the back door from where she took him past the spacious modern kitchen to a short passageway along which she guided him through to the lounge – a room that Dan already knew from previous visits and where, despite his misgivings, he held her in his arms, remaining that way until Anne, anxious to talk, gently released herself and went to sit in an armchair. Dan sat on the nearby settee.

"I'll get us some cool drinks in a moment, Dan. It's been a really hot day again, hasn't it?" She paused whilst she thought about how to move beyond the usual small talk.

"I'm sorry that I haven't contacted you for several days. I've been longing to see you – but, well – with the way things have been here, it's been impossible."

"I've had the same problem," replied Dan.

"And I don't suppose it will help if George – or Sue – find out that we've been together this evening."

Dan was silent for a moment whilst he wondered if the situation with Sue could be any worse, but then, he had yet to hear about what had transpired between Anne and George. "Strange, isn't it," he said, "that the two people this most affects are you and me but we seem to be almost powerless in the face of other people's thoughts and opinions."

Anne, however, had already been educated in the realities of social pressure.

"We won't be able to change that, Dan. I'd rather enjoy the time that we can spend together than waste it worrying about what others think."

Having previously paused to wonder what exactly it was that they were sharing, Dan understood what she meant, but whatever it was, it now seemed that it was a very fragile thing, and, like Anne, he too was driven by a sense that their time together was precious because there might be very little of it in the future.

"I'm going to get us those drinks." He watched her graceful movements, as she went over to a drinks cabinet just to one side of them. "What would you like?"

"Mm, since it is so warm this evening a gin and tonic would go down well…"

Anne made the drinks and returned with them, this time sitting next to Dan. They nestled companionably and unselfconsciously together, sipping their drinks.

Eventually Anne said, "I wasn't sure if you would be able to come this evening, but it must be two weeks since we last saw each other."

"Well, I should be working as usual, but as things turned out, I was just wondering what to do, when your text arrived."

"So, were you at home?"

Dan related the events of the previous evening and the sequel in which Sue had locked him out of his house. Anne was very taken aback.

"Can she really do that? I mean, she obviously has – but is it legal?"

"I don't know, Anne. She will probably find a way to justify it. She may also be hoping that I won't contest what she's done."

Anne looked into his eyes. "I'm so sorry, Dan. When we first began to get closer, I didn't realise it would lead to all this. I've been very self-centred, not to mention short sighted."

"You're hardly to blame though, are you?" replied Dan. "We've both wanted to be together – but then, when you stand back and look at the situation, what have we actually done?"

Anne gave a small laugh. "That's the irony, though, isn't it, Dan? We've actually done very little – apart from having the odd kiss and cuddle here and there."

"Well, that being the case," he said, "I actually fancy one of those right now."

She smiled and they turned to each other. As they drew closer together, he found himself studying her face for a moment.

"I almost hate to ask you, Anne," he said, "but I can't help noticing that there's a dark area in your make-up. Is that a bruise?"

She hesitated but then saw little point in denying it. "Yes, it is," she admitted but instinctively dropped her head so that it could not easily be seen. He responded by gently putting his fingers under her chin and lifting her face towards him.

"Are you going to tell me how it got there?"

She hesitated, initially reluctant to do so, but then shrugged in resignation. "You've probably guessed anyway. Someone, almost certainly my neighbour, must have seen us, or perhaps saw your car on the drive. Anyway, when George was here he began to question me about you – and about how long you've been coming here. He was angry and at first, I lied, saying that you'd come here on school business – but that only made him angrier – and it was then that he hit me. In the end, I told him that we're friends and wanted each other's company. I'm not ashamed of that, Dan – we'd done nothing to be ashamed of. But, when he's as angry as he was then, I'm seriously afraid of him and of what he might do."

Dan said nothing but felt his own anger beginning to mount. Seeing the effect of her words, she placed a hand on his arm.

"Dan, please, please don't…" she pleaded. "It's hard enough to manage George. I don't want the two of you at each other's throats –

or, for that matter, at mine. If we give him time, he'll probably calm down again."

He took in what she had said and waited for his temper to subside. She had not, though, for the moment, explained by what process George would 'calm down' and a sense of futility slowly began to replace Dan's diminishing anger.

"So," he asked at last, "what are we going to do? Are we just going to give everyone what they want – and simply stop seeing each other?"

She hesitated and turned a little away from him. "Unless I'm much mistaken, neither of us want that. But then, it was never my intention to wreck your marriage." She paused. "I think we should just try to be careful, to be very discreet and not let our feelings run away with us. That way, whatever the gossips have to say, we'll both know we have nothing to be ashamed of…"

Dan nodded. There was good sense in what she was saying – except that… He looked away. His anger with Sue's acceptance of what she had heard and her unwillingness to let him tell her the truth still rankled. And besides that, he had no idea when he would next be able to see his children. They would no doubt have heard the gossip – and were possibly being taunted with it at school. Both of them had enough knowledge of social media to be able to access the hideous comments online and, most damaging and destructive of all, a deep fake video of him and Anne. Such evil things had long been possible – but despite that they were still effective tools for those who wanted to wreck careers, marriages and lives.

There was still more to worry about with Josh and Emily because the very last thing that they needed was their parents splitting up. The school's summer break was fast approaching and in the autumn, Josh would be wanting to make a good start in the sixth form whilst Emily was hoping to make good choices about her GCSEs.

The whole situation seemed to have blown up out of next to nothing in such a short period – just a few weeks and now… and now, he could not even begin to see what his next step should be. He gazed through the lounge window at the evening sky beyond. The sun was sinking towards the horizon. Anne followed his gaze.

"Do you have anywhere to stay tonight? You haven't said."

"No," was his simple reply.

"Well, you could stay here…"

"But George…"

"George is in London, still trying 'to calm down', I expect. After all, not only am I supposed to be cheating on him, but his factory was also severely damaged during the Climate protest."

"I had nothing to do with…"

She stopped him. "I haven't supposed for one moment that you did. But I shouldn't worry anyway, Dan. He has lawyers crawling all over the situation."

"Okay – well I hope for both our sakes that they're committed to the truth and not simply to calming him down."

"Ah no," said Anne. "I wasn't referring to his lawyers in the context of 'calming him down'. No – to do that, he's probably spending the night with one of his many women."

Dan was taken sharply aback. Was that the means by which George habitually 'calmed himself down'? Now that, surely, was taking 'double standards' to a whole, new, breath-taking level.

He started to speak but Anne placed a finger firmly on his lips. "No, Dan," she said. "We're all capable of being hypocrites at one time or another – but for the time being, let's leave that to George."

"But don't you find that very humiliating?" he said before he remembered that Sue had accused him, the day before, of humiliating her. "Have you ever challenged him about his behaviour?"

"I've certainly tried – but if he has the slightest suspicion that I'm accusing him of double standards, he flies into a rage."

"Perhaps his violence is the real reason that you haven't left him. Are you afraid of him?"

He suspected that the situation was worse than she was admitting, and he wanted to provoke her into 'opening up'. But she had lived with the situation a long time and answered him in a calm and level voice.

"I think I've already told you that I am… He's a very forceful man and I don't know what he might do if he becomes sufficiently angry about…well, about us. A beating might be just the beginning…"

"There are people who could protect you from him…"

"Are there? You don't know George – not as I do." She paused. "He hates the thought that someone might be capable of taking me away from him. And if I ever did leave him, I'd lose everything I have here. I could never afford a place like this – not on my earnings. I'd lose everything I have and besides, although he has such a violent temper, he's also very strong – and in the kind of world we used to live in, he protected me..."

"But is it really worth sacrificing your self-respect by clinging to someone so violent, and possessive that he uses force to keep you, even whilst he's being disloyal to you?" He stopped, aware that in his frustration, his voice was rising.

Anne sat silently with her head bowed but then turned her face towards him and said, "I know you're concerned about me, Dan, and I love being with you. We're soulmates and that's something that I'll never be with George. But could you offer me all this? Did I tell you that he often takes me on his business trips with him? He takes me on flights to Europe, the US and the Far East. We meet all sorts of amazing people. With George, life is full of boundless possibilities. Is that something that you think you and I would do together?"

She left her questions hanging in the air because he had the sense to see that he could never offer her the life that she shared with George. And she knew that although it often tormented her, she was unable to accept the limitations of Somerset, of England, and of the constrained and decidedly finite possibilities that the Climate Crisis seemed to be forcing upon her and everyone that she knew.

They were at an impasse – but it was one that at that moment she believed she had time to live with.

Whilst they had been talking, they had been sitting very close to each other. She realised that she would not find it easy to disentangle herself from the warmth and intimate closeness that she had been sharing with him – but George was already in the process of spitefully disrupting Dan's life and there had to be a limit to it...

With as much grace as she could muster, she slid away from him and picking up his glass, and her own, silently indicated that she was going to pour them both another drink.

Although it was a summer's evening, Dan could see through the lounge window that the light had nearly faded from the sky. Anne returned with the drinks but then went to switch on a large table lamp. It gave a soft yellow glow to the room.

Once more they sat close together, sipping their drinks. She could not help noticing, however, that in a very short time Dan had drunk most of his wine and she felt bound to ask him, "Where had you originally planned to stay tonight?" she asked.

Forgetfully, from within the haze induced by the wine, he replied "I was planning to go back to the Withy Cutters. I think they offer B and B."

"You wouldn't be able to drive back safely through those lanes, Dan. Besides, you'd be lucky to get a room now. The 'Withy Cutters' is usually fully booked at this time of year."

"So...?"

She laughed. "So...you need to let me finish my sentence! I was trying to remind you that I've already agreed you can stay here tonight – but I'm afraid it can only be for just the one night."

A broad smile of relief – and gratitude – spread across Dan's face. He put down his glass and put his arms around her, kissing her on the neck and face and finally, the lips.

She tried to push him away. "Dan, come on! I only said that you can stay here tonight. I haven't said anything about...well, anything else!"

Slightly embarrassed, Dan withdrew and picked up his glass again.

"I'm really grateful, Anne." He looked reflectively into his glass. "All the same, I have to find a better arrangement than simply hopping from one place to the next each night."

"Yes, of course. But I might be able to help you there, as well."

"Oh?"

"Yes – one of my relatives has a holiday cottage not far from here – and not that far from your school, now that I think about it."

"That would be brilliant! Oh, Anne, you are so..." He began moving towards her once again, but she carefully fended him off.

"I mean, I would probably only need it for a short while – just while I get things sorted out with Sue."

She smiled but refrained from commenting and drained the last of her drink. Dan followed suit. He stood, putting his glass down on a side table.

"I need to go back to the car. I've left my bag in the boot."

"Really? What do you need from your bag?"

"Well, there's my toilet bag – and my pyjamas."

Anne laughed again. "I have plenty of everything here," she said. "You can leave the bag in the car. Besides, you won't need much, it's such a warm night..."

Dan did not feel inclined to argue but he still felt concerned about Anne's suspicion, voiced earlier, that George had someone spying on her. He voiced his concern, but she was not about to change her mind.

"Well," she said, "there's really only one person who can be spying on…"

"So who's that?"

"It must be my neighbour – as far as I'm aware, George hasn't got any cameras or microphones hidden around the place. I've never seen any cars hanging around outside – and realistically, the only way that anyone can get out here is by car. So that only leaves my neighbour. I know that he can see parts of this house from his – so that's who I think is spying on us – and then informing George."

"…And that means we're taking quite a risk."

"Perhaps, although if we're careful, he'll find it hard to see anything suspicious."

"He sounds like a real creep."

"Oh yes, he is. I think he's spied on me ever since we came here. But he's very careful and it's hard to catch him out."

"So what are we going to do?"

"Well, first I'll draw all the curtains – which is something I always do about now but that also means that unless he's prepared to sneak into the garden, he won't be able to see a thing – and he'll have nothing he can report to George."

"He's bound to be suspicious though, isn't he?"

"What if he is? One of the few times that I've ever caught him out was yesterday when I saw him at his window with his binoculars. I was undressing to get into the bath… I don't think George would be very pleased to hear about that…"

"Okay then, Anne, I get the picture. So, where do you want me to wait?"

"If you stay in here, he can't see into this room – and when I've finished pulling curtains, I'll call down to you."

"All the same, it does seem a bit ridiculous…and what about when I leave in the morning?"

"I'm pretty sure you'll be much too early for him. I've never seen any signs of life next door until about ten o'clock."

Dan nodded his agreement. It was something of a risk, but it was one that they both seemed prepared to take.

"So," she said, "when I've drawn the curtains, you can follow me up. It's a gross intrusion that this 'neighbour' sees fit to spy on me – but better safe than sorry."

She gave him a smile and then went off to begin the rather bizarre procedure that they had agreed upon. Dan watched and waited as she closed the last of the curtains downstairs and then he waited a little longer while she dealt with the curtains and blinds upstairs.

Finally, she called down to him that she had finished, and Dan went to meet her at the top of the broad staircase. Most of his visits had been on weekend afternoons when she had usually taken him into the lounge. This evening, he would get to see something of the upper storey of the house.

She led him along a thickly carpeted landing to a small door on their left. She opened it and went in. "I forgot to close the curtains in here," she said. She went ahead of him and stood briefly at the window, watching the last of the light fade from the landscape.

Dan waited for her at the foot of the large and very comfortable looking bed as she turned from the window. She came back towards him, and he held her briefly. She did not resist.

After a moment or two, she detached herself from his embrace, unbuttoned her blouse and skirt, discarding them to one side of the bed and slid beneath the duvet. Dan had watched her, his heart in his mouth. A moment he had wanted for so long had arrived. He followed suit by pulling off his outer clothes and slipping in beside her.

From there, it was Anne who took the initiative – though not quite as Dan would have imagined. She drew in close to his side and then, smiling, kissed him gently on the lips.

"Well, Dan," she said, "there are so many things we're supposed to have done – so as the expression goes, we might as well be hung for a sheep as a lamb."

* * *

The next morning, Anne put some breakfast together for the two of them. They had both slept well after the wine they had drunk the previous evening but looked bleary-eyed and rumpled in the sunlight which, at that time of day, streamed into her kitchen. Dan sleepily munched his way through some cereal, whilst she made scrambled eggs which she then shared onto two plates, before coming to sit next to him.

For a while they ate in warm, comfortable silence with Dan reflecting that breakfast time at home had rarely been this calm or peaceful. Anne went to make some coffee and then brought the cafetiere back to the table. Whilst they waited for the coffee to finish brewing, Dan turned towards her and gently slid one knee between hers. Her dressing gown slid back, revealing her slim thighs. She laughed.

"Dan, you know we're not going to...well, you shouldn't be doing that! You need to get off to work."

He nodded. "I know. Being so close to the end of term, activity at school is fairly frantic. I'll just have a coffee and then get going. What are you doing today?"

"I have four pupils for tuition, I have to go to Fairfields for a concert rehearsal and then later, I'm joining up with some colleagues for our weekly get-together, a musical one – strictly for our own enjoyment." She smiled but then looked a little more serious. "Somewhere in amongst that little lot, I'll phone my aunt. The last I heard, she hasn't let the holiday cottage yet so, no doubt, she would be grateful for the business."

"I really appreciate that you're willing to do that for me." He thought for a minute, and then asked a little anxiously, "Will George have anything to say about it?"

"No, Dan," she reassured him. "George and my aunt have never seen eye-to-eye, so they have almost nothing to do with each other. And besides, the cottage belongs to my aunt so it's nothing to do with him anyway."

He leaned across to kiss her on the cheek, but she turned her head so that her lips met his.

They lingered for a moment but then she said, "Dan, you really have to go! Come on, I'll take you through to the back."

He followed her to the door and then made his way out to the workshop hidden among the trees. She watched him from the back doorstep as he swung the doors open. Reversing out, he found enough space to turn the car around and began to get out to close the doors – but she waved him away and quietly called across that she would shut them when he had gone.

He drove carefully round to the front of the house and, checking left and right, out into the lane. There were no other vehicles in sight, and he was able to make his way steadily down to the main road and then to complete an uneventful drive to the collection of temporary classrooms of which Wellsprings School now consisted.

* * *

Despite his chronic lack of preparation, the day went well. He felt tired despite having slept well but memories of Anne helped him to pass through the first few hours of work like a surfer riding a wave.

It was not until mid-afternoon that the wave began to break. He was listening to a group of readers when he became aware of several giggles from the children close to him. He lifted his head from the book they were sharing. "What is it, Simon?" he asked, knowing that he would get an all too candid answer.

"We thought you were falling asleep, Mr 'Olroyd!" piped up Simon Nuttall in a voice that Dan wished was a number of decibels quieter.

"Ah well," Dan replied. "Sometimes I like to close my eyes so that I can focus even more clearly on listening to you."

"But what about the book, Mr 'Olroyd? Don't you need to see the words to know if we're readin' 'em proply?" It was Amelia, the class sceptic.

A thought flitted across Dan's brain. "Amelia Parkin, I wonder what life holds in store for…" He did not bother to finish the thought. Faces were turned towards him, waiting for his reply.

"Amelia, you're absolutely right, of course I do. But I've read this book so many times, I know all the words by heart."

"Really, Mr 'Olroyd? Do you?" Her eyes were round with amazement. There was a rustling of voices as children began to consider whether or not it was truly possible that he knew all the words of the story by heart. Things were clearly getting out of hand.

Dan shut his book and sat up straight, folding his arms as he did so. The readers around him quickly did the same and the rest of the class followed suit, the question of Mr 'Olroyd's phenomenal memory apparently having been placed on 'hold' for the time being.

He took them straight into their 'Home Time' routine and breathed a quiet sigh of relief as the last child exited the classroom door and was met by her mother at the foot of the steps.

* * *

Dan invariably kept his mobile phone on 'silent' whilst he was in the classroom. He took a moment to open it and then saw that Anne had left him a message. She had been right. Her aunt's holiday cottage had not been let – and would he be able to visit the cottage that evening at 7.30? He quickly replied that he would be there.

It took him a little while to find the hamlet of Goosewick, even with the help of his 'satnav'. The cottage was part of a small group of houses, the back gardens of which ran down a gentle slope towards the River Sedge. Dan left his car in a small parking area just off the road and went to explore.

Anne had sent him the address and a picture of the cottage. The evening sun was still strong, so he stood beneath a tree to study the image on his phone. The cottage was not hard to identify amongst the other houses since it stood on its own plot of land and was the only one in that group of houses to have a thatched roof. The sun lit the warm colours of its local stone.

He pushed the phone into his pocket and walked across to a white painted gate that gave admittance to the garden. Following the stone flags that formed the path to the front of the house, he found that the door was already ajar. He opened the door a little further and called into the twilight of the interior.

"Hello!"

By way of answer, he heard hurrying footsteps and a small, grey-haired woman with a lively, smiling face made her way towards him. "Ah, you must be Dan?"

"I am indeed," responded Dan.

"Yes, ah, good. I'm Phoebe!" She extended a hand which Dan shook, expecting frailty but meeting with a firm and wiry grip.

"Do come in! It's much cooler in here. Isn't it hot his year! So hot! And after all the rain and storms of the winter. Now, Anne has told me a little about you but do come and tell me a little more. Then, hopefully, we can do business."

Her words were poured out in a torrent so that Dan felt he had to wait before he could say anything.

He explained his present predicament, although he resorted to euphemisms when it came to his problems at home.

Phoebe, surprisingly, waited patiently and without interjection whilst he finished his explanation and then said, "So, you'll be needing the cottage right away then?"

"That's right. If that's not a problem…"

"Oh no! No problem at all! In fact, it'll suit me very well. Come on – I'll show you round!"

Dan, all too aware of his physical bulk, followed Phoebe as she hurried along narrow passageways, upstairs, downstairs, through the kitchen and dining room until they found themselves once more in the lounge.

"Oh!" she exclaimed. "I'm feeling cooler now! Would you believe it?" She hitched her cardigan up round the shoulders of the light floral dress she was wearing and moved towards the still open door, where the evening's warmth was penetrating the coolness of the room. "Why don't we go into the back garden to finish our discussion?" She led the way through to the back door, leaving it ajar for Dan to follow her. At the back of the cottage was a large patio on which stood a picnic table, surmounted by a parasol and surrounded by picnic chairs. They sat next to each other in two of the chairs that gave them a view down to the river.

"Now that you've had a look around, what do you think?"

"It's a lovely cottage. And it's in a charming spot… but it's also, well, rather off the beaten track."

"Yes, of course, but then it's not that far from where you work – and it would certainly give you some peace and quiet at the end of the day."

Dan smiled. Other than being located in a rather isolated hamlet, he had thought that the cottage would be just right for him from the moment that he saw it – but there was a process to go through. They haggled a little over the monthly rent, with Dan recalling that she had not been able to let it in the early part of the 'season'.

Phoebe acknowledged that he was right.

"It has been a poor start. The storms did a lot of damage to the hamlet, including this cottage. Fortunately, we weren't flooded up here, but I had to have a lot of repair work done."

Finally, they settled on a rent that was well within Dan's monthly salary and Phoebe agreed that they could complete what she referred to as the 'paperwork' the following day. She seemed happy that she had been able to let the cottage and that, given Dan's circumstances, he would need to stay for some months to come. Having handed Dan a set of keys, for which he had to sign a receipt, she left him to settle in. Dan went to retrieve his suitcase from the car and began to think about getting an evening meal somewhere. Having studied a local map earlier in the day, he recalled that it was not far from Goosewick to the 'Dog and Duck'.

* * *

The last few days of the summer term passed in something of a blur. Dan was struggling less because, despite being very unhappy about the separation from Sue and his two children, he had managed to get several nights of sound sleep and, with the school's summer break just ahead, there was the prospect of having more time to resolve the issues in his private life. It was late Thursday afternoon, and the school was due to close for the summer break on the following day.

He was sitting at his classroom desk, poring over class lists and other details for the autumn term, when Amanda slipped into the room. Seeing him with the class lists, she said, "I shouldn't spend any more time on those, Dan. We've dealt with all the details relating to class lists and the next time we'll have to think about them will be just before the autumn term. I would like a quick chat with you though. Do you mind if we go to my office? It's a bit more comfortable there."

Dan readily agreed; although they sometimes met in their capacities as Head and Deputy, it was rare for Amanda to have time for an after school 'chat'. They walked together across to the Administration hut and then along to Amanda's office. She motioned him to a comfortable chair.

"Thanks, Dan. I just need a few minutes of your time to catch up with you."

Dan wondered if Amanda had heard about the events in his private life or whether she was going to bring him up to date with the Wellsprings situation. He would surely know in just a few minutes.

Amanda did not waste any time in getting to what she wanted to say.

"I hear, Dan, that you and Sue have split up."

"Yes," replied Dan sadly, "we have."

Amanda hesitated before continuing. "So, did it come as a surprise – or have you been having problems for a while?"

"Strange as it may seem," replied Dan, "I hadn't really thought about it. I certainly had no intention to be living apart from Sue and the children – and it's not what I want."

"Have you been in touch with her then?"

"No... I haven't spoken to her – or heard from Josh or Emily for more than a week..."

"That must be difficult for you..."

"Yes...of course, Amanda...bloody difficult, to be frank."

Amanda waited. She could see that Dan was close to tears and although she had thought it inevitable that Sue would hear about Dan's alleged affair with Anne, she was sad to see the distress that the situation was causing him. She did not, though, feel judgemental about it.

"I'm sorry, Dan – naturally, I weighed up whether or not I should speak to you about what is, after all, your private life, but there is a school aspect to it..."

"I cannot imagine what that would be", replied Dan warmly. "I've made every effort to keep my work and home life completely separate."

"But we both know it's not that simple," replied Amanda. "I respect that you want to keep them apart but, unfortunately, it does seem to me that your personal life is affecting your work."

Amanda gave an inward sigh. Despite her best intentions, they had somehow arrived at a difficult juncture – one that she had hoped to delay. It was clear, however, that Dan was not about to drop the subject.

"What makes you say that?" he demanded. "As far as I'm aware, I'm well on top of everything that needed doing this term and I'm well ahead with the planning for the autumn."

"Yes, Dan, I agree you've done well with that aspect of your role – but, unfortunately, there are other areas – ones which, I have to say, you usually handle well but where things are going awry."

This comment caught Dan unawares. He genuinely thought that his home life had not affected his work.

"So, what are you talking about, Amanda?"

Amanda paused. She had hoped that Dan would realise but now, it seemed, she would have to spell it out.

"I'm talking about your relationships with other staff, Dan – and the way that you've been handling what are sometimes referred to as 'tricky situations'.

"Do you have any particular instances in mind?"

"Yes, Dan – I do. It was some days ago now, but I found myself dealing with a small deputation of staff complaining about the matter of classrooms getting too hot for both staff and children."

"I did try to deal with that, Amanda – the issue is really one of supply. The heat this summer has affected everyone and obtaining even such basic things as fans has become a problem. I was trying to deal with it before coming to you – although I do need to talk to you about the costs."

"I understand that, Dan – as do the staff. But their complaint was as much about you as about the heat. They complained that when they approached you, you dealt with them in an impatient and thoroughly bad-tempered manner."

Dan felt deflated. He remembered the situation that Amanda was referring to and knew that he had let his temper get the better of him. He had left himself no room for manoeuvre.

"I'm sorry, Amanda," he said. "I will go back and apologise to anyone I've upset. I would, though, really appreciate it if we could look together at the difficulties caused by the temperatures this summer. We need to come up with solutions – and they won't be cheap."

"I will certainly go through the problems with you, Dan – and I feel somewhat remiss myself. We should certainly have discussed them before now. Meanwhile, I think it will be appropriate for you to apologise to those staff you've upset – and, I would suggest, try to get a clearer picture of the problems they are dealing with. The classrooms are not uniformly the same." She smiled faintly. "The ones next to the trees by the playground seem to be managing quite well."

Perhaps by depersonalising the discussion, she could make space to have a more constructive conversation. There was an appreciable silence – which, finally, she thought she should break.

"I hope you don't mind, Dan, but I think it would be better if we returned to the point from which we started. Of course, I do have a better understanding of your situation than your other colleagues…"

"I don't want them to know. I'd much rather keep it to myself…"

"I can understand that too…but if you are going to keep any knowledge of your personal situation away from the staff, then you also need to make sure that you can still manage issues that arise with… well, with the sensitivity that, in fairness, you have generally shown in the past."

Dan recognised that Amanda was, in turn, being very patient with him. There was, though, something he felt he should broach with her that did not relate directly to his role. It was the matter of the problems at the Wellsprings School site.

"I appreciate that I've let my personal problems affect the way in which I've dealt with staff. I'm hoping that with the summer break ahead of us, I can begin to make a difference with regard to my problems at …well, at home."

Amanda smiled. It was the perennial hope of teachers that the time and comparative leisure afforded by 'the summer break' would work their magic on all concerned.

However, Dan had not finished.

"There's pressure on both of us," he continued. "Staff are constantly asking me… 'When on Earth will we be moving back to the Wellsprings site? Surely the problems have been fixed by now?' They're surprised when I say I don't know – and, of course, in all honesty, that isn't true."

Amanda pursed her lips. A decision about the school's future was imminent but that was something that she could not share – even with the school's Deputy Head.

"I'm afraid there's nothing more I can say on that subject. As soon as there is, Dan, I'll let you know immediately."

He nodded. It was the response he had expected.

He took a quick look at his watch. He needed to be on his way.

"I'm sorry, Amanda – I have to go but I would really appreciate a chance to talk to you more about the problems we have with…well, the extremes of the weather and the temporary classrooms."

"I'm sure we can make time for such a meeting. It will have to be during the summer break now, but I'd prefer that, Dan, because we'll both be in a more relaxed frame of mind – and more likely to find some constructive solutions."

"I agree," he said, making his way to the door.

"I'll see you tomorrow then. 'The last day of term' – a phrase that always has a certain ring to it – don't you agree?"

"I certainly do," said Dan with a laugh.

He sometimes grumbled to himself that he came a long way down on Amanda's list. But this time, at least, she had made an effort. At least when they met during the Summer Break, she would not be 'at everybody's beck and call'.

He left Amanda's office and returned to his classroom. It took him a few minutes to gather up things he needed for the following day and then he drove to a supermarket in Sedgewater to buy food and, after a short debate with himself, a bottle of whisky.

Then, his detour complete, he drove back to the cottage. Strangely, the change in his route 'home' was almost welcome because, as the summer had settled into a prolonged spell of hot weather, the days had seemed to blend into each other. He drew up outside the cottage and listened briefly to the air conditioning; it had become a familiar background to his journeys, no matter which route he had to take.

* * *

Amanda remained in her office for a few minutes more. Unusually, she did not have an evening meeting to attend – and James would not be back until late. She picked up the bag containing her notebook computer and headed for the car park.

Now that the heat of the day was gradually fading into a warm evening, her drive through the lanes was delightful. Her Audi was better suited to motorways than the slow and narrow byways of Somerset, but she took delight in the beauty of the countryside and the music playing through the sound system.

As soon as she crunched her way onto the drive, she triggered the door on the garage and drove carefully into its cool, dark space. Then picking up her computer bag from the passenger seat, she decided not to go in through the garage side door but to have a look at the garden.

The gardener she and James had employed for years had retired, but his son was now running the business and seemed to be making a good job of managing the problems of heat and drought. The borders and beds were delightful, and she felt very fortunate to have such a garden in which to relax.

Amanda did not credit James with knowing much about garden designs or planting schemes, but he did know about employing people who had such knowledge and skills. The heady perfume of the flowers seemed only to be intensified by the still lingering heat of the day.

She wandered along the path that led round to the other side of the house and made her way to a small arbour where her favourite seat was located. There she took a little time to enjoy the peace of the garden that she and James had earned through their constant hard work and which, together with the large house amidst the beautiful space that was all around her, she reminded herself was the reward for all the years that she had worked whilst others had frittered away their time and thus found themselves in the constant hand-to-mouth struggle that now seemed to characterise the lives of so many.

There, she paused, knowing that, for her, this was not an authentic line of thought. She had come a long way in her life, but she had not forgotten the place from which she came. She rested her eyes on a bed of tall flowers resplendent in their summer colours and wondered why it was that in her thoughts she was not truly enjoying or celebrating the wealth that was manifested all around her; instead, she was at best, taking a brief respite from the pressures and anxieties that were an integral part of the work that she did. And it did not help that, over time, she had begun to feel that her marriage to James was, as she had once thought of her time with Dan, a matter of convenience rather than of the love that, she reassured herself, she had felt for her husband in the first years of their marriage.

Where, for example, was he on this beautiful summer's evening? Wherever he was, he was not spending it with her. No doubt he was either engaged in earning more money – or, at the very least, creating more opportunities to add to the fortune that was already his.

Her present house with its beautiful gardens was, indeed, a far cry from the flat her mother had rented to provide a refuge from the abuse of her husband – Amanda's father – who was now a non-presence in her life, the father who should have been her rock, her touchstone, but who was now just a bad, leftover memory from the poverty-stricken years of her early childhood.

Fortunately, there had been others who had shown her that it was possible to be happy… She had thought that James would be one of them but in that, it seemed, she had misled herself.

She paused to reflect. Was she too harsh in her thoughts about him? After all, if he was feeling her disenchantment with him, it was small wonder that he had other places to be on such an evening.

She recognised, of course, the core of her dissatisfaction with the house, garden and husband that so many women would have envied her. At first, she could be forgiven for thinking that it was the emptiness that seemed to be at the centre of it all – but she knew all too well, that the emptiness was born out of silence – a lack of voices, a lack of children's voices. That was the heart of it; for all that she had, she did not have a child of her own – and she was acutely conscious that time was passing.

* * *

Phoebe's words about the 'peace and quiet' of the cottage came back to Dan as he cooked his evening meal. Now that the day at school had plenty of space into which to recede, his thoughts turned to Emily and Josh. He desperately wanted to keep contact with them. When he could get his thoughts together, he would text them to see if they could, or would, meet him. As for Sue – it had been just three days since they had split from each other but, already, contacting her would require an effort that he was reluctant to make.

Seeking distraction, he fiddled with his phone and found a radio station from which, as background to his thoughts, he could listen to some music. He munched away at the stir fry he had made for himself whilst his thoughts returned to his conversation with Amanda.

In recent years, he had never understood her consuming preoccupation with her career. Assuming that they did meet during the summer break, there might be a chance for him to gain some insights into what was driving her these days.

His mind went back to the year in which they had lived together. She had certainly never shown any such preoccupation during that time. Of course, he understood the reasons for the formality that she insisted on in their present working relationship but there were times when it seemed quite bizarre, given their previous intimacy. Admittedly, she had chosen to marry James instead of him, but even so, the extent of the pretence when it was just the two of them together, often seemed more than a little ridiculous.

He was learning, however, that he was no judge of such things, and it was he, rather than Amanda, who was proving to be the more naïve in the matter of other people's opinions. He finished his meal, took his plate through to the kitchen and then returned to the lounge to slouch in an armchair.

His mind strayed to the previous night at Anne's house. Whether he had wanted to admit it to himself, he had longed for their closeness to express itself in a physical relationship but, up until his visit to her the day before, there had seemed to be little prospect of such a thing.

Her husband, of course, had already spread lies about Dan's behaviour towards his wife – and Dan also knew that his feelings for Anne were such that he had found it hard to hide them. At that point, he stopped to think about his previous behaviour towards Anne. Perhaps that was where George Moresby had genuine cause for complaint. If someone had told him about the kind of 'obvious behaviour' to which Amanda had previously drawn his attention, he would have been far from pleased about it. In fact, from what Anne had told him about George, he would have been furious.

George, though, he reflected, had deliberately spread lies about him. He had ensured that Sue believed her husband was having an affair with his wife – and had also, meanwhile, taken part in the destruction that had put his factory out of action.

From there, he wondered, once more, how his love for Anne was proving to be such a destructive thing when, at its core, it was something of beauty – and a door through which he could slip away from the humdrum of daily existence.

He brought his thoughts in that area to a close. He had to hold his life together somehow – and part of that lay in contacting Emily and Josh. He pulled his phone from his pocket and began composing carefully worded messages to them.

Then, having sent them he waited, wondering if either of them would reply that evening. A few minutes of silence from his phone, however, was sufficient to send him in search of the whisky he had bought at the supermarket. He poured himself a modest measure and returned to the armchair, his mind, as he thought, clearer and more focused than it had been for a long time. Time seemed to slow down and reality to come a little closer. He poured himself another, larger measure.

He woke a little after midnight. Leaving the whisky and empty glass by the armchair, he found his way up the stairs to bed. Somehow, he persuaded himself that it would be a good idea to undress and to put on his pyjamas. The room was stuffy, so he opened a window. It made little difference to the temperature, but he lay for a while, listening to the small sounds of night in the countryside.

He woke again, a little after two in the morning. His head had begun to throb; he rarely drank whisky and now he was paying for his brief enjoyment and supposed clarity. Work would be tedious, full of clearing up and survival to the end of the day. After lying awake for some time, his mind straying across issues personal and general that he could do little to change, he dozed off again and woke to the sound of the birds in the trees outside his window.

* * *

Some days later, the long spell of hot weather had still not broken. Dan sat once more at the picnic table in the cottage's back garden looking beyond the garden hedge and across to the river. The river was running at a noticeably lower level and, as he went to explore the grass area stretching down to the garden's bottom hedge, he could see that the grass was slowly beginning to turn brown and that the earth was cracking. The contrast with the winter months could hardly be greater. He had heard something in the television weather news about a 'blocking pattern' and the eastward passage of cooler, wetter weather being prevented; he mopped his forehead and sipped at a cold drink.

Sandals, shorts, tee shirt and sun hat had become his familiar mode of dress since the end of the school's summer term. Eventually, following his text messages, he had heard from Josh and Emily. At first, Emily had been dismissive of any approaches from Dan but then had eventually agreed to talk to him – though they had not fixed a time or date. Josh, too, had been cool towards him but then he had agreed to meet his father at a café in Sedgewater. Dan glanced at his watch. He would need to be on his way shortly if he was going to be in time to meet up with him.

Finishing his drink, he went through the cottage to the front door, locking it as he went. His car had been standing in the sun for several hours and a small wave of hot air greeted him as he opened the driver's door. The driver's seat was uncomfortably warm as he settled into it and the steering wheel almost too hot to grip. He switched on the air conditioning and waited several sweaty minutes until, at last, cool air began to lower the temperature of the car's interior and the steering wheel.

As he drove towards Sedgewater, the countryside shimmered in the heat. Trees and bushes drooped in the strong sunshine, their foliage more reminiscent of early autumn than mid-summer. Fields of wheat and other cereals had been toasted brown – although whether the harvest would be good or bad, he had no idea.

There was little traffic on the roads into Sedgewater and he had no difficulty finding a space in a car park near the town centre. From there, it was a short walk to the café Josh had suggested as a place in which they could meet. Bizarrely named the 'Flying Pumpkin', it was housed in a group of buildings that had been modernised to accommodate various niche retail businesses. The door had been propped open and, as Dan entered it, the café felt only a little cooler than the summer's day outside. He looked around and spotted Josh already sitting at a table near the front window.

He made his way over and Josh, who had been looking at his phone, left it on the table and rose to give his father a hug. "Dad, I've missed you!"

Dan was not quite prepared for Josh's response and, although he was conscious that the other customers were watching them, decided to disregard them. He threw his arms around Josh and said, "I've missed you too, Josh!"

They stood hugging each other for several moments until Dan moved to sit down. Josh followed him, returning to his seat, but said, "Em' and I have both been missing you!"

Dan hesitated but then said, with a faint smile, "That's not the impression I've had from your messages…"

Josh looked abashed. "I'm sorry about that, Dad. But we were really angry with you."

Dan felt encouraged by Josh's use of the past tense.

He paused. "Most of all, though, we want you to come back. Life at home is not the same. It's awful, just horrible!"

"I'm deeply sorry about that, Josh." Dan hardly ever succumbed to tears, but he felt them rising. He tried to keep control of his voice. "What has your mum told you?"

"That you've left us. That you've gone off with another woman!"

Dan was aware of other customers looking in their direction. He hung his head. He had expected that there would be difficult moments with Josh, but he had not been ready for the awfulness that George Moresby's lies had created.

"I…I have not gone off with someone else…" he tried to explain.

Josh had believed his mother but now it seemed that his father was also admitting what she had said.

"But according to Mum you've been having an affair with someone else!"

Dan was acutely conscious that they were in the middle of a café. He briefly wondered why he had not foreseen such a situation.

"No!" he said emphatically. "Someone told your mum a pack of lies…and she believed them. I didn't leave. Your mother threw me out!"

To Josh, however, it seemed that his father was prevaricating or trying to avoid being blamed for the split with his mother.

"What's that supposed to mean?" he demanded.

"It means what I said, Josh. I had absolutely no intention of leaving. But, just before the end of term, I came home as usual, and I tried to get into the house, but I couldn't – because your mum had changed all the locks. I was locked out!"

This time, Josh listened intently. His father's explanation at least tended to confirm his impression of events.

"Mum just said she would be taking us to Gran's house," he said. "We asked her if there was a problem at home, but she refused to explain. She just told us not to catch the bus and to wait for her."

"I thought that was what had happened," Dan replied. "Anyway, after I'd been at the house a while, I had a text from her, telling me what she'd done."

Josh listened to him but, fundamentally, it was already too late for it to make any difference. "Em and I didn't agree with what Mum did – but – when she told us what you'd done... How could you, Dad? How could you? You've wrecked everything!"

Dan looked at him; Josh's mood had changed, and he could see that his son's anger on learning about his father's supposed affair with Anne Moresby was rapidly recharging itself. He tried to avert the explosion that was coming.

"Nothing's happened, Josh! I never intended hurting any of you – and there's no reason that anyone – you, Emily, your mother – should ever have been hurt! If your mum had given me even the smallest chance, I would have explained the whole thing to her...but nothing should have happened... because I have not been having an affair!"

He was trying not to shout but his frustration was rubbing off on Josh.

"You don't seem to realise, Dad. Whatever rubbish you were expecting her to believe, she was so humiliated that there was never the slightest chance she would listen to you. She was in pieces! You completely smashed her world – and ours with it!"

"I know... I mean, I guess she would have been. I could see how she felt."

Josh's mouth fell open. What had happened, he wondered, to the person he loved – and trusted. Fury was written across his face; his voice rose in a crescendo.

"You guess she would have been...? You guess? Didn't you know? What on Earth did you think would happen if you went off and...and... started fucking another woman?"

This time it was heads and not simply eyes that swivelled towards them. Stony glares were coming from the staff behind the counter. An elderly red-faced man leaned across from his table and hissed loudly, "Language!"

This only served, however, to make Josh even more angry and frustrated.

"Oh, I've had enough of this...this bullshit!" he yelled. "I didn't come to hear such a feeble load of rubbish! And it is feeble. Unbelievably feeble ...and pathetic!"

By this stage, he was almost spluttering. He leapt up, knocking over his chair and, pushing the café door widely ajar, strode into the street.

Despite feeling utterly humiliated, Dan decided that he had better go after him. The tumbled chair was blocking his way, so he quickly righted it and rushed out, but Josh was keeping a very brisk pace. Ahead of him, Dan could see him walking parallel to a line of black, ornamental iron railings that bordered the town park. When he reached the park gates, Josh strode onto the path that ran parallel to the route he had just followed, thereby doubling back on his previous direction, until finally Dan, having now entered the park, had to run to catch up with him. Finally drawing level, he put his hand firmly on his son's shoulder so that Josh came angrily and very reluctantly to a halt.

"What?" he yelled. "What can we possibly have to say to each other?"

"Just – just hear me out. There are some more things I can say – things that are not excuses but which might help you to understand."

Josh supposed that, at least he owed his father that. Despite being in summer clothing, they were now both red-faced and sweating. A yard or two further on, there was a park bench in the shade of a large plane tree. Dan drew his son towards it, and they sat down at almost opposite ends of the seat.

Josh slumped angrily, glowering in sideways glances at his father and waiting for him to speak.

"This whole of this misbegotten saga began more or less by accident."

Josh gave an impatient snort, but Dan continued. "It was during the floods. I went to help someone who had run out of vital medication…and I just found that, well, I had feelings for her. That's all there is though, Josh! That's all there is. We've not been having an affair.

"You have to remember as well that it happened at a time when we were all under each other's feet at your gran's house, there seemed to be no end to the problems from the flooding and your mum was completely taken up with her work – as always. She seemed to have no time for me – or for that matter, for you and Emily either."

He paused. There were elements of truth, Josh thought, in his father's words but it all sounded far too glib.

"All I can say, Dad," he said impatiently, "… is that Mum has never been any different. She must have been like that when you married her!"

Dan could not deny it. She had always been very focused on her work.

"Yes, she was, Josh, but I couldn't object to that too much because I was also wrapped up in my work …and at least I could come home and listen to someone who, when we did spend time together, could talk about something other than education and teaching. It was a kind of relief. Also, at that time, work had not become the 'be all and end all'. In the last few years, though, it does seem to have taken over…"

"So, was work all you were interested in? What about me and Emily? Weren't you interested in us?"

"Oh, Josh, of course we were interested in you! We loved you both from the very beginning! You know that we did!"

"Then what changed, Dad? Why have you decided, after all these years, to go off with someone else?"

"Josh," he said, "for the thousandth time…! I have not gone off with someone else. I haven't decided on anything yet and certainly not on going off with anyone. Look, I just don't know what I'm doing at the moment – okay. I haven't the faintest idea…!"

It was part of the torment of his situation that whatever kind of relationship it was that he had with Anne, it almost certainly had no future but that was something that he could not explain to Josh at that moment.

To Josh, however, on the brink of adult life, his father's frank admission was at least something he could understand. His anger began to abate. He sensed that his father was 'lost' and would need time to find his way again.

It was a day of inadequate words and gestures. Finally, he shrugged. "Alright, Dad, I'm deeply disappointed…Life will never be the same but at least you've given me some idea of what's happened. I think I also know who this other woman is – the one that you've mentioned – but I don't want to hear anything about her – nothing at all."

Dan could understand Josh's feelings. There were other things he had wanted to talk about, but he decided that they would have to wait. He said, "I hope you'll still go into the sixth form."

Josh nodded. "Yes, my plans haven't changed. I still want to get my A-levels – although I need good GCSE grades…"

"How did they go? You must have finished them when this all blew up?"

"Yes, fortunately I had. And thanks to the floods back in the winter, I had no choice but to get my head down." He managed a wry smile. "I probably did more revision this time than I've ever done."

"So, you think you've done well?"

"I don't really know – I didn't have problems with any of the exams. But like everyone else, I'm just waiting for the results."

Dan nodded. There was no way in which he could make things happen any faster. He would have to wait whilst the various parts of the present situation played out to a conclusion because there was a sense in which he, like Josh, was waiting for results.

Meanwhile, Josh, having initially hoped that his father might try to get together again with his mother, had begun to have a clear sense that such a thing was very unlikely. He felt sadness and loss for them as well as himself but 'home life' as it was now would also push him to think about his future – and that would lie elsewhere. He took out his phone to check the time.

"The bus back to Monk's Hill is due shortly," he said.

Dan had assumed as much. The bus station was a short distance from the park.

"Can I walk to the stop with you?" he asked.

"Why not?" Josh's anger was played out – and largely behind him now. The journey home would give him some more time to think and the outlines of what was likely to happen had begun to emerge. Now, more than ever, he wanted to get his A-levels – and then a degree.

They walked together to the bus station, saying little but, in the last minutes before Josh's bus arrived, Dan said, "You might want some help with your A-levels from time to time – or anything else you want to talk about. I'm still your dad, Josh – that hasn't changed. Just text or phone me. We can easily meet up – here or out at the cottage, I don't mind which – although we should probably give 'The Flying Pumpkin' a miss for a while."

Josh's face reddened but he gave his father a wide grin. "I'm sorry about...the café but I... just lost it for a few minutes. All the same, it's good we've talked – I'll send you my GCSE grades as soon as I know them."

He glanced away to where his bus was drawing into the bus station. Then, turning to his father, they briefly hugged before he went to join the queue of passengers as it began moving forward.

Dan waited a minute or two and then waved farewell to Josh as the bus drew away.

Setting off for the car park, he reflected on the relative clarity of Josh's future compared with his own.

Back at the car, he opened the door and was greeted by the familiar rush of hot air. He should, he thought, have taken time to find a shadier spot in the car park – but then, he had been in a hurry to meet up with Josh. His son's outburst at the café would shame him for a long time to come, but then their meeting had not been an outright disaster, and he felt sure that they would now keep in contact.

After several minutes, the interior of the car had cooled to the point where he could hold the steering wheel without burning his hands. The driver's seat was also at a temperature that was tolerable.

He would drive back to the cottage for a solitary lunch. Solitude was something to which he knew he had to accustom himself. It was an element in everyone's life. Loneliness, however, was another matter; unfortunately, recent decisions he had made meant that loneliness was also likely to be part of his daily life for some time to come.

He drove slowly. The heat induced lethargy and there was no particular reason for him to rush now that there was no-one he was rushing to meet. It was also impossible to drive quickly through the long, winding lanes – which, for the time being, would never lead back to anywhere that he would truly think of as 'home'.

* * *

CHAPTER 18

OBSESSION

If Dan had thought that he was on his way to establishing a new equilibrium in his life, he had reckoned without the twists and turns that he would find himself making over the next few weeks.

He entered into the first twist as soon as he arrived back at the cottage. His thoughts had been of a quiet lunch in the back garden but, having parked the car on the drive of the cottage and opened the front door, he looked back across the road and saw, parked discreetly amongst several other vehicles, a car that he recognised as belonging to Anne.

He wondered briefly what had made her decide to visit him that afternoon, but he did not have to speculate for long because, with some quick glances around her, Anne left the car and came across the road to meet him in the garden of the cottage.

He moved to catch her in his arms as she came through the gate, but she refused him saying, "No, Dan, it's risky for me to be here at all. Let's go inside."

She went ahead of him, into the lounge. He followed and almost as soon as he put his arms around her, they drew each other into a passionate kiss. Moments later, they had aroused each other sufficiently for Anne to be hurrying ahead of him, up the stairs towards the bedroom that she thought Dan would have chosen to use.

Having previous knowledge of the cottage, she made the correct choice and as soon as Dan had followed her into the room, she opened a window and closed the curtains. Then she quickly and efficiently pulled off her clothes and slid, naked beneath the single sheet that Dan had left on the bed. He took a little longer and worried that she was becoming impatient but when he slid in beside her, she simply said, "I'm sorry, Dan – I didn't want to wait."

For the next few minutes, they said little, engaging each other instead in silent acts of passion until finally they lay side by side, slowly returning from the focal point of their ecstasy to the summer's afternoon that they had briefly left behind.

Involuntarily, Dan began to doze but she came close and said, "Don't fall asleep on me. I don't have much time, and I want us to make the most of it."

"I thought we'd already done that."

"We have… it was lovely. But just stay with me a little longer."

Dan did as she had urged him until they both lay once more silently side by side, perspiring in the heat of the afternoon, each lost in their own separate thoughts.

Eventually, Anne reached for her watch on the bedside cabinet. She gave a small groan. "Oh dear…I'll have to get going in a few minutes. George is due home this evening. There's also something we need to talk about before I leave. Perhaps we could have a minute or two downstairs? Then I really will have to get home."

Dan roused himself and moved to sit on the side of the bed. Reaching for his clothes, he dressed quickly.

Anne meanwhile had also hurriedly dressed and gone down to the kitchen to make cool drinks for them both. Dan waited for her in the lounge. He sprawled on the settee until she arrived with the drinks and then he pulled himself into an upright position.

Seating herself next to him, she said, "I'm afraid I'm not going to be around for the next three weeks."

"Oh, why?" Dan was surprised and a little taken aback.

"George has told me that I'm going with him on his next trip to the US."

"I see. Presumably he didn't give you the chance to say 'No'?"

"Not really."

There was a long pause whilst Dan thought about what he was going to say next. Finally, he could only falter his way into what he so badly wanted to ask her.

"Is there any way, Anne, that we could ever be together. I mean, not just for an hour or two here and there, but I…" He left his sentence hanging in the air, not knowing how to finish it.

She did not immediately answer. Although it might have surprised him, it was something she had already thought about. "I wish there was a way, Dan. When you started to ask me that question before, I gave you what I later thought was a foolish answer. I think I said that you couldn't give me what George provides me with…But then there are some things he can't provide me with – and that his wealth can't buy."

He moved closer to her until she eventually stood, and he held her in his arms. "Then, do you know, Anne, what I feel for you?"

She in turn, holding him gently said, "Yes, Dan – I think I've always known."

"Then…?"

"Then, I would still have to ask, whatever our feelings, will we ever be able to do anything about them?"

Defiantly, he kissed her on the lips. "I can do that!" he said.

She smiled. "That," she said, returning his kiss, "is something about which I'm only too ready to agree."

They let go of one another and Anne said, "Now, I really have to go. I'm not totally sure how long I'll be away and because George is, uh, the way he is…and contacting you may be difficult. But as soon as I'm back at Blunden's Knoll, we can meet…"

She moved towards the door and, as soon as she opened it and stepped outside, the summer's heat enveloped her. She turned briefly to him. "Texas will be even hotter than this," she said. "And I shall be in the wrong place with…" but he lost the end of her sentence as she drew closer to the gate and crossed in the shimmering haze of the afternoon to where her car was baking in the sun.

Dan, not worrying about discretion, waited for the slow minutes that it took for the air conditioning to begin doing its job and then waved as she disappeared along the dusty lane towards the home that she sometimes thought more closely resembled a prison.

* * *

As the afternoon wore on, he remembered that it was a number of hours since he had last eaten. He went into the kitchen and then returned to the picnic table with the remnants of salad he had made the previous day. He contemplated the lacklustre plate of food before him and then briefly picked at it before pushing it away and going to get a drink. The warmth of the day had barely abated even though it was approaching five o'clock and a glass of water would have been best suited to quenching his thirst. But he returned with a glass of whisky in his hand. He sipped at it, gazing down to the fields where the cows had gone to lay down beneath the trees and where the ever-shrinking river wound its torpid and meandering course across the meadows.

Later, Dan knew, the whisky would probably make him drowsy but for the moment, he needed to dull the deep ache that throbbed relentlessly inside him. How had he come to be in this place, pleasant though it was? What was he doing there away from his family and the few friends who might have been of help to him? The answer, he knew, was quite simply that he had turned from family and friends and so, unsurprisingly, he could not go running to them now that he needed them.

His love for Anne had begun simply enough. She was talented and beautiful; it did not take a person of any profundity to admire her. And although she was not independently wealthy, she had access to her husband's wealth and therefore, to a lifestyle that Dan could only aspire to.

That was the tantalising aspect of his relationship with Anne; she was, he had slowly begun to realise, a lover to whom he could only aspire because she could never truly be his. On one level, the source of the ache was a simple one. Their physical relationship was such that he lusted after her in a way that he had never experienced before – and yet...and yet, there was so much more. Seen from Dan's perspective, she was not simply beautiful in her physical attributes but, in mind and spirit as well.

He realised, of course, that he was seeing her through a lens that idealised her in every way and that therefore, his image of her must be false. But, for however long his image of her could continue to exist, he would remain beyond the reach of reason.

Ironically, he was by no means certain that he wanted to dwell in a place of such elevated sensibilities, for in one moment, his spirits would soar into previously unknown heights and then, at others, plummet into depths of misery. Heaven and Hell, he was discovering, were next door neighbours.

The whisky in his glass was diminishing far too quickly. Clumsily, he made his way into the house and returned with the bottle. Now he would no longer need to interrupt his thoughts by going to fetch another drink.

The clarity and self-honesty of his earlier thoughts had begun to cloud over but lasted long enough for him to realise that there was no long-term future in his relationship with Anne. They could be, as Anne had once said, 'soul mates', but Dan wanted more than that; more than that, though, was beyond his reach – and beyond his abilities.

He finished his glass of whisky – which also signified the end of the bottle. He tried to stand but found that his legs would not obey him, so, being already very drowsy, he lowered his head onto the table and fell into a ceaselessly repetitive dream.

He eventually woke to find himself in darkness and bathed in sweat. He made another attempt to stand, and this time succeeded. It would be many hours before he was sober again, but he managed to stagger as far as the settee in the lounge. There he stretched his length and in the all-pervasive warmth of the summer night, he fell once more into a heavy sleep.

He did not wake until mid-morning the following day. A foul taste in his mouth and a painful headache reminded him that his way of getting down to serious thinking carried with it a serious price tag. He followed the trail of open doors through to the back of the house where his glass still stood on the table, but the whisky bottle lay, appropriately, on its side.

He had no idea what time it was, and he seemed to have mislaid his watch, so he checked his phone instead. In the process, he noticed that there was a message from Amanda. He decided to look at it when he had managed to freshen up.

He did not rush unduly. First, he washed his face repeatedly in cold water then ate some breakfast cereal and finally nibbled at a piece of toast. At that point, he decided that he could probably face whatever it was that Amanda had to say.

The message, when he opened it, was a little bit of a surprise. She wanted to meet him; that was not in itself surprising because she had suggested as much when she had left their previous meeting. No, the surprise was that she wanted to meet so soon after the start of the summer break; he had thought that even Amanda would have wanted a few days of complete relaxation. The meeting, she suggested, should also be at her house.

Dan thought about it for a moment or two; he could never remember visiting Amanda's house before. That was a little unusual. Unlike other headteachers he had known, she had always ensured that they met at school or, on the odd occasion, in some other place that was a good deal less than private – such as a café or the corner of a conference room.

For all that he was intrigued, he did not spend long musing on her choice of venue. His head was still throbbing and, other than the depression that hung over him following Anne's departure, the feeling that pervaded his mood that morning was one of fatigue. He had slept heavily but he had not slept well. He decided to make a strong cup of coffee and take it into the back garden.

The coffee briefly helped to lift his mood. Normally, during previous summers, he would have taken on some task related to his house or perhaps the garden, but there was nothing here for him to do. He poured himself another cup of coffee.

His mood lifted again. There would be a way forward. He might be facing a divorce and the loss of his house, but he would find a way to solve his problems, to reinvent himself and start his life anew.

There was, however, one overarching problem that spanned his mood swings and constantly brought him back to the ache in the pit of his stomach and the black wall that, in his worst moments, bounded the horizons of his world. He was in the middle of an impossible love affair, one that was already costing him dearly and which, God knew, would cost him so much more before he was able to look at it as objectively in his mind's rear-view mirror.

He glanced again at the message on his phone. There were two days before his meeting with Amanda. What on earth would he do with himself until then? There was nowhere he had to go and no-one he had to see. He had brought his briefcase out to the patio with him, thinking that he might sketch out some ideas for discussion. He pulled a blank sheet of paper from the briefcase and roughed out three or four bullet pointed ideas before, in a fit of futility, he screwed up the paper and flung it in a crumpled white ball onto the sun heated slabs of the patio.

It came to something when, in his present state of mind, he found himself looking forward to a meeting with Amanda. Still, it was at least something, other than his self-pitying emotions, to occupy his mind. He pulled out another blank sheet of paper. This time, he managed to complete his list, and the outcome of his thoughts found its way back into his briefcase rather than onto the hot paving slabs.

In one way or another, he occupied the next two days with small domestic jobs, reading and incessant watching of the 24-hour news channels. When the time for his meeting eventually came around, he reflected that his head, waking and sleeping, seemed to have been filled with the constant babble of words, but that it was only this morning that he would find himself finally engaging with a living person and not with some image created with text or pixels. Perhaps it was not so ridiculous, after all, that he found himself looking forward to his meeting with Amanda.

* * *

Dan found Amanda's house quite easily. It was about three miles from the cottage in which he was staying and, as with many of the older buildings in that area, located on land that would flood only in the most exceptional circumstances. Given the image that Amanda projected of herself at school, he was surprised to find that it was a traditional farmhouse or, perhaps, because of its size, a farm manor, complete with thatched roof externally and low beams internally. It was also, he could not avoid noticing, surrounded by beautiful gardens.

A large brass door knocker enabled him to let Amanda know that he had arrived. She pulled open the door vigorously and ushered him in.

"Do come in, Dan. I'll close this door though. It helps to keep the house cool. These old houses have thick walls, so they stay warm in winter – and cool in summer."

Dan had heard this dictum many times before, but he was grateful for the coolness after the unrelenting heat of the morning outside.

"It's a surprise, isn't it, after the flooding in the winter – such a contrast. But after the last few weeks of hot weather, I'm sure it won't be long before we'll be told there's a drought and we have to save water." Dan paused, aware that he had fallen into small talk – something he often found himself doing when anticipating a move onto more serious topics.

For once, Amanda indulged him. "I'm sure you're right, Dan. In most other years, a drought would have been declared by now. It would be ironic if we were told to use standpipes after being marooned by flooding during the winter."

Up to this point, Amanda had been a little behind him in the passageway from the front door to the lounge but now she came forward into the lighting of the lounge.

"Another feature of old houses is that they can sometimes be a bit gloomy inside. As you see, even on a bright summer's morning, I still need to have some lights on in here."

He paused to look at her. Although they had a formal daily relationship at school, they were both wearing light, informal summer clothing. She had her dark framed glasses perched on the end of her nose. Spread out on a nearby coffee table were school documents relating to the Autumn.

"Come on," she said, "I was just looking through the plans for next term."

They sat, side by side, on Amanda's settee looking through the documents.

"I know we're both familiar with all of this, Dan, and by the way, I'm sure you were probably expecting me to contact you later in the Break – but I usually like to continue in 'school mode' for a few days – and then try to get some relaxation after that. Besides, the ends of summer terms are always so frenetic that a few quiet days when I can get to do some serious thinking about the Foundation's 'bigger picture' can seem like sheer luxury."

That was something that Dan could understand. Admittedly, in this particular year, he had not contemplated anything other than relaxation from the start of the Summer Break, but in Amanda's role, he thought, there must often be a significant tension between near-term demands on her time and her desire to have a decisive influence in the strategic direction of the Foundation.

For the moment though, she pointed him towards a comfortable armchair and went off to make them both some coffee. Dan waited, gazing around the room and enjoying the taste and comfort exhibited in its furnishings.

He looked up as Amanda came bustling back into the room, bringing with her on a tray a cafetiere, cups, plates and biscuits.

"This should keep us going for a while," she said. She served Dan with a cup of black coffee as requested, poured a cup for herself, and retreated to an armchair next to the one in which Dan was sitting.

"So, Dan, how have you been during the last few days...?"

"Oh, not too bad," he said. "It's very quiet at the cottage I'm renting but of course I'm missing Josh and Emily ...and Sue as well, for that matter."

"Do you want to talk about it?" asked Amanda and then, seeing his hesitation, continued, "Or, if you would prefer, talk about school business first and then have some time – as much or as little as you want – to talk about your current situation."

Dan nodded. "Yes, that would be fine. I'd appreciate a little time on school business because we were rather preoccupied with the news about Wellsprings at the end of term – but there are some issues that I'm sure you must have in mind and that we should discuss. After that, I think I would find it helpful if I could talk to you about...how things are on the, uh, personal front."

She smiled. "I thought that's what you'd prefer. In relation to school matters, have you had time to read that recent document about 'Education for a Sustainable Society'? We could start with that. We have to set out our plans for implementing it next term, so what thoughts have you had so far?"

It was a topic in which Dan was keenly interested and he was pleased that they could share some time away from the immediate pressures of daily school business, working through his ideas about the leadership, organisation and resources that would be needed for a successful teaching programme.

Amanda listened carefully to him, making perceptive comments particularly in relation to the cross-curricular nature of the initiatives and the team working that would be necessary. They spent some time teasing out their thoughts until, eventually, it seemed to both of them that they had a good basis on which to work at the start of the next term.

As Dan ran his eyes once more over the notes he had made on his tablet computer, Amanda served them both with some more coffee and said, "I feel that's been a really useful session, Dan. I know there are two or three other items we should probably tackle, but unless you feel they're urgent, it might be more helpful for you to tell me about your current family situation. Of course, if you'd rather not, particularly in the light of our past and the present circumstances in which we work together, I'd quite understand... But, we have some peace and quiet here this morning and I can see, despite the effort that you were making at the end of last term, that recent events are weighing on you..."

Dan was not averse to talking about it, but he was aware that there could be pitfalls in such a conversation.

"I appreciate there are aspects of it that could relate to my work at school..." he began.

Amanda, though, quickly added, "Yes of course, Dan – but, most of all, I need to know how you are feeling – partly for school reasons but also because, although we have to be formal at work, we're not at work now – and we have known each other for a long time."

"No, we're not at work," he agreed, "but we have been discussing school business this morning – and it's difficult to know where work life ends, and home life begins."

"That's a familiar conundrum for both of us, but I was very sorry to hear that you have split up with Sue."

"You're right," said Dan. "I'm missing her – and the children too. You asked me first about Sue, though. I ..." He paused. "Of course, I know why she doesn't want me anywhere near her. But I don't understand how we got to where we are. It's all happened so quickly. I don't know what's happened to me. We had our differences of course, and I hated the way that work always seemed to come between us but...I almost don't know how to put it...I have a great sense of loss...of opportunities that we might have had." He stopped. He had wanted to control what he said but now, it had come pouring out.

Amanda nodded. She could readily understand Sue's anger, but she could see that Dan was still in the throes of an experience that he did not understand. She had, though, also taught both Dan's children when they were Primary school pupils.

"How have Josh and Emily been with you...?" she asked.

"As you would imagine, they think I've deserted them – which is understandable, given the circumstances."

"Have you spoken to them recently?"

"I've managed to speak to Josh," said Dan, fighting to keep his voice under control. "I met up with him in Sedgewater about three days ago. He was very angry with me at first, but I think now that we will stay in contact. I'm sure he's missed me, just as I miss him."

"...And what about Emily?"

"I've sent a message to her – but I haven't heard from her yet. I know from Josh that she's very upset about what I've done, but I'm hoping, that given time, she will get in touch."

At that point, Amanda hesitated not knowing how much more she needed to ask – or should ask. She could already see that Dan was in turmoil and that the recent events in his private life would affect him for some time to come. In a sense, she had answered the question that her seniority of role in relation to Dan required of her. There was, though, more than that involved… As she had earlier recalled, they had known each other a long time and, more than that, they had been lovers for the year that they had shared a flat in Sedgewater; it was hard for her to pretend that the year in which they had lived together had been without significance.

Meanwhile, as Amanda's memory was taking her back in time, Dan had placed a hand over his eyes. Seemingly oblivious to her, he muttered, "What a mess!"

Although it was only half-heard, it drew Amanda's attention back to him and she created a short space for them both by topping up his cup of coffee.

Gratefully, Dan took a sip from his cup.

Amanda decided, despite reservations, to pick up the conversation again.

She asked, "So, what do you think is likely to happen now?"

"It's hard to say," replied Dan. "Sue has successfully contrived to prevent me from getting back into the house; I can't remember if I've told you that but that's why I'm having to rent a cottage."

Dan had, of course, already made Amanda's PA aware that he had a new, temporary address and 'out of hours' 'phone number; Pauline, meanwhile, had been told by Amanda, to say nothing about it to other members of staff. They all had Dan's mobile phone number if they needed to contact him.

Amanda returned to the subject of Dan's eviction from his own house.

"Are you going to accept that situation?" she asked.

"Reluctantly, yes."

"I wonder if you should, Dan? Presumably the house belongs as much to you as it does to her…?"

She seemed to be straying beyond the boundaries that she had previously set for herself, he noticed.

"You're right, Amanda – but the next set of payments relating to the house is still about a fortnight away – and because she's not talking to me, I have no idea what she's thinking. At this point, though, I'm simply glad that I've got a roof over my head. I think Sue and I both need some time to work out what we want – for ourselves, and for Josh and Emily."

Dan decided that he had gone far enough with the discussion of his personal circumstances, and he did not want to mention anything to Amanda that might suggest that he could no longer do his job effectively.

Meanwhile, Amanda knew that it was George Moresby, Anne's husband, who had made it his business to see that Sue got to know of Dan's affair with his wife. That too, was not without significance and was something to which Amanda wanted to give more consideration. Moresby had been a generous benefactor to Wellsprings Primary and had set up a charitable fund on the school's behalf. Once they got to know, the Governors, particularly Eleanor Browning, would look askance at anything that might jeopardise his generosity.

She tried to be circumspect.

"I don't want to add to your worries, Dan, but I think you should know that George Moresby is friendly with one or two of the Governors – and, of course, they are all aware that he is a benefactor of the school. Anne, too, as we both know, has made some very helpful contributions to school life."

"I'm aware of all that…" replied Dan, "and I'm afraid you're right – it only makes matters worse."

Amanda, already aware that she was treading a fine line, found herself trying to pursue conflicting objectives – namely, warning Dan of the precariousness of his situation whilst also reassuring him that so long as he continued to be effective in his job, he would have her support.

"As you might expect," she said, "I have to see both sides of the situation. "I can see what the Governors' view of this will be – my job dictates that I should – but I can also see that you need time to work things out. However, as you'll be aware, it may not be too long before they learn of your relationship with Anne. They may well be inclined to see what has happened as a private matter but will also want to be reassured that you are still able to fully focus on your work. The situation with regard to George Moresby is something else – I'm afraid I don't know what he's likely to do."

He did not know how to respond to her. It was true that if, at the beginning of the next term he still felt as he did now, his personal situation would inevitably affect his role at Wellsprings.

For the moment, however, he was gratified that Amanda felt able to show more sensitivity in the privacy of their conversation than might otherwise have been possible. The problem was, though, that it was not always within her power to control the pressures placed upon her.

He realised with a start that she was speaking to him and that whilst he had been musing on this, she had asked him another question.

"I'm sorry. I was just taking a moment to think about what you're saying…"

She smiled. "I was saying that, without wishing to pry, I wondered how things stand with regard to Anne?"

Once again, Dan found it very difficult to answer.

"I'm not seeing her at present, if that's what you mean."

It was a half-truth; a dishonest answer and he suspected that Amanda realised it. She would find it easy to catch him out if she so wished. The Amanda he thought he knew would surely do so. He waited.

For some reason, however, she did not follow through. Instead, she gave him a sideways glance and said, "I realise that these things are not about everybody's convenience – if I can put it that way. No doubt, it would be much easier for both you and Anne if you had not started an affair."

Dan did not reply because he saw her comment as purely hypothetical. What had happened could not be undone – nor, to any appreciable extent, could he soften the hurt that he had inflicted on Sue. With Josh and Emily, a certain amount of reconciliation might be possible.

Amanda looked at him and realised that the conversation had gone about as far as it was likely to go for the time being. She said, "I'm sorry, Dan. This probably isn't what you need at this moment."

Dan nodded. The summer break would give him some more time to think, but whilst he was determined that he would not be pushed in any direction that he did not wish to go, he had already told himself many times that the affair with Anne had no future. The problem was that, so far, he had not been able to talk to Anne about it, and, he reminded himself, it would be nearly another three weeks before he could do so.

There was a tacit awareness between them that they had said about as much as they could about Dan's relationship with Anne and also that it had killed any appetite they might have had for continuing with any further school related topics.

Sensing that their business for the morning was finished, Dan began checking that he had everything he needed before returning to the cottage. Looking about him, he said, "Thank you for inviting me over here this morning. It's been helpful. I really appreciate it."

Amanda's sentiments were similar. She smiled and said, "I've appreciated it, too, Dan. It's been good to talk without the usual distractions. Perhaps we can do this again before too long?"

"Yes, that would be good," agreed Dan.

Seeing that he had now picked up his computer bag and papers, Amanda walked with him to the front door. There, they briefly kissed each other on the cheek and then Dan walked across to his car, climbed in and set off slowly along the drive to the road.

* * *

Amanda returned to the coffee and to her laptop. Now that she was alone, she continued to think about the implications of Dan's affair with Anne.

She was by no means sure that he was fully aware of the difficulties that he had created for himself and for the school.

Was there, for example, a danger for Dan that there were some people, school governors included, who might believe that he had exploited Anne's vulnerability to his own advantage? Knowing him as she did, she was inclined to believe that, rather than any calculated taking of advantage, it was Dan's naivety and failure to recognise possible consequences that had drawn him into the affair. Anne, she was sure, was also perfectly capable of manipulating Dan if she so wished – although Amanda could see no motive for her to do so, other than the gratification of her own desires.

Awareness of Dan's problems, however, would not necessarily help her to ensure that he continued to be an effective part of the school's management; there was likely to be a school inspection in the near future and if Wellsprings proved to be a weak link in the Academy's portfolio, it would do her credibility lasting damage. She could try to empathise with Dan's difficulties, but empathy would only get her so far; Wellsprings Primary School, having been uprooted from the site on which it was supposed to have a permanent base, needed all its staff, particularly senior staff, to be at the 'top of their game'. If, as now seemed likely, Dan still had mental health issues at the start of the autumn term, she could be faced with decisions that, on both personal and professional grounds, she would rather not have to make.

She gave a sigh, wishing that her ambitions had not led her so far away from the direct contact with children that she had so much enjoyed in the earlier parts of her career. There seemed to be a need now to distance her emotions from the difficult decisions that she was sometimes required to make, and working again with Dan reminded her that, despite the professional persona that she had developed, she was still made of flesh and blood.

Alone, with Dan on his way elsewhere and James anywhere between home and his latest project, she fell again to thinking about her desire to have a child. Having come from a background that was anything but wealthy, she sometimes accused herself of being 'greedy' and, when in a mood of self-accusation, she would see herself as being ungrateful for the prosperity and well-being that her career and marriage to James had brought.

It perplexed her that, having postponed her desire to have a family, she should now be experiencing problems in conceiving a child. Initially, James had shared her ambitions but now that she seemed to be having difficulties in becoming pregnant, his enthusiasm had waned. Their lovemaking, although it still occasionally happened, was perfunctory and dissatisfying to a degree that was having a damaging effect on their marriage.

James, meanwhile, had shown no enthusiasm at all for exploring other ways in which Amanda could become pregnant or, failing such an outcome, could enter into adopting a child. Such was his hostility at times to any of these courses of action, she wondered how the person she thought she had married could have changed so much.

In all of this, Amanda had begun to feel that there was a tacit assumption that the reasons for her failure to become pregnant lay with her. James, though, was adamant that he would not participate in any testing to find out if he was, in fact, capable of making her pregnant.

There was also a further question that Amanda often thought about – and that was whether it was wise to bring a child into the world when that world seemed to be deteriorating in so many different ways. She recognised, of course, that this was not a new question and that there must have been innumerable times in history when women had put it to themselves. The period in which she was living, however, did seem different. There was no foreseeable end to the crises that had incrementally begun to manifest themselves right across the globe.

Her work had, of course, caused her to think more widely about the problems of the society of which she was a part, and lately, she had begun to question the value of the enormous collective effort that went into preparing children and young people for a civilisation that, in all probability, was no longer going to exist. And surely, if such a thing was clear to her, it must be clear to others also? Seemingly, however, it was not.

All around her were people whose main aim in life was to load into their lives more wealth, more possessions, more luxurious holidays and to distance themselves as far as they possibly could from the poverty and often hunger that was all around them. She was not, of course, guilt-free in that respect. The stick that she had so often used to drive herself on was the insecurity of her childhood – those years of feeling hungry, of trying to stay warm in an ice-cold house, of trying to keep out of the way of a father who was perpetually drunk and ready to take out his anger on those who were closest to him – his wife and daughters.

She had more than achieved the security she had sought. Now all that she lacked was a child of her own. Regardless of what was happening around her, she longed for a child – and yet it seemed that, despite all that she had achieved and all that she had, what she now most desired was going to be denied to her. And what was the point of it all, on that hot, hot summer's afternoon if there would be no child for her to love, in the midst of all the inanimate possessions that surrounded her?

* * *

As Amanda continued in thought, Dan was still in the process of driving back to a rented cottage and the solitude that had proved to be his lot for the time being… He felt happier after his conversation with Amanda, and the non-judgemental way in which she had listened to him had led him to feel hopeful that the cool formality with which she had treated him for so long was not a true reflection of how she felt. Perhaps, now, after distancing herself so carefully in recent years, she was beginning to thaw? If that was happening, it would at least be something of an acknowledgement of what they had once meant to each other.

The road unwound before him. He was not looking forward to another solitary afternoon at the cottage. Perhaps he would try contacting Emily again although, as his conversation with Amanda had reminded him, the person he most needed to speak to was Sue. She was also, however, the person who had been most injured by his thoughtlessness. He would keep trying to get in touch with her – but he did not hold out much hope of success.

He arrived back at the cottage and, drawing onto the driveway, looked for a shady spot in which to park the car. In its most recent stages, his marriage to Sue had been as dull as ditch water – a meaningful simile in a county like Somerset – but he should not have let her down.

Having left the car in a pool of shadow at the far end of the cottage, he unlocked the front door to spend another afternoon in the company of his remorse.

* * *

The following morning, Dan drove into Sedgewater seeking some company other than his own but musing again on the fact that he had still heard nothing from Sue, and also nothing from Emily.

He parked the car and set off through the pedestrianised shopping precinct. It was not likely that he would meet with Sue there, but Emily often came on her own into the town to shop or meet up with friends.

So now, as he wandered in aimless fashion through the shopping centre, Sedgewater had become a place of hauntings and he suddenly seemed to be aware of how many teenage girls there were of medium height, had blonde hair and whose general profile and clothing could conceivably be that of Emily. More than once, he found himself the subject of curious or even irritated looks as he drew level with a would-be 'Emily', only to find that he was inflicting unwanted attention on yet another rear-view lookalike.

When this sequence of events had taken place several times, Dan recognised that by wishing to be once more in contact with Emily, he was drawing unwanted attention to himself. The seating area of a street café beckoned, so he ordered a strong coffee and was sitting quietly contemplating the surface of the table when he became aware that someone was placing bags of shopping on the chair opposite and then, unexpectedly, moving towards him.

He looked up. "Emily!" His joy at seeing his daughter was pure and unaffected. He clasped her, rocking her in his arms as though they had been separated for years rather than weeks, whilst Emily returned his hug. Then, conscious as only teenagers can be, of other people's smiles and curious stares, she said, "Dad! Could we sit down?"

He did as she asked, but slowly, looking at her as if checking to reassure himself that he had finally found his daughter – or rather that she had found him. He laughed, relieved that at last they had been able to meet.

"How did you spot me amongst this crowd?" he asked.

"It wasn't that difficult, Dad. Besides, I have my spies..."

"Oh?"

"Yes, I met up briefly with one of my friends, Lucy Pargeter. She told me that she had seen you eyeing up teenage girls, and I thought, hmmm, sounds like my dad."

"Emily!" said Dan, scandalised by her comment but then, seeing the flicker of amusement that crossed her face, said, "That's not something I want said about me, thank you – even if you are having a joke!"

His reaction caused a brief moment of awkwardness, so he decided to change the subject.

"Hmm – 'Lucy Pargeter'?" he said. "Sounds like a familiar name. Do I know her?"

"You should do. She was in your class for a whole year – although that would have been several years ago now – five years, to be exact."

"Ah yes, now that you've narrowed it down, I do remember her. Timid little thing."

"Not anymore, Dad. Rather loud, if anything."

"Oh dear. I thought you said she was a friend of yours?"

"She is. But I can still be truthful about her."

For a moment, their initial exuberance fading a little, they lapsed into silence. How easily they had fallen into their familiar relationship with each other – and how poignantly the saga that lay behind their encounter now re-asserted itself.

A waiter came scurrying by and prompted by Emily, Dan asked him to bring her a smoothie.

Then, attempting to restart the stalled conversation with his daughter, he said, "I've missed you very much, Emily."

"I gather…" she said, a strong hint of sarcasm in her voice.

"Oh?"

"Yes, Dad – I've got several cracked ribs from that hug you gave me!" She said it with an asperity that was reminiscent of her mother, but then, it had been some time since humour had underlain anything that Sue had to say.

Dan laughed with embarrassment. "I'm sorry about that, Emily. It just seems like a long time since we last saw each other."

"It's not that long…"

"Well, it seems like it to me. How are things with you and Josh?"

"Alright, I suppose…"

"The last I heard, the three of you had gone to your gran's cottage."

"Oh, yes, we did – but we were only there for about two or three days. Then Mum wanted to be back at home."

Dan waited for a moment or two. He badly wanted Emily to know that he had not intended to leave them. "I did try to get into the house…I did try to come back."

"I know, Dad. Mum told us what she had done."

They paused as the waiter arrived with Emily's smoothie. When he had gone, Dan asked, "And what did you think about it?"

"I…I don't know. I was sad. Josh and I just want you to come back but…"

"But what, Emily?"

"Mum's really angry. She won't even let us ask questions about you."

"Ahh," sighed Dan. "I'm sorry, Emily – I am so sorry…I'm missing all of you."

Emily stared at her drink. "That's not how it feels to us," she sulked.

"What do you mean?" asked Dan anxiously.

"Well, Mum says that you've gone off with somebody else and that you'd rather be with her…"

Her comment was one that Dan might have expected but it still caught him off-balance. He paused, not knowing what to say.

"It isn't really like that..." he said at last.

Emily put her hands over her eyes and from the shaking of her shoulders, he could tell that she was crying.

"I just want everything to be the way it was before. I don't understand why we can't just go back to how we were."

Dan put his hand on her arm. "I can't see how that will happen, Emily," he said. Whilst he did not want to hurt her, neither did he wish to mislead her.

She looked at him fiercely, angrily brushing away wisps of hair wet and straggly from her own tears. She looked a picture of misery.

It was, of course, hard for him to bear. He wondered briefly how there could be any other outcome to his relationship with Anne. What had he thought? He paused. That was the problem. He had not thought. He had been so taken up with his own pleasure, he loved Anne so much, that he had thrown aside his feelings for his family. Now Emily was bringing him face-to-face with what he had done.

He moved to put his arm around her thinking that she would probably push him off but, contrary to his expectations, she did not pull away or resist his feeble attempts to console her. Instead, she let him hold her, until eventually the tension in her shoulders subsided, her tears receded, and she began to regain control of herself. When she thought she could trust herself to speak once more, she said, "So many of my friends' parents have split up. I thought you and Mum would be different...I really did."

Dan could say nothing. He, too, had believed that his marriage to Sue, dull though it had often been, would never falter. Now in seeking some relief from the dullness, in trying to find out if there was anything more in life than the following of routines and conventional behaviour, he had caused his wife and children a huge amount of sadness and distress.

"I'm sorry," he said. It was all he could say.

Emily fished in her pocket for a tissue and began to dry her eyes.

"I hope all this isn't going to stop us from meeting..." said Dan.

"What – oh no, of course not, Dad. That's the last thing I want."

"It's the last thing I want, as well," he gently replied.

"I really miss you at home," continued Emily.

"And I really miss being at home...with you."

"I can't believe that I've got another four years there..."

"Why 'four years'?"

"...Because that's how long it will be before I finish my A-levels."

Of course, thought Dan. His thoughts were in the 'slow lane' that morning.

"Have you decided that you want to go to university then?" he asked.

"Oh yes, I want to go – but it all seems a long way away..."

"The time will go faster than you think..."

Emily did not reply but now that she was talking about her future, she was recovering quickly from her tearfulness.

"Will you still be able to help me with my schoolwork?" she asked.

"I certainly will – but perhaps you need to talk to your mum about it first."

Emily nodded, knowing that whatever arrangement she had with her father, her mother would have to show a measure of co-operation.

Thinking about the practicalities, Dan said, "I'd like to come to the house – but I doubt if your mum will agree to it. You could come to me at the cottage though..."

"I think I'd like that," she replied with a smile.

Dan watched as she finished her smoothie. Any remaining signs of the tears she had shed had now receded but there were shadows beneath her eyes that he had not noticed before and her face had a pallor that seemed out of place amongst the healthy faces that summer had imparted all around them. He sensed, though, that their encounter was drawing to a close.

This was confirmed moments later when, looking up, Emily suddenly caught a glimpse of her friend Lucy.

"Oh," she said, "I think it's time for me to go."

Her father smiled, they hugged for a moment and then he said, "Off you go then. Make sure you stay in touch...and don't forget to talk to your mum about coming out to the cottage."

"I will," said Emily with a final, fleeting smile – and then she was gone, heading straight for her friend who was waiting on the other side of the street.

Dan watched, returned a brief wave from Lucy, and then sat silently staring at his empty coffee cup, trying to cope with the emotional ache that Emily's departure had left within him.

* * *

Later, back at the cottage, Dan had time on his hands and, as on similar recent occasions, decided to spend it in the garden. In previous years, he would have been busy at home but whilst he was exiled in the cottage, there was little for him to do, so for once, he initially took time to think about something other than his personal life.

Despite his self-absorption, he could not but help notice the mounting effects of the summer's dryness and heat. The lawn which had been green when he moved in had now turned brown through the lack of rainfall. Cracks in the earth that he had noticed more than three weeks ago, had continued to widen so that, had he wished, he could have inserted his fingers in them. In the valley that lay below the cottage, the river had also become reduced to little more than a sluggish brown stream, making its way between the stinking contours of its slowly desiccating bed.

Dan rarely thought of the weather as much more than the backdrop to his life. He was still young enough to cope with its vicissitudes without worrying about it too much. Until now, his personal circumstances and his self-obsession had filled his view of the world – but now that he had time to notice, he could see that the situation was changing, and the drought was forcing its way forward into everybody's attention.

His mind went back to a few days previously, when, propelled by boredom, he had tuned into the twenty-four-hour news channels and had learned that it was not only the UK but also much of Western Europe that was enduring the summer's heat.

Confirmation that the drought was beginning to affect water supplies came with news reports that standpipes were being erected in various parts of the country. Following the floods, groundwater levels had been at a very high level in Somerset, but elsewhere, the winter had been much drier. When Dan had seen the measures being taken in other counties, however, he went to rummage amongst the unread brochures and leaflets that he had left on a small table in the cottage hallway. Eventually, he found a recent leaflet from the water company, which made it clear that, even in the local area, water rationing was only days away.

It was the first time that Dan could remember such a prolonged drought and he found it alarming. He reflected that the same uncertainty that had been ever-present during the winter floods had re-emerged. At that time, everyone had wanted to know how long the floods would last. Now, everyone wanted to know how long the drought would last.

Locally, the floods had been a disaster. Although superficially life had returned to normal, some of the damage done to towns, villages and countryside would take years to remedy. The drought, however, as Dan thought about it, was worse.

For a start, it was affecting a much larger area – one that went well beyond the shores of the UK. In France and Germany, people forced by their circumstances to live in buildings with poor ventilation and without air conditioning, were suffering from heat-related illnesses; the number of deaths incurred was already thought to exceed 4000. In Spain, Portugal, Southern France and Italy smoke was billowing into the skies from large and numerous wildfires.

Less dramatically, since Dan was now entirely responsible for his own meals, he had noticed a variety of vegetables disappearing from supermarket shelves. Together with most of his neighbours, he was perfectly capable of improvising different meals based on what was available rather than lamenting the shortages, but as the year moved on from late July to mid-August, concern about both supplies of food and water began to mount.

For the moment, however, the shortage of water and the diminishing variety of food were still registering with Dan as little more than inconveniences which would end, sooner or later, and then pass into history as part of an event to be recorded in online encyclopaedias or, more rustically, in the memories of those swapping yarns over pints of beer and cider in their local pubs.

There were, Dan reflected, effects of the drought that had not, at first, been apparent – not least because most people's lack of familiarity with farming meant that they took the availability of food and drink for granted. It was clear to him, though, as he travelled through the countryside that the pastures of lush grass that he was used to seeing were slowly turning into a brown wasteland that held little nutrition for sheep and cattle. Farmers, too, had begun to publicly express their anxieties about the future of their activities as a viable means of earning a living.

Whilst he was as affected by shortages as many of his neighbours, he felt grateful that his livelihood was unlikely to be directly influenced by the drought; but for the farmers in the area, it was a different matter, and for them, the shortage of water was becoming critical.

Dan's awareness of such problems was increased when, seeking company whilst Anne was still in the USA, he had rung Greg and driven across to Sedgewater to spend time with him at the Leg O' Mutton.

There had still been enough beer available in the pub to temporarily blot out their troubles, but their evening had been blighted by a strong smell from the lavatories. Greg had explained that the flushing of the Leg O' Mutton's lavatories had been restricted and that public health concerns might soon bring about closure of the pub. The family who ran it would also be in financial trouble if it closed for so much as just a few days. The drought was beginning to be a significant problem for local businesses. Greg, though, determined as ever to play the part of the stoic, had assured him that the problems of the drought were not remotely likely to exceed those of the Global Pandemic in the early 2020s.

Dan had greeted the news of the Leg O' Mutton's plight with a mixture of bemusement and an almost inevitable helping of lavatory humour – but it had all seemed less amusing the next morning when he woke with a hangover and found himself having to be economical as he flushed Greg's lavatory with a pail of water.

Now, this afternoon, he was sitting beneath the parasol in the garden, musing that the temperatures were, if anything, higher than they had been at the end of the summer term. He checked his smartphone, which told him that the temperature was 33°C. There was another 8°C to go before UK's national temperature record, set two years previously, would be breached, but it was the persistence of the heat that Dan found difficult. By this time, there had been numerous nights on which he had been able to sleep for only short periods; he felt fortunate that, for the time being, he did not have to go into work each day and he felt great sympathy for those who did not have a choice.

After a while, however, his thoughts slipped away from the drought and into remembrance of his conscience's nightly torment about the way in which he had treated Sue and the affair that he was now actually conducting with Anne. His regrets, though, were never so great as to enable him to master his own desires, and as soon he thought of Anne, he longed to be with her.

Initially, when she had told him that she would be going to the USA, he had thought that it might then be easier to follow through on his recognition that there was no future in their relationship; but now that she would soon be returning, he found himself wanting the time to pass quickly so that he could be in her company again. He longed to be sitting with her, enjoying her conversation, delighting in her sense of fun and her laughter, and slipping into the pleasures of intimacy once more.

He thought about the lofty distinctions that were sometimes made between love and lust but knew that, in the emotions Anne brought out in him, he found it difficult to distinguish between the two. They were certainly not the same, but he felt them both – and the one was inseparably interwoven with the other. He was certain, however, that his love for Anne would never involve any violence or destructive feelings towards her. If he felt any anger, it was towards George and the way in which he treated Anne.

There were times, of course, when he was able to recognise that George was also being wronged and that he, Dan, was partly responsible. For that matter, how did he know that George's abuse had not simply been triggered by his wife's behaviour? There was no excuse for such violence, but anger and frustration with Anne would make it easier to comprehend. She was, he reflected, such a profoundly attractive woman that, if she so wished, she could have her choice of men. He had no definite proof that she was engaged in any such behaviour, but he felt the stirrings of anxiety and potentially of jealousy. He wanted her for himself, and in a sense, he wanted to possess her. The rational side of his nature told him, however, that people in general were not for the possession of others and that Anne in particular, despite her fears and weaknesses, would never submit to being the 'possession' of others – no matter how the situation might appear.

At this point, he found himself hating the path along which his thoughts had led him. He did not want to disturb his belief that his relationship with Anne was uniquely theirs and that, even if she had any feelings for George or for others, they could be in no way comparable to the depths of intimacy into which she had entered with him. It was an intensely selfish emotion but also one connected to his sense of identity and to his awareness, real or imagined, of the difference between himself and others,

Then, sadly, his earlier thought that there could be no future in his relationship with Anne, returned – but this time in tension with the question of how he was going to withdraw from her when what he so desperately wanted was to be with her.

Finally at the back of his thoughts was the most uncomfortable instinct of them all – the one that told him that he was holding deep within himself, an idealised image of Anne and that it was too much to expect of anyone that she could live up to his exalted feelings about her. There was a disconnection between his image of her and his experience of daily life. Sooner rather than later, his eggshell dreams would shatter and fall to the ground – and then, would he want to live in the degraded existence that, he believed, lay beyond?

The black wall of misery that bounded these reflections had tested him in the long hours of the night – a situation that was exacerbated by the unrelenting heat. Eventually, he realised that, although he had never taken anti-depressants before, he needed to give himself a chance to cope with the darkness that had been settling over his spirits. A visit to the local GP practice brought a frank confirmation that he was suffering from clinical depression, and for the first time in his life, he found himself taking both anti-depressants and sleeping tablets.

Then, whilst he was trying to work his way through this situation, Anne arrived back in the UK. He had not expected to hear from her immediately but, in a single message, she told him that although George would be going to London, as expected, he was going to take a break of several days in the local area; with still longer to wait, Dan wasted time, drifting about the cottage, trying to pull together teaching plans for the autumn term – whilst also trying not to think about her. Not only was the situation a huge mess, it was also one from which there seemed to be no relief other than that the medication he had been prescribed was now enabling him to sleep at nights.

Strangely, by contrast during this period, he found that when he thought, if only for a while, about the drought – a situation that was so much bigger than his private troubles – it led him towards a perspective that he could regard as more rational. There was so much about the world in which he lived that was passing him by because of his obsessive preoccupation with the world inside his head.

When he was able to detach himself from his introversion in that way, he could recognise that, despite everything, the succession of beautiful summer days was helping to lift his mood and that, whatever the privations of the drought, when the dank, dark days of winter finally came again, it was the blue skies and summer heat that he would want to remember.

Past misfortunes had also taught him a certain amount of stoicism – although this time, he could not blame those misfortunes on 'Fate'; he had made a string of wrong decisions so now, inevitably, he would have to work through their consequences. The slow progression from where he was, he recognised, would have to be borne, like the duration of the flood and the drought, and was yet another piece of uncertainty through which he would have to pass with as much equanimity as he could muster.

* * *

CHAPTER 19

PRIORITIES

It was evening and Dan was, once more, at a loose end. The hot days of that summer seemed interminable, and he knew that if he did not get away from the cottage, if only for a few hours, he would find it difficult to sleep. For once, he did not brood about the solitude in which he now often found himself but welcomed it.

It was several days since he had last heard from Anne and although that made him feel more anxiety about their relationship, it also gave him time to think more clearly about what was important to him. He remembered a place – the Westmere Nature Reserve – a few miles away where he could get a change of scenery whilst also sustaining the solitude that, for the present, he sought.

The drive across country was uncomplicated and probably even quieter than usual since many local families were on holiday in other parts of the country or overseas. Although he had not been to the Reserve for some time, it was all just as he had remembered it from a previous visit and after some rough walking that took him around the margins of a large, reed enclosed lake, he found himself on a walkway most often used by birdwatchers on their way to a bird hide located at its far end. Dan, though, much as he loved to observe the birds and other wildlife for which the lake was 'home', had gone there that evening in search of a place that was in keeping with his mood and in which he could meditate.

He went just a short distance along the walkway to a point where he knew there was a viewing platform that stood well out from the bank, but which was largely hidden from the creatures of the lake. A wooden bench, thoughtfully provided for those wishing to spend more than just a minute or two in that place, gave him both a view of the lake and somewhere that he could quietly tease out his thoughts.

From the outset, he resolved not to dwell on his longing to be with Anne; he had spent so much of his solitude doing exactly that, but this evening he wanted his thoughts to reach beyond his personal situation to events as they were evolving in the natural world.

He gazed across the lake, marvelling at the unruffled surface that it presented to the sky and to which it gave back its mirrored light, shadows and wisps of evening cloud. A mute swan with her flotilla of cygnets drifted silently by, seemingly unaware of Dan's presence as they paddled unhurriedly along the reedy margins to either side of the platform.

As much as Dan enjoyed being in such a natural environment, he did not think of himself in any way as a naturalist and his knowledge of the plants and creatures around him was superficial. It filled him with sorrow, though, that the threat to both his immediate environment and to natural habitats in every part of the world had now advanced to a point where it was possible to contemplate the destruction of innumerable plants and animals which had evolved so perfectly to thrive in the conditions of the Holocene. Now, he read, scientists had taken seriously the idea that the world was no longer in the Holocene epoch but had evolved with unprecedented speed, into the Anthropocene, a new and globally disruptive epoch in which the influence of *Homo Sapiens* was everywhere to be found – in the biosphere and beyond.

At first, in Dan's life, such notions had seemed remote, academic. Now, however, the disruptive life patterns and appetites of *Homo Sapiens* were manifesting themselves at every level of existence across the planet.

It was helpful, at least for a while, to think of this disruptive species of *Homo Sapiens* in such terms – to use the Latin, scientific name to briefly distance himself from his own kind. It also helped, for however short a period, to give him a different perspective and perhaps, therefore, a little relief from the introverted dwelling on what he wanted to see as the inconsequential preoccupations of his present, inner world.

What were those preoccupations? They were, of course, if he wanted to list them, his obsession with Anne, his wife's recently stated intention to divorce him, his inability to be with his children other than at agreed times, the possible loss of his house and the humiliation that he would feel if his affair with Anne became general knowledge. Yet, here at the lake with its open expanses of water, with its wildlife going about its own business and oblivious of his, the enormous canopy of stars and planets that he would see slowly revolving about his head that night if he stayed there long enough – set in that context, such preoccupations were myopic in the extreme and, ultimately, of course, in his mortality he would pass back into the fabric of the planet to which he and all other Earthly life owed its existence. And yet…and yet…if he multiplied these foolish preoccupations of his by several billion, he might begin to understand why this species, these billions of *Homo Sapiens* were still going about their business seemingly oblivious to any significant degree that – they/we – both pronouns applied to his thoughts – were destroying the global environment and web of life of which they and he were an integral part. It seemed beyond belief – and, for that matter, beyond any scale of foolishness on which the word 'stupid' would still have a meaning.

Although it was summer, he found himself looking at the lengthening shadows near the water's edge and at the slowly changing hues of the evening sky. He had brought no form of light with him, and he had concealed his smartphone in the car. Reluctantly he decided that, in due course, it would be prudent to make his way back before darkness fell, but he could stay for a while longer before the path back to the car park became difficult to see.

He looked down from the bench on which he was sitting at the water gently lapping around the uprights by which the observation platform was supported. The water level would be much lower, he thought, than it had been during the floods of the previous winter, but the underlying pattern was one in which the water would gradually rise to inundate most of what he could still descry in the slowly fading light. That would be the fate of much of that part of the county in which he had spent the recent years of his life. Yet, it would also be returning it all to a state in which it had long existed in human pre-history and, perhaps, before that. He wondered if he should be sad about such a course of events but then found instead, that he was reassured – reassured that the Earth could and would restore all the damage, all the destruction, all the outpourings of a species that foolishly believed that it was separate from Nature – a domain that, in the crassness of its ignorance and presumed superiority, it also believed it was capable of overcoming and subduing.

Inadvertently, he had spent longer in reflection than he had intended and, like any other animal, he, too, was a creature that needed to respond to his environment and now that the light was perceptibly fading from the watery vista around him, he slowly rose from his seat and began to make his was back along the twilit walkway and path to where he had left his car.

* * *

CHAPTER 20

TRANSITION

For a while, Dan's life at the cottage finally fell into a pattern that provided him with a sense of stability – although that was not the general experience of those living around him.

So it was that Amanda had continued to be temporary Head of Wellsprings Primary School, but her situation with the Foundation had begun to falter. The news, eventually broken by the CEO, Elaine Hubbard, to the Governors at Wellsprings that there would be no return to the school's supposedly 'permanent site' led to speculation, subsequently confirmed, that Amanda had known for some time about the Hydrologist's report that had largely sealed the fate of both the school and the nearby housing estates. This created an atmosphere of mistrust between Amanda and the school's governors which led to an insistence that the Foundation should replace her with a new and permanent Head of Wellsprings School; that, however, was all before they had fully understood the implications of the loss of the school's permanent site and the steady decrease in pupil numbers that resulted from it.

Meanwhile, Dan's position as Deputy was briefly considered and some of the Governors favoured the relative simplicity of promoting him to be acting head; another faction amongst the Governors considered, though, that he had been Amanda's accomplice and therefore saw him as being tarnished with the same accusation – that important information relevant to the school had been unduly withheld from them. Behind the scenes, George Moresby had also been actively making it known to those who saw him as a benefactor the school could ill afford to lose, that Dan had been having an affair with his wife.

Whilst Dan laboured with the burden of these accusations, both openly shared and hidden, events in the wider world were moving on. The rumblings of discontent that had been so evident during the Pandemic of the early 2020s, had now become audible throughout the British archipelago. Scotland had already become independent of the United Kingdom, and the hand of the Westminster Parliament was now being forced by Wales – and Northern Ireland – which had for some time sought a different relationship with the Irish Republic to the south.

As a result of this constitutional turmoil, a variety of related issues was being discussed: the location of an English Parliament, the role, if any, of the Royal Family, the nature of borders between the countries of the former United Kingdom, how the armed forces of the constituent countries could possibly provide anything like the previous level of security, and the form of political 'umbrella' under which the affairs of the British Isles should be administered. There was, too, a substantial movement among the English regions, some of which had larger populations than those of Scotland, Wales, or Northern Ireland, for a much greater degree of autonomy.

Like many of England's citizens, Dan felt both bemused and bewildered by the changes that were taking place around him. The country that had once been such a familiar entity to him now seemed to be passing through some sort of star life-cycle process as it continued to shrink from former Victorian giant to Twenty-First Century dwarf. Particularly perplexing to Dan was the apparent urge to divide the available land mass into ever smaller units, each of which lacked any appreciable economic viability whilst, at the same time, shouting very loudly about the right to self-government.

Various names and abbreviations for the proposed political umbrella were being tossed about, including the FSB (Federated States of Britain) and the USB (United States of Britain). Dan took some amusement from the criticism of these two suggestions – namely that the first sounded like a Russian intelligence agency and the latter like a piece of computer hardware or a 'B' grade version of the USA.

There was very little amusement to be had, however, from the steadily worsening global environment and the irony of Britain's fragmentation was not lost on those who believed that only concerted international action could deal with the Climate Crisis, the military ambitions of tyrannical states, cyber warfare and the vast human migrations that were taking place in response to the continuing degradation of the Earth's biosphere.

Within this colossal envelope of disasters, Dan's most immediate concern was with his employment in a School Federation that was losing the will to live. In part, the Federation's troubles stemmed from a much wider uncertainty about the future of the society within which it was located, but the organisation of Education in England had also failed to keep pace with the implications of online learning, many of which had become apparent as far back as the time of the Pandemic. Parents, meanwhile, were deserting the formal stipulations of State Education in their droves, not least because the State itself seemed to be on the road to nowhere.

In response to falling 'numbers on roll' a decision had recently been taken within the Federation to amalgamate four of the smaller schools into two larger establishments. The work paving the way to amalgamation had been led meticulously by both Amanda and her senior colleague, Elaine Hubbard. The 'new' schools were due to begin life in their new amalgamated identities at the start of the autumn term in the following academic year.

Knowing that one of the losers in the situation would be Dan, Amanda had designated some of her weekly time at Wellsprings Primary, to a one-to-one meeting with him. Her intention was to talk to him about his options since neither of the two new schools had shown any interest in his qualifications or experience. She hoped that her mission was not going to be a difficult one.

Her hopes were partly based on Dan's disillusionment with his own career – a state of mind that, in her belief, stemmed both from personal events and from a background of general malaise that was beginning to affect much of England's teaching profession. In Dan's recollection, however, disaffection with his career – and with his marriage for that matter – had begun at some time before the flooding of the previous winter and before his affair with Anne.

The final working through of his dissatisfaction, though, did not begin until after Anne had returned from her visit to the USA. Curiously, for three days after her return, Dan heard nothing from the small group of people – his children, Amanda, Greg and, frustratingly, Anne – who, if only unwittingly, had helped to alleviate his boredom during the sweltering tedium of the drought. Then, late in the afternoon of the fourth day, he had a text message from her; George had gone to London, and would he like to spend the evening with her? Any susurrations of irritation and anxiety that he had felt when he had not quickly heard from her again, were immediately dispelled. Reading the message, he gave a small inward whoop of delight.

They had agreed that Dan would go to Anne's house for about seven o'clock. From receiving the message late in the morning to the time that he was ready to drive over to see her, he was in a state of high anticipation. It had been a month since they had last been in each other's company and it took an effort of self-discipline, when the time arrived, to make sure that he drove through the lanes at a speed that would enable him to stop if he met anything coming the other way.

The drive seemed to drag and the warm summer lanes in which he would have usually delighted frustrated him as he forced himself away from daydreaming about Anne to concentrate on the convoluted route unwinding before him. Eventually, however, he rounded the familiar bend which led to the front of Anne's house. Then he was on the drive, and she had appeared fleetingly at the door to beckon him towards the back of the house where he could conceal the car in the usual large outbuilding amongst the trees. The clandestine nature of it all brought again a sense of collusion and excitement that had been missing from his daily life during the period of her absence. He pulled open the outbuilding's huge doors and drove his car into the cool twilight of its interior. As he then closed the doors behind him again, he could see that Anne had walked through the house and was waiting for him at the back door.

Moments later he was holding her, her hair gently tickling his face as they kissed and held each other. She had planned that they would eat first and then talk and listen to music, but barely two minutes later, as they tugged off their clothes in her bedroom, her plan had become an irrelevance. Their absence from one another had heightened their desire, a desire that expressed itself in the eagerness of their lovemaking. All too soon, they lay side by side, apart but still basking in the afterglow of their passion.

Anne wondered if they would have any appetite for eating but she had previously cooked for them a meal of seafood and pasta; it was waiting for them when they could bring themselves to get out of bed. She led the way, and they showered together, joking that it was to save water, but the cool setting of the shower helped to rouse them from the drowsy warmth that had enveloped them; outside, it was another hot summer's evening and there would be light in the sky for another two hours. It was time together that they did not want to idle away when they could still be enjoying what was left of the daylight in each other's company. Besides, the hours of darkness, when they came, would bring them once more into close physical intimacy.

Anne's choice of food, redolent as it was of the Mediterranean, seemed completely appropriate to the evening's temperature. Despite their usual concern about the prying neighbour, Anne opened the French windows of the dining room, so that such breeze as there was, could bring them a sense of eating al fresco. They sat together over their meal, talking, listening to music that she had set to play in the background and enjoying glasses of white wine.

Anne recounted her experiences in the US. As anticipated, she had often been left to her own devices and so had amused herself by sightseeing, going to galleries, lunchtime concerts and sometimes dining alone.

Dan wondered aloud, "Why did George take you with him, if he needed you to spend so little of your time in his company?"

It was something they had talked about before.

"Oh, I had my uses," she replied. Dan felt a stirring of uneasy curiosity, but she went quickly on to say, "There were three or four occasions when businesspeople came to dinner in our apartment."

"So, did you have to entertain them?"

She smiled. "Yes, but George always hires a chef and professional catering staff. He told me once that my cooking is a little too erratic."

"That was to boost your confidence, I suppose?"

This time, she laughed. "He has me there to help in other ways."

"Oh?" So far Dan had the impression that George had wanted Anne with him for purely decorative purposes, a thought that filled him with indignation.

"I'm there to help him impress his guests."

Dan said nothing but raised his eyebrows, his expression urging her to continue.

"I talk to them. George says they like to hear my all too obvious English accent. It's my 'Englishness' that they like."

"So, you're – helping him to market his business. What do you get out of it?"

"A holiday in the US for a start." She smiled. "That's not to be underestimated. There's also a piano in the apartment – a very beautiful one – so sometimes I play for them."

Dan hesitated for a moment, remembering her previous account of past difficulties. "I can see that they would enjoy that, but do you enjoy playing for them – in that situation, I mean?"

"Why not? Besides, I still harbour ambitions of being able to play again for larger audiences. I suppose, I'm using them, in a sense, to try to get past my 'stage fright', assuming that that's what you'd call it."

"I've seen you play in front of large audiences…"

"I know, Dan – but that's in a very specific context, usually to accompany school choirs or instrument players. It's different."

"Hmm – I suppose school audiences are not generally composed of experienced concert goers."

Anne thought for moment. "You're right – or, at least, partly right. Previously, I was able to focus entirely on the music – its narrative, its sequences or simply its beauty – but now I've lost that focus. I don't know why. One day it was there – and now it isn't…" Her voice tailed away.

"I'm sorry," said Dan. "I'm being very insensitive, asking you all these questions."

"No, no…" She sounded adamant. "It's not you, Dan. Whatever questions you have, I will have asked them of myself a thousand times. And, anyway, it does help me to talk about it all even if sometimes it can be difficult to… to think about those experiences."

Impulsively, he asked, "Would you play something for me, Anne? I've noticed that you have a very beautiful piano here."

"Of course, I'd love to, but do you mind if it isn't just at the moment? I'm enjoying our 'togetherness' and I've already had more wine than I'd ever drink if I were planning to play for someone – especially you, Dan." She gave him an arch smile. "Besides, I have other plans for you, plans that I don't want to delay for very much longer."

Dan surveyed the table with its remnants of the meal they had just eaten.

"Oh, don't worry about all of this," Anne responded, following the direction of his gaze. "I'll just take it through to the kitchen and in the morning, it will all go in the dishwasher."

She stood to begin taking the dishes through to the kitchen. Dan moved to help her – and for a moment, he thought that she was going to stop him.

"What is it?"

"Oh nothing – or at least, nothing much. It's just that I'm not used to offers of help."

"Hmm – somehow that doesn't surprise me," he replied.

Without comment, Anne picked up the plates and dishes she had collected together and began walking through to the kitchen. Dan collected together some more of the table's contents and followed her.

He thought but did not say, that whilst the setting was beautiful, the food delicious and the prospect of spending the night with her beyond his wildest dreams, it was almost as though they were married to each other.

There was a familiarity about what they were doing, a domesticity that he found reassuring – and which was, for the time being, otherwise missing from his life.

* * *

Later that night, he lay listening to the gentle sound of Anne's breathing. The curtain was slightly open, and moonlight fell across the beautiful nakedness of her body where, in the warmth of the night, she had cast aside the sheet.

After the loneliness and self-reproach of so many nights alone at the cottage, Dan found it hard to believe in the reality of his situation. How, he wondered, had this happened to him? He placed his hand with fingers spread on her skin, to confirm for himself that she was not part of some heavenly and libidinous dream. She stirred gently but did not wake.

His mind fell again to the earlier conversation about music. As he gazed in awe at the moonlight slanting across her body, it was inevitably music that came again to his mind – music of mystery, sensuousness, and beauty.

How profoundly fortunate was he to be with her that night. He hoped that whatever the future would bring, he would always be able to recall those moments in which he was able to delight in her while she slept in innocence of his gaze, and at peace.

* * *

The following day, they sat for a while over breakfast. It was still quite early but although Dan had nowhere to go except back to the cottage, Anne had business in Sedgewater.

"What time's your appointment?" asked Dan.

"Eleven-thirty," replied Anne. "I'm not in a huge hurry but it's probably best if you leave whilst it's still quite early."

Dan sighed. "I wish we didn't have to be so secretive about our meetings."

She gave a sad smile. "I've often wished the same. But at least, we are still managing to meet." She paused. "If George had his way, I'd be locked in a high tower."

Dan, though, remembered her previous comment and began to get up from the table.

Anne laughed. "I didn't mean that you have to leave this very minute! Anyway, last night, you asked me if I would play something for you – so, if you don't have to go rushing off in the next few minutes, I'd like to play for you now."

She took him through to a room that was similar in size and furnishings to the lounge in which they had often spent time together except that it had a view of the garden at the rear of the house. Between the centre of the room, and the windows looking out over the garden, was a grand piano. With a smile Anne gestured towards a comfortable armchair just a short distance from the piano and Dan seated himself in it.

She adjusted her position on her music stool for a moment and then began to play. Almost immediately, Dan was enraptured. The music poured out into the room, and he followed in his imagination as the mood and tempo of the piece ebbed and flowed. Flawlessly, Anne moved into the passionate climax of the piece, which, as Dan listened, expressed itself through an intricate interweaving of the bass and treble notes.

Then, silence – the piece had come to an end. He sat in silent awe both at the piece itself and Anne's playing of it. Then, as habit moved him towards applause, he checked himself and went to stand next to her.

"Anne, that was beautiful...Your playing is absolutely wonderful!"
He paused, feeling again the inadequacy of words. Instead, he drew her
gently to her feet and kissed her. To his surprise, a blush suffused her
cheek. They let go of each other, and she bobbed a curtsy.

"Thank you, kind sir..." she said, gently satirising his gaucheness
before her.

Dan smiled, thinking that his intensity had embarrassed her. There
was a short silence between them.

Then she asked, "Have you heard that piece before?"

"I think I have – but I don't know what it is."

"It's a Brahm's Intermezzo in A minor – I learned it long ago, but I
still enjoy playing it."

She looked away and said, "I'm sorry, Dan – about all the secrecy
I mean. But it's probably best if you leave before my neighbour realises
you're here..."

Dan nodded and smiled ruefully.

Moments later, she led him through the house to the door at the back
where he slid out into the garden and thence to the outbuilding where
his car was hidden. Then, having followed his by now familiar routine,
he drove the car round to the front drive and was about to turn onto the
road when another car approached from the left, so that he had to briefly
wait whilst it passed. As he checked again before driving off, he thought
he saw a small movement in the upper window of the neighbouring
house. It was barely perceptible, and it seemed unwise to hesitate any
longer, but he had the impression that he had been watched as he had
waited at the entrance to Anne's drive.

* * *

Back at the cottage once more, the day stretched emptily before him.
He drifted indecisively between rooms, finally settling on the settee in
front of the television set. Picking up the handset, he skimmed across the
news channels, pausing just long enough to learn that there had been
a terrorist incident in Birmingham, that there was a severe drought
and famine in Ethiopia, and that a boat load of migrants had been
apprehended whilst coming ashore from a boat anchored off the coast
of Dorset.

Dan pondered each incident as it was reported but, once he had flicked off the television, his focus returned once more to his own daily existence. Depressed though he was about recent events in his life and, even though he felt that he was staring at the failure of his marriage and career, here he was on this summer morning, well fed, still engaged in his affair with Anne and, for the time being at least, still able to rely on regular slices of income going into his bank account.

He went to the table in the kitchen where he had left his computer and tried to engage once more with lesson planning for the new term, but concentration eluded him; his was such a small world, and out there, the 'larger world' was disintegrating.

* * *

The autumn term of the new school year duly began and shortly after its inception, the prolonged drought of the spring and summer finally broke. As rain poured down from dark clouds overhead, there was celebration across the UK and in Europe. People danced semi-naked in the streets and wallowed, where they could, in spreading pools of water.

In all other respects, though, the school's autumn term seemed totally familiar and set to continue in the pattern of so many years before it. Dan found it hard to settle to the routine, however, because he had gradually begun to realise that his position at Wellsprings Primary was being squeezed out of existence. As he understood what was happening, it added to his sense that change was coming at a personal level and although he was frequently preoccupied by the insidious, creeping evolution of the Climate Crisis, the loss of his teaching job would be a much more immediate problem because, as always, he needed to feed and clothe himself and to have a roof over his head.

Of course, he continued to be concerned for his future in the longer term – and that of the people around him – but for a while, events on that timescale were not on his horizon. For much of his adult life, he had been completely absorbed in the demands of his work, and he felt that he had always striven to teach his pupils to the best of his ability and provide clear leadership to more junior colleagues. Now, however, as he began to see that his future at Wellsprings would be of limited duration, his motivation began to slacken. He entered a loop in which he thought about his work and routine with a detachment that only served to further reinforce his sense of alienation. He understood that it was time to move on – but then there was the question; move on to what?

Used to planning the greater part of his daily life, Dan found it difficult to consign himself to the winds and tides that lay outside his professional work – but, as time passed and he still had no idea what he wanted to do, such an eventuality seemed increasingly likely. Staying in his current job, or even a modified version of it, was not an option for him. He would have to follow his fate, wherever it took him.

Meanwhile, the autumn term progressed, it seemed to Dan, as autumn terms had always done. The vestiges of traditional English events, together with a variety of multi-cultural festivals, punctuated the term's curriculum and then were gone. Soon, he found himself thinking about Christmas with its associated social events, cards and presents.

Christmas Day, though he spent it on his own, was not experienced by him as a time in which he was particularly aware of his solitariness. He had texts and messages from friends, including both Anne and Amanda, and from Josh and Emily – who would be coming to spend time with him the following day. Television reminded him that he was part of a larger world, and he kept his meals to a pattern that he had long been used to with his family. The day came and went.

The start of the spring term began with the familiar bleakness of low temperatures accompanied by persistent wind and rain. As usual, there was a certain amount of flooding on the Levels, but the drought of the previous summer had ensured that the land did not achieve the saturation that it had in the previous winter. There was inconvenience – but never complete inundation.

For a while, the intensity of the effort needed to raise children's formal learning to the level of the expected outcomes, continued to propel him – as it always had. Somehow, he managed to keep touch with Anne, and their affair, with its rollercoaster ride of joy and anxiety, also continued although whether he was truly able to separate the highs and lows of his private life from the steadiness of temperament needed in his work was something, perhaps, about which he was deluding himself.

Amanda, however, eventually came to spread the dark wings of the Federation over his future. One afternoon, he was tidying his classroom at the end of the school day, when he received a message from her on the mobile phone that he had been presented with at the start of the autumn term.

The meeting that he believed it presaged, was one that he had been expecting. He took his computer bag and briefcase with him to his car before he went to see Amanda, anticipating that the last place he would want to return to, however briefly, after their conversation, would be his classroom.

Having put his bags in the boot of his car, he then went across to the administration block, such as it was, went through the entry procedure and joined Amanda in her office. As he entered, she rose to meet him and ushered him to a comfortable chair. That done, she seated herself in a similar chair at a slight angle to Dan's and then reached across to a folder that she had left on the end of her desk.

Dan had a shrewd idea what the folder contained. He waited patiently, knowing that Amanda was going through the motions of treating him as she would any other employee. Since they both knew the situation, it seemed bizarre, but going through such rituals was something that he had learned Amanda needed to do – and simply because the orderliness of his own little world was breaking down, he had no desire to inflict the same sense of normlessness upon her.

Having examined her papers for a requisite amount of time, Amanda put the folder back on the end of her desk, took off the spectacles that had been perched on the end of her nose, crossed her legs, and contrived to assume a more relaxed posture in her chair than she had so far been able to achieve.

"So, Dan, thank you for coming to see me – and for being patient whilst I made sure that I was up to date with your situation."

Dan nodded, smiling benignly but knowing full well that she was already very well acquainted with his 'situation'.

"I'm afraid, Dan, that I don't know what to say…" She looked up at him, as if appealing to him to help her out.

"I don't know that there's much that either of us can say," he replied.

"I think, knowing you as I do, you must have anticipated the present circumstances?"

"Yes," he replied. "I'd also hoped that at least one of my job applications would provide me with another option but I'm not surprised that I didn't get anywhere with them."

"Oh?" Amanda did her best to sound surprised but knew that Dan had lost conviction in what he was doing and from his own viewpoint, and that of the Academy, needed to move on.

He looked at her with a faint smile that had a tinge of sadness to it, and Amanda realised that this was not a time for the elaborate façade of formality that they had erected between them.

"I'm really sorry, Dan," she said. "I've hoped for a long time now that someone with your commitment and ability would find a new niche – and preferably one within the Foundation but, as we both realise, it hasn't worked out that way."

"No," he agreed. "Teaching is not a job that can be done half-heartedly. I've known for a while that the commitment you kindly referred to was no longer there so…I've been looking around for a new direction, although to be candid with you, I haven't found it yet…"

Amanda hesitated but then said, "It might have been otherwise for you here, had it not been for the Foundation's need to rationalise its staffing. I'm afraid your offer to accept redundancy has been taken because, to be frank, it will simplify one aspect of amalgamating Wellsprings and Lakeside Primary."

She stopped, not because she felt that she was giving hostages to fortune but because she thought, that even if her words ran the risk of sounding hollow, he deserved better than to be seen as a convenient way out for the Foundation.

"It's not a problem for me, Amanda. Really, it isn't. It's felt like 'time to go' for a while now."

"Under the circumstances, I probably shouldn't ask you this, but does your decision have anything to do with Anne…?"

"Well, yes it does," he replied. "But I'm afraid she can't completely claim the credit. As we all know, none of us is short of reasons to feel unsettled at the moment."

Amanda nodded. He had made a good summation of the situation – but she decided that a slight change of direction was needed. "I'd like to talk to you about all of that," she said, "but I don't think – this is the place for such a discussion. I think we'd both prefer more comfortable surroundings where we could have a drink or two."

"I'll certainly agree with that," replied Dan.

She smiled. "Then that's what we'll do – I promise. For the moment though, we still have to go through the redundancy procedure so you will receive a letter about that and, meanwhile, I would suggest that you need to contact your Regional Representative. He will help you to get the best terms although, in my view, he should not have to work too hard…"

She stopped. She did not want to say anything that would mislead him or begin to sound like a willingness to influence the process. Dan was moving on but, for the time being, she was not.

He understood that they had reached the end of what she was required to do that afternoon. They both got up from their chairs and moved towards the door.

He opened the door to let himself out and then turned back toward her. Even when the redundancy process was complete, he would not be saying goodbye to her – and at last, they would then be able to return to the informality of the friendship they had shared before.

For the moment, though, he took Amanda's hand to shake it but found instead that they were holding each other in a hug.

* * *

Later, at the cottage, Dan distracted himself by cooking a meal and then catching up on the day's news. Idly flicking between channels, his attention was drawn by pictures of long lines of people trailing across a European landscape. Having missed the introduction to the news segment, he could not identify the country in which the video had been recorded but, as far as he could tell, the scenes before him were in Southern Europe. His thoughts were confirmed a moment or two later, when a map identifying the 'trails' being used by the migrants was shown; the countries of Northern Europe were failing to load responsibility for migrants from Africa and the Middle East onto Turkey, Greece, Italy, and the Balkans. A mass migration into northern Europe was taking place.

The numbers of people, Dan recalled, had always been substantial but had rapidly swollen in recent years because conflict and famine in Asia and Africa had become more widespread and more intense. The long running concerns of countries in the North, however, had not translated into co-operative action to grapple with the problems of the regions from which the migrants came. Instead, there had been a rise in Nationalistic movements intent on using force to hold back the tide of humanity that was now flowing from the areas most severely affected by the intensifying effects of the Climate Crisis.

The concluding part of the segment focused unsurprisingly on migrants' attempts to cross the English Channel. Allegedly, England's government had 'failed' in its efforts to force migrants back to their countries of origin and to eliminate the multitudes of people smugglers. The consequences were that large numbers of desperate people were now encamped in the Southern Counties of England and were resisting attempts by the local authorities to enforce any form of law or regulation upon them. The numbers and the disorder were overwhelming the meagre resources available to the county authorities and the camps had become 'no go' areas.

Although Dan was surprised that he had gone so long without being fully aware of the pressure building up in the counties to the East of Somerset, it seemed to him that the phenomena that were being reported in fragmentary fashion only made sense if the dots were joined and they could be seen as part of a colossal picture and, he worried, as a factor in the development of a 'perfect storm'.

He switched off the television. For the moment, his own problems felt as though they were enough to deal with. Attempting to think about England's problems or greater still, those of the British Isles, was a long way beyond his scope. Even more remote was the possibility that he would be able to board a plane and escape to a tourist paradise where he could forget his troubles – not to mention, those of the country into which he had been born.

* * *

The prospect of redundancy remained in the background of Dan's life until the summer term arrived. Late one afternoon, Dan was taking part in a meeting with Amanda and Eleanor Browning, in which there was an agenda item relating to the amalgamation of schools planned for the following school year.

Unknown to Dan, Amanda had tried to ensure that he did not have to participate since she saw it as potentially rubbing salt into the wound of his redundancy. Eleanor, however, had insisted that he needed to be present since she wanted to be sure that events which would precede the amalgamation with Lakeside were all in hand and that the school's pupils would all have good reasons to remember their last term at Wellsprings Primary. Amanda continued to think that Eleanor was unhelpfully taking up Dan's time but finally gave way to her apparent need to be directly reassured that her Deputy Head was well and truly on top of the last pieces of work that he would do on the school's behalf.

The agenda items were dealt with fairly quickly, as Amanda had hoped they would be, and she felt a small sense of relief; she had a further meeting scheduled with the Foundation's Principal before she could make her way home. Dan and Eleanor were both aware of Amanda's intentions and remained in their seats when she reminded them that she needed to get away.

Dan presumed that he would find himself waiting for Eleanor to leave before he went to check that the cleaning staff had finished and that the school's buildings were secure for the night. There was a brief pause whilst he watched her shuffling her papers together but as he prepared to follow suit, she indicated to him that she had something further to say and she wanted him to stay where he was.

"I know this might seem rather out of the usual way of doing things here, Dan," she said, "but there is something I must speak to you about. We've had words about it before and it relates to the disquiet I've felt ever since I first heard about your relationship with Anne Moresby. Of course, I know about your intention to take redundancy and so for that reason, if for no other, I have so far thought it best not to involve Amanda or the Foundation in any way."

Eleanor's preface to whatever it was that she was going to say was more than sufficient to cause Dan to have an all too familiar sinking feeling in his stomach.

Inevitably, however, she ploughed on.

"I was recently at a social function with George Moresby – and despite the warning I gave you some time ago, he told me that you are still pursuing a relationship with his wife…"

Dan saw little point in denying it although had he tried to describe the true sequence of events, it seemed unlikely that Eleanor would have believed him. He also had fewer grounds for indignation than when his alleged affair with Anne was still a piece of fiction invented by her husband. But then, somehow, he had to defend himself.

"I can understand your concern, Eleanor..." he began. "And I know that George Moresby has a strong connection to the school, but from my viewpoint, my relationship with Anne Moresby is a private matter – and one that does not relate to my role as a teacher nor, for that matter, to the fact that I'm Deputy Head here. I would also add that despite Mr Moresby's connections to individual governors, he is not actually a member of the Governing Body."

"I don't really accept your argument," replied Eleanor, "and I'm not sure that you expect me to. As I reminded you before, George Moresby has been a generous and prominent benefactor and you as much as anyone should be well aware that he has contributed significant amounts of money and resources to the school. And now what is his reward? A senior member of staff not only has an affair with his wife but also takes no notice of warnings that it has to stop!"

Dan reflected for a moment that the supposed 'injured party' was someone who had long had relationships outside his marriage to Anne and who when the mood took him, often subjected her to violent beatings.

Eleanor, however, attributed no significance to Dan's silence and continued her diatribe...

"I have to say to you, Dan, that as Chair of Governors, I try to comment on the private lives of staff members only if it is really necessary but when I see that someone's behaviour is likely to have an adverse effect on the reputation of the school, I am bound to be concerned. I believe that your affair with Anne falls well within that category..."

For the moment, Dan's will to fight back had evaporated and he lamely began to reply, "I realise that to people outside of here, it could seem that..."

By way of response, Eleanor angrily cleared her throat. "You can thank your lucky stars that, as yet, people outside of here, especially governors and parents, know nothing about it – and feel thankful too that I intend to ensure it remains that way!"

"Well, there, Eleanor, you're a little bit late. I seem to recall that just a short while ago we were discussing the amalgamation of Wellsprings and

Lakeside so I'm not entirely sure which governors – or parents – you're talking about. You seem to have forgotten, as well, that I shall soon have ceased to be an employee in this or any other school."

"As far as I'm concerned, if you had not been taking redundancy, I would have made it my business to see that you did!"

Up to that point, Dan had remained relatively calm, but this last remark angered him.

"And why would that be, Eleanor? Is that something that's come from you – or, since you know him, is it something that's come from George Moresby? All part of the 'old pals' network I suppose – the way that things have always been done around here."

"Yes, well, suppose what you like. The plain fact of the matter is that Anne Moresby is someone else's wife and your behaviour towards her is completely unacceptable. There is, of course, the further matter of your own family. Have you no thought for what this could do even now to your wife and children if your behaviour becomes general knowledge?"

"I see no reason why it should become 'general knowledge' – it's a private matter and if George Moresby wants to say something about it, he can say it to me."

"There is one respect, Dan, in which you're right. I do know George Moresby. In fact, I know him well – and I can tell you that if you think for one moment that you can cross him and get away with it, you're a fool. My advice to you is that you end this ridiculous infatuation with his wife, go back to being the non-entity that you've always been, and hope that he doesn't make it his business to come after you."

"All of which sounds very much like a threat. Is that what's happening here? Am I to take it that you're Moresby's messenger?"

Eleanor gave a snort of derision. "I'm nobody's messenger – except my own. And I've given you fair warning. The only thing I will add to what I've said is that I'm assuming that when you're looking for your next job, you will want to ask me or Amanda for a reference. I can't speak for Amanda, but I can assure you, you'll be getting no reference from me."

With that, before Dan could make any further reply, she turned and stalked out of the room.

With as much self-composure as he could muster, Dan sought therapy in his final task for the day and checked that the school was secure for the night; finally satisfied that it was, he climbed into his car and set off for the cottage where he was destined to wonder throughout the evening and much of the night how it was that loving someone could lead to so much anger and disruption.

* * *

It was a bright, sunlit morning. Dan gazed out through his classroom window and across the countryside as the children worked at their Maths. Later, he planned to take them out into the area that, together with other staff, he had marked out and developed as a school garden. They would have to be careful; although it was early May, the sun already had an intensity that could cause sunburn and easily lead to dehydration. Such hazards, though, he would take into account and the opportunity for children to spend time that day increasing their awareness of the natural world was more than worth it.

The visit to the garden would face him with a dilemma – one that he had faced for a number of years, but which never seemed to become any easier to resolve. He thought of a phrase he had come across in both his work and elsewhere; it was 'awe and wonder'. Both were to be found if you knew how to look, everywhere in the natural world. That was something of course that he wanted to encourage children to find and to feel – and yet, that was also the basis of his dilemma. Surely, with a global 'mass extinction' taking place, he had a greater responsibility to the children than simply echoing the 'Isn't Nature wonderful' sentiment that he had heard so often in his own childhood? To conceal from them the destruction that was being perpetrated all across the world that, together with all living things they would inherit, was surely a form of lying. Yet, they were still so young and, despite the constant attempts to exploit their childhood, still thankfully innocent of the panoply of ways in which human beings abused each other and the planet to which they owed their existence. How fast and how far should children such as those in his care that day go in learning about what was happening – and what was being done – to the world in which they lived? The 'Climate Crisis' was, after all, an emergency with which all the children in his class and, for that matter, across the world, would find themselves having to adapt, however long, or short their lives would be.

The thoughts behind his gaze were interrupted by Simeon, who said, "Mr 'Olroyd, I don't get this one."

"Alright, Simeon, let's have a look at it together."

He perched on the vacant, Year 6 sized chair, next to the puzzled eleven-year-old.

At least, thought Dan, Simeon's Maths problem is not something I'll be told should not be in the Year 6 curriculum.

Later, though, as he walked along to the staffroom for a break, he found himself wondering if the society for which the children were being prepared was anything like the society in which they would be living.

* * *

The following Saturday found Dan huddled in his dressing gown on the settee, munching his way through breakfast and catching up on the news. He would have the afternoon to himself, but this morning, Emily was coming to pay her now customary Saturday morning visit.

Sue and Dan had not resorted to making formal arrangements about times when Josh and Emily would visit him, but practicalities had resolved it into occasional evenings with more regular visits at the weekends.

Despite pressures at school, Dan had managed to ensure that Emily's time with him on a Saturday morning was protected. This was partly because they both still wanted to enjoy each other's company but also for the reason that Emily's work at school had dipped when Sue and Dan had separated; now, somewhat ironically, since it had been Dan who had brought about that separation, it was also his role to provide his daughter with some support for her GCSE English and Maths which she would be sitting the following year. This morning, they were planning to work on Maths.

Dan was not expecting Emily to arrive before ten o'clock. When she was not working on the latest 'project', Sue liked to have a leisurely Saturday morning – and that included a slow start. It also gave Dan plenty of time to have a shower and get dressed.

The morning news consisted of little more than an elaboration of events that had been developing for days, so he flicked off the television and went to get himself ready for Emily's visit. A little while later, he returned to the settee, armed with two GCSE Maths books. He wanted to look through the topics that she needed to cover before she arrived.

He had spent time over the previous weeks familiarising himself with the GCSE Maths syllabus again, so by now he needed just a few minutes to remember the points at which misunderstandings often occurred, or where he thought Emily might struggle. He also tried to have ready a game or a puzzle that focused on some piece of key knowledge or skill; he hoped that she would be interested in Maths as a subject – because he wanted to dismantle the panic that sometimes overtook her when faced with something that she did not understand and to help her realise the power and beauty of the ideas that she was beginning to study. Of course, he wanted her to do well in her GCSE – but he knew that she was capable of so much more and he wanted her to discover the extent of her own abilities.

Slowly his mind moved away from the morning's planned activities and his thoughts strayed to both Anne and Sue. He had heard little, in recent times, from Anne. It hurt him that he knew almost nothing about what was happening in her life and more particularly, that since their passionate encounters during the summer months she had sunk back into the previous patterns of her life with barely a thought, it seemed, about what had passed between them. Despite not having seen her for nearly two months, he still found himself thinking about her for long periods of every day, but then, he wondered, what was the point when there seemed to be no evidence of such longing thoughts from Anne? On his phone, there was now a long string of unanswered texts although, in the past two weeks, he had forced himself not to send her anymore until she responded. Despite his ongoing obsession with her, the last thing he wanted was to be accused, at some future date, of stalking her.

The breakdown that he and Anne had jointly caused in his family life was a source of considerable pain to him. He had come to the point where he was willing to acknowledge his own culpability, but he wondered if Anne felt a similar sense of guilt. She knew, because he had told her, of his separation from Sue and the consequent difficulties he now had in his relationships with his children. Did she, he wondered, have any feelings about the part she had played in that sequence of events? There was little sign that she did.

This left him with the inevitable conclusion that the person with whom he had fallen so much in love, whether he cared to think about it or not, was deeply flawed. There was an irresponsibility in her that he could not understand – unless, of course, he thought back to the signs of emotional instability of which he should have been aware from the outset. He had, after all, been the one who had fetched her medication during the difficult circumstances of the winter flooding.

It was not the case that he was angry with Anne; rather he was angry with himself for having failed to see what now seemed so clear to him. Additionally, having given so little thought to Sue at the stage where he had not taken any irreversible steps in his affair with Anne, he now had plenty of leisure in which to think about the deeply hurtful and humiliating way in which he had treated his wife.

Sadly, he remembered at the earliest stage comparing Sue to the feeblest light of the moon whilst he thought of Anne as the Sun in his delusional solar system of the time. He had lost interest in the few domestic tasks that they had shared; he thought only that she seemed drab and uninteresting compared with the beautiful and talented woman who, for however short a time, had taken an interest in him and had engaged him in the kind of passionate lovemaking that he had previously only dreamed about. Perhaps there was something about the day-by-day nature of marriage that drew couples ever further into sharing only the routines and practicalities of married life whilst also making them increasingly distant from growing the pleasure in each other's company that they had first shared.

At that point, however, although he could see his situation more clearly, it was not yet clear enough. He still longed and ached for Anne. His feelings about Sue were more in the nature of remorse and guilt although the love and affection they had still shared until a relatively short time before his affair with Anne continued to echo poignantly in his memory. He longed for another chance to put it all right and, despite the fact that he could never undo his affair with Anne, he wanted to try to develop a new and better relationship with his wife. His fear was, however, that from Sue's viewpoint the damage was irreparable; he had broken his trust with her, and it could never be restored. It was possibly that which hurt him most of all.

"Sir bloody Galahad – that's who you always wanted to be, wasn't it?" he mused to himself. He had long had a weakness for women who appeared to need his help – but what was that 'weakness', seen in terms of his own feelings? Was it a need to be seen as benevolent – or kind? Was it a need to have the kind of power that a giver has in relation to the one to whom he is giving? He recognised belatedly that it was. Perhaps that was also part of the pleasure that he derived through his work as a teacher? The world, however, would see it differently. The world would see it as exploitative, as the exercise of power, such as it was, to satisfy his own desires. There would also, however, seem to be no account taken of the power exercised over him by Anne.

His reverie was broken by a sharp rap at the front door and Emily's smiling face pressed against the window. He hurried to the door, opened it, gave her a hug and a kiss, and showed her through to the lounge.

"Ooh, it's cooler in here," said Emily.

"Thankfully it is," commented her father, knowing that it was going to be another very warm day.

She had brought her schoolbooks in a reusable shopping bag; they went through to the kitchen dining area in which there was a table capable of folding out to a size that would accommodate them. The sun also streamed into the kitchen at that time of the morning which, in the cooler months, helped to offset the somewhat feeble efforts of the central heating system.

Initially, Dan had tried to steer Emily through the later stages of her GCSE Maths course but by now, he found that he preferred to pick up on the topics she was currently studying at school and then to help her to thoroughly understand them. If they accomplished that, he liked to engage her in looking at some of the ideas that represented an extension of the work she was doing at school.

Over a number of weeks, he had been able to fill in some of the potholes left by inconsistent teaching and provide her with a more reliable foundation on which to build. He was gratified that she had steadily become more confident in her approach to the subject and would often choose to learn about Maths. Dan understood the pressures placed on teachers by the examination system, so he always kept a wary eye on his daughter's need to satisfy the 'gatekeepers', but he also hoped that she was in the process of becoming a young woman with an independent and enquiring mind.

Emily enjoyed her visits to her father. They allowed her a step aside from the routine of her week and, although she had to rely on her mother for transport, the renewed confidence that she had begun to feel with her schoolwork spilled over into a more general and growing sense of self-belief.

They worked together for an hour on the aspects of algebra that formed the current topics in her lessons at school and then they broke for a drink. As they went through to the lounge, Dan knew that the temptation would be to ask Emily about Sue. Having heard little from her in weeks, he badly wanted to know how she was, what she was doing and how she was coping with their changed circumstances. He was also keen, however, to be sensitive to his daughter's feelings and so, finally, he decided that the last thing he should do was ask Emily anything about her mother. As a consequence, his wife's welfare had to remain a mystery. It was better that way, thought Dan, than to have his daughter feel that she was, in any sense, a 'go-between'.

Instead, they sat sipping their drinks whilst Dan wondered aloud what Emily was doing for the rest of the day. "I'm going into Sedgewater," she replied to her father's question.

"Oh yes, of course. I know your mum likes to spend some 'mother and daughter' time with you on a Saturday afternoon."

"She does – we've been shopping together most weekends recently. Mum's busy this time though, so I'm going with friends – Josie and Millie. Afterwards, I'm going to Millie's house, we're having pizzas and then Mum's picking me up from there. It will probably be quite late."

"Hmm – I wonder how late? I could run you home from Millie's place if that would help?"

"Thanks for offering, Dad – but it's OK. Mum's taken up riding again and the stables are not far from where Millie lives, so it's probably easier for her."

"So, is she staying at the stables until late? That doesn't make much sense."

"Oh, Dad!" Emily felt frustrated with her father's questions. "After she's been riding, Mum is going to see some friends. They all live on that side of the town – the same side that Millie lives."

"Ah, I see – that does begin to make a bit more sense. And you'll be alright waiting until whatever time it is that your mum is able to collect you?"

"I'll be fine. The only reason Mum will be late is because next year, she's hoping to go pony trekking with her friends and I think they want to look at what's on offer – read some brochures, search online – that sort of thing."

Emily seemed to feel a need to reassure her father and to provide him with explanations. It was almost as if, momentarily, they had swapped roles. He kept his observation to himself, however, and commented instead, "They'll certainly be in good time if they're not going until next year."

Emily gave a wry smile. "That's Mum, though, isn't it? She likes everything to be planned – organised."

Dan hoped that he had not drawn any more information from her than she had wanted to give. She had voluntarily told him about her mother's holiday plans for the following year and, other than reassuring himself about Emily's safety, he had not made any attempts to fish for information. It was a pipedream that Sue would ever contact him except when it was absolutely necessary, but then, if he kept better contact with Josh, he would not need to rely so heavily on Emily's snippets of information.

Whilst he felt a sense of futility about the lack of communication between him and Sue, he believed that they would both always ensure that they took a significant interest in their children's lives. Besides, he thought, although Josh and Emily were at slightly different stages, both were gradually entering into adulthood and could be expected to develop a much greater degree of autonomy than they had previously had.

Dan had hoped that he would have Emily's company for a little longer but that was pre-empted by the honking of a car horn from the lane outside the cottage. Emily went to the window.

"It's Mum. She said she would be a bit earlier this week."

"Only..."

"Only what, Dad?"

"Only, you forgot to tell me..."

"Ooops – silly me!" She gave a slightly embarrassed laugh.

Dan gave her a smile. Her parents' failure to communicate was not her fault – but then, he too was still learning – they were all still learning – about the differences that their altered family circumstances had made. He decided to change tack.

"Have you got your books? You'll probably need them on Monday–" treating her as though she was still in Year 6 rather than Year 10.

"Yes, they're all in my little bag." Responding in kind, she held it up to make her point.

"Off you go then." He laughed and bent to give her a kiss, noting as he did that he no longer needed to bend so far as had been necessary, even a short while ago.

Having accepted his kiss on her cheek, Emily opened the door and was halfway along the path before she remembered to turn and call back to him, "See you next week!"

He smiled and waved goodbye before retreating into the cottage. Moments later, a glance out of the front window told him that Sue had already driven off. Emily's cheerful presence was gone. The solitude of the cottage fell around him like the thick folds of a cloak, leaving him to reflect that Sue knew what she was doing that afternoon, Emily knew what she was doing but he had not the faintest idea how he was going to occupy his time for the rest of the day. His questions to Emily about her day would have been better posed to himself.

* * *

It had been almost a month since Dan had last heard from Anne and left to himself again, he found his thoughts returning to the nagging anxiety about her silence – a concern that he had sought to push away by constantly keeping himself occupied. Now, however, he found himself with the unplanned remainder of the weekend before him and, try as he might, he could not prevent his mind from straying in Anne's direction.

He paused to think, for a moment, returning for the thousandth time to the question as to whether he had in some way offended her the last time that they had met – but he could think of nothing that might have upset her. Instead, his clearest memory was of her waving to him, as he pulled away in his car.

There might be some other problem, he supposed, of a completely different kind. Perhaps George had effectively imprisoned her? She had joked about such a possibility but perhaps her husband was really capable of doing such a thing. He had also had the idea that she might be having persistent problems with her mobile phone – but it was not a notion that he had entertained for more than a few seconds; problems with phones were usually resolved in a day or two. Also, during the schools' summer break, when Anne had wanted to see him, she had driven over to the cottage one afternoon. He remembered it well – it was not a memory that was likely to fade; it was, though, one that only served to make him feel more uncomfortable about her prolonged silence, and her unexplained absence from his company.

He decided that he needed to overcome his worries about being seen in the vicinity of Anne's house. He wanted to understand what was going on and it seemed that the only way to do that was to drive over there and see if he could find any clues as to what was happening.

Having made his decision, Dan climbed into his car and set out through the lanes. He thought again about the events and the various means that he had used to keep his obsession with Anne at bay; he had thrown himself into the events of the summer term; he was now in regular contact with his son and daughter, and he was attempting, however unsuccessfully, to deal with the lack of communication with his wife. He was making a substantial effort to come to terms with the almost certain loss of his marriage and with an imminent need to find a new job.

It was fortunate that, in the whole journey across to Anne's house, he encountered no more than just two or three other cars and when he came across the first car travelling in the opposite direction, he had to brake hard. There was no room, at that point, for more than a single vehicle and his mind had been far away; he quickly reversed to a wider point in the road.

The other driver scowled as Dan let him past. He was not surprised; they had come close to a head-on collision. After that, he drove with greater attention and circumspection. He was now also approaching the hill on which Anne's house was situated. There was a large entrance to a farm drive on his left and he pulled into it for a minute or two whilst he thought about what he would do when he arrived. If possible, he wanted to talk to Anne alone, but he had no idea what he would find when he got there; she might be out, she might have visitors, her husband might be at home for the weekend – there were numerous possibilities. He thought about the road outside Anne's house. It was usually quiet and little traffic went that way. He should be able to drive slowly enough to see if anyone had already parked on the drive. If there was no-one there, he would risk knocking on the door in the hope that Anne was at home and on her own.

It was not much of a plan, but he pulled back on to the road and drove the last half mile to Anne's house. As he had thought, he had the lane to himself and he was able to drive slowly past the house, thereby giving himself time to see if there were any vehicles parked at the front. There were none. He drove on a little way, found a field gate with a wide splay, turned around and drove back.

His heart was thumping hard as he pulled the car round onto Anne's drive. He knew that his actions were not at all wise – but doubts and imagined jealousies had tormented him now for weeks, particularly following Eleanor's tirade, and he did not want to leave Anne's house without discovering whatever it was that had caused her silence and absence from his life.

He would make no attempt that day to hide his car. He parked it in full view of both the house and anyone who might be passing along the road. He made his way across to the front door and rang the bell. There was no immediate response, so he waited. He was about to ring the bell again when he heard footsteps approaching the door from the other side. Slowly, the door opened.

It was Anne. Immediately, he sought to search her eyes with his but having answered the door, she simply opened it wider and motioned him to come in. As on his previous visits, he followed her along the short passage, anticipating that they would be going into the lounge; instead, she stopped at a single door on the right of the passage, opened it and went in.

Dan followed her, slowly making sense as he did so of the position of the room in relation to others that he been in before. Gradually, he recognised that they were in an anteroom at one end of the lounge. He had noticed, but not registered, the door from the other side when Anne had previously taken him through to the lounge.

The room, itself the size of a lounge in many another house, was pleasant enough. On one side of its rectangular plan was a set of windows, set beside the larger windows that ran along the front of the house. The natural light in the room flickered a little as wisteria, growing along the walls outside, was caught in the gentle breeze of the afternoon and wielded a curious dancing effect of the light, on the surfaces of the interior. Anne settled herself in an armchair, its floral fabric, high back, and enclosing arms seeming both to contain and enthrone her.

She had slipped off her shoes and tucked her feet under her. Her blue dress covered her knees and revealed just a little of her neck and shoulders, above which her blonde hair fell to the sides of her face revealing the same gentle features, firmly defined but expressive lips and smiling blue eyes that he had loved from the first time that he had been alone with her and had been able to appreciate the beauty of her reality.

Today, however, there was a difference. The eyes that his memory always recalled as smiling were not smiling but contained instead a sombre clouding of emotion. He seated himself, unbidden, on a chair that matched the one in which Anne was sitting. Now that he was finally in her presence again, he did not know where to start.

Anne saved him the trouble and asked simply, "How are you, Dan?"

"I'm ok – alright, I guess. I have been better." There was a silence that hung between them until Dan broke it again.

"I've been trying to contact you for weeks. I sent you message after message. Why didn't you reply?" His facial expression implored her to answer.

She looked at him for a moment and then away, as if casting around the room for the response that she would make.

Eventually, she said, "I did not answer you, Dan, because I could not."

His expression softened a little. Perhaps it was as he had sometimes imagined. George had imprisoned her in the 'high tower' as she had all too meaningfully joked on a previous occasion.

"George was here. He stopped you from answering, I suppose. Perhaps you've been away? Or perhaps you were ill? I don't know... I just need to know why you never got back to me." His limping speech tailed off into silence.

The firmness of her facial expression returned. "We can't do this anymore, Dan."

It took a moment for her words to sink in – and then, it was as though the ground was giving way beneath him.

"What do you mean, Anne? Of course we can continue..."

"No, Dan," she said with a deadening finality. "We can't see each other anymore. We both know that. We've known it for a while."

Now it was fight or flight. He chose to fight. What would it say of him if he let her go in such feeble fashion?

He crossed the floor to her chair and pulled her to her feet, flinging his arms around her.

She turned her head away from him, but he held her tightly round the waist and forced her to face him so that he kissed her on the lips with a firmness that lacked any control.

She spluttered and somehow struggled free. He thought for a moment that she was going to wipe her lips, but she said angrily, "There, you've had your kiss! Now go!"

"If you think it's as easy as that for me, you…!"

His words spilled out but were lost as he seized her once more by the waist and tried again to kiss her. For several moments they struggled but then, whether by accident or design, found themselves in a heap on the floor, sprawling on the carpet between the chairs.

There they continued to struggle until Dan, noticing that Anne's dress had ridden up, felt a surge of long suppressed desire. Driven by his instincts, he tried to pull her to him. This time, however, she was quicker, and she wriggled away from him, finally kneeling at the other end of the rug, her hands flat on the floor and with her feet tucked beneath her. She glowered at him, her face angry and defiant.

He had never seen her like this before. There was something profoundly attractive, even erotic, in her flushed complexion and her hair falling across her flashing eyes.

"What do you want, Dan?" She practically spat out the words, demanding an answer.

"I love you. I thought you loved me. Why have you changed?" His voice softened, ending, he barely dared admit to himself, in a pathetic plea… "I want you."

She kept her position, an angry passion further darkening her beauty.

"You can't have me, Dan! We can't be together… We both know that! There's nothing here for you!"

Her anger met asymmetrically with his desperation.

His thoughts raced at lightning speed through his choices. He could test this unexplained change in her feelings. Even if at this moment she was rejecting him, perhaps – afterwards – she might once more see things differently… She had brought him to this moment. He had to make a decision. Was he weak? Did he not love her so much that, if necessary, he would take her by force?

But that was precisely the problem... He loved her to the depth of his being, and because he loved her, he wanted her to freely choose to love him. If she did not love him, he could not coerce her into doing so. Nor was it in his love to force her to satisfy his longing; he would not do that to her, even in his present extremity. That would not be love as he knew it.

He stood, holding her gaze in his. Then he turned and walked out of the room leaving first the ante-room door ajar behind him and then the front door. He did not stop or pause. His actions followed one upon another, in mechanical fashion. He did not want to give himself time to change his mind and before he was aware of how he came to be in his car, he was driving down the lane and heading towards the road that would take him back to the brooding solitude of the cottage.

At the end of the lane, he went unthinkingly through the motions of checking left and right, deciding at the last moment that he could not face going home. He needed, then, to turn right towards Sedgewater rather than left. There were no cars in sight. Nothing. He made the turn.

Suddenly, in his peripheral vision, there was a blur of grey and a loud bang. His car was shoved violently to the right. The engine stalled.

Hastily, he checked the mirror. In his confusion, he still saw nothing. He restarted the engine and decided to pull over to the safety of the grass verge whilst he sorted himself out. He pulled over and gazed before him along the road ahead.

To his surprise, there was a young man running back towards him from a silver-grey car which, like Dan's, had been pulled over onto the verge. The road was empty, so Dan opened the driver's door and got out to see what the approaching stranger had to say. He had no idea what had just happened, other than that he must have been in collision with the other car.

As the stranger arrived, slightly out of breath, Dan began to apologise.

"I'm really sorry ...I just didn't see..."

"No, no mate, I didn't see you either. Here, let's check your car."

Dan was amazed by the apparent good nature of the other driver. He followed him around the car whilst they jointly made a show of inspecting whatever damage there was to be found. In the event, there was almost nothing – a faint scuff from grey paintwork and a panel by the wheel arch that had popped out of alignment. Without asking Dan's agreement, the stranger pushed it firmly back into place and then, checking that it was once again flush with the other bodywork, said, "There… no real harm done."

Dan nodded, as if in a daze. "No," he said, "next to nothing. But what about your car?"

"Nah, nothing either, a tiny scrape but you can barely see it. If you're ok, I say we just leave it. I'm in a bit of hurry anyway." He looked at Dan with one eyebrow raised.

Dan, in turn, studied the other driver for a moment. He was young, as first noticed, quite tall, had dark curly hair and was casually dressed in faded jeans, loose grey sweatshirt, and a blue windcheater jacket.

The stranger's apparent agitation testified that he was indeed in a hurry, but there were other things about the situation that did not make sense. Dan was sure that he had been in the wrong and had had every expectation that the younger driver would be angry. He glanced down the road towards the other car. It was a silver-grey, two seat Mercedes. It looked very expensive, and Dan wondered how likely it was that the person in front of him was actually the owner. Perhaps it was borrowed – or even stolen? Perhaps he was not insured? He quickly decided, though, that he was not going to ask, especially since he felt only too aware that it was his fault that he had not seen the Mercedes before he pulled out from the junction. It seemed that they both had reasons not to make a fuss about the accident.

His mind and gaze came back to the stranger – who was, by that time, waiting impatiently for an answer.

"No, of course," he said. "It's the tiniest scrape. Not worth making a fuss about. Are you sure you're ok?"

"Yeah, I'm fine, mate! I'm sorry about the bump but since there's no real damage to the cars – or us – I say we call it quits."

Dan nodded his confirmation. "Yes, no problem."

The stranger gave a grimace that Dan assumed was the approximation of a smile and said, "Ok then, I think we're done here. I gotta go."

With that he turned on his heel and jogged back down the road. Moments later, there was a sporty roar from the Mercedes' engine and the driver was on his way, speeding towards the hill ahead and then out of sight. Dan climbed back into his own car, still in something of a daze but forcing himself to pay attention to each and every action. For a catalogue of reasons, he needed to find a quiet place where he could sit and get himself back together – or, at least, as 'together' as he was likely to be in the circumstances.

* * *

He drove into Sedgewater where he quickly found a space in the car park that he now habitually used. It was a short walk from there into the town centre. It was early afternoon and some two hours since he had said goodbye to Emily. With the disastrous episode at Anne's house having just taken place, he did not want to bump into his daughter again – or, for that matter, Sue – but the town was busy and the chance of either of them spotting him amongst the bustle of shoppers was slim.

He found a café in the corner of a small precinct and tucked himself away with a cup of coffee. He had remained calm during the brush with the Mercedes but now, as he raised his coffee cup to his mouth, he found that his hand was visibly shaking. He supposed that it was delayed reaction and put it aside as his thoughts returned again to the incident at Anne's house.

The memory of it immediately distressed him in a number of ways. Firstly, there was his awareness that for several minutes, he had almost completely lost control of himself. He still could not understand how he and Anne had found themselves on the floor, but the fact that he had tried several times to hold and kiss her when she had clearly wanted no such thing, now came back to haunt him. She could, he supposed, take it up with the police although, as he thought about it a little longer, it seemed unlikely. It had been an embarrassing incident, but he had limited its potential to hurt them both by walking away from it. There were other reasons, too, that Anne would not want their affair to be highlighted again; seemingly, George had first wrung a 'confession' out of her some time ago and would be beside himself if he learned that Dan had been at the house again. In addition to that, Dan felt sure that the incident would have been as painful for her as it had been for him and that, as such, was a mutual humiliation that needed no further exacerbation; like the collision on his way into Sedgewater, it would probably resolve itself into a matter of damage limitation.

Other damage, however, was well beyond limitation or quick repair. As much as he might wish the pain of separation from Anne to pass, he knew that it would be a long time before it would dwindle to nothingness. So much for Love, he thought, the subject of so much poetry, song, and hypocritical twaddle. Now he was learning the hard way that it was ruled by the thoughts of others and that you could not love who you wanted to love. There were rules, social conventions to be considered and words such as 'lust' and 'adultery' that could be used to shame 'offenders' back into the ways of conformity. Truth and honesty were meaningless in such a web of deception.

Not aware of how the afternoon was passing, he continued to sit over the remains of his cold and singularly unappealing cup of coffee. A sense of desolation and unending dreariness filled his mind. The loss of his marriage, his home and for a while, his children – he had somehow been borne along through all of it by his relationship with Anne. Now, with the suddenness of death, she was gone. He would see her no more.

Absent-mindedly, he picked up his cup. Along with his feelings of loss, there was also a deep sense of anger. Time needed to pass; he had to put some distance between himself and the afternoon's events. He put the coffee cup to his lips, unthinkingly draining it to the last. It was not a matter of surprise that the dregs were bitter.

* * *

CHAPTER 21

THE SMELL OF BURNING

The summer term wore on and once more, successive dry, hot days brought with them the threat of drought; in some parts of the country, there were increasing reports of serious difficulties being encountered and hints of desperation had begun to appear in news reports. So, it was to Dan's surprise that for the time being, the school had sufficient water supply to remain open.

Dan meanwhile had striven to keep his emotions about his private life away from his work and from the other teaching staff. The heat at night, however, was making it difficult to sleep, and both children and adults were struggling to cope with the demands of school. Dan was not exempt from these pressures and found himself trying to deal with a steady growth in the number of problems that came his way until finally, the breakdown of his affair with Anne was enough to push him beyond the bounds of his self-control and patience.

A single event brought it all to a head. The weather was hot but tempered a little by a strong breeze. The whole school seemed to be outdoors. Children sat or played in groups beneath the shade of trees or under the extended canopy that had been erected at the upper end of the school's playing field. A few, dotted in small groups across the field, were engaged in games of their own under the watchful eyes of roving lunchtime supervisors.

Dan had just left the staffroom and was making his way to check on how well the arrangements on the field were working when he was met by a small gaggle of children running towards him. Something was clearly worrying them.

"Mr 'Olroyd, they've got out...!"

"They're going to run away…!"

The general gist of what the children were saying was clear and Dan was immediately concerned but needed to know more.

"Just tell me carefully, Sita, who's got out?"

"It's Edward and Claire…"

"It's more than that," interrupted George, one of the Year 4 group and one of Edward's friends.

"There are six of them! Mr 'Olroyd," yelled Evelyn, another Year 4. "They're on the road!"

Immediately, Dan felt a sinking sensation in his stomach.

"Quickly," he said to Evelyn, "show me exactly where they've gone!"

He set off as fast as he could across the field with Evelyn at his side. The other children ran along with them and shortly, they all arrived at a gap in the hedge. Mystified – Dan had never seen it before – he pushed his way through only to find to his horror, that on the far side several lengths of wood in the fence behind the hedge had been removed.

"Which way did they go, Evelyn?" Dan called back to his guide.

"I think they went to the trees, Mr 'Olroyd," replied Evelyn.

Dan looked along to his right to where a clump of large trees could be seen. It looked to be some two hundred yards away on the opposite side of the road. He turned quickly back towards the children. By this time, George had joined Evelyn at the head of the group on the other side of the hedge.

"Evelyn, George – all of you! Go back to Mrs Cook! She's just over there with Mrs Wardle." He pointed to where the two lunchtime supervisors were standing. "Evelyn, tell Mrs Cook I need her over here now! Then, all of you stay with Mrs Wardle."

The children immediately set off at speed towards the two women and Dan picked his way through the gap in the fence and onto the road. Eileen Cook's response seemed to be taking too long. Setting off along the road, he pulled out his school phone, found her number and rang it. She answered immediately.

"Hello Dan," she responded.

"Eileen, we've got a problem here…"

"The children told me. What do you want me to do?"

"Evelyn thinks the 'runaways' have come along the road towards the trees. I need your help, so I want you to follow me."

"Okay, I'll be there as fast as I can…"

"Take care – and keep an eye on the road!"

By this time, having jogged towards the trees, he was just a few yards away; as he glanced back to check that he was clear to cross the road, he could see that Eileen had emerged from the fence and was rapidly running to join him. It was fortunate that Eileen was a play leader and fitter than some of the other lunchtime staff.

Once on the other side, a large open gate led through a hedgerow and onto a dusty farm track that ran across the fields to a distant group of farm buildings. Glancing immediately to his right, Dan saw that, on the other side of the gate, a grass bank mounted to the copse of trees. He went through the gate and began to climb the bank, discovering as he did so that someone had dropped a clean tissue on the grass. He paused to listen for voices but despite the warmth of the day, there was a breeze and he struggled to hear anything other than the sound of its movement amongst the leaves and branches.

Eileen had now reached the bottom of the bank and scrambled up to meet him.

"Any sign of them yet?" she asked, puffing slightly as she reached the top of the bank.

"Perhaps," said Dan. "I found a fresh tissue on the grass. One of the children could have dropped it."

"If they are here, it should only take a few minutes to find them."

"I certainly hope so," replied Dan. "It might be quicker if you take the far end of the copse and I work from the trees nearest the road. We can use the phones to stay in touch."

"Right," agreed Eileen, "I'll get going…"

Dan had chosen to start from the end nearest the road because, if the children were playing there, they might still be straying onto the road. As he approached the trees, however, he could see that the hedgerow at that point was dense and impenetrable. He began to work his way through the trees towards the centre of the copse whilst making a quick phone call to Amanda to keep her in touch with what was happening.

Pocketing the phone again, he continued towards the centre of the copse. The noise from the trees was now significant as the breeze moved amongst the upper branches. Dan listened hard for the sound of children's voices but could hear only the constant motion of the trees.

He continued scrambling his way along until, suddenly, he stopped. He listened; still he could hear nothing. But there…there it was again…not a sound but a smell…the unmistakable smell of woodsmoke. Quickly, he rang Eileen,

"Hello?"

"Hi, Eileen – I can smell woodsmoke. Can you smell it too?"

"Yes, I can…Oh! Now I can see the smoke– it's quite thick."

"Where are you?" yelled Dan against the now incessant noise of the trees.

"I'm nearly at the centre of the copse."

"Right, don't put yourself in danger – but keep going. I'm headed that way too and I'll be there as fast as I can."

Dan tried to increase his speed, but he was hampered by tree roots and thick boughs that hung close to the ground. Then, to his relief, the trees thinned, and he began to glimpse an area where the sun was able to penetrate. Alarmingly, though, he could now see woodsmoke swirling thickly amongst the trees – and, with both relief and concern, he could suddenly hear children's voices. He scrambled faster until at last, he was fully in sunlight and standing in a clearing fringed by trees and bracken.

Peering ahead, he could see that the smoke was not coming from the clearing but from amongst the bracken at the edge. Someone was waving. It was Eileen. Together, they hurried towards the base of the billowing smoke. The children's voices were now very clear, and Dan could hear persistent coughing. A small group of children, partly concealed by swirling smoke, spilled into the clearing. Seeing first Eileen and then Dan, one of the children began shouting – almost shrieking in desperation – "Miss Cook! Mr 'Olroyd – Gemma's on fire!"

"Oh my God!" muttered Dan and meaning it. By now, he and Eileen had arrived coughing and spluttering, at the source of the fire.

"Help me, Eileen!" yelled Dan. "We've got to get her out!"

Eileen needed no bidding and began pushing through the bracken to where the fire was blazing. Dan looked to his right and could see that just behind the fire the children had built a shelter of branches and bracken and that it was from there that he could hear the screams of a child. Though partly blinded by smoke, he picked up a piece of branch and began dismembering the shelter until he could see inside. There, his heart in his mouth, he saw Gemma, her clothes already alight.

With Eileen's help, Dan pulled the panicking child out of the shelter and stumbled with her in his arms onto the grass of the clearing. Neither of them had a coat on such a hot day so they rolled the child carefully but firmly on the ground until the flames were extinguished.

Forgetful of any trouble they might be in, the other children clustered around, anxiously trying to see what had happened. Gemma sobbed and moaned whilst Eileen began to reassure her and tend her as best she could.

Dan, still coughing from the effects of the smoke, rang 999, requesting an ambulance and the fire brigade. Next, he called Amanda, to confirm that he and Eileen had found all the children but also to let her know that he had called the emergency services.

As he finished the call, however, Eileen caught his arm and pointed across to where the shelter had been.

"Can we put that out?" she yelled. Dan looked quickly to where she was pointing and could see that the remains of the children's fire had set alight to the bracken and detritus from the trees.

"No chance!" shouted Dan in reply. "We have to get the children – and ourselves – out of here!"

Eileen looked up from where she was kneeling next to the injured girl.

"Gemma won't be able to walk, Dan,"

"Ok, I'll have to carry her."

Eileen pulled a face but helped him to lift Gemma from the ground.

The children were still clustered around, so he said to them. "Do any of you know a quick way out?"

"Yes, I do," said Edward. "I come here all the time."

There was no time for further questions, so he said, "Right, Edward, you're the leader. Get us out of here!

Then, together and moving as swiftly as they could, they all set off with Edward leading the way.

Edward's knowledge of the copse was instantly apparent. He took them off on a path that was only just visible amongst the bracken, but which skirted the edge of the trees. On such a narrow path, the children fell naturally into single file. At first, they seemed to be headed in the general direction of the farm buildings but then the path bent quickly round to the left and Dan could see that their course would take them to the bank and then the farm track.

They were making good progress, but Dan was already only too aware of Gemma's weight, slight though it was, and was longing to find himself on a more even surface. With relief, he saw that they were now approaching the bank and would soon be down on the track. The children easily slid down the bank, but Dan needed Eileen's help to get Gemma and himself safely onto the surface below. Then, as they checked that the whole group was still present, they all caught sight of what was happening behind them. Disbelief and horror spread across their faces as they looked back.

At first, they had been only aware of the thickening smoke as they made their way across to the farm track but now flames could be seen leaping up the height of the trees, setting fire to them as if they were giant torches.

"I hope the fire service gets here quickly!" shouted Dan to Eileen. As he spoke, he moved closer to her.

"This isn't a safe place, Dan," she said. "I think we need to move."

He agreed – although it meant returning along the road, with the children between them. Under Dan's instructions, the children understood the need to keep out of the road and together, they quickly set off in single file with Eileen at the front and Dan at the rear.

Such was the layout of the school site that it was an appreciable distance round to the school's main entrance so Dan had already decided that, if necessary, they would go back through the gaps in the fence and the hedge. Gemma, though, was moaning softly and clinging to him. She was badly in need of medical attention and taking her back through the fence and the hedge was not an option. He pulled out the phone to contact Amanda, but on the road behind them, they began to hear the growing cacophony of the Emergency Service vehicles, as they approached.

Despite the smoke that was now billowing across the road, the ambulance crew quickly spotted them. They drove carefully past and stopped just a little ahead of them in a small layby. Moments later, Dan and Eileen ushered the children towards the ambulance so that Gemma could be given immediate attention and the other children could be checked over. The children, though, were shouting and pointing excitedly to the fire engine that had drawn up by the copse. The fire crew were running out hoses whilst two more of their number were setting pulling out signs and barriers from a Land Rover that had now drawn up behind the fire engine.

Dan, however, was preoccupied with the safety of the children. He phoned Amanda and she answered immediately.

"Thank goodness, Dan," she said. "Where are you now?"

He quickly confirmed that he and Eileen had all the children in their care, that they had been checked over by the ambulance crew, that they needed to get them back to the school.

"Right, we'll get the minibus round to you."

"Ok, Amanda," said Dan. "We'll be waiting, in the layby."

"Is there anything else that you urgently need?" asked Amanda.

"Yes, the ambulance crew have checked the children over, but they'll be taking Gemma Harris to hospital so..."

"Okay, Dan, I'll deal with that next. We'll also arrange to check again on the other children when they get here. Now – is there anything else that you urgently need?"

"A stiff whisky?" said Dan.

"Apart from that?"

* * *

By the time that Dan, Eileen and 'the runaways' arrived back in the school, the classrooms were buzzing with news of the escapade and teachers were having to decide how best to manage children who were unlikely to focus on the afternoon's work. Amanda and her PA, Pauline, set to work contacting the parents of the children who had taken part in the incident, offering them the choice of collecting them early or leaving them in school until the end of the session; most opted to take them home. Dan did nor envy Amanda and Pauline, and appreciated that he had not been asked to share the task. Explaining what had happened would not be easy.

Meanwhile, Amanda had assigned Moira Haddon, a TA who often worked with Dan's class, to pick up the work that he had planned for the afternoon. Dan did his best to clean up but the smell of woodsmoke still clung to his clothing. Pauline had already told him that he would need to see Amanda but, with an unpleasant taste still lingering in his mouth, he went to the staffroom first, in search of a glass of water.

Emerging again into the corridor, Pauline was waiting for him.

"I thought I might find you here, Dan. Amanda's finished contacting parents for the moment – but she needs to talk to you."

"Of course," said Dan. "I'll get over there straight away – it's just that I still have the taste of smoke in my mouth and can't seem to get rid of it."

"Perhaps I could make you both a cup of tea?" suggested Pauline.

"Oh, yes please – that would be really helpful."

He hurried on ahead, arriving at Amanda's office door. It was slightly ajar, and she beckoned him to go in.

"Thank goodness you're here, Dan. I'm hoping you can help me clear up the details of what happened at lunchtime." She motioned him to sit down and moved to sit next to him, taking her tablet computer with her. She gave a wry smile and wrinkled her nose as she drew closer to him, saying, "I could guess where you've been – even if I didn't know."

Pauline arrived with the tea and placed it on a small table in front of them.

Dan gratefully took a sip from his cup but then went through the entire incident, pausing just occasionally to answer Amanda's questions.

Finally, she said, "Thank you, Dan – in fact, thank you to both you and Eileen Cook for acting so decisively. It's fortunate that we've managed to get all the children back, although I'm still waiting for further news about Gemma."

Dan nodded. "We did the best that we could, Amanda. As soon as the flames began spreading to the trees, we simply had to get out..."

"Yes, of course – you and Eileen did exactly the right things. And had you not managed to get there when you did, I hate to think what would have happened... Meanwhile, the farmer who owns the copse has reported the fire to the police so we can expect to hear from them."

"It was already well alight when the fire brigade arrived."

"Yes – it seems as though it was. Although they tried to save what they could, I think there's little of it left. With the drought and the breeze that's blowing today, conditions for a fire must have been almost perfect." She paused but then said, "As soon as we can, we'll have to speak to the children about it. We need to know exactly how the fire started."

Dan nodded in agreement. "I think two of the children have been taken home, but we could speak to the other three."

Amanda nodded thoughtfully. "When we talk to them," she said, "I want to know how it came about that none of the lunchtime supervisors saw them by the hedge. Then, secondly, I want to know how they were able to remove the planks in what was supposedly a childproof fence."

She glanced at her watch. "There's just an hour before the end of the afternoon session. We'll see the ones who are still here, and the others will have to wait until tomorrow morning."

"I'll get straight on to it," replied Dan.

* * *

By mid-morning the following day, Dan and Amanda had interviewed all the children other than Gemma who had been kept in hospital overnight as a precaution.

It emerged from the children's account that, inspired by a television programme they had seen, Claire and Edward had wanted an 'adventure'. In talking about the programme, several of the other Year 4s had decided that they also wanted to share in the adventure and had followed Claire and Edward, through the hedge and fence and along to the copse, where they had decided to set up camp. Between them, the children had built a 'bivvy' or bivouac and then decided to light a fire so that they could cook some food – although they had no idea where the food was going to come from. It was Gemma's misfortune that she had been in the 'bivvy' when it caught fire – which was also the point at which Dan and Eileen had arrived.

Events had then followed a path that both Dan and Amanda were still working through. Unsurprisingly, the landowner and local wildlife groups were livid about the destruction of the copse and there was talk of legal action being taken against the School Trust. Lurid comments and speculation had begun to appear in 'social media' conversations in several of which Dan was accused of assaulting the child whose clothing had caught fire and the Academy Trust was also facing a campaign under the banner 'How Safe Are Our Children?'.

Dan sought to keep a sense of proportion about it all by doing as much as he could to respond to Amanda's questions. A community police officer was helpful in confirming that, two days before, a late evening car accident had impacted the school's fence and that because damage to the fence was thought to be minor, follow-up with the school had not been thought to be necessary. It had then been easy for the children to remove the laths of wood loosened by the accident.

The situation with the lunchtime staff, though, was a little different. When he reviewed it, Dan had to conclude that since the area in which the children had been allowed to play was large, adequate supervision was difficult. Before the incident had occurred, parents had expressed their appreciation that the children had a large amount of 'green space' in which to play – and the freedom that the children had was thought to have minimised the usual squabbles and disputes between them. Now, however, there was a widespread view that lunchtime supervision had been inadequate and that the children's play activities should have been confined to a smaller area. He found it difficult to disagree.

He fed his responses back to Amanda, doing his best to time-share between his class and the need to get to the bottom of the incident. Ironically, although he was concerned about what the children had done, it seemed to him that the children, especially Edward and Claire, had been motivated by exactly the kind of imagination – and even creativity – the school generally tried to encourage. Although the incident was bound to be seen as utterly irresponsible by adults, it was clear to Dan it had been born out of childish innocence and not from any mischief or malice.

Fortunately, news from the hospital about Gemma was good. Her clothing had been alight long enough to have caused minor burns to her skin, but Dan and Eileen's prompt action had saved her from any long-term harm or disfigurement – something for which Gemma and her parents were appreciative now that the immediate shock of the incident was receding.

* * *

Amanda, meanwhile, was caught in a dilemma. She was pleased and grateful for the action so quickly taken by Dan and Eileen – but, unfortunately for Dan, had it not been for the situation created by the children's escape and the ensuing fire in the copse, she would have been dealing with a series of complaints that had been made against him. It seemed to her that the timing of the complaints was unfortunate, coming as they did shortly before his redundancy and against the background of his unsuccessful job applications to other Academies in the area.

Over the week following the fire incident, she was increasingly aware that Dan's mental health was continuing to deteriorate. Reports came to her of him snapping at staff, of lack of tact in dealing with parents, and of a decrease in his patience with children. More seriously, he had shown his appreciation of a TA's offer of assistance by kissing her on the cheek. Excessive reactions such as this and his general unpredictability were said by some staff to be making them anxious about working with him.

Dan, meanwhile, believed that he could not share any of his thoughts or feelings with Amanda – or, for that matter, with anyone else. Ever since the end of his affair with Anne, he had been fighting a losing battle with himself. The long heat and drought of the spring and summer had affected everybody's patience, including his own – and now it had all come together in the latest events at school – in which, despite his best attempts to do his job conscientiously, ill-founded complaints were being made against him. It was also difficult for him not to dwell on the separation from his family and the pain that he felt through being made redundant – which he saw as deeply unfair in view of the service he had given over a number of years.

Conscious that she was pacing up and down the space in front of her desk, Amanda decided that she could no longer postpone a discussion of the situation. The staffing in the school that afternoon was also such that if she had a short chat with Dan, there was a chance that she might be able to head off problems that she could now see looming before Dan's official send-off at the end of the term. There was also a risk, though, that the situation would misfire, particularly if the reports of Dan's volatility in the last few days were not exaggerations… She decided that, however reluctant she might feel about it, she had better ensure that the various eventualities were covered.

* * *

Given the events of previous days, Dan was not particularly surprised when he received an internal message from Amanda on his school mobile. She needed to see him right away. A senior teaching assistant would supervise his class until lunchtime. Could he ensure that his class had sufficient work to take them through to the end of the afternoon?

He felt uncomfortable about the message because he disliked having to leave his class mid-session and at short notice, but he had to comply with Amanda's request. Moira Haddon, a teaching assistant Dan had often worked with, arrived about five minutes later to find his pupils engaged with the tasks he had set for them. Dan assumed that whatever it was that Amanda wanted to speak to him about, it was a matter of some importance, so he hurried across to the administrative building.

He entered and paused at the school office but there was no sign of the school administrator. It made no difference, he thought; Amanda was expecting him. He walked a little further along the corridor, knocked at Amanda's door, easing it open as he did so. She beckoned him to go in and pointed to the chair that, in recent days, had almost become identifiable as his. He seated himself, listening expectantly for whatever it was she had to say.

"Thanks for coming over, Dan," Amanda began. "It's fortunate that Moira was available to provide cover for your class."

He nodded. Amanda glanced at him briefly, then down at the papers in front of her. Finally, she left her desk and went to sit in the chair that she generally reserved for one-to-one discussions. Dan raised an eyebrow, still waiting.

"This is rather difficult, Dan, but it's something that I must talk to you about…"

"Oh?"

"As you came in, I was glancing through a number of complaints from both staff and parents with regard to your behaviour towards them."

Dan's expression indicated surprise but he said nothing, so she continued, "Unfortunately, one of the incidents in question was relayed to the Principal before I'd even had a chance to talk to you about it."

She went to her desk and picked up a paper copy of the complaint, returning with it to her seat.

"Really?" said Dan, quickly rummaging through his memory in an attempt to identify whatever 'incident' it might be that Amanda was talking about.

"Yes – the complaint that went to the Principal was that you forced yourself on one of the teaching assistants, Bryony Pascoe."

He remembered it then but found himself spluttering in disbelief. "Forced myself on her!?" He took a moment to draw a deep breath. "I remember kissing her on the cheek. I did nothing else to her."

Amanda knew though that, according to the complaint, there had been more to it.

"The complaint I have in front of me here says that you pinned her arms to her sides and tried to kiss her on the lips. In addition to that, your behaviour was witnessed by another TA who was in the room at the time."

"It wasn't like that at all," protested Dan. "Bryony had just helped me with the Year 4s when I went to speak to them about last week's incident."

Amanda looked at him with an expression of disbelief. "I can understand that you may have felt grateful to her – but giving her a hug and a kiss seems well beyond the usual expressions of gratitude. Don't you think that, to put it mildly, that was rather excessive?"

"For a start, I dispute that I gave her a 'hug'. As for the kiss, it is true that I gave her a kiss on the cheek – and, admittedly, I could see I'd offended her. I did apologise to her – immediately."

"Her complaint says that you tried to kiss her on the lips but that she twisted her head away from you so that, as a result, you kissed her on the cheek…"

"There's nothing else I can add to what I've said." He gazed wearily at the carpet in front of him, wondering how he could have made such a 'spur of the moment' misjudgement.

"Unfortunately, Dan, however you see the situation, Bryony saw it differently. She has said that she's considering taking it up with her Union as a matter of 'sexual harassment'."

Amanda waited, trying to read whatever reaction was taking place inside Dan's head. For his part, Dan was experiencing a deep sense of futility – and frustration. It was all too clear to him that he had offended Bryony – and he was not altogether surprised that she had refused to accept his apology. Beyond that, there was little he could say. He had behaved stupidly. And now this latest offence would be added to the steadily accumulating pile of misdemeanours that was being heaped around him.

Frustration began to build into anger. He said, "It's bad enough being made redundant, Amanda. Why can't the Academy just leave it at that? For goodness' sake, a few more weeks and I'll be out of everybody's hair. Isn't that enough?"

Amanda sighed inwardly. She had known that working with Dan would be difficult – but she regretted that it was testing her professionalism to an extent that she had not previously appreciated.

"A complaint has been made, Dan. It has to be pursued by the Academy. I'm sure that you can see that."

He made no reply but sat glowering before her until, after a long, angry silence, he said, "So, what happens now?"

"That's not altogether for me to decide," she replied. The matter's being dealt with under 'The Grievance Procedure' and it has to run its course. As yet though, I've still to hear from the Principal. However, Dan, it seems to me that you are struggling at the moment – and that, perhaps, recent events are blurring your judgement. My suggestion is that you go home – and also, that you book an appointment with your GP."

Intended to take some of the heat out of the situation, her remark seemed to come without sufficient preface so that, instead, it had the opposite effect.

"Book an appointment with my GP? What on earth for? I'm not ill – I'm perfectly well! And what about the children in my class? What's supposed to happen to them whilst I'm sitting around at home?"

"You are not well – and, in my belief, you're suffering from depression. The last thing you should be doing this afternoon is teaching your class and I'm trying to tell you as your colleague – and your friend – that you need to go home."

Dan, though, was no longer listening and failed to recognise the sense in Amanda's plea.

"I'm not depressed!" he exclaimed, his voice rising almost to a shout. "Although I soon will be, if you force me to stay at home, twiddling my thumbs!"

Amanda flushed with irritation but held her nerve. "Nobody's forcing you to do anything, but I do strongly suggest that you make an appointment with your GP."

"And if I go back to my class, what then? What are you going to do?"

"Dan, in my judgement, the last thing you should be doing this afternoon is teaching a class of children!"

"I never thought I'd hear such nonsense from you, Amanda!" He was almost spluttering with rage. "I'm going back to my class. You can't stop me!"

It was, of course, a foolish thing to say and he had barely uttered the words before he began to regret them.

"I can stop you, Dan! And I will if you force me!" Amanda had risen from her chair.

He considered the situation for moment; as things were, he could only make it worse. He turned to her, glowering in fury, but knowing that he had to retreat. If nothing else, it would serve no good purpose if the children in his class saw him in his present mood.

"Alright! Have it your way. I'm going to the staff room. Then – don't worry yourself – I'll go home and get out of everybody's hair!"

She looked as if she was going to reply but he slammed out of the room before she could say anything more. She went to the window and watched him stride across the school site, in the direction of the staffroom. Hopefully, there would be no-one else there at that time of day. She would let a minute or two go by and then she would relieve Mrs Haddon. Dan had always had a 'soft spot' for Moira Haddon – one of those things that was more apparent to others than to Dan himself. She would send Moira across to the staffroom with Dan's beloved briefcase (how old-fashioned he was), but tell her not to get into conversation with him about what had just taken place. Then she would phone the supply teacher she had in reserve that afternoon to cover just such an eventuality as the one that had arisen.

Dan, meanwhile, sat in the staffroom drinking a glass of water. It was taking a while for his anger and indignation to subside, but he knew that there was little he could do except go back to the cottage and reflect on what Amanda had said. He remembered that his briefcase was still in the classroom. It would not have to matter. There was nothing in it that was of importance to him now. Any information that he needed about his professional association could be found on the internet – or via the phone.

He looked up as the staffroom door opened to admit Moira Haddon, rather clumsily lugging his briefcase as though it contained lead weights.

"What on Earth do you keep in this thing?" she asked. She dumped the briefcase next to the chair in which Dan was sitting.

Dan made no reply but smiled appreciatively. "Thanks, Moira."

Amanda had calculated well; Dan did not want to exhibit any signs of anger in front of Moira. Amanda had also told her not to linger in the staffroom, but she said, "I hope that you don't mind me saying so, but you look a bit 'out of sorts'. Would it help if I made a cup of tea?"

"No thanks, Moira. You're right though. I am 'a bit out of sorts'. Amanda has told me to go home. I was wondering about my briefcase – but now that you've brought it, I guess I have no excuse for staying."

He stood, picked up the briefcase and walked across to the door. Moira touched him on the arm. "Take care, Dan," she said. "You're better off out of this place."

Though intended as a kindly remark, he wondered what she meant. Perhaps there had been staffroom gossip? He decided, though, to give himself no time to ask.

"You're a good 'un, Moira," he commented and moved to give her a peck on the cheek – only to stop himself at the last moment. Instead, he smiled, patted her on the hand and then set off towards the car park. Now that he had begun to calm down, an hour or two at home taking stock of his position might be the best course after all. He was certainly not in the mood to spend any more time at Wellsprings that day than was absolutely necessary.

* * *

CHAPTER 22

DRIFTING

Slowly, he began to take Amanda's advice. No-one was making any demands of him and so, like a boat which has lost its moorings, he began to drift. Where Wellsprings Primary had provided the small world in which he worked and where he found some meaning in life, he now began to be increasingly detached from it. It was not where he was going to be in the future and, although he still had one or two obligations to fulfil there, he wanted to move on with his life.

At first, such a sentiment seemed oddly out of place because his life was almost static. The days came and went. He spent hours sitting under the parasol over the picnic table in the cottage's back garden. Now that he was no longer having to pacify staff who had become irritable in the continuous heat, he found that he could relax and return to noticing what was going on in the wider world around him.

That summer, though, people were finding it easier to recognise that the Climate Crisis was a reality and not some form of hyperbole invented by overwrought climate activists. The television twenty-four-hour news programmes were managing, for once, to get outside the immediate realms of human activity and to cover the almost complete loss of ice in the Arctic Ocean. There was much belated discussion, scientific or simply speculative, of how this long-anticipated event would affect the Earth's climatic regions, but also, incredibly to Dan's way of thinking, a certain rubbing of the hands at the prospect that shipping could now sail freely through the Arctic region and that communication between the countries of the Atlantic and the Pacific had become progressively easier in the Arctic's summer months. For some who saw the prospect of untrammelled wealth before them, there seemed to be nothing but celebration to be found in the newfound accessibility of oil, gas and minerals that had previously been locked away beneath the ice.

In the midst of such sentiments, Dan felt himself to be increasingly alienated from those around him. Far from any sense of celebration, he felt instead a sense that the Earth was careering towards states of existence in which there could be no certainty of any kind that the planet would continue to support the myriad forms of life that had evolved in the course of its history. If he thought about it like that, what was the point of worrying about the things that were filling his waking hours – books, television, meals, the internet, job applications? It was, he thought, becoming a matter of deliberate effort, to see any importance at all in the things that had for so long preoccupied him and, for that matter, preoccupied millions more across the world.

More immediately, though, people throughout the British Isles were worried about the drought that accompanied the long spell of hot weather. There had been a foretaste of it all in the previous summer, but this year, the drought had begun in the spring and had now persisted into early summer. Unused to such conditions, there was widespread anger at the Government's attempts to limit water consumption whilst, paradoxically, there was also a growing sense of fear as water levels in reservoirs began to drain to the size of little more than shallow pools amongst the remnants of formerly drowned landscapes.

Soon, there was talk of importing water, and news presenters were to be found administering daily roastings to government ministers for their perceived slowness to implement such a course of action. There was a reluctance to believe that the drought was so widespread that other countries were also trying to conserve their stocks of water and were not at all willing to export their own scarce resources to a thirsty Britain.

In the isolation of the hamlet and the cottage, Dan did his best to cope with the water shortage and with the daily foray to a standpipe that had now been set up a short distance away, on the main road. Helping his neighbours, most of whom were elderly, also gave him something else to think about other than his own immediate problems.

In the background, meanwhile, he had done as Amanda had suggested and had made a phone appointment with his GP. Late in the afternoon that he made the appointment he occupied himself by trying to put a meal together from the assortment of food left in the fridge. As the afternoon wore on into early evening, he found himself seated once more beneath the parasol in the back garden, gazing across the parched fields behind the cottage and down to the steadily drying bed of the river which was now little more than a succession of dwindling, isolated puddles.

He picked at his scrappy meal until eventually, pushing it away from him, he drank the last of the fruit juice he had poured for himself and then went in search of something stronger, resorting finally to the whisky bottle that he kept at the back of his now depleted drinks cupboard. With no-one to see and nowhere to go, he occupied himself by working his way through glass after glass of whisky and watching the long, slow sunset. Eventually, as darkness fell, an irresistible drowsiness began to overtake him and determined not to spend the night in the open air, he drunkenly hauled himself up the stairs and into bed.

The shrilling of his phone woke him the next morning to an early call from his local surgery. A weary and rambling response to the question from the GP at the other end of the call led to a firm request that he should make an appointment to see him in person. Dan reached back across the bed to put his phone back on the bedside table and, instead, sent it clattering to the floor. Why, he wondered, when he was feeling so ill, was he being asked to present himself at the surgery?

He did, though, attend his appointment at the surgery a day later and was told by a tired and slightly fractious GP that he was going to prescribe anti-depressants for him. Having disciplined himself to leave the whisky alone, Dan was able to focus clearly on the middle-aged, greying and somewhat rumpled doctor seated at the desk to one side of the room. In the light that penetrated through the carefully adjusted venetian blinds, he watched as he returned his tie to its central position and slumped, in his grey well-worn suit, into his chair and began to write out the prescription. Dan had queried the need for medication, but his GP was in no mood to be told his job. He raised his head from the task of writing, peered over his glasses and said curtly, "I'm in no doubt whatsoever, that you're suffering from clinical depression. You need to take this course of anti-depressants and then phone the surgery again in time to renew the prescription. At that point, I shall want to talk to you again about further treatment."

Dan muttered a "Thank you", picked up the prescription and then drove into Sedgewater to collect the tablets from a pharmacy in the High Street. Although he waited wearily in the queue, it took just a few minutes to collect the medication and then he was free.

* * *

Such freedom in the middle of a working day felt strange. He was used to an intense pattern of routine that took him from early morning to early evening and usually left him wondering where the time had gone. Now the hours stretched before him through the day. He drove slowly back towards the cottage until he came to a small car park at the entrance to a bridle path. The path was popular with ramblers and dog walkers, but the car park was deserted as he manoeuvred the car so that it sat next to the hedgerow.

It was broad daylight, but his interior world was cloaked in darkness. He dreaded the thought of the solitary night that he would spend when a few more hours had elapsed. There seemed to be no way out. Since the confrontations with Sue and Eleanor, and then the end of his affair with Anne, he had somehow managed, despite the sleeplessness, the remorse and the anger that he had directed against himself, to retain a sense of momentum. But now there seemed nowhere to go. He slumped over the steering wheel and involuntary sobs shook his body; having previously wondered why, even at such occasions as his parents' funerals, he never wept, at that moment he could not prevent himself from doing so.

The tears lasted for several minutes. He had to wait until he was calm again before they subsided, leaving him red-eyed and slipping into thoughts that he had never before allowed himself to dwell on; briefly he thought about racing the car towards a brick wall at a speed driven by his self-hatred and anger. He envisaged speeding towards the wall – and then the blinding rapidity of the last split seconds.

It would be a way he could convey to others how he felt about his failure and the damage he had done not just to his own life but also to the lives of others.

But then his thoughts moved on again. If he was killed outright, there would be oblivion; if by chance, however, and despite his efforts, he woke to find himself in a hospital bed with life-changing injuries, his lot, arguably, would be worse than it was at that moment. He questioned, if he had the courage for such a course of action, given its potential for failure.

Although he dismissed his first thoughts about the method of committing suicide, his mind stayed with the use of his car as a possible means. Perhaps if he chose a place similar to the car park in which he was sitting? He knew of several such places – except that they were more isolated and where it might be some time before his body was found. In all its perversity, the idea began to take hold of him in a way that the violence of his previous thoughts had not.

His mind began to work through the details. There was a place out in the hills a short distance away where a small woodland road opened into a car park intended for the use of such people as walkers and woodland wardens. In practice though, the woodland was neglected and not many people went there. It would be a suitable choice.

Then there was the question of the precise method that he was going to use. He would need a hosepipe that could be connected to the exhaust, blankets to prevent leakage at the point where the hose would be fed into the car and perhaps some form of sedative to counter last minute moments of panic.

At this point, he began to pull himself back. Why was he thinking like this? His thoughts, it seemed to him, were like those dark moments in childhood where someone had thwarted his will and he had stormed off in a temper. He had made some bad mistakes, driven by his own personal areas of weakness. He was not, as it turned out, the person he had thought he was. So then, if he did what he was contemplating, what would be its effect on the lives of Josh and Emily or even of Sue? Then, again, there was Anne. How would it affect her? He knew that she already had a history of emotional instability and the action he was contemplating, assuming that she would be unable to simply wave it away, could only have a negative effect on her.

It had to be recognised that, by their very nature, he was not solely responsible for the acts of adultery that he had committed with Anne; she had been a willing and eager partner in those events – and, together, they had both used George's violence against her to justify their own wrongdoing.

The black landscape in which his thoughts had been imprisoned began to recede, to be replaced instead by a grey light of misery. His self-hatred began to assume a different proportion. In place of fury, came a sense of futility and further questioning.

If he was to take his life, was it really 'his' to take? It was through no act of his that he had come into the world. Eventually, he would die anyway; for all living things, there was no dodging Time's bullet. As he thought about it, he remembered again his father's death. In his father's exit from the world, the idea of a 'bullet' seemed appropriate; his death had been sudden and unanticipated.

For all that his father's death had been unexpected, his time had come. Dan's thoughts returned to himself, to his own situation. Was this, then, now his time? A few moments before, he had been in despair but, as he asked himself the question, he knew that it was an unconvincing one.

If this was not the experiencing of hope, it was not, by the same token, an experience of utter despair. Rather, it was a form of resignation. The desolation that had enveloped him a short time before had transmuted itself into a grudging willingness to continue putting one foot in front of the other, to carrying the burden that he had placed upon his own back.

The realisation that he had willingly taken actions that had been damaging to others carried with it the heavy recognition that he could never undo those actions. For a moment, his mood sank back towards his previous state, but then, having recognised the immutable nature of what he had done, he made the decision that he would have to carry it with him as best he could.

A teaching colleague, he remembered, had once said to him that "We all take ourselves too seriously". Surely, this was what he was now doing. It was ridiculous to take himself so seriously; he was, after all, as his mother had sometimes reminded him when he was child, another 'grain of sand' amongst the many millions; at the time, it had seemed like just another of her all too familiar phrases drawn from her bottomless store of folk wisdom but now her words returned with a force they had never had when he was a child.

Then, despite the depth of his self-absorption, Dan's attention was suddenly drawn back to the world outside the confines of his own head. From the corner of his eye, he became aware that a slim, ginger haired and rather gawky woman in a pink tracksuit was being dragged towards his car by a dish mop of a dog. Her face was red with frustration and exertion as she fought unavailingly to prevent the dog from dragging her towards Dan's car.

The reason for the dog's urgency immediately became apparent. No sooner had it arrived next to Dan's front tyre than it lifted its leg and relieved itself with a blissful pee. Becoming aware that Dan was sitting in his car, the woman evinced a rather anxious and wincing smile before being dragged off again towards the bridle path at the far edge of the car park.

Dan was no great believer in serendipity. It was sufficient that, for the moment, the brooding darkness of his interior mood had been broken. As the woman was dragged reluctantly along the path, he started the car's engine and continued on his journey back to the cottage.

* * *

The episode at the car park forced Dan to recognise the truth of what others were telling him – but which, in his instinct to 'keep going', he had not wanted to acknowledge – that, for a whole variety of reasons, he had become mentally unstable. As the days passed after his visit to his GP, he began slowly to feel more motivated about getting started on changes that he needed to make.

It was at about this time that Josh decided that he wanted to meet up with his father for one of their periodic 'chats'. The cottage did not, of course, belong to his father but still it represented a place where he was free of the demands of his mother and grandmother and where he was more likely to be able to talk about things that interested him – and which lay outside the narrow confines of his mother's world of legal work, of Emily's perpetual fretting about 'friends' and the round of neighbours' business and 'ailments of the aged' that preoccupied his grandmother.

This time, Josh did not even need to rely on his mother for transport. A slightly older friend, 'Spiffy', had recently passed his driving test and was always looking for excuses to drive his new 'Starflash' and so was more than willing to drive Josh out to the cottage, provided that Josh was prepared to hang out with him, later that morning, in Sedgewater.

Dan watched with faint amusement as Josh attempted to lever his gangling frame out of the low and sporty interior of the Starflash. Then he was at the front door, where he briefly hugged his father before going through to the lounge. Gravitating to the settee, where he sprawled across the cushions, he asked, "How's it going then, Dad?"

"Oh, not so bad," said Dan, engaging as ever in the English habit of understatement. "Can I get you something to drink?"

"No – I'm good, thanks," he said. "I brought my own." He fished a can of cola from his jacket and put it on the coffee table in front of him.

Dan went briefly out to the kitchen, retrieved the cafetiere, which was still almost full, and seated himself in an armchair opposite Josh.

"How are things at home?" he asked.

"Ok, I guess," replied Josh.

"You guess...?"

"I'm not there all that much, Dad. I spend a lot of time with friends or round at Jayne's place... Her parents like having me there..." he added by way of explanation.

Dan felt a twinge of guilt. Jayne's parents, it seemed, were supplying Josh with the family life that his own parents were no longer providing.

"Hmm," said Dan, "you and Jayne must have got to know each other very well by now..."

Josh caught the direction in which father's comment was going. "Yes, we have...but we also spend time apart. Jayne has her own circle of friends and I still see mine."

"Was it a friend who brought you here this morning?"

"Oh – yes – that was 'Spiffy'. He's doing an engineering course at Sedgewater College but we met up through football."

"I'm guessing he's older than you..."

"Yes, Dad, though not much older. He dropped out of school and did an apprenticeship for a while – but now he's full time at the College."

"Sounds interesting...a footballer and an engineer..."

"He's not an engineer yet. That's a long way off."

"And what about you? How are your plans for university going...?"

Josh smiled. "They're going quite well. I've been looking at the courses offered by Bristol Uni this time."

"Right," said Dan, quietly pleased. "You're much more organised than I was."

"I don't know about that," replied Josh. "Jayne's parents want her to go to university but I think they're hoping that she won't go too far away."

"So...?"

"She's been looking at courses in several universities but I think the one she's keen on is Bath."

"Which, of course, is not a million miles from Bristol."

"Exactly…" Josh laughed. "Seriously, though, I have checked out the course I want to do at Bristol. It's a really good one."

"At least you know what you want to do…which is more than I ever did…?"

"Don't put yourself down, Dad. I might never have been interested in Science if you hadn't encouraged me…all those little experiments we used to do and the walks we did in the countryside."

"I thought the walks used to bore you – that's what you always said."

"I expect I did – but it wasn't what I meant. You and mum always took us on such long walks that you made our legs ache. Me and Em just wanted to go home."

"Hmm, sounds like we discouraged you…"

"No – not at all. It was only when we were very young that our legs ached… Later on, we went on our own walks or bike rides."

Dan nodded, remembering that he had encouraged both his children – but that he had also made judgements about when to stand back and let them do their own exploration.

"So now, what does all this have to do with wanting to study electrical engineering?"

Josh grinned. "Haven't you heard, Dad? 'The future's electric'."

"Yes, I have heard – a few more times than I'd care to mention. But, from the things you used to enjoy when you were younger, you could just as easily have chosen Biology or Physics – or, for that matter, Maths."

"I don't really look at it that way. Besides, you could argue that all the Sciences are connected to Maths in one way or another."

Dan nodded, pleased that Josh's younger self was clearly giving way to the kind of thoughtful young person that he and Josh's mother had always hoped he would become.

"So why not Maths, then – or Physics perhaps?" prompted Dan.

"Hmm, it's a really hard choice but in the end, I want to solve problems in the real world. I will be using Maths and Physics – but we have to change the way we all live, and I want to help with that, so I'm going towards engineering because it's practical and I want to solve practical problems."

"It sounds like you've given it a lot of thought, Josh…"

"I have – but I don't do all my thinking on my own. I spend a lot of time talking to my friends about…well, about the future, I suppose. After all, if we don't think about it, there may not be a future."

Dan sat in silence for a moment or two, aware that he was gazing at Josh – but at the same time not wishing to embarrass him. He turned his gaze aside and said, "I feel like my generation owes you – and all the children and young people in the world an apology – the biggest apology that one group of people could ever make to another…"

"You wouldn't be alone in that, Dad. Several of my teachers at school have said something similar…"

"Oh," said Dan, a sad expression on his face. "And what do your friends think about that?"

"Some are angry – very angry about it. But…"

"But what, Josh? What do you think about it?"

Josh hesitated, not knowing best how to express his thoughts and feelings. Eventually, he sighed and said, "I think that, in the end, people are just people. We can't suddenly stop being what we are and suddenly turn into some other kind of creature.. And like all living things, we can adapt. But because we're human, we can adapt extremely quickly when we have to." He paused but then continued. "If there's anything I worry about when I read or see something new about it, it's the way in which animals and plants are becoming extinct because they can't adapt as fast as we can. They can only live in the ways that they've evolved to live – and since living things all depend on each other, that's something that humans have to worry about because we're all part of one gigantic web of life."

Dan nodded thoughtfully and silently. His own son had articulated more sense than he had heard or seen in most of his life from those whose vocation was supposedly to communicate and to inform.

Josh, still lost in thought, sipped at his drink. Dan looked at the time on his phone. Whatever he had thought they might talk about that morning, it was not the future of the world…

From outside, there was the tooting of a car horn. Josh stood and went to look out of the front window.

"Spiffy's back, Dad. He wants me to go into Sedgewater with him."

"Ok," Dan replied. "I'll come to the door with you."

Josh crumpled the cola can in his hand and took it through to the recycling bin in the kitchen. Then he returned and went to the front door, letting himself out. Dan, just behind him, called out, "I really enjoyed our chat! See you soon!"

Josh turned back towards his father and gave a brief wave. Then he engaged himself in the business of shoehorning himself into the Starflash. Instinctively, Dan listened for the roar of a highly-tuned internal combustion engine but heard only the remarkably quiet sound of a powerful electric motor as the Starflash accelerated away from the kerb.

Now that he was alone again, a momentary flicker of the darkness that had lain across Dan's mind so much in the last two years briefly returned to cloud his thoughts, but with Josh's youthfulness and energy still pervading his thoughts, he quickly dismissed it and felt that there was still reason to hope that, through its young people, there might still be a way forward for the human race.

* * *

Amongst the more hurtful communications that Dan received in the next few days was a letter telling him to stay away from Wellsprings Primary School. He experienced, yet again, the feeling of sinking in his stomach – and, in addition to the hurt that arose from the injustice of it all, a sense of irony. What exactly was the point of a letter telling him to do what he had been doing for the past two weeks?

Paradoxically, another of the 'hurtful' letters told him to do exactly the opposite thing – not to stay away from Wellsprings Primary but, instead, to ensure that he attended a meeting to discuss and finalise the terms of his redundancy. He was also requested to contact the Headteacher if, for any reason, he was unable to get to the appointment.

Yet another letter, confirming the details of an earlier e-mail, told him that Mr Simon Ashley, the regional representative for his professional association, needed to talk to him prior to the redundancy meeting at the school.

It became clear to Dan that being made redundant was not so much a procedure as part of a substantial ecology; it reminded him of a natural history film he had once seen in which deep sea organisms were scavenging on the ragged carcass of a fish.

Despite his inward negativity, he replied to all the correspondence in an outwardly constructive manner. He wanted only to deal with the immediate process – and to be done with it as soon as possible. Before the end of his affair with Anne, he had felt strong; now he felt as though the succession of events in his daily life was sapping his strength to deal with them.

The regional representative duly arrived late one morning and, over cups of coffee, they discussed Dan's situation – and, for once, Dan found himself paying attention to the sort of information that he so often found tedious, having decided that, above all, he wanted to start again and that the financial outcome would be an essential part of his ability to do so.

Simon Ashley was well practised in his role. He took Dan calmly through the settlement that the school was prepared to make and went into the terms that he could reasonably expect. For a while, emotional overload and thoughts of suicide in a remote car park began to recede.

Dan, Simon told him, was fortunate that his occupation as a teacher had ensured that he was part of a good pension scheme. Consequently, he could take his pension early and, although it was nothing like as generous as it would have been had he gone through to retirement, it would be enough to see him through his immediate situation. Like so many before him, Dan breathed a sigh of relief.

There was, however, a condition; agreement from the school was subject to a 'gagging clause'. Dan was not to talk, write or communicate in any way about the situation which had led to his redundancy, or he could be subject to 'legal action'.

Hearing this, Dan's mood began to revert to a sense of injustice and anger. What if he decided to go to an industrial tribunal? Simon laid out the options but on the whole, it was clear that he was rather cool on the subject. Did Dan, in his present state of mind, have the resilience to go through with such a long and challenging process? The chances of success were not good and the costs of failure could be very high.

For the time being, Dan's independence of judgement had deserted him. Simon seemed to be a solid, trustworthy individual. By all appearances, he was one of the very few individuals trying to help rather than undermine him. If Simon said that he should sign the 'gagging clause' it would be much the safest and most reliable choice to do as he suggested.

It was settled then. Simon would be in conversation with Amanda and the school's governors but, he thought, agreement would largely be a formality. As he left, his handshake with Dan was firm and reassuring.

* * *

The morning had gone. Dan drifted back to another aimless afternoon. He ate the reheated remains of an evening meal for lunch and then looked out of the window; the dry weather and hot sunshine had continued. He decided that he wanted to clear his head and to get away from the feelings of claustrophobia that hours spent at the cottage tended to induce. He walked out to the car, climbed in, switched on the air conditioning, and drove away with just a vague idea of where he wanted to go.

As the car nosed along the narrow lane out of the hamlet, he remembered that just a short distance away, there was a popular local landmark. It was one of the few hills in an area that was gently undulating or otherwise flat and criss-crossed by a network of drainage channels and ditches. He decided that, if there was a road to the top of the hill, he would take it. He pulled into a passing place and, preferring his Ordnance Survey map to GPS, got it out and checked; there was a road that ran almost to the summit and a car park nearby. There were also, apparently, the remains of an ancient hill fort. It would be a good place from which to survey the landscape – which was one of the principal reasons for its popularity. With redundancy and possible divorce marching towards him, sunshine and fresh air would remind him that life was still worth living.

Some minutes later, the car was crunching its way across the coarse gravel of the car park. At weekends the car park was often full, but it was midweek and no-one else was there. He left his car parked next to a green embankment and climbed a set of wooden steps to a path that would take him the rest of the distance to the summit of the hill. It was not far but recent inactivity and a strong breeze left him breathless as he made his way to a triangulation point around which were marked the directions and distances to significant places both near and far.

He had brought with him a thin jacket that he had thought was too warm a few minutes ago but now, it felt inadequate in the stiff breeze blowing across the summit. Induced by the wind, tears ran from the corners of his eyes as he gazed down at the landscape below him, the embodiment of the map he had looked at a few minutes before. He had gone there to brood again over his innermost thoughts. Instead, the wind and the sun, the toasted patchwork hues of farmland, the glinting of the June sunshine on those few places where small areas of water still remained, took him away from his introspection and reminded him once more of the expanse and beauty of the world. He sat for some time on a large rock, set for such purposes, into the viewing area. Other than the beating of the wind and the flight of light and shade across the land below, nothing disturbed him.

Such was his depth of his thought, that it was only sometime later that the wind's buffeting caused him to find a more sheltered spot. He stood and drifted back round, to a place where a wooden seat facilitated a brief return to the inward turning of his mind which, of late, had become so much a habit. It was, though, a productive turning. Somewhere at the back of his thoughts, probably in the very moments that he had been drawn outwards by the world around him, a resolution had formed itself. Whatever the failures, the pain, the injustices, the lies, and deception, he needed to move on.

Walking back to the car, he decided not to return to the cottage that afternoon. Although Sedgewater would be a hot, crowded place that afternoon he decided that he wanted the bustle of human company around him, he wanted a sense of people going about their lives. He wanted to get out of his self-imposed wilderness.

* * *

It seemed odd to be wearing a suit. Perhaps it was also an odd decision that he had chosen to wear it. This was, however, the morning on which his redundancy would become formalised; even if the loss of his work also came to signify the loss of his own sense of self-worth, he wanted to preserve within himself, the ability to make a dignified exit.

He drove through the lanes to Wellsprings in silence. Amanda's PA, Pauline, had been looking out for him and when he approached the office block from the car park, she met him at the entrance.

"Hello Dan, I'm sorry this is happening. But I've been asked to meet you and take you along to Amanda's office. It's good to see you again although I wish it was in happier circumstances."

"Thank you, Pauline," he said and gave her a bleak smile. "Who's there this morning?"

"The Chair of Governors, Amanda of course, and your representative, Simon Ashley. Eleanor and Simon arrived more or less together, about ten minutes ago."

Pauline went just ahead of him to knock on, and then open, the door of Amanda's office. Light flooded into the gloomy corridor and Dan found himself blinking as she ushered him to his seat. She then went to a chair slightly removed and to one side of the 'panel', if such it was, in the centre of the room, and sat with her laptop at the ready. Dan gathered from this that the meeting was to be minuted.

The members of the panel had arranged themselves in a crescent with Amanda at its centre, the Chair of Governors to her right and Simon to the left, though also a little closer to Dan's chair, which had been placed centrally to face them.

The proceedings began as soon as Dan had seated himself. He fished the papers he needed from the pocket inside his jacket. "So, this is it," he thought. "The end of six years here and twenty years in teaching."

Amanda, rather superfluously, thanked them all for attending and reminded them of its purpose. She reminded them that the rest of the meeting would follow a protocol which, Dan knew, had to be adhered to. He found himself listening in silence to much of it, only responding when he was asked to do so.

At the point where he was required to sign the document that would prevent him from communicating with others about the details of the redundancy, Simon asked for a brief adjournment of the meeting. He stood and led Dan out to the path that led around the garden behind Amanda's office.

As soon as they had started along the path, Simon said, "I'm sorry Dan, I thought we might have communicated about this before now but unfortunately, for whatever reason, that hasn't happened. I need to know if you're willing to sign the document that's on the table at the moment, bearing in mind that it contains the so called 'gagging clause'?"

Dan had thought carefully about it and voiced his objections, knowing that, unless he wanted a long and difficult fight, he had little choice. He also knew that, psychologically, he was very poorly placed to begin such a battle.

Simon waited patiently but then said, "I hear what you're saying, Dan – and, if you want to follow the alternative path, there will be support available to you, but I need to know for this morning's purposes, whether or not you are going to sign the document?"

Dan nodded and then answered, "Yes," and with a look of resignation said, "Let's just go and get it over and done with."

They made their way back to Amanda's office. Amanda and Eleanor were standing at the far window, peering through the partially opened blinds at the school buildings beyond. Dan noticed that they were drinking coffee and thought that, as he and Simon re-entered, he heard some reference to Eleanor's garden.

The two women put down their coffee cups and returned to their seats. As soon as they were all attentive to the situation again, Amanda said, "So, Dan, your signature is needed on the agreement, the importance of which I'm sure Simon has explained."

The copies for signature had been set out on Amanda's desk. Dan stood to sign them and Amanda handed him a pen. He had read his copy a number of times at home so now, before he had time to think again, he quickly signed the documents and then left them, together with the pen, on the desk. Feeling slightly awkward, he drifted back towards his seat.

Amanda, also now back in her seat, glanced briefly at Eleanor and Simon.

"I think that's all we need to do. Pauline will take charge of the paperwork."

They stood, stiffly and formally. Eleanor advanced towards him and briefly shook his hand.

"Thank you for your service to the school, Dan. I'm sure we all wish you well for the future."

Dan nodded in acknowledgement, feeling that nonetheless, there was always an element of hypocrisy in such proceedings.

Amanda too, advanced to shake his hand. He raised his eyes to look her in the face. Given their relationship at an early stage in their careers, working together had not always been easy but he had enjoyed it.

"Thank you, Dan," he heard her say, "...for everything you've done here. I know that everyone, staff, children and parents have all appreciated your work."

She stepped back and Simon stood forward. He also lightly and briefly shook Dan's hand but said, "This is just a brief 'goodbye', Dan. I need to visit you again in two- or three-days' time – but I'll phone you first."

Not knowing what else to do, Dan nodded, turned and let himself out of the room. He supposed that the 'panel' still had a few remaining things to mop up.

He had gone only a few paces when he heard the sound of Pauline's heels as she hurried along behind him. She was waving a piece of paper at him.

"Dan, I can't let you leave this behind." She handed the paper to him. "It's your copy of the agreement!"

He let her put it into his hand. "Oh yes," he said. "How could I forget that?"

Pauline pressed his hands in her own and said, "Good luck, Dan. If you need anything, you know where we are."

She was referring to herself and her husband Jeff. Dan gave her a faint smile and said, "Thanks, Pauline. I expect I'll see you again soon."

He folded his sheet of paper and fed it into his inside pocket to sit with the copies he had brought with him. He began walking towards the car park and looked back only briefly to see Pauline hurrying back into the office building. He stood for a moment taking in one last glimpse of the school.

As he did so, he directed his gaze at the windows of his former classroom. A row of small faces was pressed against the glass. A single hand shot into the air and began waving to him, followed by a small forest of other waving hands. He grinned and waved vigorously back. Immediately there was a hubbub of voices followed by more faces pressed to the glass and yet more waving hands.

He knew only too well that his presence on the path to the car park was causing chaos in the classroom. This was confirmed seconds later when the shriek of a mealtime assistant's whistle was followed by the not too dissimilar shriek of a mealtime assistant's voice.

He gave one last wave and then, thinking to spare the frustrations of the staff trying to manage the children, he headed once more towards the car park. The sight of the children's faces and their waving hands would be forever an embedded snapshot in his memory. He wondered if anyone would think to tell them that it had been his 'goodbye'? But then he preferred to think of their faces and waving hands not as 'goodbyes' but as a collective act of goodwill – the only appreciation that he really wanted.

* * *

The heat – and the drifting – continued. The sound of fire appliances heading through the local network of roads to deal with fires in fields and woodlands became a frequent feature of Dan's daily life. Seemingly it was difficult for people to separate the idea of long, hot summer days from that of barbecued food. Most of the fires, though, began simply through the presence of heat and a plentiful supply of natural fuel. The winds that summer also seemed to be predominantly from a southerly direction so that hot air from the aridity of the countries in southern Europe and Northern Africa continued to desiccate the woods and fields right across the country. Everywhere, the landscape dried from green to sepia and became a tinderbox.

Towns and cities were far from immune. The local fire brigade in Sedgewater found itself regularly turning out to fires in back gardens where barbecues or bonfires had caused fires to start in neighbours' gardens or on nearby wasteland. After one Saturday afternoon barbecue party in Sedgewater, a number of residents had to be rescued as first their gardens caught fire and then burning material from fences and garden waste spread to houses. Smoke inhalation also led to a number of people being treated at Sedgewater Royal Infirmary.

Dan, though, in relative isolation at the cottage took care to avoid situations that could lead to a fire. He spent a good deal of time in the back garden, sunbathing or, after too much sun, seeking the shade of the parasol or house with the doors and windows thrown open. His medication worked unobtrusively so that, despite his social isolation, he began to feel steadily more positive about his own fortunes – although as he read more and took in more downloads of Climate Crisis research and records around the world, the optimism that he had felt after talking to Josh was always under attack. Amongst the situations that he found most difficult to handle was the disinformation and denial that had always been present in the various media but which seemed particularly perverse and destructive in the light of the succession of climate related crises that were now unfolding everywhere. He sensed, though, that amongst the worst aspects of the Crisis was one that he shared with billions of other people – and that was the feeling of powerlessness. Why, he wondered, should he not simply immerse himself in his own affairs because at least in those he had some measure of influence if not always control – whereas with the madness that was unfolding everywhere, only God, if he could ever persuade himself to believe in such a being, could save the human race from self-destruction – and, steadily, mercilessly and insidiously the tide of that destruction crept ever onwards.

Sometimes, out of a sense of weariness, he would simply turn off the television and the various devices that seemed at times to hold him in thrall. Then, instead, he might pick up a novel – possibly one from the nineteenth century only to discard it again because of its apparent irrelevance to the ongoing destruction of the civilisation around him – and the very civilisation out of which such novels had been born.

One afternoon, in the shade of the parasol, he chose neither a novel nor an electronic device to divert himself. Instead, he had in front of him his school diary – of the paper and card variety and which he had persisted in using despite the fact that almost everyone else around him now used electronic versions.

The diary lay open at the events that had been planned for a few days' time – including the final assembly of the term which would take place on the last afternoon before the summer break. It had been intended to use it to mark both the closure of Wellsprings Primary School and the impending transfer of staff to the new enlarged district school that would open in time for the autumn term. There would also be a staff social event in the evening.

On the face of it, the reasons for the creation of the new, larger school were related to economics and greater efficiency in the use of resources but, as Dan believed, Amanda and the Principal had both wanted a veil to be drawn rapidly over the mistakes and corruption that had resulted in the siting of Wellsprings Primary and the housing developments that it served. Dan briefly entertained the thought of carrying out his own investigation as to whether or not James, Amanda's husband, had been involved, but he knew enough about Amanda's relationship with her husband to believe that she would have been ignored if she had said anything to him about the hydrological problems in that area – but then, Dan reminded himself, he had always had the impression that James had not been a key player in the development and that, instead, the work had been done by a much larger company.

He brought his mind back to the events that had originally been listed to take place on the last day of the summer term. He was not, he knew, the only teacher who would not be transferring to the new school; two older members of staff had also chosen to retire – but, for both of them, age was much more of a factor than it had been with Dan. He toyed briefly with the idea of turning up at the staff social; he had, after all, more than earned his right to be there and it was unlikely that any move would be made to exclude him, despite the letter he had received banning him from the school. Such was his anger, however, about the way in which he had been treated that the thought of having anything more to do with Wellsprings School was repugnant to him. He wanted to put it all behind him as quickly as possible.

* * *

CHAPTER 23

WHAT FUTURE?

It was unusual that the Principal had decided not to hold meetings that day – but Amanda was quietly content to accept that now that her work on the amalgamation of schools was almost complete, she would not ignore the start of the summer break.

James had left earlier that morning, eating a quick, solitary breakfast and seemingly eager to get away to his latest project. The journey there would take him two hours, he had told Amanda, and he was not sure what time he would be back that evening. Amanda had tried not to feel resentful, telling herself that it was rather immature for someone in her position to allow her husband's activities to define her day – but, when she was later sitting over her own breakfast, she admitted to herself that she was more than fed up that on those few days of the year that she was not working, she had only herself for company.

Having finally got as far as her cup of coffee, she pulled her phone towards her and opened her calendar. It confirmed what she already knew – that she needed to spend time in her office later in the week, that she had arranged to meet her mother and her sister in a few days' time but for that morning at least, she had no commitments. She pulled a wry face to herself; there had been points during the term that had just ended in which she would have given a great deal for a few hours of leisure – but now that the opportunity was here, she found herself at something of a loss.

She toyed briefly with the idea of phoning Dan. It had been three weeks since she had last seen him – and she felt strongly that she needed to follow up on the final meeting at which arrangements for his redundancy had been completed. But – and it was a substantial 'but' –

she knew that he would be feeling resentful for some time to come, and it would be a while before she could talk to him without a certain amount of ill-feeling intruding into the conversation.

Her thoughts moved on, prompted, as in the past, by the quietness of the house. Since she spent so much of her time in schools, it seemed unnatural that here there were no children's voices. How had it come about that, as yet, she had no children of her own? It was almost a rhetorical question. She knew, of course, that there were obvious answers. In the first years of their marriage, James had seemed as keen as she was to have children; they had certainly spent plenty of time trying.

Now, though, it seemed to her that James' priorities had moved on – and that only one of them wanted to have a child; she toyed momentarily with the word 'wanted'. It hardly seemed adequate to describe the quiet desperation that she felt. She thought of the alternatives that were available to childless couples. She had tried long and hard to persuade James to think about the various steps they could take to find out why it was that she had never yet become pregnant, but he would never co-operate with her. Whilst in recent years, she had generally felt a great deal of satisfaction with her home and her career, her longing for a child and her inner frustration that James did not share her desire, had brought about in her a yearning that was becoming visceral.

Of course, there were many women now who were choosing not to have children. Their reasons varied. Some wanted to uninhibitedly pursue their careers. Others believed that the present world was such a dangerous and uncertain place that it would be morally wrong to bring a child into such a life.

She was not, though, a pessimist by nature – and although she had shown a single-minded determination in climbing the ladder of her chosen career, it was not all that she wanted to achieve. She briefly wondered why she felt as she did. Of course, the home into which her child would be born would provide her or him with many advantages, and she had at least managed her life with sufficient skill to ensure that any daughter or son that she might have would not have to endure the privations that she had suffered during her own childhood.

As she looked back yet again over her early life, it had been the insecurity and the fear of not having the most basic elements of life

– food, shelter and clothing that had so deeply troubled the years of her early childhood. Even love had been problematic, although her mother, fortunately, had somehow pulled together the strength to extract herself and her two daughters from the abusive situation into which their father's perpetual drunkenness had taken them all. Her aunt and uncle, thankfully, had also shown her the love and resilience of family relationships that had helped her to flourish, as she grew from childhood into her teens and adolescence.

Her mind had drifted, and she brought her thoughts back to the present. Waiting on her tablet computer was the latest document from England's Government – 'Our Children's Future'. Before talk of Dan's redundancy had emerged into the full light of day, he had already been talking to her about it – although, in her view, very selectively and only picking up on those aspects that had particularly concerned him.

She remembered the scorn with which he had viewed the Government's extremely belated attempts to introduce to children the beginnings of an understanding that the planetary environment that they would inherit from their parents was one that was steadily deteriorating and that, without titanic efforts from the world's younger generations, was also one in which the civilisation they had been born into would no longer be sustainable.

She mentally stepped aside for a few moments from the magnitude of it all because the instance in which she had found herself talking to Dan about it had thrown new light on what she had long seen as his lack of ambition and a rather unappealing failure to engage with the life of the society of which he was a part.

She remembered too, that before more recent events, he had talked again about the brief period in his life when he had dropped out of his degree course and spent time travelling; the journeys he had made at that time had had a pivotal influence on him. The poverty he had seen in East Africa was far worse than anything she could imagine from her own childhood, whilst the journeys he had made to places as diverse as Iceland and Morocco bore testament to the ingenuity of people who had learned to live within environments that had both great harshness and a beauty that defied indifference. After that, the life of England, he had told her, had become to him trivial, widely despoiled, polluted, overcrowded and frequently bizarre in its preoccupations. He had found it very difficult to readjust to – and to re-engage with – a country that, despite all its problems, he still loved.

Even on that recent occasion, though, they had not talked in depth. He had only outlined for her the diversity of his experiences – but she was both insightful and intelligent; she had also travelled and had not always stuck to the usual networks of tourist traps. She could understand what an influence his journeys would have had on both his sensitivity and intelligence, and she could see, that without all the fanfare that had accompanied some of the social trends of their student years, he had, in a sense, dropped out and disengaged though with nothing generally stronger than beer or whisky to back his disengagement; he had never, as far as she knew, even remotely been drawn towards the use of drugs other than alcohol. So there, in plain sight, he superficially conformed whilst being all the while, someone who endured and detested the superficialities of a society that he knew was badly serving its people and considerably under-performing in its contribution to the world.

But then, she asked herself, what was the use of such views when he had never found his own way to influence those around him, to make his presence felt? People around James were influenced by what they viewed as the very visible signs of his success. They took notice of him when he talked. With Dan, though, what did those around him see?

Perhaps at first, she thought, they saw someone of whom they were dismissive – who appeared overly serious and intense, was not particularly interested in the passing fads and fashions of the time and who could be moody to the point of surliness. She had known colleagues who saw him that way – and she herself had sometimes thought of him as rather 'old fashioned' in some respects.

If they took the trouble to look a little longer though, she reflected, there was much more to Dan than met the eye. The aspects of his character that some saw as weaknesses were also those, she saw now, that had come to appeal to her own better nature. He was generally disposed to be kind towards others and because he understood the importance of children's early educational experiences, he had chosen that as his contribution to life, rather than pursue the more conspicuous and more widely understood symbols of success wielded by those with money and overt influence.

She sighed. All the way through the recent period that they had worked together, she had erred on the side of caution, keeping to formality even when there were only the two of them in a room. She had also been disconcerted by his apparent abandonment of Sue in favour of Anne Moresby. Amanda could understand all too well what Dan had seen in her, but she judged that he had shown a shallowness and a weakness that previously she had not associated with him. Eleanor had seen Dan as 'immoral', but her ideas of morality seemed rather strange when, Amanda reflected, she was perfectly happy to associate herself with someone such as George Moresby. Notions of 'morality' seemed all too often to relate only to sex.

She paused. There was more than a little discomfort in her train of thought. Somehow, whenever others spoke of the poor and the disempowered, she had generally seen herself in the guise of her childhood and the years before her marriage to James; she had not habitually associated herself, at least in her own mind, with the wealthy, powerful people that she sometimes met when accompanying James at the sort of social events that he sought in order to extend his reputation.

Where, though, was 'morality' in the way that James attempted to evade or bypass rules relating to safe working practices, building materials, the choice of development sites, the scorn for those who did not see money as the most telling measure of success, the roughshod treatment of employees who had shown, when circumstances required, independence of mind and judgement?

It all seemed a very long way from the future world that, in the early part of her career, she had hoped for on behalf of other people's children and perhaps, still possibly, for her own child. Somehow, she had associated herself with a man who, by the nature of his ambitions, was destructive rather than creative and exploitative rather than empowering.

There were other anxieties, too, that she would have preferred to share with someone else that morning rather than have to dwell on them in solitude. She knew that if, instead of going straight to 'Our Children's Future', she lingered over either the domestic or international news, the picture would be largely the same; it would, she thought, be one of decline, of disintegration, of the sort of insecurity that many had first experienced during the Pandemic that had dogged the first years of her teaching career. What, though, she wondered, was the point of her success in the world that was now beginning to emerge?

Before the Pandemic, it had been the approach to life exemplified by James that had attracted her, but now it seemed to her, he was no more than a part of the great delusion that had gripped the human world for so long. Dan, by contrast, who had generally seemed to her to be one of life's mavericks, was the one who had always had a view of the future that was both clearer and more prophetic than that of people such as her husband.

Where, though, she wondered, did that leave her, the career that she was still seeking to advance and the child that she knew would need to be born in that part of the future that was now rapidly approaching – if it was ever going to be born at all? Would she find any solace or reassurance in the official document that she was now about to locate through her computer's file explorer? She already knew enough about the document to recognise that it was yet another piece of deception rather than of the reality that had needed to dawn on everyone long before that morning.

From the screen of her computer, the cover page of 'Our Children's Future' finally beckoned her – but she felt little sense of urgency about ploughing through it again – and then, in the autumn term, she would be one of the people expected to begin implementing the document's expectations. How on Earth, she wondered, could she expect herself to do that when she had begun to see the future in much the same way as Dan must have seen it for all the years that she had known him?

* * *

It was several weeks later and shortly before the schools were due to return from their summer break that Dan opened his phone to find a text from Amanda. The message was an invitation to visit her for coffee on the Wednesday morning of the following week.

At first, he thought about rejecting the invitation but, as he continued to think about it, he realised that it would be difficult for him to blame Amanda for the course of events when he had already told her that it felt as though it was time to move on. He found it difficult to explain the loss of control over his own feelings that had then followed, but he knew that

Anne's ending of her relationship with him had had a devastating effect, particularly since he had already wrecked his marriage and partially lost contact with his children as a result of his desire to continue his affair with her. He was also full of remorse for the way in which he had treated Sue.

Reluctantly, he admitted that Amanda's judgement had proved to be more reliable than his own – a point that was driven home when his GP had told him very clearly that he had clinical depression and that he was prescribing medication to help him cope with its effects.

As he thought about her course of action, he found it difficult to continue being angry with her; now that he could think more calmly about it all, it seemed to him that she had been acting with his best interests in mind even if he had found it difficult to see it that way at the time. He decided that he would accept her invitation.

So it was that on the following Wednesday, he drove across to Amanda's house and crunched over the gravel of her drive to park at the top near the house. The knocker on the huge oak front door was heavy to use – but effective; Amanda quickly arrived to let him in and ushered him through to the spacious reception room at the front of the house.

Minutes later, he watched from the armchair to which he had gravitated as she busied herself with the cafetiere, cups, milk and sugar. Although she was unaware of his gaze, he looked at her searchingly as she perched herself in the armchair opposite him. Even in the dim light of the room, he thought that she looked pale and tired – and that that in itself was something that concerned him and caused him to wonder about, given the hot sunshine and the weather's now longstanding invitation to spend hours of every day out of doors rather than in.

He wanted to suggest that they should go into the garden but since he was there at Amanda's request, he decided that, for the moment, he would wait. She sipped gently at her coffee before saying, "I'm glad you agreed to come over, Dan. I have been concerned about you."

He stared for a moment at his cup before answering. "It hasn't been the easiest of times. I didn't realise that I'd got so low."

She smiled. "It happens very easily, Dan. And I could see that you were not your usual self."

He nodded. "On the afternoon that you told me to go home, I was very angry – but I could see the sense in what you were saying – and I agreed with you. I didn't want to risk making things worse."

"I'm glad you see it that way. It wasn't easy for either of us. I'm sorry that we won't be working together anymore, but it will simplify both your situation and mine..."

Dan reflected for a moment before responding. He supposed that he could take exception to Amanda's turn of phrase but there seemed little point in doing so.

"I think I know what you mean..."

She put a hand to her mouth, realising the apparent insensitivity of her remark. "I do hope so! That must have sounded awful. I simply meant that we shall find it easier now to continue being friends than when we suddenly found ourselves being pushed together as work colleagues."

"I hope so, Amanda. Unfortunately, it was difficult for us even to talk about it at Wellsprings. Did you ever tell the Principal about our previous relationship?"

"No, I didn't, and if she did hear anything she never mentioned it. How relevant would it be anyway? It was years ago, and I would think very few people even remember anymore."

"You could well be right and even when we were together, only our closest friends knew about it – and most of them have moved away now..."

"Yes, we were probably worrying unduly – and that was my fault, Dan. But we both know how malicious gossip can be and I didn't want it to damage my career or yours. Social media is still just as much a problem as it was then."

He shook his head. "Well, it's all irrelevant now – to me at least."

"And increasingly to me..."

"Oh? What makes you say that, Amanda?"

"There's a great deal of uncertainty in the Academy at present – and not just there. If recent surveys are correct, large numbers of teachers could be leaving the profession in the next two years."

"That problem has existed before..."

"Yes – we both have reason to remember it. We were in the very early stages of our careers and schools were trying to cope with the Covid Pandemic..."

"This is quite different though. We all gradually learned to live with Coronavirus, but the Climate Crisis has been steadily getting worse through the whole of our lifetimes. And, so far, we haven't found a way to stop Global Warming."

"I know what you say is right, Dan. I think, though, that it's taking a very long time to sink into everyone's consciousness – decades, in fact. But now that most people are at last 'getting the message' it's creating great uncertainty."

"– Which is like the Pandemic."

"Yes – only the uncertainty of the Climate Crisis is here to stay, and we have no 'roadmap' out of it."

"We've all known this for so long though, Amanda..."

"I agree with you there – but most of us have just been getting on with our lives and doing what we've always done."

Dan could hardly disagree; he knew that his own life so far had followed a pattern that was well within the bounds of conventional behaviour. He had drifted away from the conversation for a moment and became aware that Amanda was asking him a question.

"You and Sue must have thought about all this before you decided to have children...?"

"Yes, we did think about it – although I think in Sue's case, it was timing rather than uncertainty about the future that was important to her."

"That's a rather cynical thing to say..."

Dan glanced across at her. Was the conversation straying into areas that were private and 'off limits'? He decided that it hardly mattered anymore. His relationship with Amanda had now completely changed and his marriage to Sue was almost certain to end in divorce.

"You may say that, but it was one of the reasons that we had no more than two children."

"I would have thought that was in keeping with your views about population, Dan?"

"Well, it was – but I don't think that was the deciding factor. I think it was simply that Sue did not want to go through childbirth again and also that she was keen to get on with her career."

"So, are you saying that you did not want to limit the number of children you had to two?"

Dan thought for a moment. "It might seem hypocritical – but I would have liked more. I was an only child and I think I had a clear idea that if we had three or four children, it would create a much greater sense of being a family and that siblings would provide company – and support – for one another."

Amanda gave a gentle laugh. "It all sounds rather idealistic, Dan – and quite the opposite of what I thought your views would be."

She paused, wondering if Dan would be offended by what she was about to say or how she said it.

"It's not too late for you though, is it? Surely there's still some chance that you and Sue will get back together?"

"I really don't think there's even the slightest prospect of that happening …At the moment, we're not even talking to each other, except perhaps when we have to…you know, if there's something about Josh or Emily that we absolutely have to discuss."

He stopped, wondering if the conversation was becoming too personal and yet aware as well, that Amanda was making him think about questions he wanted to think about and that, now that they no longer worked together, he would sooner talk to her about children than anyone else he could think of.

There was silence between them for some moments. Dan sipped at his coffee.

Eventually, Amanda said, "I hope my questions are not upsetting you. Now we'll no longer be working together, I'd rather think of you as a friend than as a former work colleague. We have, though, wandered away from the uncertainty that I feel in the Academy – and which, for that matter, seems to be everywhere at present. You might think that, in such uncertain times, people would think twice about having children but so far there's no sign of that. I haven't noticed any falling away in the numbers of Nursery or Reception children – and I've always seen children as a sign, an indication, that people still have some hope, some faith in the Future?"

It was Dan's turn to laugh. "Now who's being idealistic? Unfortunately, I think that all too often, parents are simply thinking about the pleasures of the moment…"

Amanda raised an amused eyebrow but said, "It's a serious point though, isn't it, Dan? Since we – sorry, I mean 'I' – since I often work amongst young teachers, I hear these conversations going on. The conversation is not generally intended for my ears, of course…"

"I don't see why, Amanda. Since you raised the questions about children, I mean, you could still…if you wanted…"

To his surprise, Dan was suddenly aware that Amanda's complexion was colouring.

"It's complicated," she said in a subdued voice. "I wish it wasn't but that's how it is…" She peered at his cup. "Would you like some more coffee?"

Dan decided that he would like some more. So far Amanda had asked most of the questions, but he still felt that he needed to get a clearer sense of what had driven the conversation along in the first place.

* * *

CHAPTER 24

THE ROUGH WITH THE SMOOTH

Dan did not see Amanda for some while after his visit to her that summer – and so, despite his best efforts at the time, did not learn what it was that was troubling her. The summer itself wore on, the heat and dust intensified and, as it stretched into the beginning of the autumn, tested the resilience of Britain and much of Northern Europe.

The anxiety that had characterised Dan's previous summer, though, was no longer there, now that his affair with Anne had ended, and his redundancy from Wellsprings School made it necessary for him to begin looking for another job. As a result, he spent much of his time filling in job application forms and reflecting that although he was well qualified in his own sphere, he seemed to be qualified for little else. The medication he was taking helped to keep him out of the pit of despair into which he had previously fallen, but a stream of rejections continued to erode his motivation.

It was fortunate that he had sufficient money to sustain himself for some time. Knowing that he could still pay the rent and feed himself helped to stave off feelings of aimlessness and insecurity, but he began to appreciate how desperate and trapped people with little or no money would feel. On his own at the cottage, he whiled away the time following his obsession with the Climate Crisis by endlessly researching the floods that had affected the area in which he lived.

Whilst the daily television news was devoting a good deal of time to the drought, Dan spent much of his time poring over video of flooding in his own small part of the world. There had been, he was very interested to find, plenty of research into the effects of flooding and sea level rise on his own county – much of which, it seemed, might well be under water in the not-too-distant future. But then his attention spread to flooding elsewhere in places that, at times, seemed unlikely locations – such as Australia or Spain. The truly global nature of the Climate Crisis became ever more apparent as his trawl through the internet produced a growing list of extreme and unprecedented weather events.

Initially, he found himself getting frustrated with the daily news coverage because so much time was spent on items that he saw as trivial – primarily sport and celebrities – but he gradually found other places to look for his information and so began to build a picture of events that was quite different from the disjointed and incomprehensible view that emerged if he allowed himself to be drawn into the endless following of the broadcasters' 'stream of consciousness'.

He realised, of course, from an early stage that, despite his medication, his relative isolation at the cottage and his obsessive researching of the Climate Crisis ran counter to his need to stay mentally healthy. Sedgewater was not much of a place but he decided that both his job applications and his 'researches' could be carried out there just as well as at the cottage. Going into Sedgewater, though, would impose upon him the need for a certain amount of self-organisation and would get him away from the seclusion and isolation of the cottage.

Accordingly, he resolved that despite the ongoing heat and discomfort, the next day he would travel into Sedgewater and that he would work from there – primarily on his job applications but also, perhaps, when he was able to do so, to continue building his picture of what was happening in the world around him – and, where possible, trying to make sense of it.

* * *

The following morning, after a leisurely breakfast, he had a shower, dressed more tidily than usual, pushed his papers and notebook computer into his briefcase and then, as he had planned, drove into town. By the time he arrived, most people had been at work for nearly two hours.

Once out of the air conditioning of his car, Dan was immediately reminded that it was yet another hot day. Meanwhile, he needed a 'base'. There was an independent coffee shop in the High Street and, for want of anywhere else, he chose to go there. The café's door was closed, presumably to maintain the coolness of the interior, and as he pushed it open and looked around for a table, he found himself feeling self-conscious, almost as though he was a teenager once more; work had always previously given him a sense of identity and he was also aware that, in recent weeks, he had spent long stretches of time on his own. Then he had to juggle his briefcase, his coffee and money as he made for the table that he would use as a temporary desk.

Finally, feeling hot and overdressed, he tried to arrange himself, his computer, a small sheaf of papers and his cup of coffee in such a way that he could access them without knocking any of them onto the floor or spilling his drink over himself or the table. As an experiment with 'mobile working' it was not an encouraging start.

The café's wi-fi was easy to access and he found several websites carrying information about vacancies. He read carefully through the various details, only to feel that if he decided to apply for any of the advertised jobs, he would be clutching at straws. He looked up, deciding whether or not to buy another cup of coffee, when he saw that the spiky haired barista, who had served him some half an hour before, was weaving his way towards Dan's table.

"Sir," he said. "I'm afraid that we don't encourage people to use our premises as a place of work."

"I wasn't aware that I was doing that," responded Dan.

"You've been here over two hours, and I've served you just twice. This is not an internet café, and we do like to give a variety of customers the opportunity to use our premises."

If that was the owner's policy, it seemed a rather flimsy one, but Dan shrugged and began packing away his papers and computer. He had not quite finished, however, so he commented, "Your advertising says that you provide 'Free wi-fi'. It was one of the things that brought me in here."

The itinerant barista was not to be beaten. "We provide free wi-fi for the convenience of our customers," he pronounced loftily. "But it's not our intention to provide rent-free office space. I'd also point out that you're occupying a table for four – and we have customers waiting."

Dan looked around. It was true. The café was otherwise full and a group of customers was waiting at the counter. "Fair enough," he said. "But why didn't you say so in the first place?"

He shuffled his way to the door and made his way into the street. From the corner of his eye, he saw the barista resume his place behind the counter and the customers begin to settle themselves at the table he had occupied.

The heat was now quite oppressive and, far from feeling isolated, he was now all too aware of the bustle and the crowds. He clutched his briefcase and looked up and down the street, seeking inspiration as to the next place in which he might perch for an hour or two.

He remembered that a few yards further down there was a small seating area and a map of the town centre. He wandered along to the large street map but then recalled that at the bottom of the pedestrianised area in which he was standing there was a leafy square in which the town library was located.

A few minutes later, he had found a table at the edge of the library's reference area. It housed a number of computers; a handful of people of various ages and appearances were busy at the keyboards. He would be inconspicuous amongst the library's customers – and at least no-one would be expecting him to buy a succession of coffees as 'rent' for the table on which he now began to spread his computer and sheaf of papers. Behind a service counter to his left, two librarians were absorbed in whatever work they were doing and seemed neither to notice his entry nor his presence at the table. With any luck, he would be able to stay where he was, with just a short break for lunch, until the library closed which, he noted from a sign above the librarians' work area, would be at 5pm.

He managed to continue working on job applications for about another hour before boredom and a desire for something to eat overtook him. With his briefcase tucked under his arm, he went in search of a kiosk which he had noticed next to a seating area on one side of the square. He joined the small queue of people waiting to be served and then, armed with a hot sausage roll and coffee in a cardboard cup, he found himself a space on one of the public benches; neither food nor drink were well suited to a hot day, but they would keep him going for a while.

Sandwiching his briefcase between himself and the bench, he munched away at his sausage roll and sipped at the scalding coffee. A glance at his watch told him that it was 1pm. By now, he reflected, pupils at Wellsprings Primary would be settling down to their afternoon session.

After lunch, he returned to the library; the table at which he had been working was still vacant, so he set himself up once more and began work. He managed to write a letter, but it was uphill work and despite being fairly meagre, his lunch had begun to make him feel sleepy. He left his computer and papers on the table and went to explore the nearby bookshelves.

There seemed to be little of immediate interest but then, as he explored further, he came across a collection of books about the Monmouth Rebellion. He knew that people from Somerset had played a significant part in the Rebellion and its aftermath, so he took down three of the books that looked to be of most interest and carried them back to the table at which he had been sitting.

His drowsiness had disappeared by now and, for a while, he immersed himself in the events, religion and politics of the Stuart period. The extent to which the upheaval of that time had foreshadowed thinking and development in the modern world, intrigued him – but then, despite having time on his hands, it was not the past that preoccupied him.

Instead, it was the contemporary world that drew him back. The library's resources seemed to be focused on the region's history, and it was the present and the future that were central to Dan's curiosity. He took out his computer and returned to the internet exploration that he had begun the previous day. In place of the worldwide span of his previous 'trawl', he decided to look at a small number of specific locations.

The first he found amongst the articles that came up as 'results' was one which referred to South Florida. There had been, he learned, a huge increase in recent years in the flood threat there – a threat which arose from rainfall, sea level rising at a rate faster than in other parts of the US coastline and the possibility of storm surges if tropical storms or hurricanes were to strike. The limestone geology of parts of the state was also contributing to groundwater flooding, a factor that, Dan remembered from experiences in Somerset, was not always taken into account.

A second result led him to look at flooding in Bangladesh. It seemed to suffer in so many ways. River flooding was common and much of the land was very low lying, particularly the myriad tiny islands in the delta of the Ganges, Brahmaputra and Meghna. With both the monsoon and flooding as annual events, Dan wondered what it was that accounted for dense population of the region – but, as with volcanic areas, that which often brought death also, more frequently, brought fertility; the silt-laden rivers determined that flood plains of the delta were fertile places in which to grow rice.

Running counter to this was a problem with increasing salinity of the soil. The fingers of the sea were reaching into the soil and affecting both fresh water supplies and the ability to grow crops. Sea level rise was an insidious and unstoppable influence that was tipping the balance from a situation in which people had long balanced the threats against the benefits to one in which their lives were constantly at risk.

Dan paused in his reading of the internet article. His sight was beginning to blur and the sun was no longer finding its way into the library. He looked around in the gathering gloom as a librarian began collecting the books he had left scattered on the table. She approached him and, in the slight chill of the room, pulled her light cardigan around her.

"We're closing in ten minutes," she trilled. He peered at the clock above the librarians' work area. As so often, he had not noticed the passage of time. He watched as the woman who had spoken to him loaded books onto a library trolley. She was small, thin, birdlike in her movements. He surmised that she was in her late forties but her close-cropped hair was already greying and her thin blue dress hung upon her; she seemed of a piece with the sparse functionality of the library.

He had, however, been grateful for an afternoon's sanctuary. He hoped that he had done enough during the morning to increase his chances of being employed once more but he felt guilty as well, that he had not devoted all the time he had available, to searching for jobs. He stood up, his briefcase in hand, and made his way to the library exit. Once in the car, he would join the late afternoon exodus from the town centre. He had a notion though, that rather than feel like one of the town's workaday employees heading for evening sustenance at home, he would, instead, be all too aware that he was trying to cloak himself in a sense of normality.

* * *

Dan managed to sustain his new routine until the end of the week. By that time, he had sent off a large number of job applications and felt justified in having chosen a strategy that made him feel more like one of the town's working population. He was not, however, at all confident that any of the applications he had made would come to a fruition which would provide him with sufficient income, let alone anything that approached job satisfaction.

The librarian who had come to usher him on his way at the end of the previous three afternoons made her usual appearance, collecting up his earlier selection of books about the English Civil War, about which he had gleaned a little more information and an opportunity to understand the country in which he lived, a little better.

Since it was Friday afternoon, her usual laconic message had a slightly different content to it.

"We're closing in ten minutes. The library will not be open at the weekend, but we will be open as usual on Monday, at 9am."

She gave a Dan a slightly bleak, sideways smile, as if already anticipating that she would be seeing him again at the start of the following week. Dan, who was pleased simply to have someone notice him, returned the smile.

He packed away his papers and computer, resolving that, since it was Friday evening, he would spend an hour or two in a local pub. Mid evening would be quite early enough to return once more to the solitariness of the cottage. He thought for a moment or two about his choice of pub although he had only a passing knowledge of the ones in Sedgewater's town centre. 'The Feathers' had something of a reputation for rowdiness; 'The Monmouth Arms' and 'The Pitchfork Rebellion' had similar reputations. Then he remembered that on the other side of the town centre was the 'Wheatsheaf' which he knew often drew in staff from the College of Arts and Technology (or CART, as it was often known). It was some distance from the library, so he decided to drive there.

The 'Wheatsheaf' was not the only pub which benefited from the College's trade but Dan had been there several times before and knew that some of the lecturers often frequented the place after what they called 'the graveyard slot' – a reference to the difficulties that arose from trying to get students to attend lectures on a Friday evening, let alone to focus on their content.

He parked his car in the pub's spacious car park and walked across to the entrance. The pub, he guessed, had once been a large and rambling farmhouse that had slowly been enveloped by the spreading urban development of Sedgewater. It was one of the few within the town's boundaries that had flint walls and a thatched roof. He went to the bar and bought a soft drink. Looking around for somewhere to sit, he spotted a daily newspaper left on a table by a previous customer, so he scooped it up and then sat with his drink, perusing its crop of crime, scandals and trivialities.

He had been there only minutes when he realised that someone was heading towards him. He looked up. The person now in front of him was wearing a blue suit that seen better days, a red tie loosened at an open top button, a striped shirt and tan shoes – which Dan thought seemed ill matched with the rest of his clothes. There seemed to be something familiar about the slightly reddened face, short, tousled hair, furrowed brow and the lively, rather toothy smile. Behind the thick lenses of dark framed glasses, the eyes of the person before him seemed a little larger than was natural. Dan strove for a minute to recognise the person in front of him – who was already extending a hand toward him.

"I'll bet you don't remember me," said the owner of the proffered hand, in which surmise Dan thought he was completely accurate but did not like to say so. Fortunately, his memory for faces suddenly made the necessary leap and came to the rescue just in time.

"Dave – Dave Andrews?"

"Right first time! I think we worked together when some of your staff needed IT training."

"Yes," thought Dan. "That was it." The details were coming back to him although he had only been Deputy Head at Wellsprings a few months and that meant that it was several years ago.

Dave, however, was already moving on.

"So, what's brings you in here on a Friday night?"

"I was down in the town centre and wanted a bit of company before going home."

Dave nodded. "I often come here after my Friday stint. Friday evenings are hard work. I think I remember that you teach at Wellsprings Primary. How are things going?"

"They're probably going well," said Dan, frowning a little. "But I don't work there now." Honesty seemed to be the best policy.

"Oh, why's that?" Dave's curiosity was aroused.

Dan described the circumstances of his departure from Wellsprings Primary but decided that it would be best to leave out any references to his personal life; the restructuring of local schools was, after all, the main reason that he now found himself out of a job.

Dave listened attentively. "Hmm, that's a bit rough," he commented. "What are you doing now?"

"Not a lot – other than filling in job applications. But I've also started looking at college courses. I was thinking of re-training because although I'm qualified to teach in Primary Schools, I don't seem to be qualified for much else."

Dave was surprised. "I'd have thought there would be plenty of other Primary teaching jobs around here. There's certainly a large number of Primary schools." He looked at the expression on Dan's face and took the cue that seemed to be there. "But perhaps it's not for you anymore?"

"That's right," replied Dan. "I've done my time with schools. I need to move on."

"I sometimes feel like that about the College – so I can understand. All the same, it takes a lot of hard work to qualify as a teacher. Do you really want to start all over again? I mean, there must be other jobs in which you could use your teaching skills?"

"I'm sure there are, but I've been combing through local job opportunities and there doesn't seem to be anything that I can relate to."

Dave thought for a moment. "Well, you may know that the College has an 'Education and Training Department'?"

Dan shook his head. "No, I'm afraid I know very little about the inner workings of CART."

Dave laughed. "I shouldn't let anyone from the hierarchy hear you referring to the College as CART. For some strange reason, they seem to have overlooked what is, after all, a rather obvious acronym. However, I'm digressing. I'm sure that if you enquired about vacancies in the Education and Training Department, there could be something there that would interest you."

Dan wanted to hear more but, after several mind-numbing days of combing through the details of jobs in which he had very little interest, it seemed best to be cautious.

"Perhaps…" replied Dan. "But I've never taught adults. I've only ever worked with Primary school children."

"Yes, of course – but don't let that put you off. What you have that could be useful to the College is your teaching skills and your knowledge of schools."

Dan was still doubtful. "Managing children is one thing. But adults – I don't know if I could make the transfer."

"You'd probably surprise yourself. A helpful thing to remember is that most adults on courses have specific reasons for being there. They either need or want to be there – often it's both – whereas in schools, the kids don't have a choice."

Dan nodded thoughtfully. Dave's rather 'down to earth' comments made sense. He felt the stirrings of a genuine interest.

"So how do I find out if there are any vacancies?"

"HR is easy to find. It's on the same site as the rest of the College – and well signposted. Otherwise, you could contact them online. The details are on the College website – as are job vacancies for that matter."

Dan had one last question. "Would there be any advantage to paying HR a visit?"

Dave thought about it for a moment. "Well, there could be. I happen to know, for example, that the College is about to advertise some new courses for people training to be lecturers. You might get to see those just as they release them. And then of course, it would do no harm to have an informal discussion with someone in HR – if only to see if they would be interested in your CV."

It sounded like a good idea. However, Dan thought he knew the courses to which Dave was referring. "You mean teaching qualifications for lecturers? I thought the Government had scrapped those?"

"You're right, Dan – they did. But you know what it's like in Education. HMG changes its mind every five minutes. All I know is that teaching qualifications for lecturers are back in fashion and there will be vacancies because the Education and Training Department simply does not have enough teaching staff of its own at present."

If nothing else, Dave's enthusiasm had been convincing and Dan felt grateful that he had been willing to share some helpful background information. He gazed pointedly at the empty table in front of them.

"Do you realise, we've been nattering here for a good ten minutes and neither of us has a drink. What can I get you?"

Dave looked at his watch. "Hmm," he said. "It'll be another half hour before my wife comes to collect me – and I have done a lot of talking today. A drink wouldn't go amiss."

"No problem – it's been a very useful conversation from my viewpoint."

"They've just introduced a new bitter here – it's called 'Rooster'. I'll try a pint of that."

Dan smiled as he contemplated asking for a pint of 'Rooster' – but turned and made his way to the bar; he would have liked to try it himself, but he had to drive back to the cottage because, unlike Dave, he had no-one coming to collect him.

* * *

CHAPTER 25

DIVERGING PATHS

With the index finger of her left hand, Sue pushed a paper clip across the desk top whilst with her right hand, she manoeuvred a cup of strong black coffee towards her mouth. She liked to be busy and that morning was tedious because there was little to do; everything seemed to be in limbo. Her most recent project was all but completed and the negotiations for new work on a similar development in Gloucester had slowed down; key people were on holiday or going out of the country to get away from the drought – and from the incessant heat. They would have to travel a long way, she reflected, and possibly go north rather than south, for once. The summer was drifting on, but she vividly remembered the events of the previous year – memories of such immediacy that she could still feel something of her former fury with Dan.

At first, when she had learned of his affair with Anne Moresby, she had been white with anger. The colleague who had told her had instantly regretted what he had done. She had stormed out and driven home in a rage, terrifying other drivers she passed on the way and, once in the house, had proceeded to smash every photo frame and then, every picture that they had jointly bought. After that, she had torn up the bundle of letters that she had kept from the days when people still wrote such things to each other. Finally, she tried to delete every reference to him from her phone and the array of mobile devices that she kept in the house, in her bag or in her car.

Temporarily exhausted by so much furious activity, she had poured herself a gin and tonic and slumped into the nearest armchair. Curiously enough, the G and T had seemed to last barely more than a few seconds and she found herself revisiting the bottles again and again until eventually, tired of fiddling about with the tonic, she began to down a succession of neat glasses of gin. Normally, she would have found gin on its own far too strong but in the uncompromising anger of that day, it suited her mood.

For a while, she had given way to hysterical sobbing. How could Dan have so completely betrayed her? How could he have made her look so stupid in front of her work colleagues and all their neighbours? And what about their children? He had wanted a sexual relationship with her badly enough to make her pregnant – twice! Then there was the fact that she had slaved all the hours that God gave to provide them with a lifestyle that, on Dan's salary alone, they could only have aspired to. Had he given even a moment's thought to that when he was so busily screwing Anne Moresby?

It had taken her some considerable while to get past the sobbing. She must have passed out because she had 'come to' again when the phone began to ring; she had let the call go to the answering machine and had listened as an 'anxious' colleague left a message hoping that she was alright and asking her to let them know her whereabouts as soon as she felt able to do so.

Her head had been pounding as though it had a regiment of road drills inside it. She had gone to the medicine cupboard to find some paracetamols but, instead, found herself dashing to kneel in front of the lavatory with her head halfway down the pan. Her body had taken over. Unable to control the spasms, she had vomited again and again until she had been totally drained and could vomit no more.

She had rolled away from the lavatory. The smell was revolting. As soon as she had had the strength, she had dropped the lid on it all and flushed it away. To her disgust, however, the smell of gin had still lingered so, despite her fragility, she had filled a bucket with water, armed herself with the loo brush and had done her best to eradicate the last vestiges of her anger-driven binge.

For a while, her nausea had threatened to return but as soon as she had felt she could withstand the taste of toothpaste, she had gone to brush her teeth. Finally, emerging from the bathroom, she had felt able to take on the task that she had gradually been setting herself – making the house so secure that Dan would never again be able to get into it.

At first, Sedgewater Security Systems had prevaricated, insisting that it was not their policy to survey a property, decide on the security resources needed, price them, advise the customer and then fit them all in the space of just a few hours. When she had reminded them, however, of all the business that she had previously directed towards them on behalf of the various solicitors for whom she had worked, an SSS van had rolled onto her drive within the hour.

Of course, she had to direct the technicians scurrying about the house and occasionally they had needed to consult her about which monitor she wanted where, and then had wanted to talk to her about the wireless connection to the app that she would need to install on her various mobile 'devices'. In between times, she had diverted away from all the bustle and had busied herself in other ways by removing empty bottles to the recycling box and attempting to clear away the wreckage that she had left behind during her angry rampage through the house.

As they worked, the security technicians had studiedly failed to notice any remaining mess, but she had been glad, several hours later, to see their van rolling off the drive in a cloud of dust that, at that time, had seemed so much a part of the summer's drought.

If it was at all possible for anything to please her on such a day, she had drawn a modicum of satisfaction from the fact that she had achieved everything that she had wanted in terms of the new security system. Now all she had to do was try to occupy herself until Dan came home; it would not be long.

She had gone across to the answering machine. It would be best, she had thought, to deal with her colleague's phone call while she still had enough patience to smooth away any forced anxiety and unctuousness of people at the office. Above all, she had wanted to free her mind of all clutter – so that she could deal with Dan as soon as he arrived. If she left the front door open and a bag by the door, packed and ready for him, the chances were that he would not even notice the new security measures that she had caused to be so rapidly installed. "After that?" she had then asked herself. After that, she would never let him in again. Despite her wish for mental clarity, her earlier feelings of nausea had passed, and, out of habit, she had poured herself a glass of chardonnay. Then she had waited…

She came back to the present. The paper clip she had been lethargically manipulating with her index finger came to rest as she reached across to answer her desk phone; she looked at the number on its display. It was a call from one of her colleagues in another office – but from a private number, a number that she had got to know very well.

She picked up the phone, letting any vestigial anger from her former home life slip away. An educated voice on the other end of the phone asked if she would like to go out to lunch. Automatically, the tone and timbre of her voice echoed that of the caller. Lunch? Of course – that would be delightful. One o'clock. Usual place? No – but his suggestion was one she knew was even better. For the sake of discretion, he would drive his car to their pre-arranged meeting point, two streets away, a place that people from the office rarely visited.

The call ended. With just a moment's hesitation, she pulled the document that lay in the middle of her desk towards her. She had to occupy the time until lunch somehow – so she might as well read it. That said, the day was suddenly no longer so boring that she had to distract herself by pushing paper clips around the desk.

* * *

The windows of the Science Lab looked out across the School Games Field. Emily was packing her books away in a leisurely fashion because the lesson that had just finished was her last one for the day. The other pupils had already left but she had to catch the service bus home and it was not due at the stop opposite the school for another twenty minutes. She gazed momentarily out at the brown expanse of grass that spread away from the school and towards the River Sedge. Everything was parched and dry. There had been a succession of summers like this now – although confusingly, the winters had still been so wet that there was the constant threat of flooding. At such times, the river upon which she was gazing took on a very different aspect.

Her bag was packed. She swung it over her shoulder and then went out to the corridor that led to the stairs. A glance at her phone told her that there was still plenty of time before the bus was due; it was a hot day and there was no reason to rush. She would walk slowly down the path to the school gate and wait in the bus shelter. Steve Barratt had offered her a lift that afternoon in the car that his father had bought him, but she was wary of Steve and did not want to incur the wrath of her mother.

It still seemed odd to her that pupils in the Sixth Form could pass their driving test and then own and drive their cars to school. She did not want to dwell on thoughts of Steve because she knew well enough that a large part of his motivation in learning to drive and to own a car was so that he could pick up girls. There was, though, little else to think about as she waited for the bus, so her thoughts drifted back to him.

Emily had known Steve for as long as she could remember. Even at Nursery, she had been vaguely aware of him as someone who was in that hazy group of children who were just a little older than her and her immediate friends. Her parents also knew the Barratts. They had met them at a party organised by Mrs Ashworth, one of her teachers when she was in Primary School. Of course, she and Josh had spent the night of the party at their grandmother's house, but she had learned about some of the details when she had later talked to her father about it.

She learned for example that Mr Ashworth and Steve's father often worked together and that they had both played a large part in the building of Wellsprings School and the neighbouring housing development. Now that she was fifteen though, Emily needed no-one to make her aware of the media attention that was being given to the problems at Wellsprings and to the belated arguments that had been raging about the siting of the entire scheme and who was responsible for the inadequacy of the initial flood prevention measures. Her father had also told her that, partly because of the problems, the school was being closed whilst she knew from other pupils at her school that a large and expensive scheme of flood defences was now being built to protect the houses in the Wellsprings area.

Emily naturally surmised that her own father might still have his former job if the measures that had been part of the original scheme had been properly put in place. That in itself, she thought, was a good reason for staying away from Steve. She did not, of course blame him for his father's behaviour, but now that she knew more about how Steve had been able to afford a car, she was even less inclined to want his company.

Then, of course, her mother had other objections to Steve; Emily was well aware what they were and thought, in part, that she was being overprotective, but she went along with them because, since her father had been forced to move elsewhere, she had become even more dependent on her mother. She was also planning to go eventually to university and entanglement with Steve was not part of that plan.

The green service bus, a double decker, rumbled around the bend that led to the bus stop outside the school. Emily flagged it down since she was the only person waiting for it. It drew to a halt in a cloud of dust, she hopped on, showed her pass and found a seat just across from the driver. She had barely settled before the bus driver had to brake sharply as a car, driven recklessly, overtook and streamed ahead, leaving the driver to mutter and curse as he tried to see his way forward.

The cloud of dust gradually cleared, and Emily caught a glimpse of Steve's car; the bus drew away and trundled along through the lanes, the loudest sounds of its progress coming from a loose section of bodywork. Emily looked around her; there was one other passenger on the lower deck and, she thought, no more than one or two more on the upper deck. It did not seem like a very economical way to run a bus service, but she supposed that the bus would have many more passengers when it made the return journey to Sedgewater.

The dull, dusty green of the hedgerows blurred past the windows. When she was able to catch a glimpse of the fields beyond, she could see that the crops were already a dark brown despite not having had time to develop and ripen properly. The harvest would be a poor one.

The bend in the road and the tree that signified to her that she was nearly home came into view and the bus drew up just outside her house. She scrambled out of her seat, called a 'thank you' to the driver and stepped down onto the road, moving quickly away from the bus in anticipation of the cloud that she knew would billow into the air behind it.

She would start on her homework and hope that she would get a message from her mother to say what time she would be back from work. Tonight, she and Josh were responsible for cooking dinner. It took just a minute or two for Emily to cross the road but there, sitting just a yard or two from the drive was Steve's car. It was covered in the fine dust that covered everything, and she found hard to see inside but a text message pinged into her phone:

"Beat you! Last chance tomorrow!"

Emily quickly decided that she would be going nowhere near the car. She slid round to the back of the house, unlocked the door and dumped her school bag on the kitchen table; hopefully, it would not be long before Josh arrived.

* * *

Jayne was finding it difficult to concentrate. Her parents had said that unless at least one of them was at home, they would not agree to her and Josh studying there together. She would have to make sure that he left before her mother returned from the office. Normally, because it was a Wednesday, her mother would have been working from home but, typically, she had been called in to deal with some problem or other and would not be back for another hour and a half. The timing of the message had been unfortunate because, when it arrived, she and Josh had been climbing out of a friend's car, having been given a lift home from school.

Jayne decided that she could hardly tell Josh to wait at the bus stop until the next bus came along because that would be nearly an hour's time – and the next one after that would be about another hour again. But now she found herself hoping that her mother was not in hurry to get away from work; if she found Josh in the house when she got back, she would be furious.

For the moment, they were supposedly engaged in working through their Maths homework together although their body language belied the seriousness of their efforts; at that moment, they were lying head-to-head on the lounge floor with her Maths textbook between them. True, they had been discussing the questions they had been told to answer for some while now, but their concentration was flagging. Jayne was almost certain, for example, that Josh's eyes were consistently wandering towards her cleavage which, since she had changed her top for something lighter and cooler as soon as she got home, was rather more apparent than it had been at College that day.

Without being fully conscious of it, Josh was engaging in what, he had recently learned, was called a 'displacement activity'. He had understood the Maths topic easily enough and now it was a matter of working through the exercise they had been set for homework. It would be much easier for him to focus on it at home than here with Jayne – and, in a contest with Jayne's attractions, the homework activity stood little chance.

"You know, it's a good thing that we're planning to go to different universities," commented Jayne with a faint smile.

"Hmm, I know." Josh generally tried to be philosophical about it. "There are just one or two problems with our plan, though."

"Oh, and what would those be?"

"Well, for a start, if we're going to get our first choices, we both have to get the grades that we need."

"Is that a problem?" Jayne always seemed to be over-confident.

Josh rolled onto his back. "Come on, Jayne! We both know that predicted grades quite often turn out to be wrong…"

Jayne paused to consider what he was saying although they had talked about it all a number of times before.

"Well, even if you ended up in York and I got a place in Exeter, we would still go on seeing each other. We would have to travel further – which would be a nuisance – but I hope you're not thinking it would stop me from coming to see you?"

Josh said nothing, so she continued.

"So far, though, you've always said that the course at Bristol is the one you want to get onto, which, since I'll be striving to get an offer from Bath, seems to me to be a pretty good solution."

Josh still made no reply. Occasionally, the gap between their plans and their achievement seemed more obvious to him than it did to Jayne. He knew, as well, that she was only thinking about the problems that it was within their ability to solve – but that was something that they were both reluctant to talk about.

"I guess you're right," he said eventually, "but between now and the exams, there's still an awful lot of work to do."

"But we'll do it, Josh. Remember, we went through all this before when we were doing GCSEs. We agreed that in the month leading up to our exams we wouldn't see each other – at least, outside of school."

He remembered it well and gave a groan. "A whole month, Jayne…!"

"What's a month – especially if we do as we've planned."

Josh said nothing but replied with a smile. Staying together was something that he would never take for granted especially since his parents had split up. He also wondered in moments of self-honesty about the durability of teenage romances.

"Do you ever think, Jayne," he asked, "that we're making it more difficult for ourselves by being together now rather than waiting until we've finished our university courses?"

"I haven't really thought about it," she said. "I just know I want to be with you."

"And I want to be with you – but don't you ever wonder about the things that may lie ahead of us?"

"Of course."

"So, what do you think about this future that we're hoping to share?"

"I think it could be difficult…but I hope that whatever happens we'll face it together."

Josh waited frustratedly, not surprised that she had described their future as potentially 'difficult' but expecting to hear more. Instead, she suddenly wormed her way across the carpet so that she was beside him. He raised himself so that he could look into her eyes. Then, after kissing her he said, "Simply telling me it might be 'difficult' isn't an answer. I thought you would have much more to say than that and you're usually the one who wants to talk about all the details…"

He stopped. She was smiling up at him and seeming almost to laugh at his earnestness. He reached out a hand which strayed predictably to the top button of her blouse and which she immediately intercepted by grabbing his fingers.

"That," she said, "is precisely the reason that I'm not saying any more."

"What do mean?" He looked at her quizzically.

"I mean that we don't have time – either for long answers or for – well, for whatever you seem to have in mind."

He pretended to pout, as though he had not anticipated her response.

"Besides," she added, "my mum will be home in about forty-five minutes – and she won't be very impressed if she finds us here together whilst she's been at work."

She leaned across to where her phone lay on the carpet and checked the time. "Your bus is due in about fifteen minutes and it will take you five minutes to walk to the stop."

Josh gave a sigh and heaved himself into a sitting position. "Yeah," he said, "and after that it's either a long wait or a bit of a walk. And I'm also supposed to be 'baby-sitting' my sister."

"I'll tell Emily what you've said," replied Jayne.

"Don't you dare!"

Josh grabbed her hands and pulled her to her feet.

She laughed at him and said, "What are you going to do about it if I do?"

"I...I'm going to wait until next Wednesday."

"Why, what's happening on Wednesday?" She stopped, suddenly, abruptly remembering what they had arranged.

"It's the start of our 'month', isn't it!" replied Josh indignantly. "After that, we're locked away with our revision – for four whole weeks!"

By this time, he had walked through to the hallway and was in the process of scooping up his backpack. Jayne waited and then walked with him to the door.

As he placed his fingers on the door handle, she drew him to her and said, "Don't worry, I won't forget about Wednesday."

"Okay." He smiled. "I'll see you tomorrow."

He turned and made his way along the walkway to the flight of steps at the end of the house that led down to ground level. On Wednesday next, Jayne's mother would be working from home so they planned to be at 'Moorside'; Josh's mother had never thought to talk to him about any plans he might have to spend the day there, with Jayne – and she, as usual, would be at the office. Emily would not be back until the end of the school day, by which time Jayne planned to be meeting up with friends in Sedgewater.

Jayne watched him go, reflecting that it seemed strange in the midst of a drought that her father had designed the house to cope with the problems of flooding – a design that had proved very prescient two winters ago when the whole of the surrounding area had remained under flood water for several months. She waved to Josh as he made his way out to the nearby lane, a small cloud of dust rising to mark his passage along the path below.

* * *

Dan had thought about phoning Amanda – and then, had thought again. It was mid-evening, and it was already several hours since he had been told that his interview for the post of lecturer at Sedgewater College of Art and Technology had been successful. To have told Amanda of his success in finding a new job, he should have done so before he had bumped into Dave Andrews in the College's Refectory. Dave, though, had an evening class to teach and so could not take him up on his invitation to join him at 'The Wheatsheaf'.

So it was that at that moment, he was sitting near an open window in his local pub, 'The Raven Arms', enjoying a celebratory pint of beer, the relative coolness of the evening and the fading light of the day but wishing all the same, that he had someone to celebrate with. His thoughts briefly turned to Anne but although it was still just a short while since she had cut him out of her life, he knew that there was not the slightest prospect that they would ever be together again.

A tinge of regret stole into his thoughts as he remembered that neither he nor Amanda had followed up on the conversation they had had when he had gone to visit her at her house. His relationship with Anne, he was now able to recognise, had always been aspirational rather than based on anything that she would prefer beyond the things that her wealthy husband could already offer her.

The same was true to some extent of Amanda, but then, he had already spent a year of his life living with Amanda. He remembered that they had been happy together and that it was by some strange twist that she had ultimately chosen to leave the love that was deepening between them and go off instead with someone who could provide her with the material security she craved but not the emotional fulfilment which, like Amanda's father before him, he had failed to supply. Dan had certainly envied Amanda's professional success, but he had never envied her the failed dream of a family that so obviously hung about her when, however briefly, she forgot to sustain her professional image. Even there, though, he reminded himself he could hardly claim to be any sort of model example. He had two children whom he loved but although he still had feelings for Sue, he recognised very belatedly that he had probably been on the rebound from his relationship with Amanda when he had met her.

So, it seemed in Dan's estimation, that neither he, nor Sue nor Amanda nor Anne had teamed up with the person most likely to make them happy. Strangely, it occurred to him, it might be the reason that he often preferred to spend time in his geographical world of data, of statistics and the immutable laws that controlled the fate of the planet rather than the small but convoluted world of his private life. If he had any responsibility at all for the fate of the Earth, he shared it with many millions of other people; the responsibility for recent events in his family, however, he believed was largely his, and his former family life might well have continued undisturbed if he had not fallen in love with Anne.

It was hardly a celebratory thought. He gazed out of the window at the rapidly fading light and took a sip of his beer. He had, at least, a chance now to do things differently and, perhaps, to do them better? He wondered again how Amanda was spending her evening.

* * *

Amanda had lost count of the number of evenings that she had found herself waiting for James. He had said he would be with her no later than eight o'clock; it was now nearly ten o'clock and she had heard nothing from him.

He always had some excuse, of course, and so far, she had always pretended to believe him. It was now months since she had waited for him. She would wait another half hour and then go to bed, knowing that when she woke in the morning he would still not be by her side.

It was all so far from what, in recent times, she had begun to crave. Despite her mother's ill-fated relationship with her father, they had still been happy for a short period – happy for long enough to have children. And her sister Edith now had children of her own. Of the women within her immediate circle, she was the only one who was childless.

Her bedside lamp gave the bedroom a warmth which, in human terms, it lacked. She undressed quickly, putting on a fresh pair of pyjamas and then slid between the cool sheets. Their coolness was something that in the year's persistent heat, she welcomed; as she drowsed before sleep, it enabled her not to dwell on her husband's inconsiderate, some would say 'cruel', behaviour.

Amanda, though, had qualities that not everyone possessed. In the darkness of the room, she decided that, like her mother so long ago, she was well past the point where she was prepared to endure the feeling of being a 'victim'. She wanted her small world to change – so she would change it. At that moment, she had no idea how she would turn her determination into a sequence of events that would take her away from the unwanted solitude of her private life, but she knew that she would.

She reflected briefly that even in her professional life, events and connections that she had known nothing about, were turning against her. She remembered with embarrassment the afternoon on which she had told Dan about the Hydrologist's Report; it seemed almost unbelievable to her now that when the school and housing development had been built she had had so little detailed knowledge of James' involvement in those projects – and, therefore, in the train of events that had now led to the closure of Wellsprings Primary, the enormously expensive measures that were now having to be taken to protect the houses in the area – and, by a curious turn of events, the end of Dan's employment at the school. Dan, if he knew or suspected anything, had never said so.

It seemed to her as her thoughts began to drift, that the more she learned of James' behaviour during the years that they had been married, the less she felt any loyalty – still less any love or respect for him.

It was not a good thought on which to go to sleep, but it was one that coloured all her feelings about the life she had worked so hard to build for herself and for James. There had been a time when she would never have thought that she could become disenchanted with her work and her career, but that too had now become a dead thing – and something that she wanted to relinquish as soon as there was an opportunity to do so. Now, in contrast to her previous 'self', she was becoming an angry 'rebel'. She had 'played by the rules' but where had it got her?

The tablets that her GP had given her sometimes took a while to have their desired effect but soon, despite the unhappy nature of her thoughts, she fell asleep and when she woke the following day, it seemed to her that she had slept without dreaming.

James, of course, had not arrived home and there were no messages waiting for her. It was of little consequence; she was used to the solitude and, alone in the house, she would have plenty of time to give some thought to the solution of her problems.

* * *

CHAPTER 26

LEARNING CURVE

Psychologically, Dan felt that he had moved on a long way since the debacle with Anne in the summer of the previous year. That morning, he was working at his desk in the large open-plan office in which the majority of the lecturers had a workspace where they could plan their sessions and respond to the various pieces of administration connected with their role.

He looked away from his computer. His view was mainly of the heads of other lecturers, the vast majority of whom were working at computers or talking on the telephone. He turned his head to the large windows that ran along the far side of the office and gazed across the gardens of the houses next to the college. The office was on the second floor and his view now was one of the backs of houses, roofs, and the tops of garden trees. Since it was early spring, he could have imagined that he was in a garden suburb; buds, flowers and fresh green leaves were everywhere to be seen on the trees and anyone so minded could have spent pleasurable minutes watching and identifying the garden birds. The College was, however, on one of the arterial routes into the town and the road on the other side of the row of houses was continuously busy with traffic.

He had paused whilst trying to think of an interesting way to present some otherwise 'dry' material – but he had nearly completed the session planning that he needed to do, so he decided to take a mental break, gazing out of the window to get his mind away from the computer screen in front of him.

The outlook from the window was a pleasant one, but his thoughts soon strayed to the move he had made in terms of having previously spent many years teaching Primary school children; there were, of course, numerous differences between working with children and working with adults. He knew that it would be some time before he could feel that he had fully adjusted to the range of abilities, prior learning and diversity of backgrounds that he now encountered amongst the adult learners in his sessions. He was, however, still able to use his existing skills in the area of learning – an area that he had always thought of as being of both value and enjoyment. He had found, too, that he could relate well to the majority of his colleagues and that the sense of being part of a large teaching team was a good antidote to the many hours of solitude spent at the cottage.

He went back to his work for a few more minutes and then having finished his planning, glanced at the time shown at the bottom of his computer screen; it confirmed what his stomach was already telling him – that it was lunchtime.

There were two refectories on the ground floor and a café next door to the College. The first one that he would pass would be the one adjacent to the main lecture theatre. He remembered, too, that there was currently a series of free lunchtime lectures, open to both College staff and members of the public. He did not remember the topic listed for that day but knew that the details could be gleaned by looking at the display screen next to the lecture theatre entrance. He logged out of his computer terminal and made his way down the stairs to the ground floor.

As he had expected, when he reached the lecture theatre, the title of the lunchtime lecture was clearly displayed. It looked somewhat forbidding – 'Climate Change: Implications for the UK'. He thought for a minute about whether he wanted to spend his lunchtime listening to someone talk about a topic that he so often found seriously depressing. Since he had been made redundant from his previous job, however, he had had more opportunity to read about climate change, and he would have time after the lecture to have some lunch since his first teaching obligations did not begin that day until early evening. He pushed open the swing door in front of him.

He was almost late. The lights in the lecture theatre were being dimmed and he looked for a seat that was close to where he was standing at the back of the auditorium. The lecture had attracted only a small number of people, so finding a seat quickly would not be a problem. He looked around. There was a partially empty row of seats on his left. A young woman was sitting in the seat nearest to him but beyond that were several spaces. He said in a hushed voice, "Excuse me."

The woman quickly stood and moved momentarily into the aisle so that he could pass. He seated himself further along the row and nodded in thanks to her, as she settled in her seat again.

By now, the only lights in the room were focused on the lecturer's podium. One of the senior lecturers from the Science Faculty had moved to the centre of the stage whilst the person giving the lecture was waiting just within the lights. Dan vaguely recognised the staff member but could not put a name to him.

"Welcome to today's lunchtime lecture, the third in our current series in which we're committed to keeping staff and students in touch with topics in which they may not themselves be specialists. We're particularly pleased to have with us Professor John Briggs, who is a distinguished member of the Met Office's team of climate researchers at the Hadley Centre in Exeter. Professor Briggs has co-authored many reports on climate change topics and has also published a substantial number of peer-reviewed articles on the subject in scientific journals. He is a widely respected researcher and spokesman, and we feel very privileged that he has been able to give us some of his time today...Professor Briggs!"

There was scattered applause as the Professor stepped forward to the podium.

"Well, thank you, Jeff, for your introduction. It's a pleasure to be here and also to have been invited to participate in this series of lunchtime lectures. People in my line of work believe that only their immediate academic colleagues are able to understand the data that we routinely produce with our satellites and 'super-computers'. They may be right about some aspects of it but, whilst the data is complex, I believe that scientists such as myself have an obligation to ensure that members of the public are fully aware of both the phenomena we refer to under the broad umbrella of 'climate change' and the implications that those phenomena will have for our lives and our world – so whilst the research team in which I work is at the forefront of gathering the data, climate change will affect – has always affected – the whole of the planet on which we live."

Dan's interest was now fully focused on the lecturer who, he thought, looked remarkably young given his academic title; he was, in many ways, very different from Dan's image of a 'professor'. The light focused on the lectern seemed to throw into contrast his pallid complexion and his thick black hair. He was tall, almost lanky and had an energy in his movements that was at one with his youthful yet earnest facial expression. His grey jacket hinted at formality that was belied by a loose-necked black sweatshirt and dark, slightly baggy trousers.

Dan redirected his attention away from the lecturer and into the content of the lecture. At that moment, the Professor was outlining the global implications of the steadily rising carbon dioxide content of the atmosphere and the significance of the ice loss from the Arctic, Antarctic and Greenland. He pointed to the slow advances in reducing the carbon dioxide emissions directly attributable to human activities. There was, he said, a certain level of insanity entailed in publicly espousing carbon reduction whilst continuing to search for, and exploit, new reserves of fossil fuels.

The audience, though small, was riveted by the speaker's comments; as Dan cast his eyes across the auditorium, everyone was listening intently as he described and quantified the huge 'deficits' worldwide between the aspirations expressed in the 2015 Paris Climate Change Agreement and the data portraying the reality of carbon emissions. It was now, he reminded his audience, more than two decades since the participant nations, including the UK, had signed the agreement, but evidence had accumulated from the Glasgow 2021 'COP' Conference onwards that the world would miss the 'targets' to which the Conference participants had agreed in an attempt to limit the global increase in temperatures to $2.0^{\circ}C$ – let alone the aspirational international aim of $1.5^{\circ}C$. Indeed, based on the data he and his colleagues were currently working with, it was looking probable that by mid-century the increase would be close to $2.5^{\circ}C$. He used a series of charts and graphs to illustrate his points.

Despite the small size of the audience, those that were there seemed to immediately grasp the significance of the charts and other 'visuals' being presented to them. For Dan, it all became particularly disturbing as the Professor began to quantify and describe some of the characteristics of a $2.5^{\circ}C$ world; although many had failed before him, he had a gift for communication. Several times, he found it necessary to wait whilst the spontaneous reaction of the audience subsided.

Dan, who had only recently begun to seek out detailed information about climate change, was shocked by the data driven scenarios that were being set before them.

By this time, the lecturer had begun to move on to the increasingly observable effects of global 'tipping-points'. Methane emissions associated with the now well-established thawing of the permafrost in the Arctic regions were causing, said the Professor, marked feedback effects, measurable from satellite data, that were vastly amplifying the effects of steadily rising CO_2 emissions.

At this point, the lecturer began to move more specifically to the implications for the UK. There were, he said, both future costs and benefits to the effects of climate change. For example, amongst the benefits some had claimed for a warmer climate in the UK was that it might became a more attractive place as a tourist destination. A further benefit could be that it might be possible to grow a range of crops previously unsuited to the British climate.

The costs, however, in his view, far outweighed any spurious benefits. These included, paradoxically, the impacts of both flood and drought. He cited the accentuated behaviour of the jet stream over the UK, including the development of blocking patterns which, in turn, brought about extended periods of intense rainfall or contrastingly, prolonged periods without precipitation. Such periods of flood and drought, he said, had become much more probable. He pointed to the effects they would have on transportation and infrastructure. Pests and diseases previously associated with climates further south would also establish their presence here whilst plankton food sources for sea life were steadily migrating north; fish stocks in British waters were already being seriously affected.

Dan listened glumly, recognising the realities that lay behind the lecturer's words. During the winter a little over two years ago, he reminded himself, he had found himself coping day-to-day with the effects of prolonged flooding. Rail infrastructure on the south coast of Devon had also been pulverised once again, completely cutting off rail connections to Devon and Cornwall.

It all seemed a far cry from the measured and reassuring tones of government reports and policy programmes that Dan had found during his internet searches – and yet, he noted, Professor Briggs was doing no more than adhere, in a very disciplined way, to the phenomena that he and his colleagues were directly observing through their data collection and analysis. What was it about the lecture that was having such a markedly different impact on him from the anodyne effects of government documents? From his sixth form years, Dan recalled a Robert Graves poem 'The Cool Web'; perhaps it was partly the intention of the language in all those reports, policies and plans to constrain and enmesh the power of meaning? But, then, what was the alternative, Graves had asked – volubility, madness?

His thoughts had taken him briefly away from the lecture's central theme; he refocused as the Professor concluded that the hopes of our civilisation – therefore of our children and future generations now lay in redoubling the efforts to reduce carbon emissions and to totally replace fossil fuels with renewable energy sources. The message was one of mitigation and adaptation. We all needed to change our 'lifestyles' – 'our daily ways of doing things'; it was not a matter of inconvenience but one of the utmost necessity – indeed, of survival. It was a message requiring a step change of even greater magnitude and urgency than that made during the Coronavirus pandemic of nearly two decades before – a change of which the world had shown itself substantially capable at the time. It was in that proven human ability that the world needed to place its hope, if it was to avoid a calamity of far greater scale and duration.

It was a sobering note on which to end. There was silence across the auditorium which was only broken, after many seconds, by closing applause from across the scattered members of the audience; it was as if they were waking themselves from a state of shock.

'Jeff' whose name Dan had now recalled and who had welcomed the Professor, returned to earnestly thank him and to hope that the audience would take away with them and share, wherever they could, 'the extraordinarily significant message' that the College's eminent visitor had delivered.

The Professor thanked his audience once more for listening to him. There was a repetition of the earlier applause and then he was ushered away from the podium and towards the stage exit. Dan, also needing to make his exit, glanced along the seats; the woman who had been sitting at the end of the row had left so he made his way along to the aisle and out to the lobby.

Once there, he tried to focus on the events of the day, although it was hard to return to the relatively mundane circumstances of his surroundings. He reminded himself that he had still not had any lunch and decided to see what was on the menu in the café next to the theatre.

It was not an extensive menu, so it took him just moments to decide. The café's automatic door slid open. He went straight to the counter and ordered his meal, taking a coffee with him as he found a seat.

He sipped his drink but was aware that the lecture was still playing on his mind. As he waited for his food to arrive, he looked around the café and noticed the woman who had been sitting just a few seats away from him in the lecture theatre. He turned his attention once more in the direction of the counter, beginning to wonder what had happened to his food but, at that moment, his eye was caught by a movement outside the café window. A man, in his twenties Dan guessed, was peering through the window and into the café. It seemed as though his attention had come to rest on the young woman a few seats away from him. Trying not to be too obvious in his movements, Dan sought to get a better look at the stranger outside. He had a rather wild appearance. A dark mop of unruly hair contrasted vividly with the pallor of the stranger's unshaven face. He now seemed to be so intent on staring at the young woman that he was unaware of Dan's inquisitive gaze. Dan wondered if he was a student at the College but then, the stranger suddenly ducked down from the window and Dan's attention was simultaneously drawn away by a woman's voice.

"Excuse me – do you mind if I sit here?"

Taken by surprise, Dan turned towards the voice.

"Do you mind if I sit here?"

It was the woman the stranger had been watching through the window – and whom he had already seen in the Lecture Theatre.

"No – please do," he answered. "I'll only be here a few minutes, then you'll have to the table to yourself."

"Oh – I hope not."

It seemed a curious thing to say. He peered at her. She was wearing a blue denim jacket and long black hair trailed down over her shoulders, framing a not unattractive face. Her expression at that moment was a mixture of anxious smile and perplexity; Dan shuffled around the table a little to give her more space and she settled herself on the neighbouring seat, placing the bag that she was carrying on the floor beside her.

"...It's just that the person who was outside has been following me."

"Oh – I see," he said tentatively although, as yet, he had only a vague idea of what was happening. There was a moment's silence, so he prompted her.

"Do you know him – the person at the window?"

She hesitated. "No – not really – only by sight."

The conversation was awkward, fragmentary; Dan decided to try starting again.

"Well," he said, "given that we're also strangers to one another, perhaps I'd better introduce myself? I'm Dan Holroyd and I teach here, in the College."

She gave a slightly nervous smile but followed suit. "And I'm Karen," she replied. "I came in here because I saw an advertisement for the lunchtime lecture. I'm sorry if I took you by surprise. As a rule, I wouldn't have dreamed of bothering you, but it was that man who was outside the window... he's been following me and I thought that if I looked as though I was with someone else, he might go away..."

Dan glanced back towards the window. There was no sign of the stranger.

"Well, the trick seems to have worked," he commented.

'Karen', as he now knew she was, looked at him, pulling her coat around her shoulders. "All the same, do you mind if I stay here for a few minutes?"

"Of course not," responded Dan, "I'll be glad of the company." He tried not to glance at his watch despite the time it was taking for his food to arrive.

She continued, almost as though she had not heard him and as if her anxiety was finding relief in conversation. "It might help, as well, if we look as though we're in conversation..."

"I rather thought we were...."

She looked at him quizzically.

"In conversation, I mean," he added.

She smiled. "Oh, yes...I suppose we are!" Her smile became a small giggle. "It's just that when I saw that man's face in the window I panicked, and I didn't know what to do. I'd seen you of course in the lecture theatre, so I thought it would probably be alright to come and sit next to you for a few minutes."

Dan nodded and then asked, "Has he followed you before?"

"Yes – several times but I've only seen him in this part of town – and I don't come here every day by any means. This morning, though, I had some work at 'Pilgrims' – and when I came out, he was standing near the school gate, almost as if he was waiting for me."

"Hmm, it does sound rather odd." He paused before asking, "So, are you a teacher then – or a teaching assistant, perhaps?"

"Key Stage One," she confirmed. "I'm a supply teacher."

Pilgrim Primary, the school to which Karen was referring, was at the end of a quiet side street off the avenue in which the College was situated; Dan knew little about it but he had sometimes seen pupils, recognisable by their uniforms, making their way with their parents, along the road outside the College.

He thought a little more about what she had said. "Have you reported any of this to the police?" he asked.

"No, I haven't – or at least, not yet."

"Perhaps you should."

"Oh, I will if I need to – but so far, he's only followed me. He's never tried to pester me or get in my way. I mean – all he's ever done is make me feel uncomfortable – so what would I say to the police if I went to them?"

There was a momentary silence. He could see that she might have difficulty convincing the police that the stranger was also, perhaps, a stalker. There were several people, after all, that Dan saw regularly 'on the street' outside the College; invariably, they were begging and were probably also homeless. Maybe the stranger outside the window was one of them.

Sensing, though, that speculation might be unhelpful and that they had only just met, there was only so much he could say to reassure her. He decided to change the subject.

"What did you make of the lecture?" he asked.

She shrugged and repeated his question, wanting to reframe it. "What did I make of it? I know how it made me feel…"

"Ok – so how did it make you 'feel'…?"

"Alarmed – depressed – and angry, all at the same time – although I also wonder why I should react in those ways. We've all known for many years about the dangers of Climate Change."

"We have…" said Dan, "But until quite recently, it's always seemed remote. Now it doesn't feel remote anymore. In fact, it feels like we all need to wake up – and the sooner, the better.

"So, what's made you change your mind – about it all seeming 'remote', I mean?"

He thought for a moment. "Oh, a variety of things I suppose. Previously, I'd always put Climate Change in the large category of 'Things I Can do Nothing About' – things like overpopulation, pandemics, nuclear war and all the rest... The list could be a long one. The winter before last, though, my house was flooded. It's been flooded before but this time, the flooding was deeper and lasted longer than on previous occasions. Being marooned for several days changed my attitude more than anything else. I had plenty of time to think about what's happening... Now, even if I don't know exactly what to do, I feel we must try to do something – otherwise, despite all the concern, I'll be no better than the 'Deniers'."

Karen nodded sympathetically.

"I know how you feel – especially about not knowing what to do – and having your home flooded for weeks on end must have been awful."

She paused and then said, I guess that means you live out on 'The Levels'?"

"Yes, about a mile and a bit from Monk's Hill..."

"I live on the other side of Sedgewater. We weren't affected so badly there although it was bad enough. I can't remember a winter in which we've had so many storms. Living out on 'The Levels', though – surely you must have thought of moving?"

"I must admit I have..." he replied. "Being stranded in a flooded house certainly reminds you how weak we are compared with Nature. It made me realise that the Crisis is here – and not just in the news."

Karen was sympathetic but recalled some of the comments she had heard at the time.

"I agree with you completely," she said, "but I remember that, at the time, there were plenty of people who argued that flooding has always happened on the Levels and that if you choose to live out there, that's what you can expect..."

"Well, up to a point, I suppose that's true – but most of the time it doesn't flood. And it's a beautiful place to live and work. At the time of the flooding, there was a lot of anger – understandably so. Most people thought that, yet again, the Environment Agency hadn't done enough dredging. And some of the phrases trotted out by politicians – and even the weather people – caused a good deal of scoffing."

"What did they say...?"

"Oh, there were comments that suggested the flooding was a 'one in fifty years event' – or even sillier, that it was a 'one in a hundred years' event. My house has been flooded three times in the last ten years and the last time was worse than any of the previous events, including the terrible flooding of 2013 and '14.

"Yes, I thought that some of the discussion was unhelpful – even insensitive," she said. "The reasons for flooding are not as simple as many people suppose," adding by way of explanation, "I'm no sort of authority but the seriousness of the flooding and the controversy about the Levels made me want to find out more."

He nodded, reflecting that she seemed to be quite a thoughtful young woman and that she had already shown more interest in his former predicament than many of his colleagues had done at the time.

Karen, however, was becoming aware of his attentiveness so when finally, his food arrived, she took the opportunity to check her watch. It prompted him to ask, "Can I get you another coffee?"

"No, thanks," she replied. "That's kind of you and I've enjoyed talking to you – but I have to go."

She hesitated for a moment and then, fishing in her bag, pulled out a leaflet and placed it on the table, using a salt cellar from an adjoining table as a paperweight.

"...That's just in case you're interested. If you are, we might meet again."

"Well, thank you," said Dan, and then rather tentatively, "I hope you don't have any more trouble with the stalker..."

Karen looked anxiously at him for a moment and then, again, at her watch. "I hope so too but I really must catch the next bus – I've got someone waiting for me at home. Maybe see you at the meeting?"

She pointed in the general direction of the leaflet as she made her way between the tables and chairs. The opening and closing of the café's automatic door sent a momentary gust of air across the room, causing the leaflet to tug at its salt cellar paperweight as if wanting to escape. Dan picked it up – and decided that he was interested. What was this about the meeting that Karen had referred to?

The leaflet was an A5 sheet of paper, printed in a variety of coloured inks and inviting its readers to attend a meeting of 'Sustainable Sedgewater'. Dan took out his smartphone and put the date, time and place in the calendar app.

A few minutes later, he pushed his plate away. The food had been rather nondescript, and he needed to do some more work before his early evening session with a new group of students. As he went out into the vestibule again, he thought that he would find it difficult to return to the routine of his daily work. The professor's lecture and the subsequent conversation with Karen had unsettled him.

* * *

Back at his desk, he spent some minutes reorganising himself and then sat gazing out of the large window on the far side of the office. What could he do? He was just one person in a world population of billions. But if people across the world, people like him, lost hope, then all was lost… Somehow, he had to continue…to continue… Reluctantly, he pulled his keyboard towards him.

Time passed. Almost without noticing he became absorbed, once more, in his work. Teaching adults was different in a number of ways from teaching children but, as he had reflected previously, he still had to prepare sessions, carry out assessments and record data relating to his students' learning. There was still a familiar routine to his work at the College – a routine, he could hardly fail to notice, that served to anaesthetise the acute sense of urgency that the lunchtime lecture had aroused in him.

* * *

For the next fortnight, the routine ran its course until the day of the meeting advertised on the leaflet. Dan had nearly forgotten it by the time it came around, but his smartphone pinged to remind him.

It was a Wednesday and, fortuitously, a day on which he had no evening lectures. The meeting had been arranged to take place at a pub on the eastern side of Sedgemoor so Dan decided to eat there earlier in the evening and then stay on afterwards.

He found the place easily enough. It was called, rather appropriately, 'The Greene Man'. A dimly lit passage led to the bar. A row of pumps bearing the logos of various lagers provided refuge for the barman who seemed more interested in his smartphone than in his customers. A rack on the bar contained menus so Dan took one, found a seat and made his choice.

By that time, the barman had remembered why he was employed by the brewery and called across to him. Dan went to the bar.

"Yes," pointing to the menu, "I'd like the chilli, please."

The barman grunted and pressed the appropriate button on the till. "Anything to drink?"

Dan glanced along the bar. There was another set of pumps, less brightly lit. He preferred local beers to lager and from where he was standing, they looked more interesting.

"Yes," he said, after a moment or two. "I'll have a pint of 'Old Brock'."

The barman grunted again; Dan felt a tinge of sympathy, wondering if he had a problem with his throat. He glanced at him, taking in his appearance.

He was wearing a black shirt, open at the neck and a pair of black trousers and blended into the shadows behind the bar so that Dan mused that he could just as easily have been a stagehand.

He set Dan's beer down on the counter, a comma of greasy black hair falling across his pallid, pock marked face.

"That be all?"

"For now," said Dan. "But I'll be here a while."

"Ok, I'll open a tab." The barman went to the till again and pressed some more buttons. Dan returned to his table and sampled his drink. First impressions of the pub were that it was just one step away from the days of spit and sawdust but at least the beer was good.

After a while, a large, frumpy young woman, with a short black skirt that seemed to emanate from just below her ample bust, came hurrying across the room, bearing Dan's plate of chilli. He tried to read the logo on her grey tee shirt; in the dim light of the bar, it was not easy to make out but eventually he was able discern the words "Come on Baby…"

She set down the plate and, having arranged the cutlery with a delicacy that was belied by her size, scooped up a dirty beer glass and used napkins.

"Can I get you any sauces?"

Dan surveyed his meal. He had not had time to taste it but decided that he would spare her a second visit. She went off round the other tables, gathering up cutlery, more dirty glasses and napkins before disappearing through a swing door and into the kitchen just beyond the end of the bar.

He picked up his knife and fork and tried a mouthful of chilli. It was hot in both temperature and taste – which was the way he liked it. If it had come out of a packet, it was a good packet. He took another sip of beer, remembering one of his mother's multiplicity of proverbs. "You can't judge a book by looking at the cover," was the one that had come to mind.

He took his time eating and drinking. The barman had retreated to a stool at the far end of the bar and continued to play with his smartphone. Every so often, Dan heard laughter from the kitchen. Eventually, the young woman who had brought his meal, re-emerged and minced up to the table to ask, "Is everything alright with your food, sir?"

She was already moving away to another table that was apparently in need of her attention before he was able to reply, "Yes, fine, thank you!"

He was no-one's idea of a food critic but, for once, he meant it. She smiled and continued on her loop back to the kitchen. This time, Dan could see the second half of the logo which was on the back of her tee shirt, framed by orange 'flames'. It said, "- Light my fire!" As with the offer of the sauces, Dan decided that he would decline.

* * *

He was just deciding that perhaps beer was not the best liquid to cool the temperature of his mouth when he heard the voices of customers coming into the bar. He looked at his watch. It was nearly time for the meeting.

A tall, thin, elderly man emerged from the passage and into the bar. Behind him came a white-haired individual, also rather thin but wiry and, from the ease of his movements, someone accustomed to exercise – running or cycling perhaps. They went to the bar to buy drinks.

A little behind the two men came a woman, round faced and smiling – someone in early middle age, Dan guessed, whilst also noticing that she had brown hair and was wearing a lumpy and colourful cardigan, black trousers and flat shoes. She had a laptop under her left arm and a sheaf of papers in her right hand.

He could hear another woman's voice; he recognised it as Karen's. At first, her head was turned towards the bar but as she turned to look around her, she caught sight of Dan with his now empty plate and beer glass.

"Hello Dan!" she greeted him. "I'm pleased you could come."

He got up to return the greeting, giving her a light peck on the cheek when she offered it to him.

"We'll be going through to one of the back rooms in a minute – when the committee have finished buying themselves drinks," Karen continued.

"Are you a member of the committee?" asked Dan.

"No, just one of the 'foot soldiers' – but I often get involved in the events and campaigns."

They chatted for a few moments before Dan remembered that he had yet to pay his bill, so he excused himself from Karen's company and went to the bar.

He had just re-joined her when she looked around suddenly; the committee members had begun to leave the bar.

"It looks as though they're going through," she said. "We usually meet through there." She indicated an open doorway to her left.

The 'Greene Man' was not a pub he had been to before, so he left Karen to show the way.

An extended gaggle of people began to wander through to the room in which the members of 'Sustainable Sedgewater' were meeting. They filed patiently into what Dan guessed was the pub's skittle alley where serried ranks of wooden chairs had been set out. He heard someone exclaim, "Who set these out? There's no room to sit down!"

Gradually, the members of Sustainable Sedgewater teased the chairs apart although in the process, the neatly assembled rows became a higgledy-piggledy mess orientated, at a variety of angles, towards the committee at the front.

Karen and Dan randomly picked a couple of adjacent chairs and sat down.

There were several more minutes of complaints about the chairs and the noise of them being rearranged before the chairman called the meeting to order. He did this by knocking loudly on the committee's table and when this failed, he was helped by various people coughing and calling for quiet.

Eventually they were ready and the chairman began to speak.

"Welcome, everyone, to this meeting – only the second time that we've met here at the Greene Man. I would just remind us all before we begin that the pub manager has agreed to us having this room for free – for which we're very grateful. I assured her that the members of Sustainable Sedgewater have healthy appetites for food and drink, particularly if it's locally sourced, and on that basis, she's happy to have us here."

There were brief sounds of laughter and agreement before he moved on to the evening's business.

"I believe Moira has put out batches of tonight's agenda and there should be a small pile on a chair near you."

Karen picked up a pile from a chair on her left and handed them round to the people next to her.

Dan studied his for a minute or two whilst waiting for the other people in the room to do the same.

There was an assortment of items, most of which Dan thought he would find interesting – Regeneration of Sedgemoor's High Street; contractors' traffic associated with Hinckley Point; changes to local bus services and Sustainable Sedgewater's participation for that year in the town's 'Earth Hour' event. Planned activities for which the Committee sought the meeting's approval were also listed at the bottom of the agenda.

"It looks like we'll be here for some time," muttered Dan in a hushed voice to Karen.

"About an hour and a half," responded Karen. "Don't worry – Michael's a good chairman."

Dan looked again at the committee, having previously recognised the tall, thin, elderly man he had first seen in the bar, as the person to whom Karen was referring. Altogether, there were four people fronting the meeting although it was clear, that at that moment, progress was being led by Michael and the round-faced woman in the lumpy cardigan who, he had gathered, was Moira.

Dan listened as the various committee items came and went. As Karen had said, Michael seemed to be effective in his role and Moira also appeared to know what she was doing. Together they nudged the meeting along, pushing the participants to put together resolutions (if there were any) that were realistic for the group.

It was clearly the non-committee members who provided the less predictable element of the meeting. Dan saw Karen wince when one of them, a stocky, red-faced, tweed jacketed man he guessed to be in his fifties, stood to protest about plans for a new 'solar farm' on the edge of the town.

He began presumptuously, by saying, "I think I speak for everyone here…" only to be hissed at and reminded by another member that he did not speak for him.

Michael directed him back to the agenda and to the minutes of the previous meeting when the plans for the solar farm had been thoroughly discussed. He sat down heavily, redder in the face than when he had stood up.

Karen looked at Dan and gave a resigned smile. A little while later, during the item about bus services, another smaller and rather bird-like man stood to make his views known about the proposed ending of the 'Number 30' bus service. Dan sat bemused by the energy with which the little man attacked the item, noticing that he was wearing a blue jacket of the kind favoured for drivers by some bus companies. A collection of enamel badges festooned his lapels.

This time, there was more general sympathy since a number of the people in the room would be adversely affected by the closure of the service. Various proposals were made from the floor of the meeting and gradually, a workable resolution to apply as much pressure as possible to the bus company, was agreed.

Recognising that the group could do little to influence such things as traffic movements in and out of Hinckley Point, Michael offered the committee's services in making the views of the meeting known. Since the project had been pushed through by people known to be generally dismissive of groups like 'Sustainable Sedgewater', he did not hold out much hope that they would be listened to, but he suggested a social media campaign to propagate local people's viewpoints, and the majority were willing to accept his proposal.

Dan saw Karen glance at her watch. There were just ten minutes left – time usually taken for reporting on actions taken since the previous meeting. The remaining item – 'Earth Hour'- needed more time than was available and Dan wondered how it would be dealt with, but Moira, recognising that 'Sustainable Sedgewater's' contribution would be made through the work of a small number of activists, proposed a smaller meeting the following week, to thrash out the details.

Michael closed the discussions on the dot at nine o'clock. Dan was impressed – with the time keeping, if not exactly with the scope of the issues that the group felt it could handle. There were appeals to help stack and put away the chairs – with which Dan and Karen dutifully helped. Then they went to the bar, to mull over what most of the group's members would perceive as a positive meeting.

They bought more drinks and found a table away from noise of others.

"So, what did you make of the meeting?" asked Karen.

"It was interesting."

As yet, he felt that he barely knew her and a non-committal answer seemed best.

"How about you? What did you think?"

"Oh, I was interested in tonight's issues. It's also a chance to mix with some like-minded people…"

Dan sensed that there was more to come so he waited.

"All the same," she continued, "our meetings can be frustrating. It's just that I wish I could find a way to make a real difference. I've been to quite a few meetings of Sustainable Sedgewater – and at the end of each one, I've always found myself feeling dissatisfied."

Dan nodded sympathetically. "If I was a regular member, I'm sure I'd feel the same. But can any of us really make much of a difference?"

"I've thought a lot about that too. Individually, no-one can do much but I'm hoping that gradually people like us can create an overwhelming tide of opinion that will bring about change."

"'Amen' to that!" replied Dan. "What worries me though, is how long that might take. The Climate Crisis is already here and yet we seem to have very little idea about how much time we have before we reach the point of no return."

"We all worry about that, Dan – but Greta Thunberg and Extinction Rebellion have had a huge impact over the years. Surely that must give some ground for hope. I also believe that whatever situation we're in, we can still choose to make things better or worse."

As a broad sentiment, Dan agreed, but he paused to think about instances where Karen's belief in the power of human beings to influence their destiny might not apply; the nightmares of Nazi Germany and Putin's hold over Russia came to mind.

His thoughts were interrupted by Moira who came to their table to ask, "Karen, how are you getting home?"

"I was hoping that someone could give me a lift."

"Right…well the thing is, Bill Bledlow was given a lift by someone who didn't stay for the meeting. We can all squeeze into my car but it would mean that one person would be without a seat belt."

"I can give you a lift," volunteered Dan, "…if that would help."

Karen hesitated. She barely knew Dan although her instinct was that she could trust him.

"Would that take you out of your way?" she asked tentatively.

"Depends where you live," replied Dan.

"Highwick – a bit further round on this side of Sedgewater."

"I know it," said Dan. "I came that way earlier this evening…"

"Well," said Moira, "sounds like you have yourself a lift." She winked at Dan and leaned in towards them both to whisper conspiratorially, "Bill is, shall we say, rather large – and it would be a real squeeze for everyone."

Then she looked at Karen. "Will you be able to get to next week's meeting? Wednesday, 7.30 as usual? I'll get the details out tomorrow."

"Yes, I think I'll be able to get there. It will just depend on being able to make suitable arrangements for Dad."

Moira nodded, aware of Karen's situation at home. "Hopefully see you then…and perhaps you as well?" Her question was aimed at Dan.

"I'll do my best," said Dan, thinking that his 'best' might depend on what Karen decided to do – and then wondering why he should think anything of the kind.

Moira slipped away to where the chairman and two other people were waiting for her. They waved to Karen as they left.

Karen was still worried that she was inconveniencing Dan.

"It is a real nuisance that there are no buses at this time of the evening – but we try to encourage car-sharing – although it does sometimes have its little problems…"

She was sounding tentative and almost apologetic again.

"Don't worry," said Dan. "I usually drive around on my own these days. It will make a pleasant change to have some company."

"Well, thanks Dan, although I'm afraid I need to get home soon. My dad's carer will have made him comfortable for the night but I'm not keen on leaving him for too long."

Seeing that they both had empty glasses, Dan suggested that he could drive her home straight away. Karen had only ever alluded to her father incidentally, but he decided that he would ask her about him when they were in the car.

The car park was almost empty as Dan led the way to his Toyota and then set off, following her directions when necessary. Their drive to Karen's house took them around the northern edge of Sedgewater, where the ring road formed a boundary between town and country. The road was lit at intervals by the baleful glow of orange streetlamps. Here and there, were clusters of development – industrial units, low rise office blocks, vehicles and gas canisters in security pounds – and then again, trees, hedgerows and unbounded spaces where the streetlights came to an end and where the countryside beyond the road fell away into darkness. As their route began to loop westwards towards the motorway, Karen said, "It's not too much further now. Hopefully, Dad will be asleep but I'll need to check on him before I go to bed."

"What's the situation with your dad?" asked Dan. "You mentioned that he has a carer but it sounds as though you're one of his carers as well?"

"Yes, I am. He has a carer who comes in the morning to help him get dressed and have some breakfast and then another one who comes in the evening to get him ready for bed."

"Doesn't sound too bad. But you must be pleased you have some help."

"Oh yes – without them, I'd find it hard to cope, although it was Dad's idea to have two carers. Having someone to get him up and then someone to help get him ready for bed really helps."

"I can imagine," said Dan who by now felt himself warming to her as someone who was not only trying to 'do her bit' for the wider community but also for her family.

"Do you have any brothers or sisters?" he asked, wondering if there was likely to be anyone else whose help she could draw on.

"One of each," she replied, "but they live a long way from here. And besides, they're both career people."

They drove on in comfortable silence for a minute or two and then Karen said, "Almost there."

"You've had to give me a few more directions than I thought," commented Dan. "Perhaps I should have used the 'satnav'?"

"Depends which female voice you prefer."

"How do you know it's a female voice?"

"Most of them are."

"Well, I definitely prefer your voice."

Dan looked sideways and saw her smile.

"Here it is. On the right." She pointed to a double gateway that gave access to a drive on the other side of a tall hedge.

He pulled up at the kerb. As they came to a halt she said, "Thank you, Dan. It's been good to talk to you."

"Perhaps we could talk again soon – when we're somewhere other than a lecture or a meeting?"

"Mmm, I'd like that." She fished in the pocket of her coat and brought out a card, which she placed on top of the dashboard. "Why don't you text me – or give me a ring?"

"Yes, I will," agreed Dan.

She smiled again, touched him lightly on the arm and slipped out of the car. "'Bye, Dan."

He watched as she crossed the road, opened the left side of a pair of double garden gates then closed it again and disappeared from view. He reached across to her card and put it in his trouser pocket. Then he pulled away and set off back to the ring road that would take him to the south of the town, under the motorway, and into the maze of lanes that led homeward.

* * *

Later, he lay awake in the stillness of night, his mind playing over the events of the last few months.

Working at the College was helping him to take his mind off Anne. He had also gone, for a short while, to a counsellor. He only remembered fragments of the sessions – usually when something happened to trigger his memory, but amongst the things the counsellor had said that had stayed with him was the thought that, at first, he would think constantly of the person with whom he had fallen in love and then gradually the memories and the attachment would recede until eventually he barely thought of her at all.

In one part of his mind, he found the idea that he would ever cease to think about Anne abhorrent; in another part of his psyche, however, he longed for a cessation of the torment that accompanied the memories of his affair with her.

He also had to recognise, as something that was helping him to restore his mental health, the hours of each day for which his mind was now occupied with his work. Indeed, he was conscious that he was often dragging out some of the tasks entailed in his job in order to keep his mind away from unwanted thoughts.

It was, though, more than a matter of trying to block out his memories and desires; there was also a great deal that he had to learn and to assimilate. Firstly, there was the very different approach that he now needed to adopt in relation to teaching adults – as compared with children. He was becoming very interested in the current theories of learning – his knowledge of which, he now had to extend and then incorporate into his teaching.

Secondly, and by contrast, navigating his way through the College's bureaucratic organisation entailed a variety of learning for which he had far less enthusiasm. It was the aspect of his new environment that he found most frustrating and difficult to engage with. Consequently, despite getting on well with most of his colleagues, the sarcasm that some of his administrative tasks drew from him had already caused his line manager to be exasperated with him.

It concerned him too, that he was in the midst of his working career but was currently having to work part-time. In terms of his income, that was not 'good news'. However, there was no doubt in his mind that his new role was enabling him to put time and space between himself and the situations he yearned to leave behind. Previously, he had willingly shouldered a good deal of responsibility, but he was still sensitive that he had 'let people down' and he shrank from taking on anything that would increase the demands made upon him. He needed time to get himself back together despite having a much-reduced income.

There was also the point that the reduction was not all bad. Many of the things that he had previously thought of as essential now proved to be readily dispensable. He no longer drank so much alcohol and had ceased to give in to the urge to fill his living space with electronic gadgets that quickly became redundant – or to fill his fridge with too much food, some of which, therefore, went into the food waste. He also bought clothes that were cheaper but just as well suited to his everyday activities.

Even living by himself had become less of an anxiety. He had learned to distinguish solitariness from loneliness and although when he was first on his own, he had passed through a long spell of going out simply in order to seek the company of others, he often found now that there were times when he positively preferred to be by himself. Beyond the requirements of his job, he now had more freedom and more independence, and he had begun to attach a greater value to both.

He mused, for a while, on more recent events. He had started to read much more widely in areas to which his enquiring mind took him, but it seemed to him that human induced climate change was the issue that was of paramount importance to the world in his time. It deeply puzzled him that most of the society around him wanted to ignore it, when, for all its profoundly disturbing existential messages, he was drawn to it, like a moth to a flame.

Better to understand the flame, he thought, and better to understand its deadly and endless consequences if humanity was ever going to be able to advance beyond it and continue seeking out its destiny. There was, however, to his ongoing despair, little sign of any such thing; instead, much of the society around him seemed to want to divert itself with absolutely anything other than the truly essential – and the more trivial and infantile that 'anything' was, then so much the better.

The madness of it all wracked him but, for the sake of his mental health, he brought his thoughts back to memories of the evening. He had enjoyed being in Karen's company. The meeting he had found tedious and frustrating because, he wondered, how any small-scale, local organisation could ever play a meaningful part in setting humanity on a safer and less destructive trajectory. To believe any such thing, he had to resort to partly understood, and possibly unreliable, analogies concerning the beat of butterfly wings becoming the initial turbulence that summed with other turbulence to eventually become a hurricane. The reassurance that such analogies provided was, he thought, more 'Category One' than 'Category Five' on the Saffir-Simpson hurricane wind scale.

He came again to thoughts of Karen although – strictly speaking – his remembrance was more in the realm of feelings than thoughts. If there were, indeed, the first beats of butterfly wings, they were unlikely to turn into the hurricane of emotions that had churned through him during his time with Anne. Getting to know Karen, if that was where he was headed now, would involve feelings that were gentler, less stormy – but possibly more enduring. He wondered briefly if he truly wanted 'gentle' rather than 'stormy'. Stormy was certainly far more exciting at the time; but then again, it was also more likely to lead to destruction. If he went down the route of destruction, he would never know what lay in the years beyond – and, above all, his enquiring mind wanted to know – at least, for as long as he was going to be able to survive.

He mildly reproached himself for spending time on thoughts of Karen; it was much too soon to be dwelling on them. He turned over to check the time on his phone; it was 1.25 am. He needed to get some sleep. As ever, there was never a way to entirely shake off the imperatives of daily life.

* * *

CHAPTER 27

FARE FORWARD BUT NOT FAREWELL

It was a Saturday and four years since Dan and Sue had separated, and then, in the autumn that Emily had entered the sixth form, had agreed to divorce. Josh, despite the worries he had expressed to Jayne, had gained the grades he needed and had taken up the place he had been offered at Bristol University.

Prior to Dan and Sue's divorce, there had been some of the usual wrangles over property, but with one exception, their disagreements had now been settled. Meanwhile, Emily had gained a place at Exeter to study History and Modern Languages. Neither Sue nor Dan had shown any reluctance to help her financially whilst she was there.

That morning, Dan was scratching his head over 'the one exception' – the piece of property that he was pondering at that precise moment; the inflatable boat had remained for some time at what had, if effect, become Sue's house until she told him very firmly that she had no use for it and wanted him to accommodate it at the cottage. So reluctantly, that was where, with Phoebe's agreement, it now resided, but his disagreement with Sue had been, after all, as much about where the dinghy might be needed rather than who should own it.

He hoped that one day he would feel like using it again and although, for the moment, retention of the boat seemed illogical, he was reluctant to sell it. Fortunately, the cottage had a double garage, and with a small amount of reorganisation, it would be easy enough to find space for the outboard motor and the large container in which the deflated dinghy was stored. He was also now the outright owner of the trailer that they had used for transporting the fully inflated dinghy; Sue had insisted that it belonged with the boat and that it, too, had to go. For the moment, he had secured it to a steel post at the side of the garage.

The major piece of property over which agreement had not been finally settled was the fate of their former family home on the Levels. Through their solicitors, an interim arrangement had been made that Sue should continue to live there until Emily had finished her school education and that, after that, they would negotiate over its sale; Dan had agreed, reasoning that, whatever feelings he harboured about the way in which Sue had effectively made him homeless, Emily still needed some stability during the two years of her A-level course.

Now, however, Emily had finished her A-levels and final agreement about the house was pending. Latterly, Sue's mood seemed to have lightened and since he had originally shown flexibility in not pressing for its sale, she seemed inclined to be co-operative about its future ownership. For his part, Dan had always loved the place and wanted to return there. Besides, he knew that Sue had now started a relationship with someone else, a work colleague apparently, and was now hoping to marry him.

It would not have been a surprise to Dan that Sue had already had a detailed conversation with her intended future husband about the house on the Levels – although there were aspects of that conversation that would also have had a sense of 'déjà vu'. They had, for example, speculated about the ease, or otherwise, of selling the house if there was a recurrence of the flooding that everyone on the Levels had endured some four years previously. They had agreed, too, that if a similar event were to occur again in the near future, property values would be severely affected.

For the time being, Dan shelved his thoughts about it all. Karen, with whom he had been spending a good deal of time in the past year, had gone to visit relatives in the London area, for a few days and he had not made any arrangements for his own entertainment. He was at a loose end.

He thought for a moment. There was always television – or perhaps he could read a book? The choices did not seem very attractive. Instead, he decided to drive into Sedgewater where perhaps, he would see a film or look in at one or two of the pubs. If necessary, he would leave the car in Sedgewater and get a taxi home. It would be expensive but better than taking a risk.

He ate a quick meal, put on some casual clothes and then drove into Sedgewater.

* * *

The film at Sedgewater's Roxy cinema had managed to divert him for a couple of hours. Emerging into the glare of the lobby, his watch told him that it was close to ten o'clock; the sickly-sweet smell of popcorn seemed even stronger there than it had during the film and he decided to go in search of somewhere with a more adult taste and smell to it. 'The George' was just a short distance away and he made his way there, aware of a keen wind that was reminding him that autumn had passed and that winter had already begun to make its presence felt.

'The George' was an old pub built in stone and with an entrance at the dining area where diners were seated at wooden tables and from where they were served by the kitchen on that side of the pub. A wide doorway led into a spacious bar and beyond that, into a succession of young staff scurrying to and fro across the flagstone floor. Dan bought himself a pint of beer and settled at a table in the bar.

The pub was busy with Saturday night customers and he had been there only minutes when another customer perched on a seat opposite him.

"Mind if I sit here, mate?" enquired the newcomer although he had, by that point, already installed himself. Glancing around the pub, he stretched out his long legs, so that Dan found himself avoiding the battered pair of brown shoes that emerged next to him, on the other side of the table. The newcomer took a sip from the tall glass of lager he had placed on the table.

"Busy here, ain't it? Is it always like this?"

"I'm afraid I couldn't tell you," replied Dan. "I've only been here once or twice before."

"Not a local then?"

"Well I'm local in the sense that I live just a few miles away."

"That's 'local' in my book."

Dan took a sip of his beer, noticing his companion's brown, weather-beaten complexion. He thought he also detected an Australian accent.

"Where are you from?"

"Brisbane, Australia."

Dan nodded. "That is some way from here," he acknowledged. "What brings you to Sedgewater?"

"My wife's English. She had a hankering for the 'Old Country' and she comes from these parts."

"Oh, I see," said Dan, adding, "although if my previous address had been in Brisbane, I'm not sure that I would have chosen Sedgewater as my next place of residence."

"Love's a wonderful thing," commented his companion, giving a dry laugh and taking another swig of his lager. "By the way, I'm Kevin – or, preferably, 'Kev'." He offered his hand across the table and they shook.

"And I'm Dan."

"Good to meet you, Dan. So, what do you do when you're not drinking beer?"

"I'm a lecturer," replied Dan. "I work at the local college."

"I know it or, at least, I know of it. My wife's in Education as well."

"Oh?" Dan raised an eyebrow in curiosity.

"Yes, she teaches at Mile End Primary. That's why I'm in here as a matter of fact. She's having a 'girls' night out' at the 'The Black Swan' and I'm waiting for her – but I think they must be having a few. I've been hanging around for a while."

"Are you the chauffeur?" asked Dan, glancing at the gradually disappearing glass of lager.

Kev followed his glance and said, "Oh don't worry about this stuff, mate. It's as weak as piss water. And, yes, I am 'the chauffeur'."

Dan winced at Kev's directness of self-expression.

His companion looked at his watch and ran his fingers through his dark and profuse head of curly hair. "They should be here soon – if she remembers, that is."

Dan noticed the reference to 'they', deciding that he would move on before Kev's wife and any tipsy companions she might have with her arrived.

"What's the 'do' then?" he asked. "It sounds like they must be celebrating."

"Not celebrating exactly. No. One of her friends has been made redundant. Someone she's got to know since we arrived, a couple of years ago. She's called 'Amanda'. The wife often talks about her, but I've never met her. Officially, it's a 'farewell' but Jess was talking about 'helping her to drown her sorrows'."

Dan took a slow sip of his beer. Having taught in the local area for a number of years, he knew many of the local teachers. Several of them were called 'Amanda' – but only one of them that aroused his interest; it would not be good, though, to let it show.

He decided to change the subject. A customer theatrically complaining at the bar about the cold weather outside provided the pretext.

Dan smiled an ironic smile at that. "I'd imagine it's generally a good deal warmer than this in Brisbane?"

"Just a bit," agreed Kev. "It was one of the reasons Jess wanted to come back to England. It was way too hot – not only in the summer but all year round. When we left about two years ago, there were wildfires on the outskirts of the city."

"That must have been terrifying."

"It was. Houses just a short distance from ours were burned to the ground. Into the bargain, Jess and me want to start a family. I loved Brisbane when I was a kid, but I wouldn't like to bring up children there now."

"Because of the heat?"

"Yeah, absolutely because of the heat. Day after day, always the same. It was really getting to Jess."

"So, you decided to take your chances in post-Brexit, post-Pandemic UK?"

"You mean 'Out of the fire and into the frying pan'?" Kev laughed at his own rather contorted joke. "It was a bit of a 'culture shock'. That I will admit."

He noticed that Dan's glass was empty. "Can I get you another?" he asked.

Dan shook his head. "Thanks, but no. I ought to be getting on. All the same, it's been good talking to you."

"Ok, mate – perhaps we'll meet again sometime?"

"We might," said Dan. "I'm often in Sedgewater these days."

He felt a little reluctant to leave. The conversation had interested him, but he still felt resolved that he did not want to meet a group of 'worse for wear' teachers on a Saturday night.

With a nod of acknowledgement to Kev, he made his way back to the street.

His instinct had been right. He had barely left 'The George' when he saw and heard, just a short distance further down the street, a group of scantily clad young women; he paused long enough to see that the 'Amanda' he knew was not amongst the noisy group of revellers. Then again, although he had heard recently that she was more than fond of a drink, he could not imagine her wanting to participate in a late-night pub crawl. She would also probably feel like the 'odd one out' in such a youthful group, the nearest members of which had now lurched and stumbled to within a few yards of where he was standing. He pulled his waterproof jacket around him, zipped it up to keep out the cold, and crossed the road to the opposite pavement.

From there, he was just in time to see the women making their way into the warmth of the pub. Kev would not be short of company now. Perhaps, thought Dan, they would meet up again and it suddenly occurred to him that, although Kev had asked him about his job, he had not shown a similar curiosity about whatever it was that his Australian companion now did for a living. If they did meet again, he would have to make up for his omission.

As he hurried along the street, he rehearsed again with himself the reasons that he had made a quick decision to move on from 'The George'. Firstly, the chances were that he would know some of the teachers in the group that had gone into 'The George'. Secondly, being in amongst a group of drunken people would only seem like 'fun' if you were part of the group; if not, it was more likely to be both tedious and unpleasant.

He returned to thinking about 'Amanda'. If it was reasonable for him to believe that she was the same Amanda that he had known since his student days, had lived with for a year and had worked with at Wellsprings Primary, then he wondered how it had come about that the event at the 'Black Swan' was her leaving 'do'. His own departure from Wellsprings had been an angry one but he no longer resented her role in the events of that time.

He had, though, through his absorption in his new role at the College, lost touch with Amanda. He had supposed that her climbing of the Academy career ladder had continued apace and that her next role would be that of Principal – but he had not kept in touch with her, linked as she was, in his mind at least, with one of the few episodes of his adult life that he preferred not to talk about. Now, here he was, led by his own untoward curiosity towards a pub in which he would find himself enquiring about someone who would probably turn out to be a complete stranger.

There were, however, Dan reflected, occasions when his curiosity had a perverse twist to it. This was one of those times. Anyone with an ounce of common sense would simply have flagged down a taxi and headed for the warmth of their own bed at home. Instead, here he was, trying to answer his own set of silly questions – like a moth drawn to a flame.

Kev had let drop that his wife had been at 'The Black Swan'. It was within easy walking distance of 'The George' and it took Dan just a few minutes to find his way there. He was also grateful for a chance to clear his head in the cold night air.

By the light of the streetlamps and a nearly full moon, he found his way along the narrow lane that would take him to the forecourt of the pub. He had not been there for some time so when he arrived, he gazed up at the building for a moment or two, taking it in. He had been a frequent visitor there many years before when it was a friendly but down-at-heel hostelry; now, however, by all appearances, it had been transformed into a renovated pub and restaurant on which a good deal of money had been spent.

The 'Black Swan's' building formed two sides of a square that contained the pub's gravel forecourt in which stood a number of heavy iron tables and chairs, principally used in the summer months. The upper stonework of the building, other than the illuminated, glossy black sign with its gold lettering, was lit only by the eerie light of the moon. By contrast, the white rendered walls of the ground floor stood out clearly. Dan could see that the interior of the restaurant was in darkness, but the neatly framed double window of the lounge bar still glowed with light. He followed the paving slabs that formed a path to the door. Ducking his head in the low entrance, he went inside.

He had barely gone two paces when a barman replacing glasses behind the bar called out, "We're closed, sir."

Dan smiled thinly to himself. It had not used to be a pub where he might expect to be addressed as 'sir'.

"No problem," replied Dan, "but perhaps you can help me. I'm looking for a woman…"

The barman interrupted him sharply. "We're not that kind of an establishment. Now, if you don't mind…"

"If you'd let me finish…" continued Dan, faintly amused. "I'm looking for a woman who used to be a work colleague of mine. I believe she was with a group of teachers who were in here earlier."

"Hmm, that lot. Yes, well they said they were teachers…not that I'd want a child of mine taught by any of 'em."

He turned and called across to a colleague who was clearing up in a dimly lit area that served an area at the back of the pub.

"Hey Joe, there's a gent here says he's lookin' for a woman who was with that rowdy bunch, earlier on."

"Oh aye," said Joe. "Send him through. I'll see 'im."

Dan made his way along the bar to the back area. Joe, a rather dumpy individual with red face and thinning hair, but shoulders broad enough to impress potential troublemakers, was wiping down the bar.

"So, what can I do you for?" he asked, cocking an eyebrow at Dan.

Dan repeated that he was a former work colleague of the woman in question and that he thought she might need some help in getting home.

Joe continued to look suspicious. "How do I know you're on the level?" he asked. "Do you have any ID?"

Dan walked over to him, taking out his driving licence and his College work pass.

Joe examined them closely, handed them back and then stood to one side.

"This the woman you're talking about?" he asked.

In the dim light of the bar, Dan could see a woman slumped at a table, her head resting on her arms. He went closer and sat down on a chair next to her. He peered at her closely but he knew already that it was the 'Amanda' he knew so well from his past.

Dan looked back at the barman. "This is her," confirmed Dan. He cast about him, looking a for a coat.

"If it's her coat you're looking for, it'll still be in the cloakroom. I'll get it for you."

Dan nodded. If possible, he needed to get some sense out of his former colleague.

"Amanda," he said, "it's Dan – Dan Holroyd. I need to get you home."

Amanda turned her head, slowly, blearily and said, a little waspishly, "Dan? What you doing here?"

"I'm going to take you home," he said.

"Home? Home? I don't wanna go home."

Dan struggled to understand Amanda's slurred speech. He looked at his watch. Getting her outside might take some minutes and the bar staff were almost certainly wanting to get finished for the night.

Joe came back into the bar, carrying Amanda's coat. With Dan's help he managed to get her to her feet and, taking it in turns to hold her upright whilst the other fought to get her into the coat, they laboriously prepared her for the cold night outside.

"Cor," muttered Joe at last, "I want a thousand pounds for that."

"She'll thank you for it in the morning," commented Dan.

"Lookin' at the state of 'er, I don't think she'll be saying anything to anybody in the morning."

"Ok, well maybe it'll be the day after that."

"Go on with you," said Joe. "I'll give you a hand in getting her outside. After that, you're on your own."

"I shall just phone her husband," continued Dan. "I don't suppose he'll be very happy but, hey, what are husbands for?"

"Well, I hope he's got a sense of humour."

Together, with Joe on one side of her and Dan on the other, they half-walked, half-carried her to the door.

As soon as Dan was outside, Joe began closing the pub door. Standing in a small remaining gap of light, he said, "I'm sorry, mate – she's not exactly 'a slip of a lass' is she, but we want to get away to our beds. Mind how you go."

"Thanks," said Dan, grateful that the gruff and initially suspicious barman had turned out to be a lot more helpful than he had first supposed. Feeling Amanda's weight against him, she was not as heavy as Joe had implied but then, in her drunken state, it was going to take an effort to move her any distance at all.

He looked around. They were in one of the more salubrious parts of Sedgewater and it was possible that he could find a bench for them both where the cold night air might help Amanda to sober up and thereby prepare her for the rest of the journey home.

He looked down the street. There was no bench in sight but there was a bus shelter about a hundred yards further on. With Amanda alternately seeming to regain some use of her legs and then losing it again, he guided them into a slow and lurching progress towards the bus shelter. After a few minutes that felt more like half an hour, he halted with Amanda still clinging to him, in front of their destination. Mercifully, no-one else had sought refuge there and he was able to manoeuvre her on to the bench inside.

For a moment, he felt sure that she was completely asleep and he rested with her breathing against his neck and wondering what on earth to do next. Then, she began to stir. Perhaps the cold night air was having the desired effect, he speculated. She was trying to say something.

"Who...? Who are you?"

Dan had to listen carefully. Her voice was very quiet. Resisting the temptation to remind her that he had already told her his name, he said, as patiently as he could, "I'm Dan...Dan Holroyd."

At first, the repetition of his name seemed to have no effect, then she began to produce a rather strange gurgling sound. Listening closely once more, he realised that she was giggling.

"What? Can't be! 'Dan the Man', 'SuperDan'? What you doing here?"

"I'm trying to get you home."

"Home? I don't have a home!"

She made her remark with some emphasis and in doing so, began to slide off the seat. With an effort, Dan hauled her back onto it and said, almost as he would to a child, "You do have a home, a very nice home. I've been there – if you remember."

He waited whilst she began to giggle once again.

"You've been to my home? Ooh, you naughty man!"

Her last remark, he felt sure, had been made with a tinge of irony, of mischief; that, at least, would be something more characteristic of the Amanda he knew. If she was showing glimmers of sobriety, he might just be able to get her home before dawn.

She appeared to have fallen asleep again so, with her head on his shoulder once more, he began to think about his options. He could, for example, drive her home in his car. He had drunk only a single pint of beer although admittedly, it had been a strong one. No, his preferred option was still to phone her husband and get him to pick her up. If he was 'breathalysed' with Amanda as his passenger that could generate a variety of questions from those who knew them – questions that he would rather do without.

He was brought back to the present by the awareness that Amanda was trying to speak again. He inclined his head close to her lips as, with an effort, she said,

"I have another home – another home, you know."

"Oh, really?" replied Dan wearily, surprised that she now seemed able to talk in sentences. "Where is that?"

"Jus' around the corner."

He had no idea if she was telling the truth or not but then thought to himself, "What have I got to lose?" It sounded as though, at most, he would only have to haul her a few more yards – and if it was true, well, it had to be better than sitting in a draughty bus shelter on a cold winter's night.

He got to his feet and then, with some effort, manoeuvred himself so that he could help Amanda to her feet and get her right arm around his neck. Then, as soon as they were ready, they set off again.

They reached the corner of the street without mishap but once there, Amanda seemed to dither. She paused to squint at the road sign which was partly buried in a privet hedge on the opposite side of the road.

"Whassat say?" she asked.

Dan peered at it for a moment. Apparently, the person clipping the hedge had not thought the sign to be important. At last he could read it. "Prospect Row," he announced.

"Issaone," confirmed Amanda, which Dan interpreted to himself as, "It's the one."

With some difficulty, they crossed the road and made their way along the pavement. The street was lined on both sides with handsome terraced houses, built in stone and each having a small front garden that set them back from the road. Roofs tiled with slate, small, neatly painted wooden framed windows and brightly coloured front doors set in arched doorways conveyed a sense of order and integrity. The privet hedge, clipped uniformly to waist height ran along the row until the road narrowed and continued on into a small canyon of dreary, brick-built houses.

Amanda drew them to a halt well before they entered 'the canyon'.

"Here," she said, slightly impatiently. "Number 9."

Dan unlatched the wooden gate and swung it open, closing it again as soon as he had managed to get Amanda inside. Large, rectangular flagstones formed a path to the front door. Labouring a little now that there was no longer a hedge to guide them, they arrived at the front door.

The door was sheltered by a pergola but there was just enough light for Amanda to see the lock. She drew a Yale key from her pocket and tried to insert it but then after several attempts, handed the key to Dan and said, "You do it."

Dan did as he was told, and he was able to swing the door open and help her inside. With one last effort, he opened a white painted door on their left and helped her into what was clearly a sitting room. A large and comfortable leather settee beckoned, so Dan carefully lowered Amanda onto it, made sure that she was in a stable position and then lifted her feet. She had worn a pair of heeled shoes that evening which, with hindsight, had probably added to her instability as they had wobbled along the streets, but Dan now carefully took them off and tucked Amanda's feet onto the settee and beneath the hem of her coat.

He withdrew to a matching armchair just opposite the settee, where he began thinking about what to do next. In retrospect, it seemed rather stupid that he had hauled Amanda all the way from the pub before seeking an alternative course of action, but then, as so often, one thing had led to another.

He must have dozed for a moment because a loud snore from Amanda made him jump. As he looked across at her, she turned so that she faced the back of the settee; in so doing there was a clatter as something fell on to the floor. Blearily, he forced himself to pick up the fallen object, discovering in the process that it was Amanda's smartphone. That was good news, he thought, but only if he could get to her 'contacts' list. The phone was quite different from his own – and differently configured. He began to wish that he had not deleted all numbers relating to Amanda from his own list of contacts. Fortunately, in the circumstances, there seemed to be no security PIN or other obstacle to his progress and after a minute or so, he was able to scroll through the very extensive list of names. Although it had been a long time since he last met her husband, Dan remembered that his name was 'James'. He scrolled down to the 'J' section. There were five names there, of which the middle one was

'James'. He entered the number into his own phone, pressed the 'phone' icon and the number began dialling. He waited.

The phone rang for about twenty seconds or so. Then a sleepy voice answered, "Hello."

"Is that James?"

"It is. What can I do for you?"

"It's Dan Holroyd, James – I used to work with your wife. I've got her with me now. I think she needs to come home."

"Oh? We had arranged that she would phone me after her 'farewell' do. She was going to spend the night at our little house in town."

"That's where we are now. Uhh, I'm afraid she's had too much to drink and she got me to bring her here."

"Right... Oh dear, it sounds like you've been put to a lot of trouble. And you're sure she needs to be at home...?"

Dan held the phone away from him for a moment, exasperated by James' apparent reluctance. He put the phone back to his ear, determined to hide his irritation.

"I'm afraid so. At the moment she's stretched out on the settee but I don't think that's a very good way for her to spend the night – especially since she's had so much to drink. She needs someone to keep an eye on her."

Dan thought he heard a sigh from the other end of the line.

"OK – understood. I'll come down straight away, but it'll take about half an hour."

"That's no problem. I'll just wait here until you arrive."

"Thanks. I'll be as quick as I can..."

There was a click and James went off the line; Dan quickly saved the number to his own 'contacts' list, then closed his phone and put it back in his pocket. Next, he quietly slid Amanda's phone back into her coat. As he did so, she stirred, exhaled noisily and then settled again but this time with her face towards him.

Before he stopped to think about it, he found himself gazing at her. A lock of hair had fallen across her face, and in sleep her expression had a childlike innocence. Dan had to remind himself that she had been a prime mover in making him redundant. He thought a little more about his motives for rescuing her from the pub. Had there been an element of *schadenfreude*? Had he harboured a malicious desire to catch her in her drunkenness and to extract from her some expression of regret about the way in which he had been treated? If so, it was clear that, on this occasion, he was destined to be disappointed.

So then, he wondered, if it had not been malice or revenge that had taken him to 'The Black Swan', what was it that had taken him there? Was it simply his curiosity or, expressed more basically, his 'nosiness'. As he thought about it a little more, he was sure that was part of the reason – but also, that it was not the whole reason. Perhaps having previously worked closely with Amanda, there was a still a vestige of the mutual loyalty that he had once believed they shared? There was too the thought that although he had been deeply hurt by the apparent lack of understanding of the blood, sweat and tears that he had poured into Wellsprings Primary School, he still harboured a residual liking for her. But then, of course, before all that had been the year in which they had lived together, a year in which he had believed that they would place their relationship on a more permanent footing.

He looked again at her slumbering face. Was he still attracted to her? Immediately, he sought to dismiss the idea; in that respect, he had always fostered a sense of neutrality towards his female colleagues. Their year of 'living together' had made it more complicated, of course but, by mutual consent, during the time that they had worked in the same school, whether alone together or in the company of others, they had both striven to sustain a working relationship that gave no clue to any of their past connections.

In other respects, it had not been so complicated. Through many years of working in schools where the majority of staff were female, the women with whom Dan had worked had always inhabited a kind of grey area in which it was possible for him to like them but in which he never developed any feelings of attraction towards them.

He paused in his thoughts. Was he being rigorously honest with himself, and had not Amanda always inhabited a rather different place in his mind? He allowed his gaze to return once more to her face. Until the final set of events at Wellsprings, he had sometimes wished that they might come across each other socially rather than cling, as they always had, to the strict segregation of their private lives. If they had met in that way, they might well have developed a more open – and a more honest – friendship with each other.

He looked away. All that was now dead, of course. So why had he gone to help her? In the end, it had been intuition; he had always believed that eventually she would, like so many others, fall off the ever-turning wheel. Inevitably, losing her job would have hit her hard – and she was always going to find an evening, such as the one that now lay behind her, difficult to handle.

There was one last question that he had not yet resolved; why, he wondered, had the other women simply left her, knowing that she was incapable of getting herself home? The answer was probably not hard to come by. She was fiercely independent when the mood took her and she had very likely told them that James (or was he 'Jim'?) would be along in a few minutes to collect her; above all, she would not have wanted to be dragged off on a 'pub and club' crawl. There was also the barman who they knew would keep an eye on her; whilst he was not exactly Cerberus, he had taken the trouble to check Dan's ID and to satisfy himself that he could be trusted.

Dan yawned a wide yawn. It was late and he wanted his bed. He went to the window and looked out, just in time to see a vehicle, a Range Rover he thought, drawing up at the kerb.

He watched as an older version of the 'James' he had occasionally met years previously made his way up the path to the door of the cottage.

There was the sound of a key turning in the lock then a voice calling through to him. "Hello Dan!"

The door of the sitting room opened.

"Hi! Took longer than I thought. It's chaos out there – must've been a crash on the Sedgewater Road – police, ambulances, you name it! Anyway, I'm here now – so I'll take her off your hands – and then you can get away to your bed!"

"I'll certainly be pleased to get there," replied Dan.

"You'll be alright to get home?"

He inclined his head towards Dan, having asked the question as if he only wanted a positive answer. Dan obliged him.

"Oh yes, the car's just a short walk from here."

Then, having observed the courtesies, they set about getting Amanda out to the car. As soon as she was securely held in place by her seat belt, James shut the door and walked back to lock the front door of the house. Returning to Dan, who was waiting on the pavement, he placed a large hand on his arm and said, "Right then – that's it. She would probably have been ok down here for the night but thanks for your concern."

Dan grunted. "I hope she'll be alright in the morning."

He felt as though he wanted to say a lot more – but it was late and he was not about to look for trouble.

"I'm sure she will – bit of a headache I expect – otherwise, she'll be fine. We've all been there."

With a nod, he climbed into the driver's seat, pulled his door shut and drew away from the kerb.

Dan briefly watched the tail lights of the Range Rover as they disappeared round the junction at the end of the street and then began the walk to where he had parked his own car, reflecting on James' apparent lack of concern for his wife's safety.

In the cold night air, he felt both wide awake and sober. For the moment, it helped him to set aside his immediate worries about Amanda. All the same, it was just as well that tomorrow was Sunday. Then he looked at his watch and thought, "Forget about it being tomorrow – Sunday's here."

* * *

The following weekend, Dan went to see Karen and her father. After they had initially met at the College and then subsequently at various 'Green' events, they had become friends and regularly met.

On this occasion, he had barely rung the bell before she opened it and showed him through to the very spacious front room. Since Dan had been visiting the house for some time, he and Karen now had an established routine so that as he entered the room, she would go to a large and comfortable armchair, leaving him to occupy the adjacent capacious and comfortable settee. It was invariably a sign that she wanted to talk.

She slipped off her shoes and tucked her feet under her. The armchair easily accommodated her slender frame as she looked around for something on which to put her coffee cup. Dan scooped up a small table and placed it by her side before retreating once more to the settee.

He watched as she took up her cup again and began running a middle finger around its rim; it was an indication that she had something on her mind.

"I'm really worried about Dad," she said at last.

"Oh?" Dan had guessed that, other than the state of the world and the education of young children, it had to be something to do with her father. "Is he poorly?"

"You could say that," she replied, flashing him a weak and watery smile.

"What's happened then?"

"It was last night. He got up to go to the loo – and had a fall."

"Was it a bad one?"

"Well, he didn't break any bones – which was a miracle – but he's really bashed himself about." She began to sob.

Dan put down the drink he had been nursing and went to her side, moving her cup so that he could perch on the coffee table. Rather awkwardly, he managed to put both arms around her.

"Why on earth didn't you phone me?"

"It was the middle of the night. Anyway, I rang for an ambulance, and they came out almost straight away."

"So, what did they say – when they'd had a look at him?"

"They said he had minor concussion. And that he's very frail. They were surprised that he'd had the strength to get out of bed."

"They probably reckoned without his stubbornness."

Karen managed another watery smile. "They certainly did. Although, as we've said before, it's precisely because he's so stubborn that he's had so many accidents."

Dan waited, knowing that she was still holding something back. Finally, he prompted her. "Minor concussion – sounds bad enough. I wonder why they didn't take him into hospital. I would have thought that was the usual drill – at least overnight until they knew he was in a fit state to be at home. And you said he'd really knocked himself about?"

He waited again while she pushed back another sob.

"He did, Dan. He was going along to the bathroom when he suddenly slipped. He was using that stick of his and I think it must have slipped. Anyway, the first I knew of it was when I heard a bang – a really loud one. Of course, I woke immediately – and I knew it was him. I went straight out of my room and there he was – on the landing floor. He must have hit the small shelf above the radiator because it was underneath him – and with bits of glass and china ornament scattered all around him."

"What did you do then?"

"Well, I was beginning to panic a bit because he wasn't moving and – when I finally got up close to him – I could only just hear his breathing. Then I checked his pulse – which was also weak. It was enough for me to know that he was in a bad way, and that was when I decided to ring for the ambulance."

"How long did it take to get here?"

"I guess it must have been about ten minutes – very quick, as these things go, I believe, although at the time, it seemed like an eternity."

"You hear so many stories about the time it takes for emergency services to arrive."

Karen nodded in agreement. "I decided to occupy myself by trying, as best I could, to make him a bit more comfortable and clearing up some of the mess. I moved as much of the debris as I could but the worst of it was, I had to be so careful. I wanted to get the wretched radiator shelf out from under him but I could see that he'd hit his head so I thought he might also have damaged his neck. I decided not to move him, but it was cold on the landing, and I put a blanket over him, just to try and keep him warm."

Dan nodded. Now that she was talking, her words were flowing in a continuous stream. He could readily picture the anxious time she must have had as she waited for the ambulance.

"So, what happened when they arrived?"

"There was a loud rap on the front door – and, as I'd already unlocked it, one of the ambulance crew stuck his head inside and called up the stairs. Then they came in, a tall skinny chap and a little bird of a woman with a ponytail, and came straight up to where I was waiting at the top of the stairs. After that, I watched them for a minute or two but then, I'm afraid and anxious though I was, I left them to it. I could see that they really knew what they were doing – and I was simply in the way."

Dan gently pulled her closer to him. "I wish I could have been here to help you."

She sniffed into a tissue. "Well, I must admit, there were several times in the early hours of the morning when I heartily wished that you were, but I knew you were coming here first thing so I decided not to drag you out of bed."

"All the same, you should have called me. I would have come, no problem."

"I know that, Dan, but really, there was very little that you could have done. And the ambulance crew were excellent. As soon as they arrived, I knew Dad was in competent hands."

There was a slight pause after which Dan said, "How is he now? Will it be alright for me to see him whilst I'm here?"

"Oh yes, of course – but when I came down a short time ago, he was fast asleep. Let's say we give it a little while and then we can go in and check on him. After that, if he's awake, he'll probably want to see you."

"Are you sure?"

"Yes – he may be physically frail and doddery but he's still quite alert and aware of what goes on around him. He looks forward to your Saturday morning visits – a bit of male company, I suppose. Most of the time, he only has me to talk to."

As usual, she was being unduly deprecating about herself. He looked forward to talking to her father, but he was doubtful that he would be in any shape to do so that morning. He looked at Karen, wondering how much more to say.

* * *

For a while, Dan busied himself, helping Karen with small jobs around the house but also enjoying being with her and all too aware that if he went back to the cottage, he would have only himself and the television for company.

Periodically, she went to check on her father but returned each time with the unsurprising 'news' that he was still sleeping. When Dan had listened to Karen's account of her father's fall and the ensuing episode with the ambulance crew, he had been surprised that he had not been admitted to hospital – but then, even before 'Brexit' and the Covid 19 pandemic, the UK had endured years of austerity and public services had been pared back to levels well below previous expectations. Now the long, formative years of a different relationship with Europe were playing through and the previous austerity had persisted. The advent of the Pandemic had only accentuated the country's economic problems so that political promises to improve social care had remained where they had been before – in the 'long grass'.

To a certain extent, Dan and Karen took the political wallpaper of the day for granted. It was plain to see that the economy was on a long, downward slide but since public honesty would probably have been viewed as political suicide, an all-too familiar contest between national delusions of grandeur and expectation management still formed the backdrop to the daily business of 'living'.

As they sat down to share some lunch, Dan would have liked to discuss the larger context, but he knew that Karen was generally not in a mood to do so. If he wanted to offend her sense of what was achievable in their immediate circumstances, he knew better than to talk about situations that she saw as hypothetical or located in the realms of abstraction. The one area where this was not in evidence was in their shared and ever mounting concern about the effects of climate change – but even in that, they no longer discussed the background. Instead, Dan believed, they could only talk about the direct implications for their own plans, for the lives that they saw themselves leading over the next few years.

Thus it was, that as they worked their way through soup and sandwiches, Karen managed to surprise him by starting a conversation about a project that was both located in their long-term concerns and in the more immediate dissatisfactions that they had begun to discuss with each other.

"I'm going to stick with the supply teaching until the situation with Dad is resolved. After that, well, I'll still need to survive but I don't enjoy my work at the moment, and I'd rather do something that would be more in line with my beliefs about what's happening in the world."

Karen had talked to Dan before about her dissatisfactions, but it now seemed that she was moving towards some idea of the alternatives.

"Well, we both have our dissatisfactions," he said, "but at the moment, I only have one idea and that's to try and develop my teaching at the College. So, what have you been thinking about?"

They had already talked about linking their futures together and he wanted to know what she might be planning.

"At the moment it doesn't amount to much more than an idea but then again, I think it's something that I could readily turn into a practical proposition."

"I'm intrigued. So, what's your idea?"

"I want to set up as a small holder."

It was the first time that she had ever voiced such an idea to Dan, and he was not sure that he had heard her correctly. After a pause, he said, "That sounds like big departure from what you're doing now…"

"It would be a huge departure, Dan…but I've been thinking about it for some time and my ideas are just beginning to come together."

"So why are you thinking about such a big change…and why now?"

Karen looked at him sceptically. "Why now? You know why."

"I know what's happening with the climate and I can understand why so many people are feeling unsafe, why they're looking for change – but are you really convinced that events have gone so far that you – or perhaps 'we' – need to make such changes in our lives?"

"Yes, I do, Dan. The changes you're talking about though, happen gradually. In the human bit of the world, they happen much faster."

"Maybe so – but what's made you think about such a radical change?"

"The Government's really struggling at the moment…"

Karen's comment was outside of her usual repertoire and took him by surprise. What had it to do with anything that related to their situation? He struggled to reconnect with the conversation. Lamely, he said, "So, there'll be an election…"

"There will – but that won't solve anybody's problems now."

"Probably not – but that's nothing new."

He waited for Karen's reaction, but he waited in vain. She continued on the path she had already chosen.

"…Only the Conservatives can win an election at present, and they don't have the ability to solve the problems."

"…Which begs the question as to why we keep voting for them."

"We don't keep voting for them! It's true that many people vote for them but there are many more who don't…"

"But that's our system – 'First past the Post'. It always means that we have a party of government with a clear mandate to govern – or at least, that's the message we keep getting."

"Unfortunately, though, Dan that's led to a huge number of people feeling that their vote doesn't count and that there's no point in going to the polls."

"Alright, I agree with you – or at least, I can see that's true. But we've got so many other problems right now. People usually rally round the Government when there's a national crisis…"

"I think you mean 'crises' – in the plural – don't you?"

"Crisis, crises or whatever, Karen – how is going off and 'doing our own thing' going to help?"

"It will help me, possibly it will help us – especially if people are losing faith in 'the System'."

"…Whatever that is. It will take an awful lot to cause some kind of collapse here. What you're saying could only happen if the whole international system of trade and economics was starting to break down."

"That is what's happening…!"

"But why? I mean, what makes you say that…?"

"Because the banking system is breaking down." She said it with emphasis and with a look of exasperation on her face as she wondered if Dan ever read anything that he could not relate directly to the environment.

Dan, in turn, realised that she was talking about something that, for some reason, had simply not registered with him. Newspapers, in physical form, had largely gone out of existence and online, he only read what he saw as significant.

"Alright, alright, Karen!" he said. "I've seen the headlines on my phone – but to be honest, I haven't taken much notice of them."

Karen, in turn, felt that she was becoming unduly vehement and decided that it was time to restrain her growing agitation. She remembered, too, that it had been her father who had talked to her about the crisis in the banking system and that, had it not been for him, she might also have failed to understand its significance. She silently counted to ten. Finally, she said, "I know what I want to do, Dan. I've thought about the practicalities of setting up as a small holder and I think I can make it work. If you want to join me in that project, it would really help us both – but if you still need some time to think about it, well, I understand. There is still some time left before I can get started but after that, I would need you to decide."

For a moment or two, Dan said nothing. He had become fairly comfortable in his bachelor existence at the cottage and his part-time job at the College but now, Karen was reminding him of the greater realities in the world beyond Sedgewater. It was something of a shock after his estimation that she was unable to engage with the 'big picture'.

At last, he said, "I will think about what you've said, Karen – and I will give you an answer, I promise. In the near future though, surely, what you decide to do has to take into account of what's happening with your dad? So, what do you think needs to happen now?"

For Karen, that was a genuinely difficult question. "It's hard for me to say, Dan," she replied, "but last night's events reminded me, if I needed any reminding, that whilst Dad has retained many of his mental faculties, his body is giving out on him. He finds it enormously frustrating, and his frustration makes me feel so sad for him."

She paused for a moment, finding it hard to persevere.

"He's been a wonderful father." She corrected herself. "He is a wonderful father but since I'm the one who now provides most of his personal care, I know how weak, how frail, he is...I can't hide from myself the fact that it almost certainly won't be long before I shall find myself living in this huge house all on my own."

Dan hesitated, not wanting to add to her difficulties but then said, "From what you've told me, your dad has plenty of money. Wouldn't it be better for him to go into a residential home? At least then, you could have more of a life of your own and he would have people around him who could care for him day and night?"

"You're right – Dad does have sufficient money. But as last night's incident showed, he's stubborn to the last. He's never wanted to go into a home – he's adamant about it – and I've never really wanted to change his mind. This house is my home as well as his, and whilst he's here, the least I can do is help him to spend his final days in a place he's always loved – and about which he has so many happy memories."

"I can understand that..." commented Dan sympathetically, "but since, as you say, this house is your home, has he given you any idea what will happen to it when he dies?"

"Yes, of course, we've talked about it quite a few times. He's always thought that the potential sale of the house could be a contentious matter – at least with my brother and sister – so he's appointed a solicitor to be the executor of his will."

"Have any of you seen the will?"

"No – but he has told all three of us that we will each be well provided for – and we have no reason to doubt what he says."

Dan looked at her in the realisation that they were now well away from their previous topic.

"I think we've gone round in a big circle…"

"Oh, don't worry, Dan. I think we're both distracted by the situation with my dad and by what's happening around us. But as I was saying before, I have to think now about what I'm going to do with myself in the future."

She looked at the time on her phone.

"Oh dear, I hadn't realised how long we've been talking. We need to look in on Dad and check on how he is. You were going to stay for a while I think – and have a chat to him?"

"Shall we just see how he is," suggested Dan, "and then go from there?"

"Ok, let's do that. Come on." She took him by the hand and together they set off up the staircase.

About halfway up Dan commented, "I like this."

"You like what?" Karen asked.

"You leading me up the stairs."

She laughed. "That's quite enough of that," she said and then added as an afterthought, "Good things come to those who wait."

Dan squeezed her hand. He certainly hoped so – and then repented of his thought, inasmuch as their plans inevitably revolved around the natural course of events now playing out in her father's remaining days.

* * *

Karen opened her father's bedroom door as quietly as she could, but he was already awake and called out to them in a shaky voice, "Come on in."

Music was playing softly from the radio which sat on a small table near the window. As they approached the bed, Karen's father raised a trembling right hand from the bed in greeting. Dan could see that his face was badly cut and bruised on the right side and that there was an all too visible bump on his right temple.

"Hello, you two," he said. "I'm glad you've come to see me at last."

"We wanted to let you have some peace and quiet," responded Karen.

"Oh, I get plenty of that," her father assured her. "Come and sit down for a minute or two."

There were two chairs standing by the bedroom wall. Dan brought them to the bedside so that he and Karen could sit next to each other.

"How are you feeling now, Dad?" asked Karen.

"I've felt better," her father responded. "Karen, love, could you just help me with these pillows?"

Karen went to the far side of the bed and began plumping up and repositioning his pillows, whilst Dan helped to support him.

"Is that better, Hugh?" asked Dan.

"Aye, I suppose so. It's more comfortable and I can see you both – although that could be a mixed blessing, couldn't it?"

"Glad to see you haven't lost your sense of humour, Dad – or sense of mischief for that matter."

"Oh no, take more than a bit of a fall to do that."

"Bit of a fall?" responded Dan. "If you look like that, I'd like to see what you did to the other fella."

Hugh began to laugh but instead descended into coughing. Karen took a glass of water from her father's bedside table. She waited momentarily for the coughing to subside and then held the glass to his lips. He sipped patiently, taking in small amounts of water and waiting between sips.

"You may want to laugh, Dad, but really, you have knocked yourself about this time. What on earth were you thinking? If you needed to go to the loo, you know I'm just across the landing. Why didn't you use your buzzer?"

"I can't keep waking you up in the middle of the night. You've usually got work the next day."

"Yes, usually I have – although in this case, it was a Friday night. I don't work on a Saturday."

"How am I supposed to know that? I don't know what day of the week it is. I lose track."

"Yes, I know, Dad. That's no surprise. But all the more reason why you should use your buzzer." Karen paused, before taking up her next issue. "Then you were using your stick again. You know you should be using your 'wheelie walker'."

"Bah! That thing. It's a contraption. I'd rather have my stick any day!"

There was brief lull in the conversation during which Hugh began to cough again and Karen held the glass of water to his lips until, once more, his coughing subsided. As she ministered to her father, Dan surmised that he saw the 'contraption' as a reminder of his ever-decreasing mobility and his dependency on others.

Karen also realised that for the time being, she was getting nowhere. She would wait for a better occasion than the present. When her father was settled again, she said, "I expect you could do with some food. You haven't eaten anything since yesterday. Do you think you could manage a little bit of something?"

Hugh hesitated for a moment but then admitted hesitantly, "Oh yes – you're right. I am a bit hungry. But I couldn't eat much. Is there any of that vegetable soup left?"

"Yes, there is. It would only take a few minutes to heat through. Is that what you'd like?"

He nodded. "It's about all I could manage at present – but it'll keep me going."

Karen smiled, relieved that at least her father was exhibiting signs of having an appetite. She made her way to the door and then down the stairs to the kitchen.

As she left the room, Dan picked up the conversation.

"What happened last night then, Hugh? How did you end up on the floor?"

"Oh, I don't really know, Dan. First of all, I felt a bit strange, not dizzy exactly but I didn't have any strength and I put my stick down near the edge of the rug. The next thing I know is that two people in uniforms are fussing over me and asking lots of questions."

"That would be the paramedics, I suppose."

"Yes, that's it – 'the paramedics' – mouthful, isn't it. I just thought of them as the 'ambulance people'. I didn't see Karen at first."

"She was the one who called the ambulance. When she saw the paramedics treating you, she just thought she would be in the way."

"Oh, I know. She's always been a sensitive girl. She's very good to me – which is more than I can say for her brother and sister. I'm lucky if I see them from one year's end to the next."

Hugh was aware that Dan was once more looking carefully at his cuts and bruises.

"You don't need to worry about me, Dan. Karen doesn't need to worry about me. I'll be alright – or, at least, as 'alright' as I can be these days."

They became aware of Karen's footsteps on the stairs and then the landing. She popped her head round the door.

"I'm sorry, Dad, but there's not so much soup left as I thought – barely a cupful. I don't know why we kept it. I'm going to make some more but it will take a few minutes. Are you two alright for a bit longer?"

Hugh answered for both of them. "We'll be fine."

Karen smiled and went off to the task she had set herself.

"How long have you two been seeing each other now?"

Hugh's question caused Dan to think for a moment.

"It must be almost two years now?"

"That's quite a long time." He hesitated. "You spend a good many hours here although Karen's never made any mention of you moving in." He chuckled, as if the thought amused him. "She's probably remembering her mother. Miriam always decreed that only people who were married could sleep together under our roof…"

Dan thought that Karen's father had got a long way ahead of the conversation. He was caught a little flat-footed, having spent part of the day wondering if Hugh would be strong enough to talk at all. Politeness and deference to Hugh's infirmity also prevented him from pointing out the substantial difference between being under the same roof and being under the same bed covers.

"I don't think we've ever discussed it," he replied at last, wondering where the conversation was going.

"Well, I guess that's your business – or, I mean, the business of the two of you. It's just that I know I'm not going to be here much longer, and it pains me to know that because I can't get about the way I used to, Karen spends many hours more or less on her own. I know she misses her mother. We both miss Miriam. When she died, there was a huge hole left in our lives. But Karen's still a young woman. She deserves better."

"She does go out to work, Hugh – although I know she often worries that you're here for hours on your own."

"She doesn't need to worry. I like my own company. And I know you'll understand me when I say I'm not afraid of dying. Some days I feel exhausted, and I simply want some peace and tranquillity. I've seen enough trouble in my life; that's one thing that never changes. We all have our time here – and I've had mine."

Dan was silent. It was not so long ago, when Anne had finished with him, that he had found himself having similar thoughts. The differences, though, were at least as important as the similarities. Hugh was weary of daily existence, worn out by its incessant struggle and willing, at last, to surrender to what he saw as the inevitable. Dan, by comparison, had wearied of himself and of those he loved but who had disappointed him. Now he had found, however, almost to his surprise, that life without Anne was still tolerable and was taking new directions, and he wanted, once more, to see what would happen next, in the unfolding events of his own time.

Hugh had respected his companion's silence but whereas he had been gazing before him, he now turned his gaze to look at him.

"From what I see, I think that you and Karen care for each other. She's had plenty of loneliness in her life but, if I have a wish for her, it is that I would not want that loneliness to continue when I'm gone."

"It won't," said Dan. "I believe I can promise you that. We already spend as much time together as possible, and I know that we both have every intention of ensuring it stays that way."

If Hugh had hoped that Dan would commit himself to anything more than that, he did not say so. He had a better idea of how little time he still had left than either Karen or Dan, and he had no desire to burden the living with the expectations of someone who was a step away from death.

"Dan! Can you help? Dad's door has stuck!"

They were both jerked out of their contemplations and Dan went quickly across to the door to open it for Karen.

"Whew!" exclaimed Karen as she came into the room. "I had no idea that would take so long. I'm sorry, Dad, I meant to put this in front of you ages ago."

Dan helped Hugh into a better sitting position, whilst Karen, having placed the tray and its bowl of soup carefully before him, seated herself on the other side of the bed, ready to give help if it was needed. Hugh picked up the soup spoon with a trembling hand and tried to convey the soup to his mouth. After he had made several vain attempts, Karen moved forward to help him and Dan anticipated objections but there were none; instead, Hugh co-operated with his daughter and allowed her to steady the spoon so that most of the soup arrived at its intended destination.

"I'm sorry, Karen – but I think I might have done a mischief to my right hand – probably when I fell over. It'll be alright again in a day or two."

The two of them persevered until only a small amount of soup was left in the bowl. Then Hugh put down the spoon, lay back on his pillows and said, "Thank you, Karen, that was lovely. But now I think I might take a nap."

Karen moved the tray and soup bowl to a bedside table and carefully rearranged her father's pillows and sheets once more so that he was comfortable enough to sleep. Then she walked across to the blinds and partially closed them, reducing the light level in the room.

She looked at Dan to indicate that she was going downstairs and he followed her quietly out of the room, softly closing the door but finally leaving it a little ajar.

* * *

Karen seated herself at the kitchen table and silently watched as Dan boiled the kettle, found the tea bags and milk and set about making two cups of tea.

For a short while, they sat sipping their drinks but saying nothing. Eventually Karen asked, "So, how do think he is?"

"Much as you said," replied Dan. "He's very frail and, in addition to that, it will take a while for all those cuts and bruises to heal."

She gave a sigh. "I wish I knew what more I could do. I've broached the subject of a residential home many times but he's completely adamant. He wants to spend his last days here. And, really, there are no reasons why I should not respect his wishes."

"…Except that he's at the point where he needs round-the-clock care. Meanwhile, you're providing much of that care whilst also trying to keep going with your work as a teacher."

Karen sat with her head in her hands. For a moment, Dan repented of his rather blunt summary of the situation; she looked close to tears.

"I could move in here, at least for a spell, just until your father feels stronger again. I could help you to look after him – and I could make a better job of supporting you as well." Hugh's earlier comments had watered a seed that had already been in Dan's mind.

Now he was almost pleading with her, and he could see that she was hesitating, thinking about what he had said.

At last, she gave a small, anguished cry. "Aaah, how I wish it was that simple…"

He moved next to her and took her hands in his. "So why isn't it that simple? You have enough bedrooms here. We needn't get in each other's way. And I would be right here when you need some help."

"But you have your work too. What about that?"

"True – it wouldn't be perfect but at least I could be here some of the time. It would be better than the present situation."

She thought about it for a few moments more but then she shook her head and said, "No, Dan, I couldn't…"

"I don't really see why not…"

"No, I've respected Dad's and – for that matter – Mum's wishes all these years, and I don't want to go against them now…"

"Have you talked to your dad recently about his wishes, Karen? I know he wants us to be together."

"I know that too. But I'm equally sure that he doesn't want us simply 'shacking up' together under a roof that is still his."

Dan hesitated. His earlier conversation with Hugh had seemed to suggest otherwise but they had gone only so far in the discussion of future living arrangements with his daughter. Frustrated, he feebly asked, "What are you afraid of? Don't you trust me?"

There was a pause. It was a question Karen did not want to answer so she tried to deflect it. "It's not you, I don't trust…"

"Who, then?"

"Myself. If you had a bed here, I might not be able to resist creeping in beside you…" She smiled.

It took Dan a moment to realise that Karen was trying to lighten the moment, but when it dawned on him, he said, "Alternatively, I could always come and creep in beside you…"

"Now that is the next thing that I'm worried about…"

"Why?" Dan appealed to her but was beginning to smile, despite himself.

She laughed. "Because my bed creaks, that's why."

This time they both laughed together.

But, when their laughter had come to its natural end, Dan knew that Karen's answer to his suggestion was still stuck at "no". He stood, intending to retrieve his jacket from the coat pegs in the hall.

She came to him, putting her arms around his middle and looking into his face.

"Don't be cross with me, Dan. My answer won't always be 'no'. I think we both want the same things."

He gazed at her for moment. "I know that..." he said reassuringly. They kissed for a moment and then Dan turned to let himself out.

From the path outside, he said, "Don't forget – if you need help with your dad – or just anything really, give me a call. If you can't get me for any reason, leave a message."

She nodded. "Of course. Speak to you again tomorrow, ok?"

The day was fading into a dank twilit evening as Dan climbed into his car and set off down the drive, getting out of the car again to go through the business of opening the gates, moving the car, closing the gates and then heading for 'home'. Karen had watched the lights of Dan's car disappearing down the drive but then, as she turned back into the house, she wondered if she had been unduly rigid with him – and, as he had asked, so she now asked herself – what was it that she was afraid of? She felt tempted to dismiss the question; the situation was as she had said it was. She did not want to sleep with Dan if, all the time, she was going to feel that she had to hide their intimacy from her father.

A little wearily, she allowed her thoughts to continue on their trajectory. Not wanting to sleep with Dan in her father's house might not, however, preclude her from going to the cottage where he was staying. She did not want to keep him waiting indefinitely. He was a patient man – but she was unsure as to exactly how long she could expect him to wait before he began looking around for someone else.

Was that, however, all of the problem? She continued her anxious self-questioning. She was sure that they loved each other, and, to her that was more important than any moral dilemmas she might have had. No, it was not that. It was simply that she wondered how well she knew him, even after the time they had spent together. Did she, Karen wondered, know him well enough to live with him and in addition to that, to share a bed with him? Those would be huge steps for her to take – and decisions that she had never found the courage to discuss with him. Then again, she knew that he had been unfaithful once, so – was he capable of being unfaithful to her?

She allowed her thoughts to stray into what it would be like to, well, be 'with' Dan because, for reasons she had never fully analysed, she had never been 'with' anyone else. That would, indeed, be a huge step.

In the gathering darkness, there was a faint call from her father upstairs. He wanted something. She had to go. She did not want him trying to haul himself out of bed again and, heaven forbid, having another fall. She switched on the light above the stairs and hurried up to his room. Putting her head round the door, in the twilight of the room she could see that he was stirring. She went to his side and switched on the beside lamp.

* * *

The light on the message machine was flashing; Dan dumped his briefcase in the hall and went to press the 'play' button. The voice of Amanda greeted him and, to his surprise, invited him to pay them (or was it simply her?) a visit in the near future – whenever it was convenient.

Having just arrived back at the cottage from a day's teaching at the College, Dan slumped onto the settee. Was this something he had the energy to even think about at that moment? The answer was probably 'no' but beyond the realms of willing thought, as he would readily acknowledge, lay the involuntary processes of a brain still active from a busy day; his mind clicked into 'auto-pilot'.

His departure from Wellsprings, of course, was now well and truly in the past but the memories of that time continued to be both painful and grossly over-rehearsed, in terms of the mental 'air time' that he still permitted them. So, it was not so much that he was unwilling to meet Amanda – but that, having already spent so much energy on continuing to turn over the same exhausted ground that he could not, for the life of him, imagine what it was that they could usefully have to say to each other.

He thought back to the evening, about a fortnight before, at the 'The Black Swan'. At the time, he had made a conscious decision that, despite some very distasteful memories of their shared past, he wanted to know more about the circumstances in which she now found herself.

Had he wanted to gloat? He did not think so. Was it, as he had told himself at the time, that he still retained a remnant of loyalty to someone with whom he had worked closely on a daily basis, and who had relied on him to provide her with the time and space to deal with the Academy Trust? He had previously thought so – but now was not so sure.

He fished in his briefcase for his dairy. There must even now, he reflected, still be unfinished business between them, things that had yet to be resolved. Around the time of his redundancy, to his way of thinking, she had fallen all-too completely into the 'executive' role that was being cultivated nationally – and by her peers, locally. Dan had not wanted such a role and despised what he saw happening to Amanda and to others like her. In his view, the developing 'business model' was entirely inappropriate to the ethos of a school – which needed to be run efficiently, which needed a sense of its own identity – but which was, at its core, a body of people centrally concerned with the education and welfare of the children in the school's care.

Others had seen Dan as 'out of step', a still relatively 'young fogey' – but 'fogey' nonetheless, whose beliefs harked back to the Mr Chips role model rather than someone fit to participate in the gradually evolving corporate enterprises that schools were becoming. People like Dan knew nothing of any substance and could be trumped every time in any decision-making process by people from the business world, people steeped in life's 'nitty-gritty' – or so it was believed.

He struggled still with his own demons. He had indeed once striven to be a role model for the children he had taught and had tried to stay well within the moral parameters that invisibly permeated such a role. Now, however, his previous marriage and career lay wrecked behind him – and principally because he had lusted after someone else's wife. His past was a mess.

He wondered: was that why he wanted to meet Amanda? Being on the scrapheap had initially felt very lonely until he realised that a 'heap' was exactly what it was – a continuously self-replenishing mass of people whose value as economic units was to be seen, henceforth, as that of additional consumers – of marginal value to the market, but no longer additional atoms of creativity. And now, Amanda, who had overseen his redundancy, was here on the scrapheap beside him. In its own way, the process had a tinge of nasty fascination about it. The lurking desire to meet Amanda was less of a mystery than he thought.

At last, his eyes came to rest on the current week in his diary which, he had previously and cheerfully noted, had been set aside for students as a 'reading week'. He still had commitments at the College, but his timetable was lighter than usual. He would need to choose the day carefully. Tomorrow, Wednesday, he had meetings to attend but the Thursday he had scheduled for work that was easily moveable to another day. It might be short notice for Amanda, but it was worth a try. After all, as far as he knew, her timetable these days was largely empty.

The poor signal on his mobile phone led him to prefer the landline and he walked across to key in the number he had noted from Amanda's message. In the event, it was James who answered the phone.

"Hello James," he said. "I'm responding to a message from Amanda."

"She hoped you might," replied James. "I'll pass you over to her."

Dan waited whilst the phone was passed to Amanda.

"Hello Dan," she said. "Have you got a time when you can come over for a coffee?"

"Yes, I have. How would this Thursday suit you?"

"Thursday will be fine," she responded with alacrity. "Shall we say ten o'clock?"

If such a meeting needed to take place at all, ten o'clock suited him very well, so he confirmed, "I'll see you then."

"I look forward to it. Bye for now."

Dan gazed at the phone for a moment as if it could somehow illuminate the lack of any further explanation – but then he would have a better understanding once he had been to see her. He put the phone down. It was time to put a meal together – because despite being tired, he was also hungry.

* * *

The following Thursday, as planned, he drove across to Amanda's house. The journey took him just a few minutes. He wondered vaguely if he would have Amanda to himself or whether James would be there as well and what, after their rather curious reunion the previous Saturday, they would have to say to each other.

Dan made use of the large and ornate door knocker and, a few moments later, Amanda opened the door to him.

"Hello Dan. Come on in!"

She kissed him lightly on the cheek and led him through to the lounge where a fire had been lit in the open hearth. Although it had been a substantial amount of time since his last visit, the room seemed unchanged. Just as Dan had remembered, the light level was low and a soft glow from two table lamps created pools of light and darkness between the furniture.

James shuffled in, carrying a tray on which there was a full cafetiere, milk, cups, saucers and a plate of biscuits. He set the tray down on the coffee table which stood in the centre of a large, rectangular terracotta coloured rug. The leather settee on which Dan vaguely remembered sitting with Amanda, stood just to one side of the rug, facing across the coffee table towards the dancing light of the fire.

"Hello again, James," said Dan.

"Hello again, Dan," returned James, "And please, call me 'Jim'."

Dan smiled. He was no friend of formality but 'James' seemed more distant than 'Jim' and Dan preferred to have a little distance between himself and Amanda's husband.

Amanda, meanwhile, poured Dan a cup of coffee and handed it to him. "I think I still remember that you prefer black coffee – but there's milk if I've got that wrong."

"No, no, that's fine," he replied, gratefully accepting the cup, and retiring with it to an armchair at the edge of the rug.

Amanda poured coffee for James and herself, and they stood slightly awkwardly for a moment before she and 'Jim' seated themselves on the settee.

Though not given to explanations, James nonetheless, felt moved to say, "I realised the other night, as I was driving back here that I didn't say 'thank you' to you for rescuing Amanda – which, considering it was the middle of the night, was not too clever." He hesitated. "So, uh, thank you, it was really helpful – and we both appreciated it."

He ground to a halt. Such sentiments were not part of his usual repertoire. Amanda must have written his script for him, thought Dan.

"I think, Dan, that what my husband has not said is that if either of us has a 'night out' in Sedgewater, our usual arrangement is that, rather than risk driving home, we go to the little house in Prospect Row and spend the night there. The arrangement works well – but I suppose that, in the circumstances of the other night, it was very fortunate that you used, ah, shall we say, your 'detective skills' to find me. We are grateful as James has said – and had you not come to my rescue the whole saga could no doubt have become even more complicated."

Dan smiled, and said with uncharacteristic unctuousness, "It was not a problem. I was glad to be of help."

He took a sip of his coffee, reflecting that although he had not sought revenge, it was in small measure at least, already his.

James, meanwhile, was looking restless.

"It must be good though," said Dan, "for you both to be able to spend more time together?"

It was as much a question as a statement.

To Dan's surprise, it was James who responded.

"It is good," he said. "Although we're both people who like to be busy. I try to be company for Amanda, but she misses her work colleagues – and we've always thrived – both of us – on the fact that we are so busy."

Dan sensed that James was being economical with the truth, but rather than contradict her husband, Amanda decided to help him out.

"Yes, I'm sure that's right. And, of course, now the situation, at least for the time being, is that one of us is busy – whilst the other is not. It's taking a bit of getting used to, isn't it, darling?"

Now James was looking distinctly pained; Dan speculated as to the cause. Was he unhappy about his wife being unemployed – or did he not like Amanda calling him 'darling' in front of a visitor? Either way, Dan found James' mounting discomfort a source of both curiosity and mild amusement. He wondered what the victim would do to ease his suffering.

James, however, was not in the habit of tolerating unwanted predicaments.

"Funny you should mention being busy," he said, with a glance in Dan's direction. "This morning is no exception, I'm afraid."

Wriggling his mobile phone out of his pocket and placing it on the coffee table, he continued, "I've got a contractor doing some work for me – and, if he rings, I'll have to go."

"Problems?" asked Dan.

"Oh, nothing too extraordinary," replied James. "I recently bought a plot of land. It was a very useful acquisition but sometimes there's a problem with flooding at the bottom end of it. A contractor is sorting out the drainage, but there are some things down there that need my input."

He reached for his coffee and took a sip.

Dan sensed that he did not want too many questions asked. Amanda rode to his rescue, once more,

"That's all right, dear," she said. "I'm sure Dan and I can still find things to talk about."

On cue, Jim's phone buzzed loudly from the coffee table. He picked it up, opened it and wandered away from the settee.

Dan heard him say, "Ok, Rob – so it's as we thought. No problem – see you soon."

James closed his phone, returning to his coffee cup to take one more mouthful before tersely explaining, "Humph! Contractors! I'll have to go down there." He grimaced, in what was meant to be an apologetic smile.

Dan tried to read Amanda's expression but failed. James was already on his way out of the room. Moments later, they heard the back door of the house bang firmly shut and then the sound of the Range Rover crunching over the gravel.

After a brief silence, Amanda asked, "Can I top up your coffee?"

Dan nodded. "Please, I could do with it."

Amanda decanted coffee into his cup and then into her own. Dan waited, wondering where their conversation would go.

"I'm pleased that you were willing to come over this morning."

"It's no problem, Amanda. You have good coffee here – as I remember from my last visit."

She smiled. "It's curious that circumstances brought us back together last Saturday. I've been wanting to get back in touch with you ever since you left Wellsprings."

Dan studied his coffee for a moment or two. "It was a surprise," he said. "If I hadn't been at a loose end that evening, I wouldn't have gone into Sedgewater."

"It isn't my usual choice either," agreed Amanda, "but whatever the circumstances, it was fortunate that you came along when you did – I think the bar staff had already had enough and were ready to go home."

"You're right about that," commented Dan. "I didn't understand, though, why you were on your own when I found you. I'm surprised that none of your friends stayed with you, given that you were 'the worse for wear'?"

"They offered – but I didn't want them to stay. And I also told them that James was on his way to collect me."

"He wasn't 'on his way', though – was he?"

"No, he wasn't but I saw it as a white lie because of the arrangement that James and I have about – well, about such occasions."

"You mean the arrangement about the house round the corner."

"Yes – it usually works well enough except that…"

"Except that you'd had much more to drink than usual." He finished her sentence for her.

"Yes, that's about it – that, and the fact that, despite the amount I'd had, I still didn't want the others to think that I was totally incapable."

Dan resisted the urge to make any further comment and Amanda wanted the conversation to go in a different direction.

"So how are you, Dan? I've hardly heard anything from you – or about you – since you left Wellsprings."

"I thought that was best and, at the time, I wanted to draw a line under what I've come to think of as my previous life."

Amanda frowned. "I'm sorry to hear that. I know that you were having problems in your private life, but you did some excellent work at Wellsprings, and I hoped you'd find another teaching post somewhere in the area. What happened to turn you away from Primary teaching?"

"I don't think there was anything that turned me away from it as such, Amanda. I was just restless. I could see that Josh and Emily would soon be independent of me and Sue, and because we both had busy careers we'd chosen to live in a quiet place where nothing – other than flooding – ever happens. And, sadly, as a couple, we were going nowhere."

"So, when Anne came along…"

"When Anne came along, for a while there was suddenly some joy, some excitement in life again."

"What's the situation now with Sue?"

"Oh – we divorced about two years ago. She's still living at Moorside although for how much longer, I have no idea. I think she's got someone else in her life these days."

Amanda nodded. There had been remarkably little gossip about Dan and Sue, no doubt because they had always taken care to preserve their privacy.

"How's life at the College?"

"Oh – good, thanks. Working with adults was a challenge at first but I'm enjoying it."

He paused. The conversation was not going as he had hoped it would and the routine they had adopted made him feel as though he was being interviewed. If they were going to make a fresh start with their relationship, he had some questions of his own.

Amanda, meanwhile, whilst quietly pleased that James had gone off to deal with a work-related issue, it seemed to her that she and Dan were still behaving as though they were still in the kind of formal relationship that they had so carefully preserved at Wellsprings. Their situations had moved on but, in relation to each other, they had not.

She smiled at Dan. "I seem to be asking the questions, Dan – as though we were still at Wellsprings…"

"I imagine that's because we haven't yet adjusted to the changes in our mutual circumstances…." said Dan.

That was it, thought Amanda; that was why they were persisting in their former stiffness with each other. Their lives had changed but they had had no opportunity to adapt to one another in their new situations.

"I can tell you more," continued Dan, "but I also want to know what happened to you. I must admit I was surprised when I learned that Saturday night's event at The Black Swan was your 'leaving do'."

"Hmm," replied Amanda, "the get-together at the pub was not my leaving do. That was held at Fairfield last Friday – and Saturday night was 'drinks night with the girls', if I can put it that way."

"But what made you leave, Amanda? The last I heard you were one of the candidates tipped to replace the Principal."

"You heard correctly, Dan." She sighed. "But it's a long story – too long for this morning. I think that, basically, I became disenchanted with the job and also with much of what I was trying to achieve within the Trust."

Dan frowned. "I don't think I would ever have known that you were anything other than devoted to what you were doing."

"I'm tempted to tell you the whole thing, Dan but I'm conscious that James will only be out for a short while – and we need longer, quite a bit longer. Really, I'd like us to press 'reset' – I think both of us need to do that – and then to see where we are after that?"

He nodded slowly. The seemingly 'new' Amanda was certainly full of surprises and he liked the idea of pressing 'reset'; the formality they had adopted at Wellsprings had never worked for him.

"There were specific situations that made it difficult for me to follow my ambition," Amanda continued. "But something you said a short while ago caught my attention. When you spoke about your 'restlessness', that resonated with me because I've been feeling restless at the Academy for the last two years – and it seems to me, that with events moving as they are, unless I get on and achieve one or two of my personal ambitions, I shall always have a sense of regret."

Dan ran his hand over his forehead. What on Earth did Amanda imagine she was going to achieve in the rapidly degenerating situation around them?

Thinking that he was simply puzzled, she said, "I will explain eventually but James won't be gone long. There were tensions between us when you left Wellsprings and I'm hoping that we can get past them and make a fresh start."

He stared into his cup. He had hoped that this morning would be the time for explanations – even for reconciliation – but James' imminent re-arrival in the house was an obstacle to any depth of conversation between them. So, what was the point of their meeting?

He raised his eyes to look at her – and found that she was already watching him. "I asked you to come over here this morning because Saturday night's episode could easily have placed me in a vulnerable situation, and I'm very thankful to you for getting me out of it." She paused. "But also, I simply wanted to meet up with you again. It's a very long time since we last had a chance talk to each other about anything other than work."

That, thought Dan, was certainly true although interspersed with his longer-term feelings about her, he still felt both disbelief and a lasting sense of humiliation about the way in which she had dealt with the complaints against him and her apparent complicity in making him redundant.

They would need to talk about those things and, indeed, his anger with her would have to be dealt with if the 'reset' that they both wanted was ever to take place.

They had lapsed into a silence which was eventually broken by the sound of James' Range Rover crunching its way over the gravel on the drive. Moments later came the sound of the back door opening and of James making his way through to the lounge.

"So," Amanda greeted his arrival, "how was the site this morning? Is there a drainage problem?"

James frowned but did not immediately reply. Dan, meanwhile, had never visited the site to which Amanda was referring and so was unaware of her scepticism about the plot of land that James had gone to inspect.

"We have many 'inconveniences' around here," she said in an apparent aside to Dan. "Flooding seems to be one of the most persistent."

Conscious that James could hear any comments that passed between them, Dan looked questioningly at her, but she took his facial expression as an invitation to continue.

"There are others, though – people with metal detectors come to mind – and archaeologists and, if you think about it, the Anglo-Saxons too, although they were not so much an inconvenience as a plain, bloody nuisance. Their handiwork seems to be everywhere."

James came across to where they were sitting and pretended to sniff the air. "Hmm," he said, "no evidence of gin this morning. You've had too many cups of strong coffee."

Dan had the feeling that he was momentarily witness to an ongoing issue between husband and wife, but he had no wish to intervene or become entangled in their disagreement. A longer conversation with Amanda would have to wait. He smiled and said, "It's been good to meet up again – and thank you for the coffee. I should be going, though, because I have to work this afternoon."

Amanda smiled and began to leave her chair with the intention of seeing him to the front door, but James intervened.

"Don't bother yourself, dear. I'll see Dan to the door."

He ushered Dan before him and into the hallway but as they approached the door, he said, "I'm afraid I've parked too close to your car. I'll need to let you out."

Dan could see that there was ample space between the two cars on the drive, so he was puzzled by James' comment, but he said nothing and walked with him across to where they were parked.

"There's no problem, James," said Dan. "You've left me plenty of space," but as he was about to climb into his car, James touched him on the arm and said, "It must have been quite a surprise to bump into Amanda last Saturday…?

"Yes, it was," agreed Dan. "But she seems to have recovered."

James gave an enigmatic smile. "Well, yes," he said. "But I'm glad that you had nothing stronger than coffee this morning."

Dan again said nothing but opened the door of his car.

James placed his hand on the top of the door. "Amanda will have appreciated your company this morning," he said. "She finds it hard to occupy herself at present."

"I'm not surprised," commented Dan. "But if you're working close to home, perhaps there's a chance for the two of you to spend more time together?"

James looked bemused, as if spending time with his wife was a novel concept. "Well, yes, there is…but of course, the site I visited this morning is just part of what I think of as my 'Home Project'. I also have a much bigger project up in the Midlands – in the Severn Valley."

Dan nodded, sensing that missing pieces in that morning's puzzle were falling into place.

He began trying to get into the car, but James was impervious to his readiness to leave, and his hand remained firmly on the top of the door. "Remind me sometime to have a chat to you about my wife's relationship with alcohol…"

"Oh, does she have a problem?"

"You could say that…" replied James.

Yes, thought Dan. And I'm looking right at the cause of that problem.

He nodded to acknowledge James' comment. James released his grip on the door and Dan got into his car. James watched with his arms folded across his chest as Dan reversed, turned the car around and headed slowly down the drive.

* * *

CHAPTER 28

TERRA INCOGNITA

O n the evening of the day that he met with Amanda, Dan felt again the need to get away to a place in which he could think about the various issues that were on his mind. The Westmere Nature Reserve seemed the best choice and once he had parked his car, it took him just a few minutes to find his way back to the seclusion of the observation platform that he had discovered on his previous visit.

He looked across the lake to where a number of ducks were dabbling at the water's margin. Creatures like ducks, it seemed to him, were always living in the moment although they had certain innate abilities 'hard wired' into them – such as the ability to follow migratory routes. He, too, drew on his memories – but then used them to think about the experiences that were currently unfolding in his life and in the world around him.

He was drawing on his memories that evening – including the one against which he measured the water level in the lake, and which led him to believe that it was higher than when he had last been there. The lake, though, was not directly affected by the sea or its tides. Instead, its level was affected by rainfall, by the streams that fed into it or drained out of it and the groundwater in the surrounding area at any particular time.

The sea and the nearby coast were another matter and very recently there had been a flurry of news about the Thwaites Glacier in the Antarctic. Now, it seemed the Glacier was melting at a rate that, over the course of nearly two decades, had steadily accelerated.

There had also been an acceleration in the melting of glaciers everywhere. Greenland's ice cap was being fed at an ever-faster rate into the oceans of the world and the mountain glaciers that had formerly watered the lands of the continents were dwindling towards disappearance. Coastlines and coastal countries everywhere were being affected, and England and the County of Somerset were no exceptions.

Although scoffed at by sceptics, the statistics for Sedgewater Bay showed that sea level in the Bay was steadily creeping upwards. The problem, thought Dan, was that on the timescales generally used by human beings, the rise was almost imperceptible – and that sadly, it was this that perpetuated the survival of the sceptics, even as so many coastal areas were steadily disappearing beneath encroaching sea water.

It was through such unstoppable phenomena that Dan shared with millions of other people a sense of powerlessness – whilst those who had the power to make a difference to the trajectory of the Climate Crisis consistently took too little action or took it too late.

The reasons for this inertia or slowness to act had been endlessly discussed but were immaterial to Nature, so that the result was that the situation was no longer retrievable. Large areas of the Earth's surface were becoming uninhabitable and what had initially been a trickle of human migration across the globe had now become a flood, an unceasing inundation.

And he, Dan wondered, was he any different from those who had failed to act or who now travelled the earth vainly searching for a place to live and a patch of land on which they could sustain themselves? England had been fortunate so far. It was still possible to believe, in the British Isles, that civilisation could survive the catastrophe that it had set in motion – but for how much longer?

His awareness of the enormous problems he could do little about, though, did not replace or reduce his worries about the needs of those around him – his children, Amanda, Karen – and, even Anne, though she was now someone, he had to assume, who had decided to eke out her fate within the bounds of her marriage. These persisted like a steady drumbeat in his life.

He paused. He had included Amanda in his thoughts – but, like Anne, there was nothing in his relationship with her that signified any specific responsibility on his part for her well-being. It was she and James who were responsible for each other – and, after his affair with Anne, he had sworn that he would never again involve himself in another couple's marriage.

Karen, too, although he had now known her for more than two years and had become someone about whom he cared, had never moved into the emotional void left in him by Anne. She was the only other person in his acquaintance who felt the urgency and the enormous weight of the irreversible crisis into which the human race had sleep-walked but, in their daily life, the most frequent focus of their shared attention was Karen's father, Hugh, whose pressing needs had become a joint concern.

Involuntarily, Dan's thoughts returned to Amanda; since they had first met, there had always been a special place in his thoughts for her and although he had accepted her rejection of their relationship so many years before, it had deeply hurt him at the time – and had possibly led him into marriage with Sue long before he was truly ready for such a commitment. However, the situation was as it was. Whatever the state of the relationship between Amanda and James – and however much he might regret the sadness that was clearly to be seen in Amanda, it was not, he told himself, any part of his responsibility, other than as a friend, to help her find again her appetite for life.

He shifted in his seat at the lakeside. He was still in regular touch with both Emily and Josh, and he found himself wondering about the kind of fate that had now been meted out to them by his own and previous generations; it was, it seemed to him, a grievous infliction, born out of greed, self-centredness, and lack of forward vision. Would he – how could he – expect them to care for him in his old age as he and Karen were now caring for Hugh? And what could he do for them in the years ahead, as the future rattled ever further from the grasp of himself and every other living person into a future that, according to most predictions, would be a living nightmare?

As he thought about his children, his thoughts had slipped into a different gear, and he needed to bring them slowly and deliberately back to the reality of the place in which he was sitting. For all the time that he had spent trying to calculate what lay ahead, he could still only live his life day-by-day – and perhaps it was no more than vanity that led him to believe that the world he saw in his crystal ball was even close to the one that would gradually become the Earth's tomorrow.

The light was fading quickly. The cries of wildfowl echoed across the evening sky and across the melting, coalescing tones of its reflection in the mere. It was a wild and solitary place, and, for that moment, he felt like an intruder there. To navigate his way without mishap back along the twilit walkway to the car park would require him to focus his thoughts on the here and now. From there, only time would tell if, in the chaos that seemed about to descend on them all, they would have the ability to survive.

* * *

CHAPTER 29

'THOUGH THE RAIN,
IT RAINETH EVERY DAY'

(King Lear – Shakespeare)

The following Monday was difficult. The visit to Westmere the previous week had become a pleasant memory as the weather during the weekend became markedly worse. The lanes were filling with water as Dan drove into Sedgewater, cursing the blocked drains and gutters along his way.

The students in his lectures arrived, looking damp and dishevelled, hanging their wet jackets and coats on the backs of their chairs so that water pooled on the floor. A clutter of sodden umbrellas adorned the assigned but inadequate area near the door.

Lunchtime in the main refectory was only a little better. Food, or the College's version of it, and an opportunity to chat with friends, helped to lighten Dan's mood. In quieter moments, he had a text 'conversation' with Karen – largely about her father's health and then it was time to teach again.

A fresh crowd of rain-soaked students arrived, and he hurried through his lecture materials, aware that there was pressure from the group to finish earlier than the scheduled time; the ongoing deluge outside the windows was causing everyone to be distracted and, in the light of the local area's history of flooding, there was a pervasive anxiety about getting home.

Dan was not exempt from this general disquiet. A strong wind was now amplifying the impact of the water cascading out of the sky and he was grateful that once he had gone out through the College's main door, he had only to travel a short distance to get to his car.

He clutched his briefcase in one hand and held on to the hood of his anorak with the other. The wind buffeting the car made it difficult to open the door, but he finally wrenched it ajar and almost fell into the driver's seat.

From there, he fumbled beneath the dashboard, trying to find a cloth with which to wipe the misted windscreen. Finally, he was forced to wait until he could see ahead. From there, he joined the lines of traffic crawling along the main road, their lights reflected in the rills of water swilling across the carriageway.

At the far end of the road, there was a roundabout preceded by a slip road to his left. Although the vehicles queuing for the roundabout were almost stationary, he was relieved to see that traffic on the slip road was moving freely. From there, he had a choice; there was a shortcut which would take him beneath a railway bridge – or the longer route which would take him out into the countryside via a level crossing. If the shortcut was open, he would take it.

As he prepared to turn right towards the railway, however, he could see that there was a forest of flashing blue lights clustered around the approach to the bridge. The line of traffic of which he was a part began to crawl along as drivers and their passengers rubber-necked to see what was happening. No special effort though was required to see that the dip beneath the bridge was flooded, and the queuing cars came to a halt as police officers almost up to their chests in water fought to wrench open a car door and then to rescue the driver, man or woman Dan could not tell, from the dark waters swirling around the vehicle.

Horns began to honk as those behind reminded those in front to keep moving. There was time to see no more – and already the dusk was deepening as Dan waited with as much patience as he could at the level crossing whilst a train thundered through, and the crossing gates returned again to their vertical resting positions.

Once on the other side of the tracks, the traffic gradually fell away and soon he was looking for the junction that would take him into the lanes through which he would have to thread his way back to the cottage. From previous experience, he knew that his main problem would be surface water although about halfway along his route there was a narrow stone bridge that was notorious for flooding during downpours. It was not a place at which to make the wrong decisions.

For a while, he made good progress, concentrating on his route and sheltered by the hedgerows from the buffeting wind. Here or there, he had to squeeze into the hedge or pull into a passing place in order to allow a vehicle from the opposite direction to get through and then, he found himself on the descent to the bridge – and praying that the water had not yet begun to wash across the road.

His headlights, set to 'automatic', lit up the wind-battered road sign, 'Weak Bridge'. He focused his attention on where the narrow ribbon of tarmac snaked through the twilight towards the bridge's parapet; the light of his main beam picked up the runnels swilling across the road but as he looked, the river had yet to encompass the bridge. He would have just moments to cross.

Resisting the urge to accelerate towards the hump at the bridge's narrow centre, Dan pushed through the flooding on the nearside and then paused for a moment as he realised that on the far side of the bridge the flooding was worse. Stuck in a moment of indecision, he felt the bridge beneath him shaking with the impact of the river's torrent.

It was do or die; get swept away or survive. He pushed forward, his heart pounding in case water should enter the exhaust pipe or, worse, that the car would begin to float. Water surged around him, and he could feel its force. He seemed to be losing traction and whilst the car was apparently being pushed sideways, his attempts to steer were achieving nothing. Then, suddenly, just as he thought he was lost, the surface beneath him began to edge upwards, the wheels found grip again and he fled forward, out of the surging waters, away from a watery death.

With his heart still banging in his chest, the car's impetus steadily reasserted itself and he was climbing up, up and out of the valley. He glanced in his rear-view mirror thinking to catch a last glimpse of the flood behind him, but he could see only the red glare of his own tail lights in the engulfing darkness. There would be 'flashbacks' later, he was sure, but as far as he could guess, he had passed his moment of danger.

By now, the rain was falling so torrentially, that Dan found it hard to believe that it was not driven by some form of supernatural fury. Water teemed down from the sky's blackness to cascade incessantly through the beam of the car's headlights. Every lane was becoming a shallow brook and water had begun to spout from the stone walls that lined his route.

Debris strewn along the route was impossible to avoid as he bumped and crunched his way through the last of his journey.

Then, in the final section of lane, he came to a slithering halt before a large branch that had been ripped from a nearby tree and had fallen across the road. He had but two choices – either to retrace his route and find some alternative way through to the hamlet or he could attempt to move the branch. The thickness and solidity of the branch was readily apparent. It seemed extremely unlikely that he would be able to lift it. He could possibly use the car to bulldoze it out of the way – but he might not succeed and anyway, it would not be possible without causing appreciable damage to the car.

Every option involved a degree of risk. Finally, he decided to get out and see if he could even contemplate trying to move the branch. Switching on his hazard warning lights, he battled against the force of the wind to open the door; then he was out and struggling to close it again. Immediately, he was plunged into a roaring chaos of sound and water, his clothes utterly inadequate for such conditions.

Somehow, he battled across to the branch, found a solid section of the wood and tried to lift it. He heaved, he fought, he strained every muscle – but it was quickly apparent that he was never going to lift its inert, brutal and slippery mass from his path. Soaked to the skin and blinded by the rain, he steadied himself against the branch, wondering if there was yet another choice.

Somewhere, he found a still centre in his brain. He noticed that there was gravel scattered everywhere across the road's surface. It was hard to retain a grip on its surface. Then a huge blast of wind smacked him hard up against the branch for a moment in which fleetingly he thought that both he and the branch would be tumbled into the flooded ditch at the side of the road.

But that was what he wanted – the branch in the ditch – and out of his way! He could not lift it but given the strength of the wind, the slipperiness of the road and the small but additional force his own strength could provide, it might just be possible to move the huge and stubborn obstacle in his path.

Buffeted constantly, he sought and found places where he could get some grip on the road's surface. Again, a blast of wind pinned him against the sodden mass of the wood but then, again it rocked and

seemed ready to roll and pivot at one and the same time; of course –
the torn end of the branch, the heaviest end, had landed on the side
of the road!

The wind was gusting incessantly; it was just a matter of waiting
because, every now and again, there would come a blast of enormous
strength. He had only to time his effort. He began to push and push
but, for all his heaving, the branch seemed just to make the slightest of
rocking motions. Then, suddenly, there at his back, was a colossal, blind
but unbelievably powerful hand, tossing both him and the branch aside
from the road.

Dazed, it took him some moments to regather his wits and to realise
that he was entangled and suspended head down in the arms of the
branch with his right hand plunged into icy cold, rapidly flowing water;
but then, the joyful realisation – the branch was out of his way! His need
now was to extract himself from his predicament and get back to the car.

Raising his hand from the water, he hauled himself upright,
untangled himself from the clutches of the branch and fought his way
back across the road to the car, which he had unwittingly but fortunately
left in the lee of a thick and seemingly impenetrable hedgerow; the wind's
turbulence, however, still reached its vortices down around the car and
he had to tug hard at the door again to get in.

Sodden and shivering, he drove the last half mile to the cottage. His
tyres crunched over the debris strewn across the apron of the garage. He
had no need to open the up and over garage door; the wind had already
blown it open. Cautiously, he edged forward, aware that there could be
garage contents and wind-borne bric-a-brac on the floor. If there was
anything, however, he did not see or feel it beneath car's tyres.

He clambered stiffly out of the car, his teeth chattering. There was
a padlock on a shelf to one side. Its purpose in being there was that it
could be used when necessary to reinforce the garage door's locking
mechanism; he used it now.

Despite the darkness, the wind and the rain, he was aware of pieces
of broken roof tile scattered across his path to the front door. Laboriously,
he forced a hand numbly into the now sodden pocket of his trousers in
which he had earlier placed his front door key. His fingers were stiff, the
key and lock uncooperative, but at last he stood in a gathering pool of
water in the cottage hallway.

Without waiting, he stripped off his outer clothing and padded through to the shower room, leaving a trail of water behind him. There, he pulled the cord that operated the shower light and fan, uncharacteristically thanking the Almighty that at least the power supplies had not yet gone down. With as much speed as he could muster, he stripped off the last of his sodden clothing and plunged beneath the revitalising stream of the shower's hot water.

It was some time before he emerged again to find a towel and then the comfort of the electric fire and his winter dressing gown. In the subdued light of a table lamp, he stared into the fire's glow, aware that the ominous thunder he could hear in the background was the sound of the river in the valley behind the cottage's garden. It had been in summer, almost four years before that night, that he had gazed down upon the river, believing that it could not be long before the summer's arid heat reduced it to no more than a succession of puddles. Monday was nearly over but surely, he thought, such extremities of drought and storm were still a long way from what they might eventually become; he shivered involuntarily, despite the warmth of the fire and his winter dressing gown.

* * *

The following day continued in similar vein. Putting on his waterproof clothing, he prepared to do what he could to prevent the intrusion of water into the cottage.

As he went outside into the wind and rain, he reflected that the summer that year had been very different from the long, hot, dry summer in which he had moved to the cottage. By contrast with the drought of that period, the year that was now drawing to an end, it seemed reasonable to conclude, would go on record as one of the wettest in recent history. It had also been one of the warmest – and the combination of these two factors had caused significant problems for the Country's agriculture, particularly in an economic world where there was a need to produce more food than ever within the islands of Britain.

Dan had noticed temporary shortages of some food items – both home-grown and imported, in each of the preceding twelve months. That was not, though, his immediate concern; instead, it was his inability to access not just shops but his place of work, or, indeed, to get into the town of Sedgewater at all.

That day, he had felt both bedraggled and dispirited as he dragged into position one of the last of the sandbags that he had stored away in preparation for conditions such as those that Southwest England was experiencing at that time. As he came to the end of his labours, he was satisfied that flooding was not an immediate threat to the cottage, but successive weather forecasts had highlighted the queue of winter storms waiting in the Atlantic. The weather forecasters made repeated reference to the comparable situation in the winter of 2013 to 2014 although Dan recalled that the preceding seasons of the year had all been wetter than those of 2013 and groundwater levels were very high indeed.

Back at the cottage, his stock of tins in the cupboard was steadily dwindling. The threat to electricity supplies was ever-present and if they went down, the food he had stored in the freezer would soon become a health hazard rather than an asset. He was hoping that, against the run of current predictions, something would happen to jolt the atmosphere in the UK's part of the Atlantic out of the rut into which it had fallen; his hopes, though, in that respect, were dwindling by the day.

The weather and the darkness of the season seemed to be weighing on everyone with whom Dan was in contact. Ordinarily, he would have been preparing to spend time at Christmas with his children and now, this year, with Karen – but he was having difficulty envisaging any kind of Christmas that was not white but flood water grey.

Karen had been in touch a number of times. She was finding Dan's inability to visit her frustrating and even upsetting. He did not like to remind her of his previous offer, which she had turned down, to temporarily move in with her, in order to help her cope, practically and emotionally, with her father's gradual deterioration; she had privately worried at the time that her decision might come to haunt her, but she had not imagined that it would be quite so soon. Dan, too, was deeply frustrated by his inability to help her just when she needed it most.

It was not surprising then, that, when the telephone rang, he hurried to pick up the call because he thought that it would almost certainly be Karen. The College having now closed until local flooding receded, it was very unlikely to be from anyone there.

To his surprise, it was Sue. She sounded as though she could only just control her voice.

"Dan, we need you to come as quick as you can get here!"

He was taken aback, not only by the fact that it was his ex-wife but also by the lack of preamble.

"Why, Sue, what's going on?"

Immediately, it seemed like a stupid question. He needed just one guess.

"What the hell d'you think is happening?" She almost screeched it at him. "It's flooding here again! We're cut off and water's already beginning to fill the lower part of the house!"

Of course – he had not forgotten about Sue, but for the last four days, he had been totally preoccupied with his thoughts about Karen and the College, not to mention his dwindling food supplies.

"Have you tried phoning Fire and Rescue?" It was an obvious first step, but he decided to risk her wrath by checking.

"Of course I've phoned bloody Fire and Rescue! Their lines are all jammed and unless someone gets here soon, there'll be no point. The water out here is rising fast – and I mean fast! I've never seen anything like it!"

Alarmed as he was by Sue's plight, it suddenly occurred to him that she was not the only one at risk. "D'you have Emily with you?" Exeter University's Christmas recess had already begun.

"Yes, we're both here – and we're both desperate. We need help!"

Dan thought quickly. It would take him thirty, maybe forty-five minutes to get there.

"What about the neighbours?" he asked. "Can they help?"

By now, Sue was nearly in tears, seeing his questions as needless delay.

"I haven't seen them in weeks!" she screeched. "We're stuck, totally flooded! We need your help! For God's sake – get the boat and help us!"

His mind raced. He had to get to them and the boat would provide his only chance.

By now, he was pacing up and down the living room with the phone clapped to his ear.

"Right, Sue – I'll leave immediately. I'll be there as fast as I can! Meanwhile, go right to the top of the house – and don't give up on 'Fire and Rescue'!"

"Ok, Dan – we'll do that! But hurry – or there'll be nothing here but water!"

"I'm on my way! Try to stay calm – and stay in touch!"

He ended the call, then quickly found his waterproofs and tugged them on. His mind, meanwhile, was already working overtime on how exactly he would get to Sue and Emily. Finding a route was not a problem – he knew the area like the back of his hand. He would go to Beacon Hill and then down the other side as far as he could before reaching the flood waters. The roads in that direction were quite wide and, at worst, he would be no more than a mile from Moorside. From there, he would have to make each decision as it came – and he would take a map despite knowing the area so well, because he had learned from previous flooding that electronic systems, including GPS, were vulnerable.

He quickly put the items he needed into his backpack, cursing himself for not having thought about what was happening out on the Levels! How had he lived there all those years – and not thought about the dangers of Sue's situation? And then there was Emily. How could he have forgotten that she would be at home with her mother? What a fool he was!

It was not the time though for self-recrimination; it would have to wait. He hurried out to where the dinghy's trailer was chained. Luckily, the situation had not caught him completely four-square. With the previous flood still branded on his memory, that morning he had looked at the boat again – though primarily with his own needs in mind. The situation had already been such, that sooner or later, his food supplies would run out so rather than sit and wait for others to help, he had begun to work out his own salvation. He had inflated the dinghy and attached the outboard motor – which he had also tested successfully.

There was plenty still to be done though. The fuel needed topping up then the boat had to be secured to its trailer – and the trailer to the car; it would all take precious minutes. On the plus side, he had done it all before – many times.

Still, he found himself fighting his own frustration. Winching the boat onto the trailer was hard work and when he climbed into the car, he was sweating profusely. He knew it would take about twenty minutes more to get to a suitable place at Beacon Hill and then maybe another five minutes to launch and be on his way.

Fortunately, the storms had ensured that the roads, lightly used at best, were deserted; any sensible person, he concluded, was indoors. There was also a lull in the rain. His journey took just a shade less than his estimated time.

Parking the car, securing it in a passing place, unhitching the trailer and trundling it to the edge of the flood all proved simpler than he had thought – easier than for some beach launches he had done – but the time taken still nagged at him. Now, however, he was afloat; the engine was as reliable as ever, despite its spell in storage, and now he was navigating his way towards the all-too familiar lanes that led to Moorside. The 'deja-vu' was overwhelming, as though a slice of intervening years had been cut from his timeline. Here he was again.

It did not take him long to discover, though, that whilst the flood was rapidly rising, it had yet to reach the epic proportions of the previous inundation. He had to focus his mind at every instance. Navigating the lanes without the boat would have been impossible, but by the same token, there were places where debris and the shallowness of the flood made passage very difficult.

Now he was in a side lane approaching the road to his destination. The water was deep enough but full of floating debris from the trees and hedgerows. The fading light was another concern. He snatched a glance at his watch; Sue had phoned at about three o'clock and it was now five to four. Daylight would soon be gone. He brought his mind back to the task in hand. His smartphone vibrated and buzzed but he was at the junction between the lane and the main road. Then he was entering the turn; his phone would have to wait.

Now he was very close and it would surely be just minutes before Sue and Emily would be getting into the boat. He could see the gateposts at the front of the house but no sign of the gates – swept away, perhaps, by the floodwater. He manoeuvred carefully into the gateway – but need not have worried; there was a wide space, and the flooded road afforded him plenty of room.

Having deliberately kept away from his former home, he no longer had any idea of the submerged geography of the garden. For all he knew, Sue might have altered the whole layout. He decided, though, to go as close to the front door as he could so he switched off the engine, raised it out of the water and used the paddle to swing in close to the concrete by the front door. Water had penetrated the house and was no doubt swilling about inside but it did not yet look quite as deep as it had been during the previous flood.

He tied the boat to the porch and scrambled out onto the concrete from where he bashed on the door. An upstairs window flew open.

"Thank God! You took your time!"

Dan opened his mouth to retort but the window was slammed shut again. He tried the door. It seemed immoveable and Sue had, of course, changed the security arrangements when she had thrown him out – so he had no key. How bizarre – he would have to wait.

The twilight in which he had arrived was now moving on into darkness. He tried to be patient as splashing sounds and intermittent flashes from a torch on the other side of the front door announced that Sue and Emily had come down the stairs and were struggling to get out.

"Damn this door! The wood must have swollen!"

It was not locked then, as he had believed – but had absorbed a good deal of water.

"Give me some space on your side, Sue! I'll try to open the door from here!"

There was more splashing from inside as Sue and Emily retreated to the foot of the stairs.

Dan tried pushing the door as hard as he could but it barely moved. With a degree of desperation, he began to shove it with his shoulder. After several more attempts, though, it began to give until finally, it suddenly opened and he barely prevented himself from sprawling headlong into the water before him. Recovering quickly, he saw Sue and Emily start forward.

"Oh Dad, at last! I thought we were never going to get out!" Emily threw her arms round her father while Sue looked on impatiently.

"No time for that! We need to get going!" she snapped. Her torch had a powerful beam and she flashed it on the dinghy; Dan moved to hold the boat whilst she helped Emily to scramble aboard. Then he tried to help Sue as she briefly hesitated but then stood back again as she made it obvious that she could manage. Releasing the dinghy's rope, he slid into the dinghy, slowly opened the throttle of the outboard engine and began to arc away from the porch in a slow turn.

They were roughly equidistant from the outskirts of Sedgewater and Sue's mother at Monk's Hill. So far, they had said nothing to one another about which direction they should take. Now Sue decided to speak.

"I think we should go right, towards Monk's Hill. We could stay at my mother's place for tonight."

Dan disagreed. "We could but it's probably cut off by now. We'd be better off heading for Sedgewater."

"Wouldn't that be more dangerous?"

"I don't think so. And we can be more help to your mother in Sedgewater than if we're all cooped up in her house."

There seemed to be a certain sense to what Dan was saying. Sue said nothing but turned so that she could face forward, pointing the torch along the route that Dan was proposing to take.

He took this as her agreement and gradually opened the throttle of the outboard motor. They began to move steadily along the flooded road that led in the general direction of Sedgewater. The first part of their route would be fairly straightforward but after that, he would find himself making moment-by-moment decisions. Above all, he needed to get as close as he could to 'dry land' on the edge of Sedgewater. From there, they could try to call on the help of friends or simply find a 'B and B' to stay for the night.

Dan knew that he was heading due north-east. He did not want to stray too much further to the east because in that direction was the course of the River Sedge. The banks of the river would almost certainly be submerged because the Sedge would be in spate, and, contrary to what he had said to Sue, the surge of its waters would place them in considerable danger.

Belatedly, he began to recognise that he had set them a formidable challenge. For the moment, though, he kept to their route through the lanes – with which he had become so previously familiar.

The outboard motor maintained its steady drone and they were making good progress. Wherever Dan could see hedgerows still bristling above the water, he tried to steer a course between them whilst persisting in his general northeasterly direction which he knew would take them to rising ground on the outskirts of Sedgewater. At several points, he asked Sue to shine the torch on the map so that he could check their position in relation to the landmarks and small villages marooned in the dark and lapping wilderness of water that surrounded them. According to the map, Withyford was somewhere to the port side of the dinghy.

Then, almost before he was aware of it, they were encountering a problem he had met before. He was following the line of a hedgerow that took them in the direction he was seeking, and Sue was warning of obstacles in the water just ahead of them when suddenly he saw that they were now very close to the hedgerow, pushed perhaps, by currents in the water. Suddenly, Sue crouched in her seat, and he heard her yell, "Look out! Low branches!"

Before they could react in any way, Emily gave a loud cry as she was struck by a thick branch and swept sideways out of the dinghy and into the swirling blackness of the water.

Sue screamed, "Oh my God!" whilst Dan immediately throttled back and began trying to see where his daughter had entered the water. Sue swung the torch around, moving its beam across the slowly moving surface. As she did so Dan had seized the mooring rope and tied it around his waist.

"Take the tiller!" he yelled at Sue and as soon as she had it in her hands and was using the outboard to keep the dinghy from drifting, he slid overboard.

The shock of the water took his breath away. He gulped and gasped, conscious now of the water moving slowly but strongly around him; he fought to suppress feelings of panic as it dragged at his clothing and immersed him in its icy grip.

Sue was able to use one hand to direct the torch beam onto the water, lighting the area around him. Momentarily, he was blinded but managed to turn his head so that he could see what was happening.

There was a current that seemed to be flowing towards the hedgerow and then through it. The chances were that it had pushed Emily into the hedge, just as it was doing to him now, and that if he worked along it, he would find her. Urgently, he began forcing his way forward from just above the point where he believed she had fallen overboard. Vegetation and tree branches clutched at him. He began to wonder if the rope he had tied around him, had been a mistake. He found himself clambering over, and then attempting to flounder his way across, the undulations and hollows beneath his feet. Half wading, half swimming, he struggled on.

Whenever he could, he yelled "Emily! Emily!" at the top of his voice. Sue joined in, but for all their joint efforts, there was no reply. Dan was now several yards below the point where their daughter had been swept into the water. The shock of the water's enveloping chill was ebbing as he continued to plunge and grope his way along the hedge.

He stopped briefly to look around. At first, he could see and feel nothing but the stems and leaves of inundated vegetation. Then, he came to point where a large, submerged piece of tree branch ran out at an obtuse angle from the hedgerow, sections of it poking here and there, above the water. Sue ran her torch over it and as she did so, Dan thought that he saw what looked like the trailing tendrils of a water plant, just below the surface. He splashed along the branch and reached down. At first, he caught only the tips of vegetation in his fingers but as he probed about along the slimy surface of the wood, he suddenly felt in his grip what he took to be hair.

"Here, Sue! Shine the torch down here!" he yelled with a renewed urgency.

Reaching down, he found his fingers clutching a handful of human hair. Plunging his other hand into the water, his fingers met with and then seized at the edge of a piece of fabric – surely the hood of Emily's anorak! He began to pull, and at first there seemed to be no movement; he decided to pull backwards against the flow of the water.

Then! Suddenly! His daughter's head and shoulders rose above the surface, bobbing into the beam of her mother's torch.

"It's her! Sue! It's Emily!"

"Thank God! I'll come closer! Hang on to her!"

Dan needed no bidding. His arm was already extended down through the water to encompass Emily's waist and he consolidated his grip as Sue brought the dinghy nosing in to where they were. As soon as it was alongside them, they began working to get Emily aboard but after several strenuous efforts, it became obvious that she was caught in the branch.

Taking a lungful of air, Dan ducked below the surface. He could see nothing in the water's blackness but gradually as he felt around, he located one of Emily's boots and then realised that it was caught between the submerged branch and trunk of a fallen tree.

It took only moments of tugging to ascertain that the boot was immovably wedged so Dan began to pull as firmly as he could on Emily's leg until her foot came free of the boot.

Gasping for breath, he burst to the surface.

"She's free! Get her into the boat!"

With Dan pushing and Sue pulling, after several attempts Emily slid over the side and into the bottom of the dinghy. Dan gave silent thanks that she was no heavier than she was, as he drew in deep breaths in an attempt to recover.

Then he began hauling himself into the boat; it took a huge effort. Water was pouring from every part of his body and clothing. Sue also helped by hauling on the rope around him and then heaving on his arms and chest until, exhausted, he lay in a sodden mass, in the bottom of the dinghy. For a short while, he was unable to move. Finally, digging deeply into his reserves of energy, he dragged himself into a sitting position next to the tiller. Meanwhile, Sue had passed the torch to him and slithered away to apply her resuscitation skills to Emily. In the torch's powerful beam, he could see that she was having a desperate time; despite his incessant trembling and shivering, he tried to direct the light so that it both illuminated the boat's interior and enabled him to peer into the black expanse ahead of them.

There was, too, an ever-present risk that they would drift further in towards the clutches of the hedgerow. He began to open the outboard's throttle.

"We need to get away from here!" he yelled against the engine's noise. "Then we need to find somewhere to land!" He tried unsuccessfully to overcome his incessant shivering and to focus on finding somewhere to beach the dinghy. There they could get Emily onto a surface where her mother's attempts at resuscitation could be more effective.

Sue's attention, meanwhile, was concentrated entirely on her daughter. At first, she feared that they were too late, that despite finding Emily quickly, she had been submerged too long in the water. Her first step was to try to wake Emily. It went against her nature to pinch and slap Emily but now, in an attempt to wake her, that was what she needed to do.

Trying to fight her desperation, she persevered. For what seemed an age, her daughter remained cold, inert, seemingly lifeless – but she could not stop. Nothing would make her stop! Then, a shock, and the first indications of relief; Emily's eyelids began to flicker, her eyes rolled open and her head moved to one side until, suddenly, she was retching up water into the bottom of the boat.

"Dan! She's coming round! Thank God!"

Sue had been preparing to move to 'rescue breaths' and CPR, but to her partial astonishment, Emily was expelling the water from her lungs unaided.

With help from her mother, she moved into a position where she was partly on her side and from which she continued to heave and cough water into the well of the boat. Her anorak was sodden and heavy so Sue helped her to get out of it, replacing it with her own outdoor jacket which she put round her shoulders.

As soon as Dan saw that Emily was now conscious and in some semblance of a recovery position, he yelled to Sue, "We need to phone for an ambulance! I'm hoping to beach the dinghy just up ahead!"

In the light of the torch, he saw Sue pull her phone from her anorak pocket. The motion of the boat made keying in '999' quite difficult, especially since her hands were cold and wet but she managed it.

Dan judged that the area ahead and to his left was close to the edge of the flooding. He began to steer in that direction. It was difficult to see anything much in the darkness when their only sources of light were the stars and the beam of the torch. Then, in the shadowy void, there it was – an area of grassland rising out of the water! He turned his attention to guiding the boat in towards a dimly perceived 'island' of slightly elevated land just to the port side of the boat.

As they drew closer, he could see that its area was larger than he had first supposed. He could see now that it was a grassy knoll, probably used as pasture, the contours of which determined that it had remained above the level of the flood water. Despite the darkness, they could make out that it was devoid of trees, buildings or any other kind of shelter and entirely surrounded by the flood; it would have to do. If they could drag the boat clear of the water, they could shelter inside it until help came. Mercifully, there was no rain falling although an icy breeze was blowing.

Whilst he focused on safely beaching the dinghy, Dan could hear Sue talking to an emergency services call handler, describing Emily's accident, their predicament and the small 'island' on which they planned to land. He nosed the dinghy towards an area of grass that was just above the water's edge and throttled back. The dinghy glided forward but then gave a sudden lurch as the prow mounted the grassy bank ahead of them.

Sue glared at him as she hung onto her phone with one hand and the side of the boat with the other.

He heard her say, "Sorry can you repeat that?" Then she turned to him.

"Dan, the call handler needs to have accurate details about where we are."

"I can get those – give me a moment." He seized the waterproof wallet containing the OS map. "We've come just beyond Withyford."

He paused. With the help of the torch, he would be able to see well enough to give a grid reference. At first, the movement of the water at the stern was causing the dinghy to rock slightly but he forced himself to concentrate. It took just a few moments to find and then check the co-ordinates from which he was able to give a six-figure grid reference.

With Dan's help, Sue relayed the reference to the call handler, having to repeat it twice. After she had given one or two further details and listened to the call handler's responses, the call ended. It was possible that she would need to use the phone again before they were once more in a safe situation.

"So, what's happening now?" asked Dan, his teeth chattering with the cold.

"They're sending an air ambulance. It's about the only way they can reach us quickly. We're not that far from Sedgewater and they thought it would be here in just a few minutes. I tried to give the call handler a good idea of the situation we're in out here."

Dan attempted to listen, unaware that his head had begun to nod. Incessant activity had filled the last hour, but now that there was a pause, sleep was stealing upon him in the mists of a guilt suffused dream. A voice was asking him what had made him so certain that heading for Sedgewater was better than taking the other direction to Monk's Hill? Another voice, Sue's perhaps, was asserting that had they gone to Monk's Hill they would almost certainly not have encountered the problems they had met on the way into their present, perilous predicament.

He was woken rudely by Sue slapping his face. "Come on, Dan! Stay awake! Don't go to sleep on us."

His face stung from the slaps but a heavy feeling of almost irresistible sleepiness continued to weigh upon him.

"Look, we're still partly in the water and the water level is rising." It was Sue's voice. He needed to listen. He needed to respond.

"We need to get out and drag the boat further up!"

He felt her pushing and shoving him, trying to get him to stay awake.

It took a huge effort of will but finally he made it back into reality. Hauling himself up he lurched forward into the bow of the dinghy and half-clambered, half-fell onto the grassy area beyond. Then he was aware of Sue scrambling over next to him, urging and cursing him into action.

"Come on, Dan. Shift your backside! We need to move this bloody boat!" Her voice seemed to come from far away.

"It's warm, stay here," was the feeling that pervaded his semi-consciousness but then he felt the sharp, percussive sting of another slap on his face.

"For God's sake, woman, what the hell are you up to?"

His voice sounded feeble, whining – but he knew that they had to keep moving. He dragged himself to his feet and saw that Sue was attempting to get Emily out of the boat. It was the spur he needed. He went to help her and with the small amount of assistance that Emily was able to offer, they helped her out and onto the grass.

Sue turned her attention next to trying to drag the boat further up onto the grass. Dan had raised the propeller clear of the water but, with its outboard engine still attached, he wondered how much difference they could make. Together they began tugging at it, striving to keep a foothold on the rain-soaked grass beneath their feet. Occasionally, wind driven waves gave a small amount of assistance at the stern but after several minutes, they had been able to do little more than inch the dinghy a little further up the slope so that the bow and now part of the mid-section were resting on the grassy bank on which they had beached.

Since the dinghy provided the only shelter from the winter breeze, they got back into it, placing Emily between them so that she was both more sheltered and able to share whatever body warmth they still had. The tilt of the dinghy also worked in their favour by draining much of the water that had accumulated inside it into the stern. By sitting in the bow, they could huddle together and help to weight the boat so that it was less likely to get washed back into the water.

Now it was a matter of waiting. Emily and Dan both succumbed to the drowsiness against which they had fought during the attempts to move the dinghy. Sue was also shivering with the cold though still conscious enough of their peril to be anxiously looking at her watch. The call handler had said that the helicopter should arrive in about twenty minutes; Sue could only suppose that demand was heavy that evening because by helicopter, it would only be minutes to the Sedgewater Royal Infirmary but she admitted to herself that she knew nothing about the logistics of the Air Ambulance Service. Twenty minutes did not seem long to wait and with the flood all around, it was the quickest way that anyone could get to them.

She placed her right hand on Emily's forehead. Even to Sue's chilly touch, her daughter's skin felt cold and by the light of the torch she looked pallid. After a moment's hesitation, Sue placed her fingers against Dan's cheek. His skin felt much the same temperature as Emily's and had a pallor similar to that of his daughter. Bending closer to Emily's nose and mouth, Sue listened to her breathing, noticing that it was both rapid and shallow. No doubt, Dan's breathing would be similar. She tried to check but he woke momentarily and muttered, "Christmas lights – where are they? I know I put them here. You must have moved them! Oh, now I can see them. You've put them on!"

His speech was rambling, confused. He must be dreaming again – a sign that worried her.

But then suddenly, she could see that he was not totally confused. Now she too could see lights! And she could hear the steady thwack, thwack, thwack of a helicopter's rotors. Her heart leapt!

Then, fleetingly anxious, she wondered if the helicopter crew would be able to find them. She pointed the torch beam towards the helicopter and used the flash button to send three short pulses, three long, and again three further short pulses. The helicopter circled around briefly and then came skimming decisively across the flood waters towards them. She was sure the pilot had seen them but for good measure, she repeated her torchlight SOS.

It flew in slowly now until it was stationary above them, its navigation lights winking at them, its engine roaring and the sound of the rotors now almost deafening. Dan and Emily had been woken by the sound of the helicopter and although both confused, were struggling to respond to its arrival. For a moment, Sue worried that the downdraught of the helicopter's blades would thrust them back into the water but the pilot, realising that they were sheltering in the dinghy, was immediately aware of the situation and rotated the helicopter away from its position above them, landing a short distance away.

It had barely landed when Sue saw two crew members carrying flash lights, jump out and come quickly towards them.

"Hello, I'm Dave. Let's see what we've got here." The second crew member arrived, Dave announcing as she did so, "This is Louise."

They spent a short time examining both Dan and Emily who by that stage, seemed to be only partly aware of what was happening. Having satisfied themselves that neither had sustained any injuries that would complicate transfer to the helicopter, Louise turned to Sue.

"We need to get you all into the helicopter and go from there. I have your name as Sue Holroyd?"

"Yes, that's me. This is Emily, my daughter, and Dan, my ex-husband."

"OK, as you probably realise we need to get them to hospital quickly. Are you aware of sustaining any injuries?"

"None at all as far as I know. I'm just bloody cold."

Louise grinned. "If you're able to get to the helicopter, we'll help you on board. We're going to assist Dan and Emily to get there, starting with your daughter. We think that, with help, Dan should be able to walk across but we'll have to put Emily on the stretcher."

Sue nodded. It just needed to happen. "Come on," said Louise, "let's get you out of this wind."

Sue was able to make her way across to the helicopter, instinctively hunching low as she came to the area beneath the helicopter's blades. A crew member helped her to climb aboard and then into a seat.

Meanwhile, Dave and Louise had begun working rapidly to transfer Emily. Sue watched anxiously as they carried her across to the helicopter and then, once inside, secured the stretcher in position. Dan was able to climb aboard with assistance but as soon as he was in the relative warmth of the helicopter, he began to feel drowsy again.

The pilot throttled the engine and the helicopter rose vertically above the flood, banking away towards Sedgewater as soon as it had achieved sufficient height. Dan tried to focus on the lights of the town slowly passing beneath the helicopter, but he had been exhausted by the episode in the dinghy and only awoke when being gently prompted to do so by Dave as they landed on the helipad at the hospital.

Later, he remembered asking about Emily and noticing the look of concern on Sue's face but then, the events that followed became a blur. It was daylight when he returned to consciousness again and the curtains around the hospital bed in which he was lying had been drawn back.

After a little while a nurse came to his bedside, announcing herself as 'Sarah'. She had just come on shift and busied herself with the bed for a moment, where Dan had disturbed the covers and then asked, "How are you feeling this morning, Mr Holroyd?"

"I've got a bit of a headache but otherwise, I don't feel too bad."

"I can give you something for the headache but a senior colleague needs to carry out some further checks. She should be here in a minute or two. Is there anything else I can help you with?"

Dan studied her a moment – black hair neatly pulled back from a pale, serious oval face, her uniform worn tidily. She smiled, bringing a lighter touch to the air of efficiency she had around her.

"There is…something else. I need to know if my daughter, Emily Holroyd, is alright. We were admitted at about the same time last night. I could also do with knowing about her mother, Sue Holroyd."

"Can you remember what time that was, Mr Holroyd?"

"Please – call me Dan. I'm afraid I haven't a clue – mid to late evening, I should think."

She could easily check but she needed to confirm his details.

"How old is your daughter, Dan?"

"She's nineteen. She's a university student."

"And Sue – what's your relationship to her?"

"She's my ex-wife."

Sarah smiled and said, "I'll do what I can. It may take a few minutes. Now, do you have any problems with paracetamol?"

"None," replied Dan.

Sarah decanted some water into a cup from a jug on his bedside table and then proffered the tablets and the cup.

Dan swallowed the tablets and sipped at the water, whilst Sarah plumped his pillows and helped him to settle into a position from which he could see more of the ward. Then she went off to find out what she could about his ex-wife and daughter.

* * *

During the previous two days, Karen had heard nothing from Dan; she had been frantic and had made continuous attempts to text and phone him, but as afternoon wore on into evening, the sinking feeling in her stomach became ever more intolerable. Something must have happened – of that she was certain. Through the night and on into the next day, she tried to distract herself by focusing on her father's needs. To a large extent, she had now become her father's nurse – a return to an earlier pattern of social care after successive governments had wasted more than a decade in pursuing one ideologically driven model after another whilst simultaneously failing to set up anything resembling an effective and compassionate system. Much as she loved her father, she felt caught in a trap – and now the one person she had relied on for support in recent months was not replying to her phone calls and messages.

She was drowsing in a chair, having had little sleep the night before, and thinking that she ought to find herself some lunch when her 'phone began to buzz. She snatched it up from the small table next to her. Peering at the display, she did not recognise the number.

"Hello?" she said tentatively.

She felt a huge surge of relief as she recognised the caller's voice. It was Dan!

"Oh, thank God, Dan! Where have you been? I've been worried sick about you!"

"I'm sorry, Karen – but it's a long story. Before I get to that, though, I need a favour."

She made herself wait whilst he explained that he was at the Royal Infirmary and, having been discharged in the last half hour, had nowhere to stay. Could he possibly come to her house for the night?

"Of course you can stay – but how are you going to get over here?"

Dan remembered that his last contact with Karen had been shortly before he took Sue's call for help.

"Well," he said, "I don't have my car. Is there any chance of a lift?"

"Of course – I'll come and get you. It's only a short distance from here and I'm sure Dad can be left for a short while. I'll just check on him and then I'll be straight over to pick you up. If you can wait in the multi-storey car park across from the main entrance, I'll find you there."

"Great!" said Dan. "I'll see you soon then."

The call ended. He put the handset of the hospital payphone back in its cradle. Karen had sounded anxious – and he would have some explaining to do. It was some story that he had to tell her – and one that two days earlier, he would not have remotely anticipated.

* * *

Karen managed to contain her feelings all the way back to the house but as soon as they were inside the front door, she clasped him to her and momentarily abandoning her self-control, began kissing him. Dan responded as best he could but then he found himself trying to restrain her and saying, "It's ok, Karen. It's ok. Really – I'm fine."

She looked at him, a little tearfully he thought – and at his anorak. "Well, you're not really 'fine', are you? Look at you – your coat is soaked. Here, let me have it."

He decided to let her 'mother' him as she slipped the anorak from his shoulders and hung it on the pegs. The anorak was on loan since his waterproofs were unfit to wear and still at the hospital.

"Why on earth did you wait around in the pouring rain? Why didn't you just wait in the car park as we'd agreed?"

"Well, for a start you would have needed a ticket to get in there – and anyway it's almost impossible to find anyone in that place. My phone was damaged when I was in the dinghy so I waited where I'd see you arrive." He shrugged. He was still tired from his ordeal and would happily have gone to sleep again.

In spite of her feelings, she could see that he had not yet fully recovered. She made an attempt at a smile.

"I'm wittering," she said, "and it makes no sense that we're standing around here. Let's go through to the lounge."

She led him through, calling back over her shoulder, "Will this rain never stop?" She added," I can't remember when we last had a break from it, even for so much as an hour."

"I think you're probably right," agreed Dan, "although having been tucked up in a hospital bed, I was able to forget about it for a while."

Once in the lounge, he flopped onto the very spacious settee whilst Karen, deciding that they could probably both do with something to drink, went through to the kitchen.

Feeling warm and comfortable, he began to doze – only to wake with a start when Karen returned with two cups of coffee. She put them on a small coffee table in front of the settee and went to sit by him.

"I thought the coffee might help," she said. "I don't know how well you were able to sleep in hospital ...and I certainly haven't been able to sleep."

Her slip-on shoes flopped to the floor as she cuddled up to him and looked into his eyes.

"I just thank God, though, that you're in one piece," she continued. "I've spent the past two days worrying myself sick about you – especially when you didn't reply to any of my calls or messages."

"I'm really sorry – but if you'd have seen the situation we were in, you'd have understood completely. And, as I said, I'd damaged my phone – so I simply couldn't get in contact."

"I wondered if something of the sort had happened – but because I didn't know, I began to imagine all sorts of things."

"Well, at least you don't have to worry any more – although I should think you've been kept busy, looking after your dad. How is he?"

"Fortunately, he's been fine. You're right though – he has kept me busy." She paused.

He drew her to him intending to kiss her but then, what started as a short embrace became a longer one. Relief mingled with the comfort and the strength they drew from each other's presence.

When they finally drew apart, Karen laid her head in his lap and said, "I love you, Dan. If only you knew how often in the last few days, I've longed for that moment."

Up to that point, he had always thought of their relationship as one of kindred spirits rather than as lovers but her concern and kindness were pushing aside his reserve.

"I love you too," he reassured her. They let the silence of the room settle around them.

It was some little while before Karen asked, "Are you up to telling me about what happened to you? It sounds as though you had a very difficult time."

Dan was by no means sure that he wanted to talk about his experience, fearing that he would find himself reliving the guilt that he felt about his decision to head for Sedgewater and the trauma of Emily's near drowning – but he had reminded himself, often enough, that it was better to talk about such things than hold them inside – so he began to relate the whole episode, from the time that he had received Sue's call for help up until the moment that he had first been able to believe that Emily would make a full recovery.

As he finished his story, he realised that there was a detail he had forgotten to include.

"You asked why I didn't phone you – and I said I'd damaged my phone," he said and gave a wry smile before continuing. "It happened when I jumped into the water. I had the phone in my trouser pocket. It sounds stupid, I know, but for that moment, I wasn't thinking about anything other than finding Emily."

Karen did not think it was stupid but rather, something that she could all too easily envisage – and she could see, too, that talking about the events during the boat journey had been difficult for him.

"You've told me more than enough to help me understand," she said. "The rest can wait. It's not actually very long since the whole thing happened…"

Having finished his story, he had lowered his head and she could feel that his body shaking beside her.

"I'm sorry," she said. "It's my fault. If I'd realised earlier, I wouldn't have asked you to go over it all again."

"No, no…" he replied, speaking with difficulty. "It's not your fault at all. I needed to talk about it – especially when I think about what might have happened."

She waited, avoiding any glib response and wanting to give him time to continue when he was ready.

There was a long pause before he managed to say at last, "The people at the hospital told me I might have flashbacks. But I thought it was better to talk about it rather than just – you know – bottle it all up."

She waited again before saying, "The great thing is, Dan, that you did find Emily and you did manage to rescue her."

Dan nodded. They were words that, years after, would continue to resonate in his memory but for the moment, he found speaking difficult. Eventually, he managed to say, "You're right, Karen… Thank God I found her!"

Karen thought that, for the time being, he had said what he needed to say and made a move to get them both another drink, but Dan put a hand on her arm, wanting her to stay.

"There is something I'm finding very difficult…"

She sat down again. "What is it, Dan?" She looked at him intently, ready to listen once more.

"My decision to head for Sedgewater…we need never have come in this direction. Sue wanted us to go over to Monk's Hill and stay with her mother. Looking back, it would have been much safer."

"You don't know that, Dan," she said, emphasising her words. "You made the decision you thought was right at the time – and you had nothing to tell you otherwise."

"Except that I did have some idea – from having had a similar experience before. The chances are that it would have been…" His words hung in the air; he seemed determined to blame himself.

Karen decided she should try to distract him, at least for the time being. "What was the last news that you had about Emily, when you left the hospital?" she asked.

"I was told that she needs to stay in hospital for another 24 hours. She has pretty well recovered from hypothermia and the effects of nearly drowning – but flood water contains a huge number of pollutants, and I think she's being assessed for any ongoing effects there may be from those."

She nodded, readily picturing the rubbish and farmyard waste that the flood water was scouring from the Levels, but she was also slightly puzzled.

"I imagine that you must also have swallowed a good deal of water…?"

"Oh, I did but nothing like as much as Emily. She ingested far more than I did. I was checked very thoroughly but the main concern in my case was hypothermia. Fortunately, the Air Ambulance got us to the hospital very swiftly and we had excellent treatment from both the Air Ambulance crew and the staff at the Royal Infirmary."

"When will you know more about Emily's situation?"

"Sue should be able to tell me more and I'm hoping to phone her in a little while. Hopefully, the hospital will be able to discharge her some time tomorrow."

"Is Sue still with her?"

"No – we agreed that Emily didn't need her mother or me to stay there tonight. In any case, Sue's exhausted. She's gone to stay with friends – just a short distance from here, in fact – people she met whilst taking riding lessons."

Karen had been completely absorbed in Dan's explanation but remembered that it had been some time since she last checked on her father.

She said softly, "I need to see if Dad's awake yet. If he is, he'll probably want something to eat. Let me just attend to him and then I'll make us both something to eat. Will you be alright whilst I do that?"

"Yes, of course," replied Dan and lay back with his head resting on the back of the settee whilst she went off to take care of her father's needs.

He welcomed having a few minutes to himself. He needed to think about what he should do next. There was no question of going back to the cottage. The incessant rain was causing serious disruption throughout the area and his conversation with Karen had at last prompted him to wonder about the situation at Monk's Hill. He decided to find out what he could as soon as there was an opportunity.

Karen went up the stairs to her father's bedroom, returning a few minutes later.

"Dad's awake. I need to get him some food. When I've done that perhaps we could think what we'd like to eat. Why don't you try to catch up on the news while I'm in the kitchen?"

"I could come and help you."

"No, I'll be fine. Why don't you see if you can find some up-to-date news about the flooding?"

She went off to the kitchen and Dan picked up the TV handset that was next to him on the arm of the settee. He decided to see if the BBC had any recent reports on the local situation.

The large flat screen of the television came to life and he waited with as much patience as he could whilst the news programme wound its way through a seemingly interminable section of sports coverage.

As it moved into interviews with tanned and healthy 'twenty somethings' in places as far away as Australia and South Africa, Dan felt a remoteness that was more than just a function of the distance. His attention waned and he found himself beginning to doze again.

He woke when he heard Karen say, "The news is just starting, Dan. The newsreader is going through the headlines. Sedgewater seems to be amongst them, so I think I'll come and join you again."

He roused himself to a more upright position whilst Karen settled herself at his side. Then they waited patiently whilst the newsreader fleshed out headlines relating to the NHS, a celebrity scandal, the never-ending detritus from long-ago 'Brexit' and gang warfare in London. Finally, sweeping panoramic pictures of flooding in the Southwest appeared in HD, filling the whole of Karen's very large TV screen.

"Wow! Just look at that!"

His reaction was involuntary and had escaped his lips before he had time to think about the implications of what they were seeing.

"That's a lot of water out there!"

"And a lot of suffering..." added Karen.

They continued to watch as the newsreader moved on to report flooding in the Thames Valley and along the course of the River Severn in Wales and the Midlands. In the north of England, small towns had also been inundated whilst roads and bridges had been swept away. It seemed to be much the same story across the length and breadth of the UK – high groundwater levels, incessant winter storms and local flood defences unable to cope.

"Storm Hector," commented Dan, "... went well to the north but look at what it's done to Cumbria." He shook his head.

"We've done no better with 'Ingrid'." Karen had continued watching as the report returned to the Southwest to show details of damage to road and railways. "I think it's as bad down here as anywhere else – if not worse."

As the coverage of the news headlines came to an end, the newsreader contrasted the UK's weather with that of destinations in the weekly 'Travel Programme', the item that was about to follow, but Dan and Karen were more intent on finding out as much as they could about their immediate surroundings.

"Shall we see if we can find the local news? That might give us some idea of the situation at Monk's Hill."

Karen picked up the handset and almost immediately managed to tune into some regional news on another channel.

Although flooding had been highlighted in the national news, the local coverage was more detailed including some additional video of the havoc being wrought by storm force winds. There were graphic scenes of lorries blown over on the M5 and of their goods distributed across the carriageways. Further west, there were pictures of trains running the gauntlet of waves in the Dawlish area and vast quantities of sea water crashing over the harbour entrance in Looe, inundating the well-known 'Banjo Pier'. Finally, as the report returned to the flooding, there was detailed coverage of Sedgewater and the Monk's Hill area.

Together they watched in silence as a video sequence shot from a drone showed the complete isolation of Monk's Hill in a steadily spreading inland sea. Sedgewater, too, was close to being encircled by water although the link along the M5 was, for the time being, still open, ensuring that transport could get in and out on the eastern side of the town.

The report went on, in extended coverage, to look at damage to the M5 and A38 westbound. The main problems seemed to be with road surface damage caused by tanker collisions, wind borne debris and storm force conditions along the strip between the coast and the southern fringes of Dartmoor.

Finally, they had seen enough. It had not eluded either of them that although they were, for the time being, warm and comfortable, they were in the middle of an unfolding regional disaster. They also had more immediate family concerns. Karen needed to check again on her father and Dan remembered that he needed to contact the hospital – and also to find out what he could about Sue's mother, Gwen.

Karen went upstairs to see that her father was still comfortable, and Dan picked up his mobile phone, hoping that he would not have too many problems finding out about Emily's progress. He and Sue had certainly been well-informed about her situation up to the time that Dan had left the hospital late that morning, but it was now approaching evening, and he knew that medical staff had planned to assess Emily's situation during the afternoon.

* * *

In the event, his phone – one that Karen had loaned him, and from which he could access his contacts – had buzzed at his side and he could see from the display that the caller was Sue; as he responded, she sounded rather breathless.

"Great news, Dan! Emily's made a full recovery!"

"What a relief! That's exactly the message we wanted to hear! Is she being discharged today?"

"No, she's still being kept in for one more night, but she should be discharged tomorrow. I think the doctor supervising her recovery wants to be absolutely sure that it's safe for her to 'go home' – although I did explain to him, that, at the moment, there is no such place as 'home'."

"What did he say about that?"

"He didn't seem that surprised, to be honest. He already knew about our escapade in the dinghy and thought that we must be amongst the hundreds of people who've been flooded out of their homes."

"How are you both going to manage over the next few days? It couldn't have happened at a worse time of year."

"You're right about that. Fortunately, Nicki has offered to put us up during the Christmas period. It's incredibly kind of her – and I think I'm going to take her up on it. I don't think there's anywhere else we can go."

"What about Josh? He's due home any day now, isn't he?"

"Yes – tomorrow. Nicki already knows about Josh, but I'll check with her this evening. I'm going over to her place as soon as I can get a bus – or a taxi." She paused. "Since we're speaking about arrangements for Christmas, where are you going to stay? I need to know because Josh and Emily will both want to meet up with you during the Christmas period. If you're staying at Karen's house, they could come round on Boxing Day. Nicki's house is just a short distance away. They could easily walk."

"I'll talk to Karen about it. I don't think it'll be a problem. She does have family other than her father but they live some way from here – and from what I gather, they're not in touch very often."

"Okay – perhaps we can confirm those arrangements tomorrow then? I'm going now because I can see the 33 bus coming in but I will need to talk to you some more – firstly, about Mum's situation and then also about the house – about 'Moorside'. Anyway, the bus is here now. Speak to you tomorrow."

She ended the call – though not before Dan had noted her change in tone compared with the way she had first greeted him on the doorstep of 'Moorside'. Meanwhile, he felt fairly certain that Karen would agree to Emily and Josh visiting them on Boxing Day and that they would get on well with her. If they resented anyone, it was Anne – who, in their perception – had been responsible for the break-up of their family;

fortunately, they were both magnanimous enough to recognise that the marriage between their father and mother had broken down but that their father still needed to be in a close relationship – rather than the semi-isolation in which he had been living for nearly three years. Dan sadly wondered if he would ever have precipitated such a chain of events if he had bothered to think sufficiently about the results of playing 'Sir Galahad' to Anne's needs – both medical and sexual. For that matter, would any such set of events have occurred had it not been for the flooding that had occurred at that previous time? It seemed like a philosophical question but one that had resulted in far from abstract consequences.

Sue's reference to the house on the Levels had also piqued Dan's interest. It would not in the least surprise him if she had decided that it was now far too vulnerable to flooding and to the vicissitudes of climate change in general; it was also more than likely that she already had other plans.

Strangely, he noted as well, the flood had also had the effect of forcing Sue to speak to him on more than her previous 'once-in-a-blue-moon' basis. There was little apparently so strange as the pathways of the Climate Crisis.

Karen came back into the room. "I've seen to Dad's food and I'm just cooking us a lasagne. I think I've cooked it for you before?"

"The vegetarian recipe? Yes, you have – I shall enjoy that."

She smiled. "It's in the oven but it will be a little while before it's ready. Perhaps we could have a glass of wine whilst we wait?"

"Sounds good to me. Sue called whilst you were in the kitchen and there are one or two questions from her call that I need to talk to you about – perhaps whilst we're drinking our wine?"

"Why not? I've got a bottle of English white wine – it's quite a crisp, dry one. I think you'll like it."

"Another result of 'Brexit' – or maybe, the Climate Crisis?"

"I don't suppose we'll be bothered either way, will we? I shall just enjoy it."

More than in need of a little light relief, he laughed. "Me too!"

Karen returned briefly to the kitchen to check on the lasagne. She had already cooled and opened the wine and, having set two glasses on the coffee table by the settee, she poured their drinks.

They chinked glasses and sat, side by side, sipping their wine until Dan said, "First question – since you've been kind enough to let me stay here, can I also spend Christmas with you?" He watched her briefly for signs of a reaction but there were none, so he said, "Ok, second question – If we can spend Christmas together, would you mind if Josh and Emily came to visit me here? If that would be difficult – well, it's not really a problem – we could probably find somewhere in town to meet up. It's just that they'll be staying with Sue at her friend's house, a short distance away, and it would make sense if we could meet up here."

Karen pretended to look solemn for a moment, if only to keep him waiting, and then said with a laugh, "The answer to the first question is "yes!" – as you should know – and as for going into town to meet Josh and Emily, I'm surprised you even thought about it! Of course they can come here."

"I didn't like to assume – it is your house after all."

"Mm, technically, that isn't true. It's still my dad's house – I'll tell him about it – but I can't imagine that he'll be anything but delighted to have both you and the 'children' here. He always remembers family Christmases from years past and often complains that it's far too quiet with just the two of us. Well, this year it'll be a little different!"

Having spent the past three Christmas Days on his own and then having endured the nightmare of the flooding, Dan felt that at least the holiday period looked as though it would turn out well. He leaned across and gave Karen a kiss on the lips.

"Thank you," he said. "You've helped solve several problems in one go! There may be mayhem going on outside, but it sounds as though in here, we'll be fine."

"I certainly hope so – and it'll be lovely for me to have you here, Dan. Christmas can be the loneliest of times so that's one problem we can solve for each other! Now, I think the food should be just about ready, so let's eat and then afterwards perhaps we can talk some more, if you are happy to do that?"

"I certainly am – and the lasagne is smelling good."

"We'd better hope it is, then. Let's go through."

They went together into the kitchen where Karen served them both, after which they sat at the places she had set for them in the dining room.

* * *

Later that evening, having cleared away the remains of their meal, they settled once more on the settee. Whilst they had been eating, however, there had seemed to be something other than the events surrounding the helicopter rescue that were still bothering Dan.

"I got the impression during dinner that there was something else you still need to talk about?" said Karen.

"Yes, there is. It's simply that as Sue was ending her phone call to me, she made mention of the house that she and I bought together – the house on the Levels."

"So, what did she say?"

"Not much – except that she wants to talk to me about it."

"Why do you think that is…?"

"I have a feeling that she wants to sell it."

"Would that be surprising?"

"No – not surprising at all, particularly after the experience that she and Emily had during the week. And it's not the first time – as you'll remember me telling you. The house was also flooded about four years ago although on that occasion, it was not so sudden, and there was more time to evacuate."

"You all went to your mother-in law's house, didn't you?"

"Yes, we did – and we were all cooped up there together for several weeks."

"Perhaps that was another reason why you didn't want to go back there this time – even in an emergency."

"You could be right! I hadn't given it any conscious thought, but the memory probably did have an influence on me."

"I am a little puzzled though," commented Karen. "I thought you said that it was part of the divorce agreement that the house was transferred entirely into her ownership and that she would pay you a legally agreed 'consideration' in recognition that you were the original owner and that you had also contributed substantially to the mortgage payments during the years that you lived there as a couple."

"That's right. That was the agreement."

"In which case, why does she still need to talk to you about it – if she is now the sole owner of the house?"

"That's where it becomes interesting – because I think it's not only Sue who is getting twitchy about living out on the Levels. If frequent flooding is going to be a persistent pattern in the future, that will affect property values right across the area."

"I can see that's a problem – for everyone living out there – but surely, that means it's her problem? Why does she need to talk to you about it?"

"Because I think she realises that selling the house could well be problematic – and she may hope that I could be part of a 'Plan B'."

"That sounds like quite a lot of guesswork, Dan – and anyway, if large numbers of people want to move away, why would anyone who had moved out – especially you, Dan – want to move back in?"

"Well, that's it, you see – that's where Sue is being very calculating. She knows how much I love the house – and she loved it too whilst we lived there as a family. She also remembers all too well the pain she managed to cause me when she threw me out so, on top of all everything else, I had incredibly strong feelings of 'home sickness'. I love that house – and the surrounding area. I've lived in many places but there's only one I've ever owned and that's the house on the Levels – 'Moorside' – and the last thing I ever wanted to do was to leave it all behind."

He turned sideways to look at Karen, suddenly wondering if this conversation about the house he had lived in with Sue was making her uncomfortable.

"I'm sorry, Karen," he said. "But since we've been spending much more time together, I think we've both tried to be very open with each other about everything – including the past."

"I know," she said, "and I appreciate that – but I'd be lying to you if I pretended that talking about Sue or, for that matter, your past relationship with Anne makes me feel anything other than, well, uneasy – even rather anxious."

"No – I'm not being very sensitive, am I? It's just that I've been nursing my feelings about 'Moorside' for several years now."

That could not be the end of it though, thought Karen – because there was one highly relevant factor that Dan had not yet discussed. Surely, he of all people would have thought about it.

"All right," she said. "Let's suppose that, despite everything that's happened, you decided to return there. Aren't you forgetting – or perhaps deliberately trying to ignore the facts – facts of which you and I are only too aware – and that say that you would be just as subject as anyone

439

else to the effects of climate change – the effects we already see – except that they're only going to get progressively worse? Stronger and more frequent storms, flooding, drought, possible summer wildfires, loss of farming, loss of wildlife – we've all talked about those things for decades now and the whole situation is just deteriorating with every year that passes. Why do you want to go back to a place where, if anything, you'll be even more vulnerable, even more at risk than we are here?"

"I know you're right. Perhaps, even though I've spent huge amounts of time thinking about it all, I still have a sense of denial."

"Aren't you afraid of the future? Surely you must be afraid?"

"Of course I am – I really am – but then, I still want to live my life. I'm here and I've no inclination just to throw away what I've been given or for that matter, what I've scratched out for myself. And desperate though the situation is, I'm not going to just pick up a shotgun, stick it to my head and end it all. I don't know how many years we all have left but however many it is, I still want to live them as fully as I can. I want to do my bit. And if there's any hope – any hope at all – that we can begin to turn the tide, then I want to live to see it!"

Karen was silent. The force of Dan's reaction had momentarily stunned her. She had thought about the situation many times and knew that in everything that related to the Climate Crisis, they were kindred spirits.

What she wanted to do above all was to 'wake up' the people all around her – the people that she often referred to as 'sleepwalkers' – the ones who were still denying the reality of rapid climate change and who were intent on living hedonistic lifestyles that shielded them from the possibility that human beings might soon be one of the species that would become extinct in what she had often heard referred to as the 'sixth mass extinction'; what price then the status of personal wealth and power, the extraordinary assumption that on a finite planet, economic growth could forever be not only sustainable but sought with ever increasing avarice? She felt herself sliding into despair as she reflected on such idiocy.

Dan moved closer to her. "We must still have some hope – surely?" he said. "Otherwise how can we carry on day by day, still keep 'putting one foot in front of the other'. We can't just give up."

"No, no, you're right, Dan. The worst denial of all is despair. As someone once famously reminded everyone, 'Whilst there's life there's hope'. I don't really believe in miracles but somehow I still keeping hoping for them."

There was a long pause until Dan said, "For the sake of our mental health, shall we talk about something else?"

She nodded and leaned across to the table so that she could pour them both another glass of wine. Then they sipped from their glasses in silence for a while. Eventually, Karen asked, "What are you thinking?"

He paused. "I'm taking a few moments to enjoy being here with you. It's such a contrast with the past week."

"Hmm," she said. "It's good to have you here. Usually by this time, I'm watching at the front door as you set off back to the cottage."

"...leaving you to cope alone with your dad."

"I've been doing it for a long time, Dan. I'm used to it."

"Well, at least tonight, you won't have to..."

He drew her into a kiss that might have lingered but after several moments, Karen's sense of duty caused her to say, a little resignedly, "This is probably not what you want to hear but I think I ought to check on Dad just once more – and then I think I'll probably want to go to bed. If you like, since I need to go upstairs anyway, I could show you the guest room."

"Good idea," replied Dan, reflecting that although he had been coming to the house for over two years, it would be the first time that he had stayed overnight, and he had no idea where the 'guest room' was.

He followed Karen up the stairs and waited as she ensured that her father was going to be comfortable for the night before coming out again onto the landing. He followed her as she took him past several bedrooms to the door at the end of the landing. She opened it and went in. Dan followed her.

She clicked on a bedside lamp, the light of which bathed the room in a soft yellow glow. He looked around. It was tastefully decorated in neutral colours. The bed was a large double. Karen followed his gaze.

"My parents' taste rather than mine," she commented, "But I think you'll be comfortable in here. And I managed to find you a pair of pyjamas," she continued with a smile. "They should be about the right size."

"Thank you, Karen. That's very good of you – especially since nearly everything I own is still back at the cottage."

She made her way to the door. "You know where I am if you need anything during the night…"

Dan raised an eyebrow and moved to give her a kiss.

Seeing his look, she added, "Yes, well, almost anything…"

"Are you sure?" he asked her teasingly.

"Dad's house, Dad's rules," she said, kissing him briefly before moving away.

"See you in the morning then."

She retreated to the landing, a brief backward glance telling her that Dan had hoped she would stay.

She wanted to say, as her parting shot, something like, "Our time will come," but that, as she had reflected before, could imply that she was simply waiting for her father to die – and that was a thought from which she shrank. Instead, she gave him a brief smile and hurried along to her own bedroom, next to her father's. She heard the door of the guest room click shut a short distance away along the landing.

* * *

Dan still felt drained after the activities of the previous week. He had also drunk several glasses of wine and thought that sleep would not be long in coming. Instead, he found himself lying awake, still musing on his relationship with Karen.

He knew her well enough to know that, although she had agreed to him staying with her during the Christmas period, it was unlikely that the two of them would immediately be sleeping in the same bed. And yet…

And yet he had hoped that she would want the warmth, the comfort, the intimacy of shared love. It had been some three years now since he had shared such intimacy, on the last occasion that he had made love with Anne. She had been so very different, leading not resisting, full of life and meeting passion with passion.

But then, it had all been a disaster, a glorious episode but one that had ended in rejection and misery. Would this then, be a different kind of love – the steady, reliable enduring kind that would outlast the 'sea of troubles' that seemed likely to beset them? If so, was it truly what he wanted – or did he still crave the self-revelation, the passion, the elation of the time he had spent with Anne?

Gradually, he fell asleep, knowing, deep within himself, the answer to his own question but also tauntingly aware, that as he drifted, there was another woman's presence touching the edge of his dreams. He felt her presence, but it was neither that of Karen – nor of Anne – and despite the turmoil in his sleep, by the following morning, he had temporarily forgotten both his dreams and the mysterious presence within them.

* * *

It always seemed curious to Dan that the demands of social convention were never more apparent than at Christmas. From autumn – or maybe late summer – the pressure to conform with the commercially driven seasonal orgy of consumption grew progressively until, at last it culminated with the stupor of food, drink and new possessions that had come to characterise Christmas Day. Perhaps it all came closer to the older pagan mid-winter festival than the impoverished manger in which the season's namesake had first laid his head?

Since the break-up of his family, he had tried to push all this away from him, observing it just sufficiently as to manage his self-awareness of the isolation that an outside observer would have attributed to him.

This year, however, it had been a little different. He had given more thought and time to the buying of presents for Emily and Josh, Karen and Hugh. He had helped Karen with the preparations and between them, they had given some thought to helping Karen's father derive such pleasure as he could from the occasion.

Outside the bubble of their own existence, the weather continued to be mild in temperature but excessive in precipitation. Dan had felt partly vindicated in his decision not to go to Monk's Hill. The problems of the hilltop village became such that the regional and central authorities took the decision to evacuate most of the population by boat or helicopter. A small number of people refused to leave, but of their fate progressively less became known, since communications had also been damaged by the persistent attrition of the weather. Gwen, Sue's mother, was brought to Sedgewater by boat. She had friends in Sedgewater, and it was with them that she spent Christmas.

Dan and Karen continued their quaint but slightly atrophied existence, emerging each morning to share the business of the day before returning once more to their own rooms at night.

Christmas Eve and Christmas Day were spent in a haze of consumption, conversation, family commitments and seasonal music. The King's speech on Christmas afternoon inevitably reflected on the growing threats and tensions being generated around the world by the Climate Crisis, although there was also widespread frustration at the attempt to blunt the impact of the message with accusations of political 'meddling'.

Boxing Day, often associated with a sense of anti-climax, brought instead a feeling of anticipation; Dan quickly found that he had underestimated how pleased and proud he would be to see Josh and Emily together. Karen watched, glowing with the reflected pleasure of seeing Dan greet them both. Their willingness to come brought a sense of acceptance that, in different ways, meant a great deal to all four of them. Dan also reflected that it was a great improvement on previous years when they had usually met him separately in the period between Christmas and New Year – invariably at one coffee shop or another in Sedgewater.

Karen proved to be a good host and deftly found things for them to do – eating, getting tipsy, watching a film, playing board games in which they all competed vigorously but in which they could all laugh at, or with, each other. Eventually, she lured Josh away to talk to her father whilst Emily wandered through to the kitchen with her father.

Emily clearly wanted to talk so Dan went to the cafetiere, poured them both mugs of coffee and pulled out two chairs for them to sit on. Emily sipped for a moment from her drink before putting it on the kitchen table and then sitting down opposite her father.

She seemed lost in thought for a moment, as if not knowing what to say. Dan waited.

At last she found her voice. "I just wanted to say, Dad, that I'm incredibly grateful for what you did a few days ago."

Dan had guessed that she would probably want to talk about the day that they had escaped from the flood, especially because, when they were both undergoing treatment, they had not been able to spend very much time together – and the last time that Dan had seen his daughter in hospital, she had been sleeping.

He fidgeted a little on his chair before looking at her very directly and saying, "That's very kind – and thoughtful of you, Emily. I think, though, that all three of us were in it together. And – well – while there was still breath in my body, I was never going to give up on you."

Tears welled in her eyes. She moved closer and threw her arms round his neck. "Oh Dad!" she sobbed but could say nothing more. Dan fought back his own emotions and, as with Emily, words stuck in his throat. He held her closely, waiting for her sobs to subside and until he felt more fully in control of himself once again.

He did not want to tell her that had he not gone into the water after her, he would never have had a moment when he would not have felt worthless – and not solely a traitor to their mother but to his daughter as well. Above all, he did not want to tell her about the visceral panic against which he had fought when he realised that she had been swept into the water and when it had seemed to take so long to find her.

After the experience they had shared, he felt sure that she would have 'demons' of her own still afflicting her.

They drew apart but he kept his daughter's long, soft fingers in his.

She said, "I'm still having nightmares about it…at least, about the bits I can remember."

"Do you want to talk about them?"

"I'll try. In a way there isn't much to tell. The dreams terrify me – absolutely terrify me – but there's hardly anything I can see in them. There's just the coldness of the water and all sorts of dark shapes surrounding me. Then the shapes start to move about and that's when I panic. That's when I force myself awake. What seems so strange though is that when I wake, I'm always bathed in sweat – which seems strange because in the dream, I'm somehow aware of the coldness of the water. It was so intense; I've never experienced anything like that before. And I never want to again."

Dan listened intently. He too had woken every night since the incident believing that he had failed to find her and, in the short gap between the dream and his return to reality, feeling the despair that might well have permeated the rest of his life.

"I'm afraid those experiences may be with us both for some time, Emily. The feelings that your mum and I had when we realised that you had fallen into the water – I can't describe them and, if I'm honest, I don't think I want to."

She started to say, "I'm sorry..." but her father interrupted her.

"Don't be sorry, Emily – it happened, it was simply something that happened. If anyone made a mistake it was surely me. When I thought about it afterwards, the journey to Monk's Hill would surely have been simpler and less likely to end in an accident."

"None of us had any idea about the pros and cons, Dad. It was an appalling night – and all the choices were risky."

"I guess you're right. Karen has said much the same thing." He smiled. "There is this, though – nightmares or not, every day since then, I've felt glad that we all survived unharmed – and deeply grateful to the helicopter crew and the people at the hospital."

"Me too," agreed Emily, with a degree of feeling that only people who have been in serious danger can summon.

The voices of Josh and Karen drew their attention as they came into the kitchen.

"Well, that was a success! Dad really enjoyed meeting Josh!"

"And I really enjoyed meeting him. If I have half the experiences he's had, I'll be lucky."

Josh turned to his father. "Did you know that Karen's dad had been a civil engineer?"

"Well, only vaguely..."

"You mean you've never talked about the projects he's run and the places he's been?"

Karen came to Dan's defence. "I think Dad usually wants someone to talk to him about football. I don't think he lets you get much beyond that, does he, Dan?"

"Sometimes," disagreed Dan "– and when he does, he loves to reminisce, and I love to listen – so I have heard one or two of his stories. But perhaps it takes one engineer to draw another out of cover?"

Josh laughed. "There could be something in that – although I'm not really an engineer – yet."

"But you're hoping to be, aren't you, Josh?" said Emily.

"Oh yes – and especially after talking to your dad." He smiled at Karen. She, however, was preoccupied with keeping them all happy.

"Would anyone like some more to eat or drink?" she asked.

"Not for me, thanks, Karen. You've really looked after us today – and I think I'd burst if I ate or drank another thing."

Josh laughed. "I'm the same" and he pretended to frame a bloated stomach with outspread fingers.

He squinted at the kitchen clock. "Much as I hate to say it, I think we should be getting back. Mum said about nine o'clock, I think?" he looked quizzically at his sister.

"Yes, it was. I think she's very aware that we're staying in someone else's house."

"Alright, if you're sure – it was good of Nicki to put the three of you up for Christmas and I can appreciate that your mum is very grateful to her. I'll get your coats..." said Dan.

Karen was pleased that the occasion seemed to have gone well.

"It's been lovely to have you both here. I hope you've enjoyed it too?"

"Ooh yes," said Emily. "You've been great – and it's been a good chance to get to know you."

"Yes," agreed Josh, "it has been great – and a big improvement on the Copper Kettle or Martha's Pantry – or any of the other places we've met up in recent years. You and your dad, Karen, have a lovely house and we're very grateful to you for having us – and for looking after us so well."

By now he had pulled on his coat, and he bent his head to give her a kiss on the cheek. Emily, meanwhile, had also finished putting on her coat, hat and gloves.

"Is this the person I was forever reminding to wear a coat in cold weather?" asked Dan, peering at her in feigned disbelief.

She laughed, thinking that after her recent experiences, it was something that she would never need reminding about again.

They shuffled towards the front door which Karen opened. There was more hugging followed by waving as Emily and Josh made their way down the drive to the lamplight of the street.

Dan gave a sigh; Karen waved the last of her 'goodbyes' and then closed the door.

Together they retreated towards the capaciousness of the settee in the lounge.

* * *

As soon as they were out of earshot, Emily asked, "Did you enjoy that then?"

"Yes," replied Josh. "I did."

"Did you enjoy anything in particular?"

Josh thought for moment. "I think I simply enjoyed seeing Dad look happy again. Every Christmas that I met him in town, I always thought how miserable – and absent-minded he seemed."

"I agree. It was good to see him smile. All the same..."

"'All the same' what?" He sounded a little impatient.

"I hope she is 'right' for him..."

"What makes you say that?"

"Oh, 'woman's intuition'. Perhaps one of the things that Dad resented was that, with the pressures of her work, Mum became a 'dragon' – to all of us. Karen's quite the opposite. In fact, when I was talking to her today, I felt as though I was really talking to an older sister."

"The older sister we never had. Yes, I can see that. She's a fair bit younger than Dad. Perhaps that's what he likes?"

"Perhaps it is – although it's not something I want to think about. But then, although I've so often wanted to forget it, were it not for whatever it was he 'liked' about Anne Moresby, we would all still be spending a family Christmas together. I could hate that woman for what she did to us."

To her surprise, Josh gave a small snort of indignant derision. "I don't for one moment think that's fair," he said.

"Why not?" It was Emily's turn to be indignant. "Why on Earth not?"

"Because, as the saying goes, 'It takes two to tango'. Much as I find it difficult to think about, let alone talk about, I think Dad must have found something in that 'awful woman' – as I've heard you call her – that he hadn't found with Mum. And whilst we're talking about it, there must be something that draws him to Karen as well. I think they've been seeing each other for over three years now. She may not be his 'ideal woman' but I didn't find it difficult to see them as 'a couple'."

For a moment, prompted by the fact that she was her mother's daughter, Emily teetered on the brink of an indignant reaction but then forced herself to think about what her brother was saying. It hurt her to think that, in certain respects, someone who had always been so special to her, and in some ways 'exceptional', had shown himself to be fashioned from the same clay as other men.

Her reply, when it came, was one of reluctant admission. "You could be right but, like you, that's something that I shy away from thinking," she said.

"I'm sure we both feel the same about that, but I just try to remind myself that being our 'Dad' does not stop him from having the same propensities as most other men I know."

"'Propensities', eh? That's a big word for an engineer to use," replied Emily, unable to resist a little sarcasm. She paused. "Whatever 'propensities' you may be talking about, I don't think it's that side of his nature that I'm going to remember for evermore. Especially since, if it wasn't for him – and Mum for that matter – I might still be floating around in several feet of filthy flood water!"

Josh detected that his sister was wearying of the conversation.

"Sorry," he said. "Sometimes I can be a bit like 'a dog with a bone'. You've reminded me anyway that we all have a lot more to worry about."

"If you mean the fact that we're currently stuck in a town surrounded by water with no way out and wondering day-by-day just how bad the flooding is going to get, I'd certainly agree with you."

"It's that, of course…but it's also a lot more even than that. You know it is…"

"Yes, I do know that Josh – of course I do – but look, we'll soon be back at Nicki's house.

"Ok, Em – though even a short walk together such as this one is helpful. We don't get that many chances to have anything other than phone conversations or social media calls."

"No, I suppose not," replied Emily, "although right now my main concern is whether or not Mum's had a good day."

Josh grinned in the darkness. "She probably has. Anyway, she's been a new woman ever since she's been with her present 'boyfriend'."

"I think you'll find he's a bit more than a boyfriend – and as for the 'new woman' bit, that may have something to do with the fact that he's got ten times the money that Dad was ever able to earn…"

She cut her sentence short and motioned her brother to notice that, as they arrived at the front door, there was a light in the hallway. She knocked lightly on the door, and it opened. It was almost as though their mother had been anticipating their arrival.

"Ah hello, Emily and Josh, I'm glad you're on time. It's just as well to remember the hospitality we're being given here. Besides, there's someone who's just popped round to see me for a while and this seems like a good time for you both to meet him..."

* * *

Dan and Karen had barely settled on the settee before Karen fell asleep. For Dan, used to the isolation of the cottage and having spent the day, however joyfully with those closest to him, it was a welcome pause. The bottle of whisky that he had been given as a Christmas present was in the kitchen so he left the settee and went through to pour himself a glass of his favourite alcohol, returning with the bottle – and a measure that would have made even a publican wince.

He returned to his seat next to Karen. He had taken just one or two sips of his whisky when she gave a sonorous snort, and he felt her head flop onto his shoulder. He reflected that as he could now be stuck in his current position for some time to come, it was as well that he had brought the bottle with him.

It was curious, too, he thought, that although Karen had proved slow to learn the ways of intimacy, her unwitting use of him as a pillow was another step along the path. He took another, longer sip of his whisky wondering, nonetheless, if he was not asking too much of this relationship which, even after nearly three years, still seemed to be at a relatively early stage.

He felt a hint of frustration infiltrating the alcoholic elevation of his mood. He had spent the whole day immersed in the interconnected bubbles of friends, family and self. Now, it was surely time to gaze on something bigger and enormously 'other' than his own existence – and had it not been for Karen's head on his shoulder, he would have stood up, gone to the front door, then outside – and from there, into the front garden where, if he could have found a gap in the incessant wind-driven clouds, he would have gazed up at the starry infinite space beyond.

But then, he reflected, why stand gazing up into heaven – when there was so much happening to Planet Earth? His intoxicated vision raced rapidly over the evolving changes in land, sea and sky – changes that were only occasionally reported, and phenomena so pivotally important to life that, through the profoundest of ironies, only a fraction of the population other than scientists saw fit to think about, let alone understand them. It was only through human beings that anyone would begin to attribute consciousness to the planet, but it was, nonetheless, well on course to removing the darkest of threats to its own future stability.

Karen began to stir. Instantly, he fell back into the more familiar scale of his daily thoughts, hoping that she would not comment disparagingly when she saw the bottle of whisky and the almost empty glass on the table.